I0691961

"Trust me, Ron."

I nod, my hands suddenly shaking. He takes them into his hand and lifts them to his mouth. He kisses my fingers softly.

"You're grieving right now—I would never take advantage of you. But…"

I take a deep breath.

He lets go of my hands and reaches out toward the still unbuttoned top two buttons of my shirt. The collar lays open, and his fingers trace the hollow of my throat. "You look gorgeous in my shirt."

His eyes are locked on me, and I feel overpowered but safe all at once. There's a strange ache in my body, answering to the hunger in his eyes.

"It is by far the most beautiful you have ever looked."

My eyes dart up as he reaches out to touch the next button. He studies me as he slowly begins to unbutton. My entire body warms, and I bite down hard on my bottom lip. He abandons my button to run his fingers across my lips once more. I try to remember to breathe.

## Praise for Cathrine Goldstein

"Cathrine Goldstein's *THE COUPLING*, book two in The Letting series, continues the epic tale of Veronica Billings and Phoenix to save the world that's only now coming into focus for Veronica. Goldstein has painted a story filled with shocking twists and turns, despicable villains, and a hero in Veronica readers will long remember."

*~Michael Murphy, Bestselling Mystery Author*

~*~

"Once again, Cathrine Goldstein has unfurled a deeply satisfying and disturbing adventure into a dystopian society. Dive into *THE COUPLING* - but make sure you hold your breath before you jump - you'll be pulled right in from chapter one."

*~Kristen Rutherford, Writer: The Nerdist Show,*
*How To Be A Grown Up*

# The Coupling

## by

## Cathrine Goldstein

*The Letting Series, Book Two*

**The Coupling**

Cover Art by *Angela Anderson*

The Wild Rose Press, Inc.
PO Box 708
Adams Basin, NY 14410-0708
Visit us at www.thewildrosepress.com

Publishing History
First Fantasy Rose Edition, 2016
Print ISBN 978-1-5092-0617-9
Digital ISBN 978-1-5092-0618-6

*The Letting Series, Book Two*
Published in the United States of America

## Dedication

As always,
for Jay, Penelope, and Sarah (Pickle).
Thank you for proving
the only real magic in life is love.

Chapter One

*...Even if this is all the happiness we are ever allowed, it will be enough.*

Happiness is a strange thing. For most people, it's intangible. For most people, it's an emotion that can be raised or razed within a heartbeat. A proclamation of love or a condemnation of hate can consequently feed and nurture happiness or potentially destroy it forever.

I've heard it said, sometimes people aren't aware of their own happiness until it's gone. But for me and those like me—the children of the Couplings, the ones sentenced to the Lettings—we know exactly when we are happy. We feel it—like the sun on our faces on a cold winter's day, or the cool summer breeze on the hottest summer night—and we hold on to it for dear life. For us, happiness is most certainly tangible, and we are deeply grateful when we experience it.

And this—this is precisely such a moment...

The waves crash purposefully around us, and the softness of the sand on the beach gives beneath us, creating an imprint of our two bodies stacked as one. I straddle him, and we sit on the beach facing one another. I close my eyes, experiencing bliss from the feeling of our bodies nestled together. Phoenix drops his hand from my face, and wraps his arms protectively around my waist.

Being with him gives me a sense of security like none I have ever known. Although my mother did her very best, I don't remember ever feeling this protected when I was a child living in the city, nor did I ever feel completely safe once I was sent to camp. There was always something—that fear of a call to a Letting or maybe a Coupling—that lived deep within each of us. But here on enemy territory, despite everything—the war surrounding us, my girls who are alone at camp, Lulu who is missing, and enemies who want us both dead—I feel safe thanks to Phoenix.

Brooke is standing behind us now with our verdict, but we ignore her for just a few seconds more. We are allowing ourselves to seize our time of astonishingly unexpected happiness. I still don't know why we are this fortunate, or how we got here. Yes, we're on Principal Leader Farnsworth's beach, and our future—whether we live or die—will be determined by him. Still it's not feasible we're here. It's not possible we're both still alive. After poisoning my blood in an attempt to assassinate Farnsworth, I survived. And after single-handedly facing an army led by Gunnar, Phoenix's one time partner and now enemy, Phoenix is here.

And we are happy.

Phoenix drags his hand to my mouth, his fingers tracing my lips. I part my lips, and my breath catches. Slowly, he leans forward and places his mouth on mine, but he doesn't merely kiss me, he gives me his soul.

We pull apart, smiling. Although she is, for all intent and purpose, my foe, neither Phoenix nor I want to hurt Brooke any more than we have already. For just a few happy beats more I nuzzle against Phoenix's hand, and he holds me tightly, his free hand clamped around my waist before he draws me to him.

Wrapped in Phoenix's arms, I feel the complete dichotomy of who we are and what our lives have become. Together and separately we are night and day, sun and moon, and yet, he tells me this is what makes us strong, both individually and together. I was the Head Leader at my camp, the girl who brought more young girls to the Lettings than anyone else in history, and he—he was my enemy, the rebel leader I fell for. Somehow, the most obedient of government workers fell for the epitome of radicals—the leader of the Peaceful Revolution.

And I fell hard.

Unfortunately, we know it is time for that balance. Our happiness must now be tempered by the news Brooke delivers. Since Farnsworth has reclaimed his position as Principal Leader, I am certain he will dole out punishments for our revolution against him. It is true we worked with him to fight Gunnar, but our plan backfired, enraging him even more. Our world is in turmoil. The war continues to rage, and people everywhere—citizens of the New World, the city, and our little camp, have been forced to choose sides and fight.

Looking up at Brooke now, her eyes wide and fearful, I know something truly awful is about to happen. I have spent enough time with Farnsworth to know it is not just our rebellion against him as Principal Leader that angers him, he is also enraged by his own mortality, his hemophilia, and quite frankly, he is jealous of my relationship with Phoenix. As far as I know, his attraction to me is neither physical nor mental. It runs much deeper than that. What he lusts after is my strong, pure, blood…that is…my blood when I'm not trying to poison him.

Phoenix releases his grasp on me, and immediately I develop that sinking feeling in the pit of my stomach. I look deeply into Phoenix's gorgeous blue eyes, and what worries me now is that Principal Leader Farnsworth's petulant behavior will be the downfall of us all.

I stand to meet Brooke, and only now do I realize we are dressed as opposing forces, good and evil, white and black.

"What is it?" Phoenix asks, standing and instinctually putting his arm up in front of me.

Brooke has no snappy answer or sarcastic remark. Instead, she looks directly at me. Her expression is one of pure devastation.

"Brooke?" I ask, making my way from behind Phoenix over to her. "Are you okay? What did Farnsworth do to you?"

"Nothing." Her eyes fall to the ground then back up to us.

Phoenix steps forward and wraps his arm around my waist, holding me tightly. I see the pain in her eyes, and I try to wriggle free.

"No," Brooke utters. "Don't. But thanks, V."

I nod, and slide back into the comfort and safety of Phoenix's arms.

"Farnsworth really is an incredible bastard," Brooke whispers, staring at the ground. She lifts her head, and stands for a long moment looking out at the misleading tranquility before us.

"What does he want?" Phoenix asks. I hear the concern in his voice. "Does he want something from you?"

"No." Brooke shakes her head. "He wants something from Veronica."

"Okay." I'm not surprised by this revelation. "That's nothing new. He wants my blood. With the exception of my girls, I'm the only one outside the New World who can supply him. He'll use the citizens of the New World if he must, but it's a last resort. He needs them on his side right now to fight Gunnar. Besides, he thinks he gains some superhuman strength when he has my blood. We just have to figure out where and when we make our next move to poison him—"

"No, Ron," Phoenix interrupts. "There has to be a better way. We can't let you keep poisoning yourself and subjecting yourself to more Lettings."

"It's the best way." I turn to him. "It's our way in."

"I am not going to stand by and watch you nearly die again." Phoenix's voice grows louder.

"Guys?" Brooke interjects.

I hear her, but ignore her. "What other choice do we have?"

"Guys?" Brooke repeats.

"Just a second," I snap at her. "We have to keep Farnsworth alive until we get rid of Gunnar, then we can go ahead and poison Farnsworth just as we plan—"

"I won't let it happen, Ronnie." Phoenix's voice is determined. "You've sacrificed enough. You've given your blood, literally, to protect the people of our country from Farnsworth's evilness—"

"And I should have done so much more. I single-handedly brought more girls to the Lettings than any other person in history, Phoenix."

"It was your job. And you didn't know any better.

No one did."

"You did." I feel the tears well.

Phoenix runs his hand through his hair. "The point is, once you knew, you saved those little girls from certain death. All the girls, Ron, not just the near-extinct O's."

"The Lettings aren't over, Phoenix. We're just in turmoil. And I promised the people a leader, a real leader, and to do that we have to continue on with our plan. I eat the poisoned mushrooms I've grown immune to, and they pump my poisoned blood into Farnsworth, it's our only—"

"Guys," Brooke shouts and we both turn to her. "He doesn't want your blood, Veronica."

"Well then, what does he want?" Phoenix asks.

"What do I have to offer except my blood?" I am genuinely confused.

"Of course it's her blood," Phoenix scoffs. "She's one of the last O's, and Farnsworth needs O to survive. With the war raging and the Lettings in abeyance, there is no blood—no one, not any of the blood types, is receiving the young girl blood that keeps them youthful and healthy. He needs Ronnie…"

Brooke raises her eyebrows at Phoenix, and out of the corner of my eye, I see him understand something she is telling him.

He squats down, resting his head in his hands. "No…" he whispers.

"He thinks it's his way back into the grace of his people," Brooke explains.

"What is?" I ask.

"He thinks it will prove to them he is on their side, and it gives him a chance to deliver more blood. He will make the rebel converts happy. Even with his condition. Two O's..." Brooke's words trail off.

"No." Phoenix stands. "No, no, no, no, NO!" He reaches down and grabs a shell. He chucks it far out into the ocean. "He can't just decide to do that," Phoenix yells. "He's breaking his own laws."

"That's why he took power again. He makes the laws." Brooke speaks carefully, "And all's fair in war—"

"All's fair in love, too," Phoenix quips. "And if I have to wring his scrawny neck myself, it's not going to happen."

"Will someone please tell me what's going on?" I demand.

"Farnsworth hasn't called you for another Letting," Brooke explains. She looks down at her feet and shifts her weight from one to the other. Finally, she faces me. "He's called you to a Coupling."

"A what?" I ask, fear running through me.

"He's summoned you to a Coupling." Brooke places her hand gently on my shoulder. "And for the first time ever in our history, our Principal Leader will Couple to serve his civic duty. Veronica," Brooke takes a deep breath, and I can see the pain in her eyes as she speaks, "Farnsworth has decided to be the one you are slated to Couple with."

\*\*\*\*

For whole minutes I stand there, not believing any of it. Quietly, I look out at the ocean that sprawls before me. I can feel Phoenix and Brooke staring at me; waiting for me to react. I stand, unmoving, struck by the juxtaposition of the peace that surrounds me, and the horrors that are waiting for me. For all of us.

Cathrine Goldstein

Slowly, I turn to face Brooke. She is my adversary, yet she is in agony, feeling my pain for me. All I feel is numb, but I know I've experienced this feeling before. I remember a time in the woods when Gunnar beat me, and yet I felt no pain. I felt nothing but concern, because I knew when the pain finally registered, it would be crippling. I am lucid enough to understand that pain will be nothing compared to this.

I look away from Brooke and turn to Phoenix. His eyes grab hold of mine, and he moves toward me. Without knowing why, I put up my hand to stop him. He stops short, watching me, waiting for me to do something. Anything. I know I have to do something.

"I have been called to Couple with Farnsworth." I find it hard to believe the words I say. It is all so surreal.

"We'll run." Phoenix decides.

"No. We both know we'll never get away. Between Gunnar and Farnsworth there is nowhere to run."

He shrinks back turning from me, trying to hide the agony in his eyes.

"I have been called to Couple," I repeat, calmly. "But I am not dead." Just saying the words, I realize this myself. "This means I live to fight another day."

I feel Brooke's eyes dart up at me. For the first time ever, her look of disdain has morphed into one of respect.

"This is personal," I whisper. "Farnsworth is attacking with laser-like accuracy. He is doing the one action that can hurt all three of us simultaneously."

"But you're the one it hurts the most," Phoenix blurts, trying to keep his anger in check.

"Maybe so, but that also means neither of you has

8

been stopped. Don't you see?" I step toward Phoenix. "Don't you see the irony of it all? The one thing Farnsworth forbade his people was to base their lives on emotions, and that's exactly what he's doing. Farnsworth is letting himself be ruled by his emotions. We can't do the same. He is so angry that he is willing to weaken his position as Principal Leader to Couple. So this is the time for you to strike."

I turn to Brooke. "This is our only chance. While I serve my patriotic duty, you must stop Gunnar and offer these people the leadership they were promised."

They are both staring at me, fixated on my every word.

"And what happens to you?" Phoenix asks, quietly.

"I survive," I respond. "Which seems to be something I am very good at." I offer a small smile, and he does his best to return it. "Farnsworth will be out of the picture for a period of time. That gives you the opportunity to strike. You worked together before," I remind the two of them. "You two are the most fearless people I know. You will make this happen."

"We are only two of the three fearless people standing here," Brooke adds, smiling at me.

"I will handle Farnsworth while you two change the world." I laugh. My eyes ache from tears, and my throat tightens.

"Ron," Phoenix mumbles.

I walk to him. He takes me into his arms and holds me for an impossibly long time. I feel every molecule in my being transfer into him and back to me. I hope I have gained even some of his intelligence and strength.

"We can run," he whispers into my ear.

"No." I pull back. "I don't know what's going to

happen, but I know this is what I must do."

I stand on my tip-toes, and Phoenix leans down. He kisses me long and hard. I hear the ocean rushing in my ears, and the small sounds of desperation we make as we devour each other with our mouths. Before I lose my nerve, I turn from Phoenix and face Farnsworth's mansion. My gaze falls to my seashell—the one Phoenix gave me as a promise. I scoop it up and hold it tightly in my hand.

I walk off the sand and across the grass toward the doors that lead back to the dining room. My toe catches against something soft and tickly. I stop only to bend down and pick the sole dandelion on Farnsworth's majestic grounds. A dandelion. I don't take the time to register what this lone dandelion represents, but I know I have found my strength. I hold the dandelion securely in my grasp, take a deep breath, and walk across the lawn toward the doors that will lead to the next phase of my life.

Chapter Two

I burst through the French doors to the dining room, and Farnsworth is standing there, smiling coyly at me. Without losing momentum, I walk directly to him and stop only when we are standing toe to toe. Before he can even say a word, I drop the dandelion and slap him across the face, hard. His head turns sharply and then ricochets back into place almost as quickly. The look in his eyes reads shock and amusement.

"You think those mud smears under your eyes left bruises?" I hiss. "Wait until you see what this will do to you." My chest heaves. I hate this feeling of complete and total lack of control.

Moments later, Phoenix and Brooke burst through the same door. Phoenix enters strong and menacing, ready to pounce, and Brooke gasps when she spots the red swelling on Farnsworth's face.

"She must have done a number on me," Farnsworth muses, reading Brooke's expression. "But we must forgive her." Farnsworth stares at Phoenix as he speaks. "All brides handle pre-wedding jitters in different ways."

"What?" I whisper.

"I'm just sorry, my love, you'll have to see me like this on the most important day of our life." Farnsworth runs his hand across his cheek gingerly.

"Your what?" Phoenix asks.

"The most important day of our life. No?" he asks, taking his time to make eye contact with Phoenix and Brooke before his gaze lands on me. "You didn't know? Oh well, let me enlighten you. My beautiful Veronica and I will be getting married. Tonight."

"What?" My heart pounds uncontrollably as I squeeze the seashell in my grasp.

"Married. The ancient custom of becoming man and wife. You've never heard of it?"

"We've heard of it," Brooke whispers.

"Good." Farnsworth looks extremely pleased with himself. "Then you all understand what I mean when I say Veronica and I are getting married tonight."

"The hell we are," I hiss.

"I do love your spirit, Veronica," Farnsworth muses, "but we do need to work on your manners. Is this the kind of respect you show your husband?"

"You're not her husband," Phoenix seethes through clenched teeth.

"Not yet, but soon. Why do you think I had you all get dressed up?"

It just then occurs to me I am wearing a long white dress.

"You are the wedding party, of course."

"This is ludicrous," I cry, my emotions getting away from me.

"You're really overstepping this time, Farnsworth," Phoenix warns.

"Why are you doing this?" Brooke asks him. "Really? I mean, what do you have to gain?"

"Her," Farnsworth blurts, nodding to me. "And that look in his eyes is just an added bonus."

"It will never happen." I move from Farnsworth and stand next to Phoenix and Brooke. Phoenix steps in front of me, protectively.

"Do you really want a wife who doesn't want you?" Brooke asks, reasoning with Farnsworth.

Farnsworth laughs hardily for what seems to be an entire minute. "Do you really think I care how I get what I want?" He walks toward the three of us, but none of us steps back.

"We could just kill you right now, Farnsworth," Phoenix tells him. "There is nothing you could do, and no one would stop us. Your people care only about themselves. That's all they've ever cared about. And with the war, they have no time to worry about anyone but their own families."

"You could." Farnsworth walks away from us, shaking an index finger as he speaks. He turns back. "But…you wouldn't want to do that."

"Why not?" I ask, with that awful sinking feeling in my stomach.

"Because the ramifications would be devastating."

"What do you mean?" I whisper.

"Well, you see, as you may have noticed on your, let's say, clandestine arrival, I still have my bodyguards at my beck and call. And the reason they're not here to stop you from doing things like slapping me across the face is because they are otherwise engaged."

"Where?" I whisper, horror filling my veins.

"You know where, Veronica. Are you really going to make me tell these two?"

"Tell us, Farnsworth," Phoenix demands..

"Well, they're with those three lovely little girls, of course. What are their names again?"

"Lilly, Violet, and Raven," I whisper, nearly crippled by fear.

"Ah yes, such nice names compared to the names my help gave them. What were those? Ah yes, cry baby, whiny, and stubborn. Their personalities show so organically under duress."

"Duress?" I eke out.

"Oh, yes. Just the slightest feeling of pain and the first one cries, the second one whines, and the third one…well, she just clenches her teeth and pushes through."

I lunge forward, dropping my seashell, and nearly grab Farnsworth by his thin, feminine neck, but Phoenix and Brooke hold me back.

"Let me go," I scream. "Don't you see? He is torturing them." The agony I feel is sending a searing pain through my gut. "He just explained their personalities perfectly."

I turn to Phoenix. "They're babies, Phoenix—only eight years old. And he knows what they mean to me. Sure he knows I've been their caretaker since the day they arrived at camp and together we're some of the last remaining O's, but he's also figured out we have a special bond." My voice cracks. "You must know how I feel, Phoenix. Raven is your sister."

He nods.

"I love those girls like they're my sisters—all of them, even Lulu who chose Gunnar over me." I wave my hand helplessly. "And Farnsworth knows I would do anything to protect them. He knows this is the only way to truly control me."

I turn back to Farnsworth. "But to use poor, defenseless children? You disgust me." I spit at

Farnsworth, and a gob of my saliva lands on his cheek and decides to defy gravity. "You are a coward."

He stares at me with pure hatred in his eyes before he reaches up and wipes his face clean.

"Wait," Phoenix cautions. "Listen, if we kill him, there will be no reason to keep those girls alive. Am I right, Farnsworth?"

"Isn't the great Phoenix, leader of the Peaceful Revolution, always right?" Farnsworth snickers.

"Don't stoop to his level," Brooke warns me, stroking my arm.

They are trying to calm me, but it's not working. I fight against their grips.

"But he's hurting them," I plead. "We have to help them." I suddenly feel weak on my feet. I swoon, and Phoenix catches me just before my knees hit the floor.

"Do what he wants, and he'll stop. Is that right, Farnsworth?" Brooke leaves me in Phoenix's care and walks over to Farnsworth.

"Something like that," Farnsworth answers, letting his eyes linger on Brooke's cleavage.

"Oh, please," she snaps, noticing his stare. "Like you'd even know what to do with them." She turns her back on Farnsworth and marches across the dining room. She heaves herself into a chair.

"Is that true?" I ask a visibly embarrassed Farnsworth.

"Is what true?" he snipes, with contempt in his voice. He is obviously mortified.

I imagine he is lost in Brooke's insult, worried none of us consider him to be man enough for…anything. He's right.

"Would you free them if you got what you

wanted?"

"Why should we trust him?" Brooke barks from the other side of the room.

"She's right," Phoenix adds. "Why should we trust him? He's already promised to free the girls."

"Because we have no other choice," I choke out, breaking free of Phoenix. I walk to Farnsworth, slowly, and Phoenix picks up my seashell and tucks it in his pocket. "Because he's not just cruel, he's lonely and pathetic, too. And the only way for him to get any kind of companionship is to force someone into it. So fine, Farnsworth. You win. What do you want?"

"We marry. Before you perform your Coupling duty."

"It's not my duty. I've served my time."

"Technically not. You never gave."

"She gave to you," Phoenix blurts.

"Too little, too late," Farnsworth quips.

"Why marriage?" I whisper.

"Because it's less...crass this way. And besides, it's time for me to marry. My people want stability in their leader. Especially now."

I stare at Farnsworth, dumbfounded. The room spins around us, yet my eyes are locked on his. For a moment, his eyes soften as if he wants me to want this. That's what I need.

I cough up another wad of phlegm and hurl it at Farnsworth. This time, it lands smack in his eye. He removes a square piece of cloth from his pocket and wipes away my infraction.

"I do wish you'd stop doing that, Veronica."

"Yeah? Well I wish you would leave the six of us alone. And anyone who may be left behind in the city.

But you won't, will you?"

"No," he whispers. He gazes at me, and his eyes soften. He smiles a small, sincere smile.

"What is there left to do?" I ask.

Farnsworth straightens up and adjusts his tie. "Meet at the chapel in one hour. Until then…well, you can enjoy each other's company."

My eyes dart to Phoenix who is staring so hard at Farnsworth, I sincerely wonder if Farnsworth might very well burst into flames. Farnsworth smiles slightly and turns away. He walks slowly to a door of the dining room and knocks on it three times. Almost immediately, the door opens and in run Lilly, Violet, and Raven. Each is dressed in an identical shiny, dark plum dress. The dresses are cut like fitted tank tops through the bodice before exploding into layers upon layers of ruffles. There is a giant flower attached to each of their waistbands. They are so beautiful I forget to breathe.

The girls run directly to me and throw their arms around my hips. Out of the corner of my eye I see Brooke smiling at us. She sees me and looks away.

"Are you okay?" I whisper to the girls.

"Yes," Raven assures me. She is taking charge of the situation. She shifts her weight and fidgets with her dress as she talks. "He didn't do anything to us. They just threatened to."

"I was scared," Lilly whispers, burying her face in my gown.

"Are you okay?" I ask Lilly.

"Yes. But I cried a lot," she tells me.

I place my hand under her chin and stroke it gently. "I'm sorry girls," I whisper. "I should never have let it—"

My voice breaks, and I step back from them.

Phoenix walks to me to comfort me. He places his hand on my arm.

"No," I snap, pulling back. "No. This happened when you and I were…ugh…" I bury my face in my hands. Once again guilt overwhelms me.

"Nothing happened. Really," Raven assures me. "And there would have been nothing you could have done, anyway. This is our journey to take. As much as we want you with us, it is still ours. You can't take responsibility for everything."

My eyes dart to her, wondering how she can be so impossibly brilliant and mature. She smiles at her brother and in that instant I know how—they were born that way. I smile at Phoenix and mouth a "sorry." He just nods at me, his mouth fixed in a pensive smile.

"Well, I really don't want to crash a happy reunion," Farnsworth states, clapping his hands together.

His action startles me. I had momentarily forgotten he was here.

Farnsworth continues. "I will send someone to collect you all." He turns to me. "I'm sorry I must go, but there's an old superstition that says it's bad luck for the groom to see the bride in her dress before they marry."

I hear Brooke scoff from her seat.

"Sir," I narrow my eyes at him as I speak, "don't worry about some silly superstition. Just meeting me was bad luck for you."

I hear Phoenix chuckle as Farnsworth starts slightly. Farnsworth straightens himself up and walks to me. He reaches out and places one hand on either side of my face. It is a completely intimate action, one that requires certainty on his part and trust on mine. Not minutes before, Phoenix had held my face in just such a way as he kissed me. Although I am not free to glance about, I feel Phoenix moving in to help me. I see Raven walk behind Farnsworth, stopping Phoenix. I squirm, trying to break free of Farnsworth, but I am unable.

"In one hour, Veronica Billings, you will be my wife. Remember that. And from that moment on, it will be your duty to love, honor, and obey me. Do you understand?"

I feel him flinch slightly, waiting for me to spit at him again.

"Veronica?" he asks, his grasp tightening on my face, my jaw sore from clenching. "Do you understand?"

I manage to shake free at last, and I look him dead in the eyes. "I understand, sir, what you are forcing me to do. But the last time I followed your orders and performed my duty for my country, it was all a farce. And I assure you…sir…any manufactured intimacy between us will also be a farce."

His eyes grow cold. "I will see you all in one hour." Farnsworth clicks his heels together, bows slightly to me, and slinks out of the room.

****

There is a collective sigh when Farnsworth leaves. Phoenix takes a few large steps toward me and pulls me close. I feel so safe and protected leaning against his chest, it's hard to remember the danger that waits, just moments from now. He strokes my hair lovingly, and then holds me at arm's length. He nods to me. There is something in his eyes, something in the way he reassures me, I know somehow we will be okay.

It is only a moment or two before the bodyguards return. They have become faceless, nameless entities representing only evil. One guard takes the three girls, and another two guards stand behind Phoenix, Brooke, and me, pushing us forward. They point their guns in the direction they want us to go.

Quickly, they walk us down a hall and into a large, windowless room in the middle of the mansion. Opulence overpowers us even here. The room is long and bulky, and crystal droplets of light hang from extremely high ceilings. There are floor to ceiling archways shaped like windows, and each archway is painted in an individual, specific scenario. I recognize some of the scenes in the paintings—the flower garden, the ocean, the front of Farnsworth's mansion. Many others remain a mystery, covered by heavy, pearl gray velvet curtains. There are fat, white chairs along the edges of the room, and the floor is a shiny, reddish wood. There is a huge amount of open space in the middle of the room, and yet, I begin to feel claustrophobic. I long for my trees and the freedom of camp.

"Well, I'll be," Brooke saunters up and down the floor. "While we were scraping for food and sending our girls to be drained, he was holding balls."

That's what this is…a ballroom. She flops down in a chair near a covered painting and pulls back the curtain slightly. She peeks underneath. It holds her attention for a second, and then she tosses the curtain back down.

"Jeez," she mutters, shaking her head. Whatever

she saw ticked her off royally.

The three girls flop down on the floor, dresses splayed gracefully around them. I sit opposite Brooke, wishing there was something I could do.

Only Phoenix continues to move. He cases the room. I imagine he's searching for an answer or a way out, literally or figuratively. Finally, even he seems to have given up hope. He stops short and runs his hand across his chin, then studies us. I can only imagine how we must appear, depressed and beaten. I offer a small but encouraging smile. He smiles back, and then something catches his eye.

"Ah," Phoenix exclaims. He makes his way to the farthest point in the room and grabs hold of something. He comes toward us, his gait much more animated, waving a tiny silver rectangle. He shows it to me and then plops the rectangle into a black square, about half the size of my walkie. He presses a button on the square then suddenly bam!

We all jump, as a fierce crash of a drum echoes off all corners of the room. All three girls climb onto my lap, terrified, and my heart doesn't slow until I realize it is only music surrounding us.

"Oh, sorry," Phoenix utters, adjusting the rectangle. The harshness of the drum is replaced with soft, sweet music, floating down to us. It calms the girls.

"Well jeez, Phoenix," Brooke barks. "Way to give me a heart attack. Thanks."

"Sorry," Phoenix snickers, smiling. He presses another button and the music style changes. There's another cacophony of instruments, but this time the music is peppier. The girls settle back down on the floor, their dresses splayed, this time resembling droplets of plum paint on an artist's palette.

"This is so not useful," Brooke snips, crossing her legs and lounging across her chair.

Phoenix is undaunted. He adjusts the music one last time, and this time it is fast, loud, happy music. He smiles a victorious smile and glides himself over to me in time with the music. I laugh, despite myself, covering my mouth with my hand. He stands before me and reaches out to me. I glance down at the girls who are all staring, smiling at us. A man is singing about never thinking he would fall for this particular girl, and the irony is not lost on me. The music grows faster as Phoenix pulls me to my feet. I stumble into him and bounce off his chest. I laugh loudly as he grabs one of my hands in his and wraps his other hand around my waist. We dance close but quickly, turning in an ungraceful circle. My head falls back as I laugh, trying to keep up with Phoenix and his moves. He pushes me away and pulls me near, once, then twice, and I'm laughing so hard I trip over my own feet. Then he lifts our arms into the air and spins me so my back is to him, and he takes my hand firmly with one hand and places his other on my lower back. He spins me and I keep going, twirling faster and faster until I fall back into my chair.

The girls are on their feet, clapping and cheering. Even Brooke smiles a tiny smile and Phoenix sees it. He glides to her, crooking his finger, beckoning her. She shakes her head in protest, but Phoenix stands before her, nodding and smiling. He puts his hand out to her, and finally, reluctantly, she takes it. As if on cue, the man sings about having "played around before," as

Brooke hesitantly begins to move with Phoenix. Within minutes she is gyrating to the beat, and when Phoenix spins her, she finds her way to him again. She slithers up to him and presses her back against his front, and sexily, she begins to sway in front of him. He laughs, tosses his head back, and runs off our dance floor to join the girls and me. Brooke dances a beautiful and provocative solo, and Phoenix covers Lilly and Violet's eyes, making a funny face at me. I follow suit and cover Raven's, but I'm laughing so hard, I'm sure she's catching glimpses as my hand bobs up and down with my laughter. Finally, Brooke quits and drops into her chair, and as the music hits the fastest beat of all, Phoenix grabs all three little girls and begins spinning them like tops beneath his fingers. It is breathtaking to watch them twirl as their dresses puff out into lace clouds around their tiny bodies. They spin and spin until they must be dizzy, and Phoenix returns them to their seats on the floor.

The music grows slower, and Phoenix comes to me, pulling me to him. We barely move, our bodies tight up against one another, swaying softly. The man singing warns he can't live without this girl, and he'd be lost without her, and Phoenix sings along in my ear. We stop moving, and he wraps his arms so tightly around me I can barely breathe. I lift my face to his, and heat envelopes us. Our arms form a sultry cocoon around one another. My breath is choppy as he leans down to kiss me. His lips are nearly on mine when a door slams. I jump and break apart from Phoenix, dazed.

I turn to find Farnsworth standing there, his beady eyes fixed on Phoenix.

"I would appreciate it if you would unhand my fiancée," Farnsworth growls.

Chapter Three

My last hour of freedom feels like a fast moving eternity. From the second Farnsworth braved superstition and collected me himself, the endless prepping will not cease. At the same time, I am overly aware with every passing tick, tick, tick of the clock, I am nearing the end of Veronica Billings—for better or for worse.

Farnsworth's assistant, Grace, fights the tears in her eyes as she places a crown made of flowers on my head. She adjusts it and straightens my dress all without making eye contact. I reach out and take her hand to squeeze, and she squeezes back.

All too soon, I am escorted toward a tiny chapel on the opposite side of the mansion. As we walk, I keep wondering why Farnsworth appears as healthy as he does, and when he'll need another transfusion of my tainted blood. What if he takes the blood soon and dies immediately? Panic overwhelms me—will the guards then murder Lilly, Violet, and Raven? There'll be no reason to keep them alive.

I walk to the closed doors leading to the tiny chapel. Grace stands next to me, and a bodyguard reaches out for the handle. I take a deep breath, and the doors open. I step inside, and there stand Brooke, Violet, Lilly, and Raven, each turned toward me. Just past them stands Phoenix. He is dressed in another suit just a tad too small on him, pulling perfectly across his chest, hugging his strong arm muscles. I gasp when I see him, a smile spreading across my face. It is almost too much to imagine that Phoenix and I...maybe, someday.

He returns my smile with a forlorn look then steps back to reveal Farnsworth at the altar, waiting for me exactly where Phoenix should be standing. My heart drops so fast I may very well step on it.

Farnsworth smiles his venomous smile and puts his hand out to me. I have nowhere to go but forward. I walk to Phoenix, but Farnsworth shakes his head, takes my hand, and pulls me to his side. I stumble forward, gasping, not wanting to leave Phoenix. As I step up beside Farnsworth, a man holding a bible appears out of nowhere. I glimpse back over my shoulder first at the girls, and then over my other shoulder at Phoenix.

"Phoenix was kind enough to be my best man," Farnsworth explains. "He's holding our rings."

Phoenix stares at me, and I can only imagine the sorrow he must be feeling.

"This is ridiculous," I mutter, turning to Farnsworth. "I know nothing about you. You don't know me at all. Principal Leader Farnsworth, sir, I am in love with someone else."

He regards me in such a way that for a moment, I think I may have gotten through to him.

"Really?" Farnsworth raises an eyebrow, seeming interested in my revelation. "Well, that's just an obstacle I'll have to overcome. I've dealt with worse. Now, if you don't mind..." he nods to the man with the bible.

"Wait," Phoenix blurts, stepping up to us.

"Farnsworth. We had an agreement. An arrangement. None of it had to do with Veronica marrying you or being forced to a Coupling."

"I changed my mind. I can do that, you know." Farnsworth turns back to the man, and nods once again.

Within seconds words are rattled off, and phrases begin assaulting me that are every bit as harmful as sharp knives. My brain fights to keep up with this onslaught attacking me. I begin to perspire, and I squint as people morph into blurry images. I swivel around toward the girls, but I can't see their faces. I can only make out tiny bodies shuffling back and forth, their oversized dresses swaying like pendulums. My heartbeat pounds in my ears, only to be replaced by a deafening squeal. Panicked, I spin around, lost, unable to make heads or tails of the situation. I look back for Phoenix, but he is no longer at his post. Wildly, I glance around as the man with the bible speaks.

"Do you, Principal Leader Farnsworth, sir, take Veronica Billings to be your true and wedded wife? Do you solemnly promise to love, honor, cherish, and protect her, to forsake all others for her sake, until death do you part?"

Desperately, I scan the room for Phoenix.

"I do." Farnsworth takes my hand.

"Phoenix?" I ask, trying to break free. I am a prisoner now, being pulled into my jail from which, I do not know how I can ever return.

"Keep going," Farnsworth commands under his breath.

"And do you—"

"I'm here, Ron. Right here." Phoenix is suddenly at my side, staring at Farnsworth. "You know this can't happen." He speaks directly to Farnsworth. "Think about our deal. Think about what's at stake."

"This is my wedding, Phoenix," Farnsworth hisses. "Do not make me remove you."

"But this is—" Phoenix protests, stepping closer to Farnsworth.

"Guards," Farnsworth yells.

"Be a man, Farnsworth. Don't call your backup every time you enter into a situation you're afraid of."

"I am not afraid." Farnsworth narrows his eyes at Phoenix. "I am simply in a hurry. In case you don't remember, there's a war out there. And I want to be sure I have my beautiful bride safely whisked away before there is any chance the rebels will infiltrate my mansion. So if you'll excuse me—"

"Whisked away?" I murmur, but no one hears me.

"I won't excuse you," Phoenix barks. "Not for any of it. And certainly not for this."

Farnsworth snaps his bony fingers, and the guards grab Lilly, Violet, and Raven.

"That's sad," Phoenix scoffs. "Hiding behind children. Threatening little girls. You are pathetic."

"What I am," Farnsworth retorts, flashing his overly white smile, "is the winner. Quite simply. So here's how it will go. Veronica will marry me, and you will let it happen."

"And if I don't?"

Farnsworth nods, and the first guard grabs Lilly. He holds both of her arms behind her back and pulls her hair to one side, exposing her soft white neck. It appears so frail and delicate, I know the guard could snap it with one try. Lilly bursts into tears.

"Stop," I plead. "Stop. Whatever you want. I'll do

it. I'll marry you. We'll leave. Just let her go. Let them all go. Just as we agreed."

"Ron—" Phoenix steps closer to me.

"It's the only way." I smile at Phoenix, choking back tears.

"You know what's making Farnsworth weak, we can still blackmail him," Phoenix whispers.

"No," I shake my head. "He'll just hurt them if I let him die. My whole purpose now is to keep Farnsworth alive. That's the only way to keep all of you alive, too. There's never been a choice. Not really. We both know it." I turn to Farnsworth. "There's never been an option, has there?"

"No," he remarks, sounding almost reproachful. "No."

"So you simply lied to us?" Phoenix asks, admonishing.

"Yes," Farnsworth explains. "It is really almost sad to see how your simple idealism assumes there is good in everyone."

"You're right," Phoenix tells him. "I was wrong once again. There really is no good in you."

"And I would also think if you love her as much as you say you do then you would want her to be safe no matter what it costs you."

Phoenix steps back. Farnsworth's words have affected him.

"No, Phoenix," I caution. I can see something in him has changed. I turn to Farnsworth. "Let them go, Farnsworth," I demand. "Let them go, for real, and I will marry you."

"Of course, my dear, anything."

"No. Spare me the crap, Farnsworth. Give them a

helicopter back to camp."

"And in return…?"

"And in return, I'll marry you willingly."

Brooke gasps behind me.

"Ron, no," Phoenix exclaims. He is at my side. "Don't do this."

"There's no choice." My voice cracks as I speak.

"Of course there is. There's a way. There's always a way. We'll find it. Together." He holds my hand, and the corners of his beautiful blue eyes crinkle as he smiles at me.

In that instant, I am certain of how much he loves me, and how much I love him.

"Trust me, Ron," he coos. "Trust me."

"I do," I whisper. "But I don't trust him." I turn from Phoenix and stare at Farnsworth. "You heard what I said. Give them a helicopter back to camp and I'll marry you. Willingly."

"It is a deal." Farnsworth answers much too quickly, and there is…something in the way he says it. Then he smiles his loving smile at me.

I inhale deeply and push the air out of my mouth. I am suddenly clear and focused.

"Get the copter," Farnsworth orders one of his guards. The guard leaves the room, and I turn back to the man with the bible.

"Go on, p-please," I stammer.

"Very well," the visibly shaken man responds. "Do you, Veronica Billings, take Principal Leader Farnsworth to be your true and wedded husband? Do you solemnly promise to love, honor, cherish, and obey him? Do you promise to forsake all others for his sake, until death do you part?"

True and wedded husband? Love, honor, cherish and obey? Until death do we part? How? How can I possibly do this? The girls are brought before me. They smile at me, each in her own special way. Lilly wholeheartedly. Violet, shy. And Raven stares straight at me, supporting me in whatever I decide. Brooke walks up behind them and places a hand on Lilly and Violet's shoulders. I turn, and there stands Phoenix. Unable to look at me.

"Again please," Farnsworth tells the man with the bible. Farnsworth scrutinizes me out of the corner of his eye, and I can tell he is wondering, as we all are—especially me—what I am going to do.

I peer at each of them again. My eyes land on Phoenix.

"Ah yes, the rings," Farnsworth adds, as if my gazing at Phoenix reminded him. "Let's start with that, shall we? May I have them please, Phoenix?"

Phoenix locks his eyes on me and shoves his hand deep into his pocket. I pray he will pull out my seashell, and we can forget all of this insanity, but instead, he pulls out two gold bands, each wide with an intricate latticework pattern. One is plain gold, and the other is encrusted with brilliant, large, shiny, clear stones. The sight of the ring makes Brooke gasp, and Phoenix's eyes dart over to her.

"Sorry," she mumbles.

To me, it seems as if that ring must weigh a thousand pounds.

"Now," Farnsworth tells the man with the bible. "Again."

"Very well." The man moves his bible from hand to hand and absentmindedly pulls on the button of his jacket. He clears his throat. "Do you, Veronica Billings, take Principal Leader Malachi Verrell Farnsworth the Third to be your true and wedded husband?"

My mind starts at Farnsworth's name, but the man's words shock me back to the moment.

"Do you solemnly promise to love, honor, cherish, and obey him? Do you promise to forsake all others for his sake, until death do you part?"

"Don't do it, Ron," Phoenix whispers.

I look from Phoenix to the girls and back to Phoenix. I imagine Phoenix slipping the ring on my finger, and then me slipping the other on his. I imagine him taking my hand and leading us all out of the chapel and far from the mansion. Away from Farnsworth, and away from this nightmare. Looking at Phoenix, I know love is the only answer. Finally, my eyes divert from Phoenix and land on Farnsworth. He nauseates me. Staring at him, I know there is only one thing to do. Only one thing I can say.

My chest heaves with anticipation. I turn back to Phoenix and for a second, the life I could have flashes before me. The life that's supposed to be mine.

"Veronica?" the man with the bible asks again. "Do you take Principal Leader Farnsworth to be your true and wedded husband?"

Time stops.

Breathing ceases.

All I want is to kiss Phoenix. I smile softly, confident, knowing it will all be okay. "Love is always the answer," I whisper to myself. And I love Phoenix and the girls more than I love myself.

"Veronica?" Farnsworth's face is flushed. I can tell he is as confused as I am.

"I-I…"

Phoenix stares at me. His blue eyes are locked on mine. He is the air and I, the earth. The room is so quiet all that can be heard is the restarting of my labored breath. I open my mouth, and the words fall out.

"I…do…"

Chapter Four

Loud, clamorous sound envelopes me. Shouts are heard, the girls are crying. Lights are flashing, and the man with the bible has disappeared from sight. Everything is going to hell, and why shouldn't it?

I am unable to move. I feel as if I'm inside a blurry bubble, and if I move, my protective cover will burst. I shudder slightly, knowing just outside my bubble is the life I must begin as Farnsworth's bride. I find it nearly impossible to shake the haze lingering inside my head. I turn to Phoenix as if I'm seeing him for the very first time. His tousled hair, the scruff on his chin, his blue eyes, so soulful and sad, they hurt to gaze into them.

I realize people are rushing about. The calm we had before the wedding is long gone, replaced with an urgency bordering on hysteria. I face my girls, huddled up against Brooke, and I shake my head, unable to understand why they are not with me. I hold out my arms for them, and Lilly breaks free of her group to run to me. Raven grabs her and pulls her back. I look at Raven not understanding, but she just shakes her head at me. I let my eyes float up to Brooke, but she simply avoids me. I cannot understand why they are treating me like I am a leper, like someone they may have feelings for, but they must keep at a safe distance. Don't they understand I'm still me? Finally, my gaze finds Phoenix who has not moved from his spot, despite the craziness surrounding him. I smile at him, but he doesn't smile back.

"Phoenix?" I ask, not understanding why my girls have turned on me. I feel that same empty ache in my soul I felt when Lulu left me. "Phoenix?" The tears burst into my eyes as Phoenix steps forward, toward me. We are close enough to hear one another above the racket. For whole moments it is only the two of us.

He stands before me and reaches out to slip my hand into his. I squeeze, but he doesn't squeeze back.

"Phoenix?" I whisper.

He leans down, toward me. I close my eyes and breathe him in, waiting to feel his kiss on my lips. Instead, I feel his warm breath by my ear. Slowly, he raises my hand to show me the oversized ring, encircling my finger.

"Why?" he whispers. "Why, Ron? Why would you say yes?"

I pull back from him, horrified he thinks there could ever have been an option. "I-I had to," I stutter, my eyes searching his. "The girls…" I mutter. "He would have…"

"Okay, Veronica," Phoenix snips. "I understand." He pulls away now, cold and impersonal.

"No. You don't."

Phoenix has distanced himself from me, so I fight to be heard above the din.

"What choice did I have? Phoenix? Tell me, please."

"You had me, Ron."

"Had? What do you mean had? Phoenix? Please," I plead.

"There's nothing left to say, Ron. Nothing."

"But don't you see? The girls will be safe now. He won't kill them, because he got his way."

"He always gets his way." Phoenix runs his hands through his hair. "Always. But this," he motions to my dress and points to my ring, "this was your decision. You made the choice, Veronica."

"It was the only choice I had."

"No," Phoenix snaps, crossing toward me angrily. He grabs my arm and holds it tightly. "You could have chosen me. Me, Veronica."

"I did," I scream. "Don't you see? I chose to keep you alive."

"No," Phoenix mutters, dropping my arm and stepping back. "You chose to trust someone else. You chose Farnsworth over me."

"What are you talking about? What could I have done?" My knees feel weak, and tears are wetting my face.

"You could have believed in me, Veronica."

"I do believe in you, Phoenix. More than anyone. Ever."

"No," Phoenix whispers through a smile, "you don't trust anyone but yourself. You believed there was no answer except the one you thought of. And so you married him."

"To keep you all alive," I repeat.

"Maybe so. But don't you see?" Phoenix appears so smart and calm. "Don't you see you just committed the ultimate betrayal?"

"How?" I whisper. My stomach clenches, and my insides radiate a dull ache. Desperation fills my every pore.

"By not trusting me. I told you we would find a

way. We would find an answer together. But once again the great Veronica Billings has to slay every dragon on her own."

"That's not true," I cry, trying to move to him.

He steps away from me. "It's not? Then tell me, didn't you just decide to save us?"

"Yes, but—"

"But maybe I don't want you to save me."

"What?" I ask, recoiling. "Why not?"

He turns to me, his eyes blazing with passion. "Because it's my job to save you."

I gasp, and he takes a breath. He looks off and then back to me.

"Did you ever think, Veronica, even just for one minute, maybe there is an answer you didn't think of? Maybe the chaos or the duress stymied your brain…? Did you ever consider I had a plan? Did you ever think of that?"

"Of course, but I didn't see any way—"

"No, there you go. You didn't see any way. But I did. I saw something that maybe I wasn't able to share with you just yet."

"But how could I know that?" I am exasperated.

"You should have trusted me. Trusted us."

"I do trust you."

"Apparently not enough."

"Phoenix," I sob. "This is me. Me you're talking to. How could you be saying these things to me?"

He lifts my hand again and shoves my ring up to eye level. "Because you have done the one thing I cannot save you from…and may not be able to forgive you for."

I step back, horrified. "What are you saying? I love

you. You."

"And I love you. But I'm devastated. Because there is nothing else I can do to protect you." He glances in the direction of Farnsworth, who is listening intently to a man in a black suit. "That's someone else's job, now," Phoenix mumbles. He shoves his hands into his pockets, and I catch my breath, waiting, hoping, praying he will produce my seashell and hand it to me. He doesn't. Instead, he looks down at his feet and then back up to me. He releases his hands, uncertain of what to do with them. "People think I have dedicated my entire life to the revolution. But the truth is that I've dedicated it to saving you. You, Ron. I have dedicated my life to saving you from rebels, from Gunnar, from bleeding to death, from mushroom poisoning, and until now, from Farnsworth."

"Phoenix…" I choke through my tears.

"No, Ron, no. You tied my hands. I can't protect you anymore. I love you, but you left me. And there's nothing I can do about it. You have your way now. You are completely on your own. Enjoy your new life, Mrs. Farnsworth."

And with that, Phoenix turns and walks away.

Chapter Five

Within minutes Phoenix, Brooke, and the girls are collected and led toward the door. Phoenix snaps his arm and breaks free from a guard who has him by the elbow, trying to lead him forward. Phoenix doesn't even stop to look back. None of them do. I am so confused and devastated I stand paralyzed, watching them go. Out of the corner of my eye, I feel Farnsworth staring at me. To his credit, he doesn't approach me.

After the door of the chapel closes behind Brooke, Grace moves toward me. "Come now, Veronica," she purrs. "Let's get you a hot bath and a cup of chamomile tea, shall we?"

I glimpse down at her, confused. I am so lost and lonely, I feel like I may crumple to the ground at any moment.

"Come," she repeats, in an even more soothing voice. "Come, Veronica."

I shift around to see Farnsworth smile at me. I drop my eyes to the ground and let myself be led from the chapel with Grace as my guide.

****

In my room, I find a bubble bath and hot tea waiting for me.

"We have very little time," Grace informs me.

"Until what?" I ask, my heart pounding for the first time since it was broken.

"Until we leave. You didn't know?"

I shake my head.

"Oh, well, Principal Leader Farnsworth has planned a honeymoon for you. Do you know what a honeymoon is?"

I nod. "He has?" I ask, my eyes finally finding their way off the floor. "Where?" Once again, panic finds its way inside me. It spreads throughout me, obviously comfortable, as I have become its permanent home.

"Well it's a business trip, slash honeymoon," Grace clarifies, busying herself with clothes from my armoire.

"And we leave…?" My words trail off, wondering if I will be called to perform my marital duty tonight.

"As soon as we're packed," Grace answers, heaving a large pile of clothing from my closet. She stops and wipes a dab of perspiration from her forehead, catching her breath.

I slump back on the bed, relieved and terrified all at once. Taking a trip will certainly delay my call to Couple, but where is he taking me? How far will we go? My heart aches when I realize I will have no way to tell Phoenix where I am going. Tears spring to my eyes, knowing even if I could tell him he wouldn't care.

Grace is next to me with a tissue.

"Thank you," I whisper, as tears flow down my cheeks.

She leads me to the bathroom and helps me out of my dress and into the tub. I sink into the warm water, the bubbles tickling my nose. I stare as she shakes out the long white dress and smooths it against her body.

"I'll send this to have it cleaned," she rattles off, but I'm not sure it was meant for me to hear.

I sit up, bubbles splashing out of the tub. "No," I yell.

Grace regards me quizzically.

"Don't have it cleaned. It was the…" I stop. Maybe I don't know Grace well enough to share this.

"The last thing he saw you in?" she asks, her head tilted sideways.

I nod. "He told me I looked beautiful. We were together on the beach…I was wearing it the last time he kissed me."

She smiles at me, wistfully. "Would you like me to leave it here for you?" Her words are gentle.

The water swirls in knowing circles around my body, renewing me and slowly restoring my confidence. My eyes fall across the graceful flow of the gown against Grace's body. I remember his hands clamped on my waist. I remember climbing up onto him, our mouths locked. I remember feeling his love for me. How strong and protective he was. I remember him assuring me no one would ever come between us. Well someone did. And it was him.

"Veronica? Should I leave this here for you?"

"No." I shake my head and take a deep breath. "No. Don't leave it. And don't clean it. Burn it."

Without even glancing at her, I feel Grace recoil from my words. "Are you sure, Veronica?"

My body tenses, and I set my jaw, hard. My hands grip the sides of the bathtub. He has left me, and the only thing I can do is to move on. "There is no need to second guess me. Thank you for helping me, Grace. But if you don't mind, I'd like to finish my bath. Alone."

Grace smiles a proper smile. She bows gracefully. "Of course, Mrs. Farnsworth, ma'am."

\*\*\*\*

I step out of the tub and wrap a slinky robe around my still wet body. The silk sticks to my back and legs, reminding me of sweaty nights at camp, when my tank top would stick to my torso as I walked from cabin to cabin, doing bed checks. I squirm uncomfortably, and pull my wet hair to the side. I leave the bathroom and enter my bedroom to find Grace has packed my entire, extensive wardrobe all while I was in the bath. My eyes scan a row of floral patterned suitcases.

"How long are we going to be gone?" I count what seems an endless amount of cases.

"That depends on how long it takes him to complete his work," Grace answers, zipping one last zipper on one last suitcase.

I walk farther into the room to find the final suitcase lying haphazardly across the bed. I run my fingers across delicate gold raised lettering: "M.V.F." I stare at the lettering until it blends into the background and the pattern of wild flowers. It is so odd, a man having gold lettering like this on a floral suitcase. But it is Farnsworth.

"You like the monogram?" she asks.

Monogram. A new word.

Grace continues. "He spent a long time choosing just the right one."

"I guess," I mumble. "But it seems odd, even for Farnsworth."

"What's that, dear?"

"The delicate gold…monogram," I practice the word, committing it to memory. "And the flowers. I mean, it's a little feminine. Even for him."

Her smile abandons her, and she studies me,

quizzically.

"The monogram." I point to the suitcase. "MVF. Malachi Verrell Farnsworth. Why would a man want a floral pattern—"

"These aren't his." Her eyes are steady on mine.

"They're not?" I ask. I survey the suitcases again. "But he has them monogrammed." Then I realize. "M.V.F. Mrs. Veronica Farnsworth," I whisper, the horror registering in me.

Grace only nods in response.

"But…we were just…m-married." I have trouble saying the word. "Even Farnsworth couldn't move that fast," I protest.

Grace looks away.

My pulse quickens, and I feel anger coursing through my veins. "These suitcases were monogrammed long before today." As soon as I say it, I know it is a fact.

"He was always hoping…" she tells me, softly.

"How…how long has he been planning this?" I murmur.

"Since the day he met you." Grace stares at me. "And maybe even before that. You are everything to him. Everything he wants, and everything he wants to be."

"That's it," I mumble, starting to rip off my robe and barging into my closet hoping to find my real clothes.

"Wait," Grace tells me, following me in.

Exasperated, I spin around inside an empty closet. No sweater, no shorts, no boots. Grace places a hand on me.

"No," I growl.

"Veronica," she warns. "Be smart. There is nothing you can do about this."

"He had been planning this all along." I am disgusted.

"Yes, and you have every right to be angry, but now you need to ask yourself the reason why."

"Why?"

"Yes…why?" This is the first time I have ever heard Grace raise her voice. "Why did he wait all this time to marry you?"

"He didn't have a choice," I answer, fuming.

"Of course, he did. He always does."

"You sound like Phoenix," I mumble, sorrow replacing the anger I had felt just moments before.

Grace tilts her head sympathetically. It is the two of us in my large, empty closet.

"I know you know the answer, Veronica. Think about it. Before, at the wedding…I know you saw it. What did you see in his eyes that, for a moment anyway, made you feel you had the power?"

"I don't know, Grace." I storm out of the closet and plop on the bed.

"Think," she tells me, following me.

"Why don't you tell me?" I challenge. "You always play these games with me. Always making me work for the answer. Like in my dreams."

"And do you find the answer?"

"Sometimes," I mutter.

"Always," she corrects me. "Always."

"If I always had the answer, Grace, right now I would be with my boyfriend, on my way back to my camp. I would not be sitting in this hellhole, waiting for my husband to decide what to do with me."

"It's hardly a hellhole." Grace speaks softly. She adjusts the buttons on her suit jacket and sits primly, next to me. "Now, think. What did you see?"

"I saw...I don't know." I flop back, exasperated.

"You're not trying."

"No, I'm not trying, because I don't care, because this is all stupid." I stand up next to the bed, towering over her. "Just tell me, Grace. Please."

"I can't tell you." She stands, her voice matching my tone.

"Why not?" I demand.

She diverts her eyes.

"Why not?" I ask, louder.

She turns to me, her movements, sharp and birdlike. "Because I still work for Principal Leader Farnsworth. And if it's okay by you, I'd like to stay alive."

For a moment, her large, beautiful gray eyes widen, and I realize she has revealed too much. My heart pounds as I stare at her.

"What do you mean, 'stay alive'?"

She busies herself by smoothing wrinkles on the bedspread.

"Grace?" Then it dawns on me. "You're an O." I back away from her. "All this time I thought you were on my side, that you cared about me, but all you were doing was protecting yourself."

"Veronica, wait." Grace tries to touch my arm.

"No." I snap my arm, breaking free from her. "No."

I think this through, speaking as I work it out.

"So if I come up with the answer, then technically you haven't helped me and you're still in Farnsworth's good graces. If you're lucky, I have the wrong answer, and this prolongs everything. I stay here to be Let and you live on happily as Farnsworth's confidante. But if I do have the right answer—like I once did about being a Leader when we convinced Farnsworth to temporarily abdicate to me, in order to gain the trust of the people—well then, I still came up with the idea myself so you're not at fault. And if you're really lucky…if my plan works, and we go forward like Phoenix and I did, you win the jackpot. You were good to me so you could have the chance to work for the new Principal Leader, and you are also out from under Farnsworth's thumb. I'll be damned," I mutter, plopping back down on the bed, recreating the wrinkles Grace has just eliminated. "It's brilliant."

We stare at each other.

"Veronica—"

"It's Mrs. Farnsworth," I snap. "I thought we already established that."

"I'm sorry, Mrs. Farnsworth, ma'am."

"Please leave," I tell Grace. "And take your packed suitcases with you."

"I'll go," she concedes, suddenly seeming saddened by our exchange. "But I'll leave the suitcases. Trust me, you're going to need them."

"Trust you?" I ask, my eyes locking on hers. "Why would I ever trust you again?"

She smiles sadly. "Because I'm the closest thing to a friend you have."

Chapter Six

Grace's words sit heavily on me. But she is wrong. She is not my friend. And neither is Phoenix any longer. So that leaves only me. Just me, married to the man I was trying to assassinate only days before. Anger, fear, and loneliness form a trinity of pain in the very place my soul used to be. I close my eyes wishing it was all a horrible nightmare, and I'm startled by a knock on my door. It is a man's knock. Undoubtedly, Farnsworth.

I stand and cinch the belt of my robe tightly around my waist. I pull open the door quickly, and Farnsworth appears startled. Then his look of surprise morphs into a much softer, kinder expression. He wears an opened navy blue jacket over a white shirt. He adjusts the jacket on his shoulders before he speaks. "I came to see if you need anything," he asks, not forcing his way in.

"My life back," I snap, slamming the door.

He stops the door with his hand. I stare at his hand, waiting for the bruising, but I see nothing. Even the mark on his cheek looks better.

"I wasn't through." Farnsworth blocks the door with his foot. "I came to see if you need anything, and, as a side note, although you are quite fetching in that robe, it would be best if you dressed in the clothing Grace set out for you."

I pull the robe closed at my neck and hold it tight.

47

"She didn't..." I mumble, not wanting to look Farnsworth in the eyes.

"She didn't help you dress?" he asks indignantly, as if this was the greatest sin any of us has committed.

"I sent her away before she could help." Although I am angry with her, there is no sense in throwing her to the wolves—or wolf. Not yet, anyway.

"I see. Well then, would you like my help?" he asks.

I study him, but there is no lechery in his expression. He is sincere.

"I have dressed myself for nearly seventeen years," I state, flatly. "I think I've got it."

"Very well." Farnsworth turns and then remembers something. "Ah yes, and the other thing I wanted to tell you, we will be leaving in half an hour."

"Where are we going?" I ask.

Farnsworth smiles, and I watch him lift his hand, fighting the impulse to reach for me. I stand frozen, terrified.

He drops his hand and shakes his head. "To your new life, Veronica."

****

Farnsworth's surprise appearance makes me uneasy. I begin pacing my floor, hearing the tick, tick, tick of the clock, knowing within minutes Farnsworth and I will be boarding his helicopter and leaving the New World, bound for...anywhere. I spy the last suitcase on the bed and unzip it to find jeans and a white shirt nearly identical to the shirt Farnsworth was wearing. The sick feeling in the pit of my stomach tells me this is the correct thing to wear, and until I am certain of my next move, I had better play by the rules.

I also find a brush to comb through my hair, and a pair of flat shoes that seem like something Margaret, the prim, former leader of my camp, would wear. Amazingly, everything fits. I zip my robe into the suitcase and try to sit still, waiting for orders.

Of course, I cannot sit still. It is only moments until my old friend and nemesis, hope, decides to show up and demand attention. The temptation hope lures me with is too strong to fight. I make my way to my window and hold back the heavy, velvet curtain. Despite the darkness, I can still see the water, and my breath catches at the emptiness of the beach below, and the sorrow I feel. One after another, the waves make their way to the sand; crashing to protest their solitude, announcing their protest to a world that cannot, and does not, care. Grains of sand struggle to find their way to the ocean, sliding in and out with the waves—a momentary dance, a second of togetherness—but ultimately, they are relegated to their place on the earth, never allowed to be carried out to sea. Each in its rightful place, never permitted to be more than what it is right now. A lone seagull flies overhead. An empty beach may be the saddest place God has ever created.

Tick, tick. Knock, knock. And so it begins.

\*\*\*\*

A large group escorts Farnsworth, Grace, and me to the helicopter. I follow, and do as I am instructed, never glancing back at the beach and my last moments of happiness. I have never before been so demure, or felt so weak. Yet the more docile and submissive I become, the stronger Farnsworth seems. I have to wonder if they took my very soul and gave it to him during our last transfusion.

"You look lovely, Veronica," Farnsworth coos, sitting next to me in the helicopter.

My head falls toward the window. I do not have the strength to answer him. We adjust our headsets as the helicopter starts. As soon as I hear the whir of the rotors, I am flooded with memories. Tears leak uncontrollably from my eyes.

"Here," Grace pulls a pair of dark glasses from her bag and hands them to me.

I mean to at least whisper a "thank you," but I cannot will myself to say even this. Farnsworth pretends not to notice our interaction.

The helicopter flies in the opposite direction it did the last time. I'm certain of it, as I feel my heart race from fear and dread. I sit up and fight to see out the window.

"No," Farnsworth comments. "We're not heading to camp."

I nod and plop back against my seat, burying my head in my arm. I think of my camp, and memories fall on me like an avalanche of fresh, wet snow. Like the eclipsed natural beauty that once must have existed in the tree-covered mountains, vast lake, and now browning, weed-covered lawns, so evil was hidden beneath the tranquility and serenity. I shake my head and steal a glimpse at Farnsworth, achingly embarrassed I ever believed in him. For seven years I lived at camp not as a girl, but as a sheep, who willingly closed her eyes in order to become a well-respected leader in his government. I led hundreds of little girls to the Lettings, and consequently, unknowingly, took them to their deaths. I let my head fall hard against the wall, thinking I should have listened to my once best friend, Gretchen. She knew what was happening, and although she didn't spell it out for me, I should have paid attention to her clues. Farnsworth is nothing more than a glorified murderer.

But despite all of that, camp was my point of revelation as well. Camp was my home, and since being separated from my mother, the people in camp were my only family. It is where I met my girls and where I grew into the young woman I have become—for better or for worse. It's where I decided to forgive myself and baptize myself as reborn. More than anything else, camp is where I fell in love with Phoenix. I catch a glimpse of my reflection in the window, and silent tears stream down my face as I think of him. Flying farther and farther away, I wonder if I will ever make it back to my camp and my waterfront to be with Phoenix as we had promised each other. My thoughts of Phoenix turn dark, and I can no longer keep my sobbing silent. I feel Farnsworth adjust in the seat next to me. I pray he does not try to touch me to comfort me. Thankfully, he doesn't.

I peek out the window from time to time, and see we are flying over more and more highways and buildings. The farther we fly, the more the water seems to close in on us. It's like the ocean is following us, and the ground becomes one long strip, pointing toward the end of the earth. Maybe we will just fly off. Soon, I feel as if I could easily reach out and touch the ocean on both sides of us. Just at that point, the helicopter touches down.

"We're here, my bride," Farnsworth whispers.

His words send cold chills down my spine. "I'm not—" I begin to protest, and then I realize, yes, that is in fact, what I am. His bride.

He smiles a self-indulgent smile.

"Don't trap me like that again," I mutter, slipping off my glasses.

The amused expression on Farnsworth's face vanishes. "Come," he commands.

I follow him out of the helicopter.

I scan my surroundings as large floodlights beam down on us. There are small red lights lined up in endlessly long strips along the ground, and in the middle of those strips is a giant, silver cylinder with huge "wings" attached to it, pointing straight at us. I am completely unsure of what I see.

A man in a white uniform runs to us. "Principal Leader Farnsworth, Mrs. Farnsworth, ma'am, we need to move as quickly as we can."

I am perplexed. Can people outside of our tiny world already know I have married Farnsworth? And what is that thing I am looking at?

"Are you ready for your first airplane ride, my dear?" Farnsworth asks, holding his arm out for me to walk before him.

Silently, I step in front of him and make my way to the silver cylinder. "An airplane?" I ask, to no one in particular as we walk.

"Yes," Farnsworth answers, sounding happy to educate me. "It can go significantly farther and faster than the helicopter."

I feel my stomach drop. I stop and swivel around to face Farnsworth. "Then we're really not going to—"

"No." He shakes his head. "We're really not." He places his arm back out to guide me, and I can tell he is irritated by my constant thoughts of camp.

I throw my hair over my shoulder and approach the airplane. There is an open door, several feet off the ground, with a large ladder leading up to it.

"Mrs. Farnsworth." A man on the plane is speaking, but it takes me whole seconds to realize he is speaking to me.

"Oh, yes, of course." I begin to climb the stairs, Farnsworth at my heels.

At the top stair the man offers me his hand to help me in. I'm amused he would think I need any type of help. Then I realize Farnsworth probably does. I take the man's hand out of courtesy, and turn to see Farnsworth smiling at me, as he does the same.

I walk on a plush, cream-colored rug, as I size up the inside of the airplane. It appears to rival the nicest of rooms in Farnsworth's mansion. To one side there is a shiny, leather, warm brown couch, large enough to hold several people. Opposite the couch are a table and four chairs. The table has a bouquet of some type of exotic flowers. I make my way past the table to find deep, luxurious chairs, and more couches. Straight to the back there is another set of stairs.

"That leads to the sleeping quarters," Farnsworth informs me.

"They have been prepared for you and Mrs. Farnsworth," the man on the airplane tells us.

Searing pain radiates from my gut all the way up to my head. Did this man really just say what I think he did?

The man addresses Farnsworth. "I think you will find them roomier and more comfortable than the last time you flew."

I glimpse at Farnsworth, and he blushes slightly. I

don't think he was behind these preparations or the plan for the larger bed. Farnsworth's eye catches mine, waiting for me to embarrass him. I remain quiet.

"Well, very well then." The man bows to us both and disappears through a door leading to the front of the plane.

Farnsworth offers a relaxed, happy smile meant for me. "Make yourself comfortable."

I glance at Grace who has set herself up on the table. She works fervently on a small machine that flashes pictures at her.

"Be careful with that," Farnsworth instructs her.

She nods, picks up the machine, and moves to the back of the plane. She disappears behind a curtain that leads to an area beneath the sleeping quarters. She is followed by Farnsworth's nurse.

Awkwardly, I move to the couch and sit. Farnsworth sits next to me.

"This is the first moment we've been alone since..." he runs his hands down the creases of his pants, "well, since, I don't know when."

I turn my head to face him. How could one person harbor so much evil?

"I..." he is struggling with his words. "I want you to know I understand you must hate me right now."

"I don't hate you now," I whisper.

Farnsworth sits up, happiness overtaking his previously stern expression.

"I hate you always."

Farnsworth recoils and adjusts himself in his seat. I set my jaw tightly and stare at him. Farnsworth reaches over and takes me by the wrist. He scowls at me.

"Don't trap me like that again, Veronica. It's not

beneficial for either of us. Do you understand?"

I refuse to speak. My jaw aches from clenching my teeth, but I feel the urge to let Farnsworth stew. I wonder how far I can push him. His grip grows harder on my wrist, and my eyes widen when I feel actual pain. I peer down at my wrist, and he immediately lessens his grasp.

"Do you understand me?" he asks, in a low growl.

"I understand." I speak through clenched teeth just as the man comes to the door and knocks. I break free of Farnsworth and turn away.

"Mr. Principal Leader, sir? It's time."

"Of course."

The man walks past us to the back of the airplane and moves the curtain aside to inform Grace and the nurse of our departure.

"This will be a feeling you've never experienced before," Farnsworth tells me. "You think you feel like you're flying on your diving board? Wait until you experience this."

The man walking through the cabin makes sure we have buckled our seatbelts. Fitting into the seatbelt makes me closer to Farnsworth than I want to be. The man removes the flowers and any other loose objects. He disappears to the front, and I hear loud winding sounds.

"The engines are starting," Farnsworth tells me with a small smile. "We will taxi down a runway for a few moments, and then we will…" He whistles and places his hands together, facing forward, and slides the top one off and into the air. "We'll be airborne." He smiles. "It's quite a feeling, actually. But it can be a bit of a surprise for your first time."

I nod and watch out the window as the airplane starts moving slowly down the strip of ground flanked with the red lights. "How do we get up, into the air? How can he get the...the speed?" I question, momentarily forgetting I am sitting next to my enemy, my husband.

Farnsworth turns to me, happy to be engaged in conversation. "Wait," he tells me.

Suddenly, I hear even louder whirling sounds, and the airplane begins to move faster and faster. I feel like I am a bullet racing through a gun's chamber. My head snaps back against my seat, and we lift off the ground. I place my sweaty palms on the seat next to me, and my hands unwittingly ball into fists. His hand is there, near mine, but it keeps a careful distance from me. Higher and higher we rise, and my eyes close. My ears feel very full, and pressure builds inside them. I rub at my ears furiously.

"Swallow," Farnsworth tells me, and when I do, it immediately relieves the pressure.

My ears unclogged, I let my head sway with the vibration of the airplane. My chest feels lighter and lighter as we lift higher and higher, away from the New World, away from the fighting, away from my memories, and my past. For a moment, gliding through the air, I wonder if I may, in fact, be able to start over. Maybe, just maybe, I will find peace once again. I open my eyes and face out the window. Behind me, the earth is falling away, so maybe, just maybe, my sorrow can too. I steel myself against the seat. Maybe I can forget everything but what is here, and now.

The plane levels and so do my feelings. I shake my head, knowing I'll never be able to leave Phoenix behind, even if he has left me.

The man knocks on the door. "Mr. Principal Leader, sir. Mrs. Farnsworth, ma'am. We've reached cruising altitude. You no longer need to be tethered down. You are free to do as you please."

I no longer need to be tethered down...? I am free to do as I please...? I look out the window and glimpse at the moon just as our airplane passes through a thick, dark cloud.

Chapter Seven

For whole moments the airplane is shrouded by complete darkness—stifling darkness. Then we break through the wall of darkness, and bright moonlight floods the cabin of the airplane. I wait for hope to come riding in on those rays of light, but the farther we race from the New World, the farther behind hope seems to lag.

"It's a fairly long trip," Farnsworth states, staring straight ahead. He doesn't face me. "But we gain back some time. It's about three hours earlier there than it is here."

My brain struggles with the idea of a place that is a different time of day. How can this be possible? I've never even heard of any civilizations still in existence except ours. "What kind of place are we going?" I swallow hard.

He avoids my question. "If you'd like to get some sleep, you are welcome to. You've had a very long day."

My body stiffens and my throat tightens. "No thank you, sir. I have no intention of ever sleeping again."

Farnsworth turns to me and takes my hand. My every instinct wants to snatch it back, but I force myself to stay still. My body bristles at his touch.

"So cold," he whispers, rubbing my hand between his two hands.

"I'm fine," I say, trying to break us apart.

He holds me tighter, but still, gently. "Veronica."

I refuse to look at him.

"Veronica, please. Please, look at me." His words are kind and not demanding.

Out of the corner of my eye I see Grace try to retreat from behind her curtain, but she returns immediately. We are alone in the cabin. I let my eyes drop to the seat between us, and they slowly make their way up to Farnsworth until I am staring him in the eyes. My chest heaves, uncontrollably.

"That's better." He smiles. "Veronica, there are some things we need to discuss before we land."

I nod, my protests laying low at the root of my tongue, waiting to fly out and rush to my defense.

"First of all, you are my wife now." He smiles a small smile, but tears spring into my eyes. He pulls a handkerchief from his pocket and offers it to me, but I refuse. "Although," he tucks the handkerchief back into his jacket, "although, I do wish you were happier about that." He chuckles, nervously. "And being my wife comes with some…responsibilities."

I pull myself from Farnsworth and stand. "It's never going to happen," I hiss.

"No?" He seems amused with my reaction. "Well I'm sure you never thought you would be my wife, either. And yet, here we are."

I storm across the cabin, wishing there was a way I could escape the airplane. I put both hands against a small, cold window.

"There's no way out." Farnsworth nods to the window.

"There's always a way," I answer, glowering at

him.

"Maybe so," he counters, "but for now, you are my wife. And I would like to explain what is expected of you."

"I hope, for your sake, it's nothing," I hiss. "Because anything more will leave you horribly disappointed."

"Come." He pats the seat next to him.

I don't budge.

"Veronica, it's not quite that simple. There will be some social graces expected of you. And one of them will be to listen when I speak to you."

I search for something to hurl at him.

"Everything loose has been removed." He knows exactly what I'm thinking. "Now, if you'll let me finish..." he smooths his jacket, busying his hands. He stops and looks at me, calmly. "And in return for listening when I speak to you, I will listen when you speak to me."

I fidget with my shirt buttons, nervously. I bite the inside of my cheek.

"Come, Veronica." Farnsworth pats the seat next to him again. "Please."

Slowly I walk back to my seat, keeping a fair distance between us.

"Thank you." His words are sincere. "And I will also ask that you be gracious toward me and our guests, whenever we should have them. Where we are heading, Veronica, I need you to please be on your best behavior toward me."

"What do I get?" I ask, my voice cracking slightly.

"What?" Farnsworth seems happy I am engaging in this conversation.

"What do I get in return for my graciousness? I will be a traitor to the one cause I believe in—"

"You believed in my cause before his," Farnsworth states, sharply.

"But I was wrong."

"When?" he asks, challenging me. "When you believed me? Or him?"

"Don't ask me these infantile questions." I stand and begin pacing.

"Then stop acting like a child," Farnsworth reprimands.

I whip around to face him. "Excuse me?"

He stands too, and seems somehow, taller. I am across the room, eye to eye with him. The empty table is between us.

"You heard me." His voice deepens. He is completely invested in this conversation. "Stop acting like a child if you want me to stop treating you like one."

"How am I acting like a child?"

"Let's see, I've caught you sneaking around, you've spat at me, you're searching for things to throw at me, and worst of all, you're pining after a little boy who you think broke your heart."

"What?"

"Move on, Veronica. Move on." Farnsworth steps around the table and closer to me. He stands tall before me, and for the first time ever, he seems physically strong, not just mentally strong.

"If you hate the way I am so much, why are you bothering with me? Just take my damned blood, and let's be done with this charade."

"I can't take your blood until you stop poisoning

yourself."

I start at his words.

"Oh please, Veronica, you think I didn't figure it out? Of course, I did. And thankfully, we had some of your previous blood to tide me over. Yes, I'll hand it to you. At the beginning I had no idea. None. Then I started to piece it together, and I asked my doctors to run some tests. It was very clever I have to say. Whose idea was it, yours or his?"

"My mother's."

He steps back, surprised with my answer. "Well that's…impossible."

I nod. "And that's the answer I needed. You finally admitted killing her."

"I've admitted no such thing. But I know you haven't seen your mother in seven years. I'm certain of it. So how could she tell you?"

"My dreams," I answer.

He smiles a knowing smile. "Tell me, Veronica. Have you ever wondered why your dreams are so vivid?"

"Aren't everyone's?"

"No." He shakes his head, smiling.

He studies me, and I can see something in his eyes.

"But we've veered too far here," he tells me.

He returns to the couch, and I work my way back to sit next to him.

"I'm sorry for saying you act like a child."

"Thank you."

"But I do need you to show me some respect. I would like you to do it all the time, but at least be kind and polite to me while we are in public. Can we agree on that?"

"And in return?"

"And in return I'll be kind and polite to you. In public and...in...private."

My breathing quickens, and my eyes fly up to his.

"I will be patient, Veronica." He softens when he speaks. "No, I don't want you to go forever without sleeping." He smiles warmly. "Knowing you, you probably could and would. But you don't have to. You can take a nap without worrying. I would never be so vile, Veronica."

I can't help but scoff, and he straightens up.

"You have a duty to perform, but I will give you time to get to know me. Away from the influence of that rebel."

"He has a name."

"Ah yes, but I'd prefer not to think of it. And I'd prefer if you didn't, either. But that I can't control. So give me a chance. I think you may like me."

"Don't hold your breath." I gaze out the window and then turn back to face him. He is not smiling. I take a deep breath and sigh. "I will give it an honest try, sir."

"Thank you, Veronica. That's all I can ask."

I nod. "I uh, think I'll go take that nap now."

"Of course. And Veronica, there is one more thing." He waits until he has my full attention and my aggressive stance softens. Then he asks. "Why do you think I married you? Really. I'm curious."

"So you could win, of course."

"I see." He nods his head, his eyes examining the floor in front of us. I turn to walk off as he speaks to my back. "It's not about winning, Veronica. I always win. I have the unfair advantage of having an army and being Principal Leader, and all that."

"Oh." I turn back to face him, honestly curious. My eyes dart out the window and then find their way to my feet. "Then why, sir? You could force me to do anything you wanted," my voice is thin and raspy, and my words are hurried. "You already have."

"I hate to think I've ever forced you into anything."

I stare at him, aware he has just given me more information than he realizes. I turn around and finally make my way to the stairs. Within a moment, he is standing behind me. My hands grip the handrails, waiting for me to step up, but he has wrapped his arms around me. His body does not touch mine, but his hands are placed higher than mine on the rails. I am unable to move in any direction. I freeze, and he whispers gently in my ear.

"I didn't marry you so I could win. I married you because I love you."

He drops his hands, and I run up the stairs.

## Chapter Eight

I toss and turn on the airplane bed. Being fully clothed doesn't help me get comfortable, but I simply will not risk undressing with Farnsworth downstairs. Lying here, I long for my mushrooms, and cry over this newly unearthed secret. I wonder over and over what Farnsworth could possibly mean. He loves me? Does he even know what that word means? Images of Phoenix flash before me and I wonder…do I?

After a long crying bout, I feel myself drift off.

I wake with a start, and I am suddenly in my bed in Farnsworth's house. I waste no time wondering how I got here, instead, I run to the window. I see Phoenix on the beach, exactly as he was that last night we were together. I run to my door, pull it open, and rush outside, my long white nightgown flowing behind me. Phoenix is standing there on the beach, his shirt opened, his gun slung around his back. He holds his arms out to me.

"I'm so sorry, Ron," he whispers into my shoulder as he picks me up. He holds me effortlessly, his lips glued to mine. His kiss is warm and strong and…right. This one kiss fills all the emptiness, and suddenly, I am full and satiated.

But as I am there, lifted in the air, my mouth locked on Phoenix's, his kiss changes. Suddenly, it does not feel warm and powerful. Now it is cold and forceful. He is pushing too hard, wanting too much. I feel my body against his, and the feeling is all wrong. He feels smooth and slick. I force my way to my feet to find Phoenix has morphed into Farnsworth. I step back, appalled, and yet utterly shocked by Farnsworth. This is the best he has ever appeared. His light blue shirt is opened, and I can see pronounced muscles on his chest. He is strong, able to lift me, and there is color to his face and broadness to his shoulders. But it is not right. Phoenix feeds me body and soul. He is my nourishment, like warm bread straight from the oven. Farnsworth is like a shiny, wet stone lining a river path, cold and untrustworthy.

I step back from the two men, holding my mouth shut to keep from screaming.

Phoenix looks at Farnsworth and then back to me. "I love you, Ron," he states, flatly. "I wish that were enough." He begins to back away.

"It is," I shriek, running toward Phoenix, but I am unable to catch him. "It is…" I crumple to the wet sand. "Please, Phoenix, please. I'm sorry…so, so sorry."

Phoenix smiles, and then disappears into the ocean mist, leaving Farnsworth and me alone on the beach.

"I can't…" I sob, as Farnsworth offers me his hand. "Go away," I yell, but he doesn't move. The cold ocean wind whips across me, and I shiver.

My eyes dart upward. Farnsworth is still there, offering me his hand.

"You are the reason he hates me," I choke out.

Still Farnsworth remains unmoving.

"Just let me go," I shout. My voice drops off as I speak. "I will never love you." My face falls into my hands.

"I know," Farnsworth tells me, putting his hand in mine and pulling me to my feet.

Quickly, he removes his jacket and wraps it around my shoulders. I try to shake it off, but finally succumb to the warmth. Farnsworth smiles at me, and I stare out after Phoenix, but he is gone.

When I turn back, Farnsworth is still here, but now we have somehow moved into his bedroom. He is lying prone on his bed, shirtless, his arms open wide, and on top of his head is a giant ram's head. I shrink back when I see it.

"Come," he whispers to me, patting one pillow.

The giant curled horns on top of his head are shiny and pointed—they are terrifying in every way, and yet, they are captivating. I walk toward them, mesmerized.

"Come," Farnsworth repeats, unmoving.

I walk closer to study the horns, and Farnsworth's eyes turn a bright shade of pink-red. He wears a distorted snakelike smile.

"What?" I murmur, confused, backing up, and suddenly—

"Veronica," Farnsworth hisses, lunging forward and grabbing my arm.

"No," I shriek, pulling away.

I wake with a start to find Grace sitting next to me holding another cup of tea. I take a moment to be certain I am no longer dreaming, or more accurately, nightmaring. The smell of chamomile assures me I am awake.

"Is that your answer to everything?" I ask, sitting up and taking the cup from her.

"You were shivering." She pulls a blanket from the bottom of the bed and covers my legs with it.

"Thank you," I mumble. I lean my head back against the headboard. Traveling with my enemies is terrifying, even my sleep is unsettling. "Was I talking in my sleep?" I am hesitant to even ask.

"Yelling."

I snap my head down to face her.

"But don't worry. You didn't say anything. At least nothing he heard." Her lips are pursed in a grim smile.

I nod, momentarily pacified.

There is a knock at the door, and I turn to see Farnsworth standing there. I sit up straight, pulling the blanket farther up onto my lap.

"I hope your sleep was restful, Veronica. We'll be landing in twenty minutes." He leaves as quickly as he came, and I have to force myself not to check the width of his shoulders, to see if it was all just a dream.

**** 

There is nothing I can do but sit and wait, aching for Phoenix—his touch, certainly, but also his companionship and his ease. The way he makes me feel everything can and will be okay. The way he enters a room and calms me at the same time he excites me.

I stare at the door where Farnsworth had just stood, and I know nothing will fill this emptiness inside me. Sadness seems to have taken up residence deep within me, in the very hollows of my bones. It is like an extra entity I carry with me, wherever I go. I know no matter what I look at or see or touch, I will never truly experience it, because sadness has shrouded me in a darkness that is unyielding. I force my thoughts off him, but it is never enough. Even if my brain strays from him for one moment, this feeling is always there to remind me that no matter who may surround me I am completely and utterly alone.

I pull the blanket up so far, only my eyes are uncovered. I feel the warmth of my breath trapped beneath the covers, and I hope it will soothe my aching muscles. It is such a cliché to say my body aches to be with him—but I can physically feel the need to have him near. There is a force surrounding me that radiates need. It is a longing, an energy that needs another's energy to be complete. And until it feels that, it continues to grow and reverberate throughout my body. A vibration surrounds me—like a game of hot and cold when you're a child. When I think there is a chance he'll be near, the energy intensifies and sends electric currents through me. When he is far away like now, the energy sends a dull vibration through me, always looking, searching, like a scout wanting more.

****

After I freshen up and make myself "presentable" in Grace's terms, I once again buckle myself next to Farnsworth.

He studies me, but doesn't smile. "Veronica," he states. "There is no way to prepare you for this. I am quite…sorry…to do this to you. But I also think…no, I believe, it is the right thing to do."

I turn to him, my eyes wide, my heart racing. Is this madman about to push me out a window?

"I'm sorry," he murmurs, patting my hand. "You look as if you're worried I would harm you. Didn't you hear what I said to you just before?"

"Yes," I whisper, through chattering teeth.

"We don't hurt people we love, Veronica."

I glance away, thinking of Phoenix and the awful things that transpired between us. Phoenix hurt me.

Does that mean he no longer loves me? My eyes flood with tears wondering if Farnsworth understands how much he has, in fact, just wounded me.

"Principal Leader Farnsworth, sir?" It is the man who sits with the pilot. He's walked through the pilot's door. "We will touchdown in five."

"Thank you." Farnsworth nods his head. He takes my hand, but I slide it back in my lap. "Aren't we growing tired of this game?" he asks.

"It's not a game."

"Maybe not. But just so you know, in about," he turns his wrist and glances at the face of a very large watch, "ten minutes, you are going to want to hold on tight and never let my hand go."

"I'll take that bet, sir." I place both hands on my lap.

"Very well." Farnsworth closes his eyes, and I feel the pressure in my ears as we drop down to the earth once again.

**** 

Our planned exit from the airplane is like a rebel drill at camp. Loud sirens are blasting, and large vehicles with armed guards are waiting for us. Strobe lights flash through our windows as the airplane taxis down the landing strip. Farnsworth calmly stands as the pilot's assistant runs toward us carrying two black, heavy vests. Farnsworth removes his jacket and slides on a vest. He replaces his jacket and fixes his lapel. He turns to me and holds the other vest out for me. I slide it on. It is heavy and squashes my breasts.

"Hard to breathe?" he asks, and I nod. He makes an adjustment to the back, and I am slightly more comfortable. Then he holds my jacket out for me, and I slide it on. He smiles at me as he pulls my jacket forward from my waist, arranging me just so. "They are just a precaution," he soothes. "They will never let anyone close enough to shoot."

"Huh," I hear myself gasp. "That's not really a relief."

Farnsworth reaches out to me. "Take my hand, please."

I hesitate. The idea of taking his hand seeming more terrifying than what's waiting for us outside the airplane.

"Veronica, for what is about to happen, take my hand."

I scan my surroundings. Grace is adjusting her own vest. Farnsworth's nurse is doing the same. Two bodyguards materialize from behind the curtain where Grace was working. They also wear matching vests.

The larger one of the men turns to me. "Please stay low, move quickly, hold your husband's hand, and do not let go unless I tell you to."

I search the man's face, trying to see if he was one of the guards threatening Lilly, Violet, and Raven, but I don't think he is.

"Mrs. Farnsworth, ma'am? I need a vocal from you."

I stare at the man, dumbfounded.

"Veronica," Farnsworth turns to me, taking my hand in his. "I know this is frightening, but you need to let us know you understand."

I nod.

"Not good enough, sir," the man states. He glances over his shoulder as the airplane slows. He checks his watch. We are clearly out of time. "Ma'am, I am Jerold.

Your bodyguard. I need an audible from you."

"Veronica, honey. Tell us you understand."

Farnsworth's grip on my hand tightens, and I turn to him, suddenly feeling like he is the only reason I am alive.

"I understand." I nod, searching Jerold's eyes for any recollection.

"Good girl." Farnsworth lifts my hand and squeezes it in appreciation.

Jerold speaks again. "As soon as the plane rolls to a stop, Lester," he nods to the other bodyguard, "is the first one out, followed by me, and then Grace, and then Ms. Patty." He nods toward the nurse. "Next will be Principal Leader Farnsworth and Mrs. Farnsworth. Do you understand?" He turns to Grace.

"Yes."

"You?" He turns to Patty, the nurse.

"Yes."

"Sir?"

"Yes."

"Ma'am?"

I look around, dazed.

"Ma'am?"

"Y-yes," I stammer.

"Good. Line up, please."

I stand next to Farnsworth as the plane comes to a complete stop. The door is unlocked, and Lester makes his way down the steps, followed by Jerold, who puts up his hand for us to wait until he gives the all clear. Peering around Grace and Farnsworth, I see a commotion outside. I hear chanting and shouting, but I can't make out what they are saying. Gunfire is heard in the distance, and I recoil, but Farnsworth does not flinch. He stays staring out the door, unmoving. Lights continue to flash, and the sound of chaos grows closer. Where are we and what are we walking into? Someone runs up to our plane, but Lester chases him off. The gunfire magnifies, and the sounds of the individual shots are clearer and more intensified.

"Get ready, sir," Jerold shouts.

Farnsworth steps closer to the door, and I feel the pull on my hand. I move forward, closer to Farnsworth, holding on out of sheer terror. Through the chaos and racket, Farnsworth turns back to me. He holds up our hands. I look at them and realize I am squeezing his hand so tight I have lost feeling in my fingers. Farnsworth smiles at me as we are ushered out into the bedlam.

Chapter Nine

Still holding Farnsworth's hand, we are escorted off the airplane with Lester and Jerold right at our sides. Sound assaults our ears as people scream. I hear the word "please," repeated over and over. I try to turn in the direction the word is coming from, but Jerold's hand covers my head, and we are immediately pushed into the back of a black, worn, long vehicle. A limousine, I suppose. We sit opposite Grace and Patty, and the bodyguards flank us, squeezing Farnsworth and I tightly together. The only sound I hear inside the car is my labored breath. Jerold moves from my side and raps a heavy gold ring against a glass partition behind Grace's head. The car begins to roll forward.

"We need to move immediately, sir."

Farnsworth nods his response.

Jerold motions to our hands. "You are free to let go now, sir and ma'am."

As I try to process these words, a woman throws herself against my window. "Huh," I gasp, moving back from the glass, and unfortunately, closer to Farnsworth.

"I'm sorry, ma'am," Jerold tells me. "They will shake off as soon as we can pick up speed."

"Shake off?" I ask, turning my head slowly in his direction.

"Yes. You have nothing to worry about, ma'am."

Nothing to worry about? I see the woman running to keep up with the car. Her clothes are tattered, and even through the window I can see she is a horrible shade of grayish brown—a combination of malnutrition and dirt, no doubt. Her face is smeared with filth and etched with worry. I use my free hand to search my pockets for a protein bar to give her, but they are empty.

"Are you looking for something, my dear?" Farnsworth is studying me out of the corner of his eye.

"Something to o-offer her…" I stammer.

"Your window doesn't open, ma'am," Jerold tells me. "And even if it did. You wouldn't want to mix with their kind. Be nice to one and you won't be able to shake any of them."

"Shake any of them?" I bite my lip, trying to process this. "How many are there?" A dull vibration courses through me.

"Thousands. Maybe more," Jerold states matter-of-factly. He raps on the window to scare off a man who is approaching. The man appears no better than the woman before him, and he has a deep red gash on his cheek. Behind the man, I see a group of about twenty people who also look as if they have just barely survived a war.

"Who are these people?" I ask, turning to Farnsworth.

"The reason we came," he tells me.

I scrutinize his expression, and best I can tell he is sincere. For the first time ever, I respect him. "We came to help these people?" I ask, wide-eyed. I feel my heart racing.

"In a manner of speaking, yes."

Grace coughs, and Farnsworth glares at her. I stare out the window as the woman and man fall away, behind us.

"There we go." Jerold sits back in his seat, seeming much more relaxed. "We should get up to speed now, sir. Once we fight through these few stragglers blocking our way."

I am caught up in Farnsworth's words. How could this monster I am married to come all this way just to help these poor people? I am perplexed. But I have to say something. I turn to Farnsworth. "I don't know what to say."

"You can start by saying you were wrong."

He couldn't possibly be expecting me to forgive all of his past sins just because we've come to offer some food to some starving people. It isn't enough. I choose my words carefully. "I was wrong? About what, sir?"

He smiles as he lifts our still intertwined hands. So I didn't let go. He was right. I feel my cheeks burn from embarrassment. As soon as he lets our hands fall to the seat between us, I discreetly slide my hand from his.

\*\*\*\*

Eventually, we begin to drive through an area that resembles a flattened version of the city back home. I am mesmerized. All this time, I never knew any other part of the world existed.

"Are you sure, sir?" Jerold asks.

Farnsworth nods his response.

"All right, sir." Jerold raps on the glass to get the driver's attention and holds up two fingers. He motions for the vehicle to go forward.

"Slowly," Farnsworth commands, facing away from me.

Jerold signals to the driver to slow down.

Although the feel is similar to the city back home, its appearance is radically different. There are probably an equal number of buildings, but they are dispersed over a much larger area. Although our city is old and decrepit, it is shiny and vibrant compared to this. This city has been decimated. All along the streets are half-standing buildings, some with boarded up windows, others, with no windows or roofs. People mull about, all dressed in tattered clothing, some carrying screaming children. They push each other. A man urinates on a street corner. Another defecates nearby. On what once must have been a stoop, a small boy sits hunched over eating what I can only imagine is a raw, dead bird. Another man comes by and pushes the boy away, stealing his bird. The man bites into it hungrily, and turns to stare as our vehicle cruises by. I see blood smeared across his face.

"Uh," I cry. "Did you see that? Principal Leader Farnsworth, sir. He just pushed that little boy and stole his food. They are eating dead birds. They are…relieving themselves in the streets. There are no buildings…no homes…no food…what is this place?" I peer around at blank faces. Grace and Patty stare down at their own feet, neither daring to look out the window. A wave of crippling pain radiates from my gut. "My stomach," I moan, as I stare transfixed out the window.

Someone throws a rock at our vehicle, and it hits the window. It startles me, and I gasp. Jerold leans forward.

"It might be better, ma'am, if you look at your feet and not out the window. We'll be out of here as soon—"

"No," Farnsworth interjects. "No. We are not rushing through here. I brought Mrs. Farnsworth here to show her the horror that exists in places other than our own. She needs a little perspective. So she realizes how good we have it back in the New World."

"But—"

"Yes, Veronica. Even at camp and the Letting facility. All of it—"

Again, I begin to speak, but he cuts me off.

"All of it was better than this."

"You did this to me on purpose?" I am even more sickened by Farnsworth.

"It was time you learned. Now, I think it's best if you continue to look out the window, Veronica. See what other worlds are like."

I tear my eyes off of Farnsworth and stare out my window. Tears roll from my eyes as I witness people walking aimlessly about, screaming and begging when our vehicle passes by. Another rock hits our car and then another. Soon we are in a deluge of rocks ricocheting off of our roof and windows. Each one sounds like a gunshot, forcing Grace and Patty to cower. But not me. I refuse to let Farnsworth think he has won.

But I can't fight off the pain in my abdomen. I clutch my stomach and breathe deeply.

"Do you need a bag, ma'am?" Patty makes eye contact only long enough to produce a vomit bag for me.

"No, thank you," I growl, my anger taking over my entire existence.

Pound, pound, pound. I refuse to react to the rocks against our car. I can feel Farnsworth's stare on me.

One rock hits my window and succeeds in making a nick.

"Look at that," I mutter, turning to Farnsworth. "They may break this glass yet."

Farnsworth narrows his eyes at me. I stare outside as a woman runs past, clutching a crying infant. They are both barefoot and in rags.

"Please," she mouths to me as she holds up the sickly skinny baby.

I put my hand against the glass to show her at least I have recognized her pain.

"That's enough, Veronica," Farnsworth snaps at me. "You can turn away."

"No thank you, sir. You brought me here to see this. And I'm going to see it. All of it."

"Very well, Veronica." I can feel him distance himself from me, defeated.

"Principal Leader Farnsworth, sir. We need to go, now." Jerold is agitated, looking from left to right, out each window. "Please, sir."

Rocks pummel the car.

"Fine," Farnsworth concedes. He sits sulking as the car picks up speed.

I take a deep breath, so horrified by what I've seen I can't revel in my obvious win. I continue to stare out the window, wondering how much longer I can hold in the vomit, but I just can't resist. I turn to Farnsworth who is red with anger.

"Happy honeymoon, darling," I hiss.

## Chapter Ten

After a fairly long drive in silence, the surroundings outside the car begin to change. Occasionally, I see a tree or a random bush winning its fight to stay alive. Soon enough, the area we drive through resembles the New World remarkably, but it is much smaller in size. There are only a few houses here and there, and each driveway is protected by a large locked gate. We drive farther still, and up in the distance, I see a mountain with what looks like the remains of a sign—letters are tottering precariously off the side of the mountain. I see an "H," then an "L," and finally, what might be an "M" or a "W" lain on its side.

"What is that?" I ask no one in particular.

"The remains of their world," Grace offers, sadly.

We drive closer to the sign and I stare at it, out my window.

"Welcome to 'HopeLess World,'" Farnsworth whispers into my ear.

\*\*\*\*

Soon our vehicle pulls down a street with a few trees, and into a long driveway that reminds me of the one at Farnsworth's mansion. I smile at the memory of charging into Farnsworth's house with Brooke, just the two of us, certain we could make a difference. I am flummoxed to think those were the good ol' days.

Our vehicle stops at the end of a long driveway.

Jerold is the first to leave the vehicle, followed by everyone except Farnsworth and me. I stare out my window as Farnsworth turns to me.

"You have to eventually speak to me, you know."

I remain quiet.

"Okay, have it your way, but we made a deal. And here is where I need you to be respectful to me. Like a good, dutiful wife should be. In return, you buy yourself some more time with no pressure."

I turn to face Farnsworth, my seething anger replaced with emptiness and sorrow.

"I'm not good," I whisper. "But I suppose I'm dutiful. So I will listen to you, especially since you have come all this way just to help these people. I owe you this much. But please stop threatening me. I'm here. I will do as you ask."

He seems confused. "Why the sudden change of heart, Veronica?"

"Didn't you see what I just saw?"

"Of course I did."

"Then can't you understand there are problems so much greater than the ones facing either one of us?"

He is about to speak, when his door is opened.

\*\*\*\*

We step out onto a circular shaped driveway and stand on large stones. Now that I can focus, I realize how much warmer it is here than it was at camp. As a group, Jerold leads us to the front door of a white house, similar in shape but much smaller in size than Farnsworth's mansion. The white paint is peeling, and green mold clings to the side of the house like a warm blanket. The front door is painted black, with small indentations marring its smooth finish. The moment we are let inside, the smell of wood and mildew accosts my senses. I cover my nose with my jacket sleeve. I look around as Jerold helps us remove our vests. There is floor to ceiling wood paneling in the small entryway and a worn braided rug on the floor. Flowered green and gold patterns cover the walls, and a single picture hangs in the hall. The picture is a portrait of an angry man, with black hair, and skin the color of mine. His cheeks are pocked, and he wears a high-collared, buttoned up black jacket, and a stern smile.

I follow the group through a small room with sparse furniture, including something made of wood with a large wheel attached to a tripod. A stool sits beside it. Against a wall is an oversized glass front armoire, its door hanging askew, stuffed full of dishes and knickknacks. We walk down a long, dark, narrow hallway, and the mildew scent grows stronger. We are brought to a brighter room and asked to wait. Grace and Patty sit on two high-backed chairs opposite a low, leather couch. Farnsworth sits on the couch, and I follow. Peering at the edges of the chairs, I see they are fraying around the seat cushions. I have sunk deeply into the couch and adjust to make myself more comfortable. I feel tiny sitting next to Farnsworth, and I don't like it. I struggle to sit up taller. Jerold and Lester stand by the door. It's dark outside, but a tree I have never before encountered brushes against a glass window. I can see well enough to tell it has long leaves that seem to grow from its center, rather than from branches.

"It's a palm tree," Grace tells me, sure I've never seen one.

My eyes dart to her as I learn the word.

Within a minute, a man in a dusty, long gray coat appears with glasses of iced tea and a plateful of sandwiches. We all take one of each, but Farnsworth puts his down immediately. He examines the nails on his fingers and checks his watch. I can tell he does not like waiting. My gaze falls on hunting arrows mounted behind glass frames hanging on the walls, and more arrows mounted at various heights throughout the room. Everyone has devoured his or her sandwich except Farnsworth and me. Just one look at the filling makes me think of the young boy and his bird. I put my glass down on an oblong shaped glass-topped table, and offer my sandwich to Jerold, who takes it, happily.

Suddenly, the door pushes open and in walks the man we saw in the portrait. The man is extremely tall, full inches taller than I am, and maybe even taller than Phoenix. He is wearing a black jacket similar to the one in the portrait, with a stiff, high collar latched at the neck. I imagine he must be incredibly hot. As soon as he enters, Grace and Patty scurry off. Jerold and Lester move to the hallway right outside the door.

The man steps forward. "Principal Leader Farnsworth, sir."

Farnsworth rises, and the man clasps Farnsworth's hand, bowing to him. Farnsworth nods his response. It's a struggle to get out of the couch, but I stand too.

"Hello," the strange man says, taking my hand as he studies my face. "My goodness, you are beautiful, aren't you?"

Something in the way he says it makes me panic. He holds my hand too long.

I step back from him, closer to Farnsworth, feeling my chest heave. I remember Brooke's story of trying to escape Farnsworth, and as a punishment, Farnsworth slated her to Couple with Lucus. Has this megalomaniac assigned me to this man? I stare at the stranger's pockmarked face and draw a deep breath.

"This is my wife," Farnsworth speaks plainly. He pulls me to him and wraps his hand around my waist. For the moment, I am almost grateful for it.

"You are a lucky man, Principal Leader Farnsworth, sir. In many ways."

"Indeed I am."

I stare at these two men, wondering what is happening.

The strange man tilts his head sideways, studying me. "She doesn't know, does she?"

"No. Veronica knows nothing about this."

I squirm in my spot, sweating even though the heavy vest is gone. "What don't I know, sir?"

"Sir? Wow. Very formal between you two, huh?"

Farnsworth sets his jaw tightly and counters. "And a little informal from you, wouldn't you say?"

The man's cheeks fill with color, and Farnsworth continues with an irritated smirk on his face. "It's only out of respect, I assure you. When we are alone, my wife calls me by my God-given name. Don't you, Veronica?" Farnsworth squeezes my waist.

"Yes," I mumble. "Um, sir? What don't I know?" My gaze falls on the low table before us, and I watch a droplet of water slide down my iced tea glass, mimicking a drop of sweat falling down my lower back.

"All in good time," Farnsworth coos, letting his hand settle in at the small of my back. "All in good time."

"For now," the strange man encourages, "why

don't we lose the formalities, shall we? I would love to hear her call you by your name. Seeing you're so newly married and all, wouldn't want you to have to contain your passion just for me."

Farnsworth gives my waist one last squeeze before he turns me to face him. He takes both of my hands. "It's okay here. In this room. You can call me by my name."

I can tell he is wondering if I even know his name.

He continues. "It gets a little tiring to hear 'sir' all the time. Especially from you."

I am stymied by the situation. I cannot fathom what is happening.

"Veronica?"

"Um," I shake my head, trying to concentrate. "Of course, sir."

The strange man chuckles, and it makes me uneasy.

"No 'sir,' Veronica." Farnsworth squeezes both of my hands and narrows his eyes at me.

I can tell this is a win he needs to secure. I take a deep breath. "Of course, Malachi. I'm sorry."

He smiles at me and lifts my hands to his lips. He kisses them gently. I pull my hands away and wipe them discreetly on my jeans.

"That's so nice to hear. When I heard about your quick nuptials, I was concerned, of course, that it was an arranged thing. But I can see by Veronica's commitment toward you that she loves you as much as you love her."

Dazed, I turn back to the man. "And who are you?" I ask, knowing I may be overstepping a boundary but really not caring.

"Ah, there's the Veronica Billings I was expecting." The man smiles. "Shall I tell her, sir, or would you like the honors?"

Farnsworth glares at the man. "This isn't a joking matter," Farnsworth mutters under his breath.

"Just tell me, please," I implore.

Farnsworth rocks back and forth on his heels. When he settles, he speaks.

"His name is Julian. He was the original Phoenix."

"What?" I ask, stepping back from both of them.

"Like Phoenix, Julian felt he could change our country. But you can see how well he's done." Farnsworth smirks, and steps forward to squash a large bug hurrying past. "He started his own world here. And it fell apart exactly as I told him it would. So we are here to help. Isn't that right, Julian?"

"Yes." The large, strange man speaks quietly, and his eyes fall to the ground before him.

"What was that?" Farnsworth asks.

"Yes, Principal Leader Farnsworth, sir."

"That's better. For you, there is no familiarity with me. You are a traitor, and you live in this filth because of it. And now here I am to save you. Once again."

"Thank you," the large man mumbles.

"Excuse me?" Farnsworth steps a bit closer as if he is unable to hear. He puts a hand to his ear. I can tell he is enjoying this.

"Thank you, Principal Leader Farnsworth, sir." The man punctuates his last word, and I watch his hands ball into fists. He sees me staring and releases his hands.

"Why now?" I ask.

"What's that?" Farnsworth gives me his full

attention.

"Why now? Why are you here to save him now?"

"She really doesn't know, does she?"

"Of course not." Farnsworth looks directly at me. "Veronica—"

This time the man steps forward, interrupting Farnsworth. "My name is Julian, Veronica. Actually, it's Julian Billings. But you can call me, Dad."

Chapter Eleven

I back away from the two men and make my way to the door.

"There's no point in running," Farnsworth warns. "You saw what waits for you out there. There's nothing but filth and slime and desperation."

"The same thing that's in here," I quip.

"Touché, Ronnie," Julian laughs. "Touché."

"Don't call me that," I snarl.

"Sorry." His eyes narrow.

"Now, one of you, or both of you, had better start talking." I turn to Julian. "How dare you tell me you're my father?" My words are breathy, and I begin to get dizzy.

"I'm not lying," Julian answers. "Why do you think Principal Leader Farnsworth brought you here?"

"I never know why Principal Leader Farnsworth does anything he does."

"Be careful Veronica…" Farnsworth admonishes.

"Me? Me?" I stomp away from them, incensed. "I should be careful? I want answers and I want them now." I point to Farnsworth. "You're supposed to be my husband. So talk." I turn to Julian. "And you, you claim to be my father? Well aren't those the two men who are supposed to love me the most in the world?"

Neither speaks.

"You can't answer that, can you? Because you

know it's not true." I turn to Farnsworth. "You know there is only one person who truly loves me, and because of your threats and my foolish actions, he has left me. So talk. Both of you. Because I really have nothing left to lose."

"You have your girls and their safety."

I hold up my hand. "Don't even start that with me anymore, Farnsworth. Because what I saw tonight cannot ever be unseen. You made sure of that. There is so much suffering and horror in the world I wonder why our ancestors ever even bothered to bring us back. You can threaten to annihilate those three little girls. And then what? Each of those children on the street? Are you going to systematically kill off every child here until I succumb to your wishes?"

"Of course not," he whispers.

"So here we are then." I point to Julian. "Talk."

Julian crosses to one of the high-back chairs. He motions to the chair asking my permission to sit. I nod. Farnsworth resumes his spot on the couch. Julian clears his throat before he speaks.

"I was young then. I was a product of the city, a boy who worked in the factories and saw the oppression of our people. I wanted freedom for our people. I wanted them to have the chance to live like the people in the New World. Years went by, and I spent my entire youth in a factory toiling away until my fingers bled."

"Don't expect me to feel sorry for you," I interject.

"I would never expect anything of the sort from you, Veronica." He sounds sincere. "Well, I was an 'O,' and as soon as I was old enough I was asked if I wanted to serve my country by…" He stares off for a moment as though collecting his thoughts.

"By working for Farnsworth Senior," I add.

"Yes. Being an 'O' is always a plus, but we were never really worried about blood types back then. There was always so much…blood." The word sounds thick on his tongue. "But then one day, Malachi over here was born, and he had a rare disease—one that made him unable to stop bleeding. And even rarer, he needed constant blood transfusions. So Farnsworth Senior panicked, like any parent, I suppose."

"Really?" I ask, lifting my eyebrow. "Like any parent?"

"Any parent who knows his child," he concedes. "So being an 'O,' like Malachi, I made my way to more Coupling houses. I produced no offspring, however, until I met your mother." He smiles when he says this, and his eyes sparkle. "Your mother was—"

"Spare me the details," I mumble, staring out a window into the darkness.

"No. Not that. She was graceful and beautiful, but she also had this fire in her. She loved ferociously. She loved me like that."

I am shocked by his words. "She loved you?"

"Yes. We loved each other."

"What happened?" I move closer to him and sit on the floor beside his chair. I curl my legs up beneath me.

"Relationships like that were forbidden. You know that."

"That doesn't mean you don't try."

"Ah, a romantic, huh?" He smiles a real smile at me.

I feel the embarrassment overtake me. "I just mean, when you love someone or something, you fight for it. No matter what. No matter what," I repeat to myself.

Farnsworth shoots me a disapproving glance.

"I did fight for her. But when she became pregnant, she knew her one job was to keep you safe. We knew what happened to those girls they took to the Lettings, and she refused to allow that to happen to you. She knew a trick, she told me. Something that could protect you when you were old enough."

"Mushrooms," I whisper.

Farnsworth's eyes dart over to me.

"Maybe so." Julian's thoughts seem to take him somewhere else, then he focuses on us once more. "So I made my way out here with a group of rebels. We tried to create a new, New World. We called it 'HopefuL World' based on the letters on that sign out there. Have you seen it?"

I nod.

"Your mother didn't trust the idea of starting over, especially with a baby. So we separated and lived our own lives."

"So what happened here?"

"It's not all that easy, starting new. Your mother was right. There was no form of commerce. Soon our food sources dwindled away. Without exchange with the New World, we had nothing left."

"Why do you live here? I mean, it's not Farnsworth's palace, but it's a heck of a lot nicer than anything else I've seen around here."

"Someone has to be the leader, Veronica. There has to be someone to follow. I am that someone."

Everything grows very quiet for a moment. I feel my heart racing and my eyes ache, but I have to know. "My mother always told me I was the spitting image of you."

"You are," Julian assures me, smiling.

I glance at Farnsworth, and he has the decency to get up and walk to the far window, giving us a moment of privacy. I turn back to Julian.

"But did you ever…wonder about me? Ever?"

"Of course I did, Veronica. Of course. And you were easy to follow once you began to make a name for yourself."

"Don't remind me," I whisper, my head hanging low.

"Veronica," he stands and walks to me. He reaches out his hand, and I take it. He helps me to my feet. "You did what you thought was right. You can't ever blame yourself for that."

A small gulp of air escapes from me, and I offer him a tiny smile. "So how do we help?" I ask.

"Help?"

"Now that we're here, how do we help these people?"

"Well, that's what Principal Leader Farns—"

Farnsworth is suddenly at my side. "I will explain everything to you, my dear. But now you must get some rest. You must be exhausted."

I yawn, as if on cue. "Yes, but what's our plan? At least tell me that, please. Have we come to feed these people?"

"Yes." Farnsworth avoids my eyes, but stares at Julian.

"Where will the food come from? The last time I was in your mansion—"

"Not having someone to cook the food is very different from not having food." Farnsworth crosses his arms in front of his chest. "The New World has plenty of food." He speaks emphatically, and it's clearly for Julian's benefit as well as mine. He must want to reassure Julian. "Veronica, I believe you were heading upstairs?"

"Uh, yes," I back up, feeling dismissed. "Um…where do I…sleep?"

"I have a room for you upstairs," Julian answers, his eyes on Farnsworth.

I hesitate. "Are there enough rooms for…?"

"Since Principal Leader Farnsworth and I have some business to attend to, I've arranged for you to have your own room. I hope you don't mind." Julian's eyes dart over to me. "I wouldn't want him to wake you in case we're up late."

I exhale.

"Grace will show you to your room," Farnsworth tells me.

I nod and walk to the door to find Grace waiting for me. I step out of the room and then turn back. I face Julian.

"Thank you," I whisper.

He bows graciously, and I leave.

****

My bedroom is a small room with more flowered walls and an old bed with a dirty white frame. The bed creaks when I sit on it, reminding me of my childhood cot and my mother. But there is something in the corner of the room under a window that grabs my attention. It is a small table made of tree branches woven together. The side of the table is open, exposing books. At least six or seven of them, and they are not the textbooks from my childhood—the only books I have ever read. These all have different colored bindings, but many of the words on the bindings have worn off. I run my finger over the sides of the books, discovering the bumpy yet fluffy feel of the covers. I remember Phoenix telling me he once read books left by the ancients and that was where he learned about a peaceful revolution. Feeling as if I am doing something very, very inappropriate, I turn away from my door and huddle up next to the far wall, clutching a book. I crack it open, and the first words that jump out at me are from Mahatma Gandhi, reinforcing what I already know…Phoenix's Peaceful Revolution is the answer, and quiet protest can have the most profound impact. I draw in a deep breath and shut the book, quickly.

I turn to find Grace is once again here, tidying up, and preparing clothes for me. She seems exhausted as she works, the flight must have taken its toll on her. She hands me a white nightgown, and pays no mind to the book in my hand. I manage to hide the book under my mattress as Grace shows me to the bathroom. It is old and tiny compared to my bathroom at Farnsworth's house. This bathroom has only a claw-foot tub and a small pedestal sink. I rinse my face with the trickle of water that drips into the brown-stained sink. I change quickly, and emerge to an empty bedroom.

I ignore the rumble in my stomach and climb into bed. I kick the old quilt off me, and begin to toss and turn. My hand reaches for the book, and I hold it to me, feeling like this action will somehow bring Phoenix closer. For an hour straight, I read through the book, captivated by the simple words and their complex meanings. When I finish, I begin to doze off for a minute or two at a time, but every time I do, the image of my mother floods my brain, and I wake with a start.

After two or three times like this, I decide trying to sleep is pointless. Soft-footed, I crouch down next to the mattress. Just as I replace the book, I'm certain I hear noises coming from downstairs.

Careful not to wake anyone, I ease my way into the hall and then to the staircase. The creak on the first step nearly gives me away, but I manage to make it the rest of the way without a sound. I hear voices coming from the room we just left. In particular, I hear a voice that belongs to neither Farnsworth nor Julian, but it's a voice I know well. My heart races faster and faster as I make my way to the room flooded with sound. Slowly and quietly, I push open the door and peer inside. I see the backs of Farnsworth and Julian, side by side, staring at a large screen. They are blocking the screen, so I strain to see around them. Just then, Julian moves enough to reveal a face so handsome, it stops my heart. He has the beginnings of a short, scruffy beard, but there is no denying it's him. My whole body aches, wanting to rush forward toward him, but I stop myself before I am seen. I clamp my hand over my mouth to keep from screaming.

Instead, I drop to my knees in the hallway and whisper, "Phoenix."

Chapter Twelve

I huddle into a ball, straining to hear every word he is saying. I listen harder and harder, sure I am wrong. I am certain I hear Phoenix talk about "fighting" and "war" and "death to his enemy." But this can't be Phoenix—Phoenix's whole existence revolves around peace. Phoenix would never hurt anyone intentionally. Well, he wouldn't harm them physically, anyway. I hug myself tightly as Phoenix shouts about "victory."

"No," I murmur. "No, no, no, no…" This can't be Phoenix. This, this is a man I do not know. I peer at the screen, and standing next to him is beautiful Brooke. She holds a gun close to her oversized breasts and smiles as Phoenix talks. She regards him with such awe and admiration it can only be love. On the opposite side of Phoenix stands Raven. My heart aches to see her. She is so beautiful and young. She remains stoic. They are all dressed in camouflage, and they look and act like a well-oiled machine.

I pull myself to standing as Phoenix shouts so loudly, it sounds as if he is standing in this very room. "Wherever Principal Leader Farnsworth is hiding, he needs to come forward and face us. He must pay for what he has done—stealing our blood, killing our children, forcing our women to the Couplings. It stops now." He raises his gun.

Brooke leans over and whispers something into

Phoenix's ear. He shakes his head, his entire demeanor suddenly changing, as if he has seen a ghost. She glares at him, clearly annoyed, and moves to the microphone.

"Principal Leader Farnsworth is traveling with his wife, Veronica Billings Farnsworth." Her words are measured and careful. "Together, they are a threat to our very existence." Brooke turns to Phoenix who looks away. I can tell he wants nothing to do with this. She goes on. "But together, we can put an end to their tyranny." She raises her gun high into the air, and the people in the audience shout in appreciation.

Then the projection scans the whole stage, and out of nowhere, I see her: Lulu. She stands beside Raven. She appears older and tired, but it is most definitely her.

"Lulu," I yell, rushing into the room and toward the screen.

Both men are startled by my sudden appearance. Farnsworth tries to stop me midway, but thinks better of it. I stand inches from the screen, lifting my hand, trying to touch any one of them, desperately wanting to be with them. I am eternally grateful Lulu is free of Gunnar and safe, even if it means they are all fighting for the wrong cause. I watch, riveted, as the camera closes in on Phoenix's face, surveying the crowd. He seems stern and angry. Then, he turns and faces directly into the camera. I know he is looking at me through the screen. His eyes soften, and I wonder if he is telling me he still loves me.

In an instant, Brooke throws her arm around his shoulder and lifts her gun to the sky. "We will fight until our last dying breath," she hollers.

"Until *their* last dying breath," a man's voice corrects. A large man steps up to the microphone, and suddenly, the face of my enemy, Gunnar, is staring straight at me.

"NO!" I scream, collapsing to the ground.

\*\*\*\*

I wake to find I am on the couch, in that same room. Farnsworth sits in one of the chairs, his eyes, locked on me. Julian is still watching the newsfeed scroll across the screen.

"Huh," I gasp, sitting up quickly. My head hurts, and I feel light-headed. "What happened?"

Farnsworth comes to my side. "You saw something on the projection that made you faint."

"Oh." My head drops backward, heavy with memories. "Was it—was it as bad as I remember?"

Farnsworth doesn't answer. I close my eyes, knowing this is one of the worst moments of my life. Not only have I lost the boy I love, but more importantly, he has lost himself.

Farnsworth offers me dry crackers and a sweet drink. I don't argue. After I have eaten, I sit up, trying to piece everything together. I push myself to focus. "He has the girls with him," I mumble.

"Who's that?" Julian asks.

"Gunnar. He—he has Lulu and Raven." My head falls back again. "How?" I question. "How did this go so wrong?"

No one answers me.

"Gunnar will teach those girls to hate. He'll teach them greed is right, and war is the only answer. Raven may not fall for it, but Lulu certainly will. We have to stop him."

Neither man answers me.

"And poor Lilly and Violet—still hostages in your

mansion—" I shake my head. "There must be a way. There must be something we can do to show Phoenix and Brooke we are still a team."

"Are we, Veronica?" Farnsworth asks, raising his eyebrows.

"Yes," I exclaim. "We have to be. How else can we stop this hell that is unfurling before our eyes?"

The men remain quiet.

"You don't understand, do you? You don't understand. Gunnar knows those girls are two of the last remaining O's. And without Phoenix to protect them, God knows what he will do to them." I choke on my words. "We have to stop this." I am standing, turning from Farnsworth to Julian and back again.

"The rebels have made their decision." Farnsworth's words are flat. "They have sided with the enemy and cut us out of the picture. There is no way we can help those girls, Veronica." His voice is softer, now. "I'm sorry."

"There has to be a way," I implore. "We can't leave those girls out there in the middle of a warzone. They'll die for sure."

Farnsworth avoids me. That old feeling of hatred settles in my mouth, and I can't shake the awful, bitter taste it's creating.

"That matters to some of us," I snarl.

Farnsworth turns back to face me. He remains calm, but I can see the anger in his eyes. "This is out of my hands, Veronica. And I think…if you want to be angry with someone, be angry with him."

Farnsworth points to the projection, and I am momentarily lost in the soulfulness of Phoenix's eyes.

"He is the one who sided with the enemy. He is the

one who dragged the girls into this. He was the one who was originally Gunnar's partner." Farnsworth takes a few steps and comes back spritely, his words animated. He lifts his hands when he speaks. "And last I checked, Veronica, we were working together. He was the one who separated from us."

"Because you forced me to marry you."

"I did no such thing." Farnsworth dismisses me with his words.

"What would you call it, then?"

"I made you a business deal."

"A business deal? You told me I needed to marry you, or you would harm those girls…all of them. And if I was willing to marry you to save them…then don't you understand I will do anything for them? I will never give up on them."

"I'm sorry, but there's nothing we can do, Veronica. The rebels have left us and sided with the enemy. They made their choice. They don't care about us." Farnsworth looks me dead in the eyes. "He doesn't care about you anymore, Veronica. You need to understand that."

Farnsworth's words sit heavily on me, and I feel the sob forming like a cyclone in my chest. "No," I mutter, flopping back down onto the couch. I can't give over to this. I also can't shake the image of fragile, beautiful Lulu, and the horrors she is potentially facing. There has to be a way. I think hard, willing to grasp at any straw that may be offered.

"You know," I mumble, thinking as I go. "If Phoenix knew what you were doing here, how you've changed your ways…maybe we could stop this whole awful war."

Farnsworth turns away from me. He doesn't speak.

I think of the image of Phoenix on the projection, and the power it held. My brain becomes alive with ideas for the first time in a very long time.

"What if we show him?" I ask, standing before the two men.

"Excuse me?" Julian questions.

"Show Phoenix what we are doing here. Publicize our work as he publicizes his war. Let people see the horror that is out here. Let them understand we are working to change it." My heart races with the idea of hope. Maybe, just maybe, I can prove to Phoenix I'm not all bad.

"Veronica—" Julian begins.

Farnsworth holds up his hand to cut him off. "I think it's a wonderful idea," Farnsworth answers, like he is pacifying a child.

"Why are you speaking to me like that?"

"Like what?"

"Like I'm a child."

"I'm sorry, Veronica. I am doing no such thing." Farnsworth's eyes briefly glance at my body before he steps back with a huff.

I look down to see the outline of my breasts showing through the thin gauze, and I realize all this time I have been wearing nothing but a flimsy nightgown. I cross my arms in front of me, and Farnsworth stares out a window. He turns back to me.

"If you want to show the rebels our good works in the hopes of restoring our nation's peace, then I am all for it. But if you are simply searching for a way back into his good graces, Veronica, that time has passed."

I drop my arms and bite my bottom lip, nodding.

"Don't you think I know that?" My eyes flood with tears. "But I can't lose my girls, too. I just can't."

Farnsworth walks forward and stops just before me. I face him, feeling my eyes widen, wondering what he is doing. A lone tear escapes my eye, and Farnsworth reaches up to wipe it away, ever-so-gently. He removes his hand, and quietly leaves the room.

I drop back down onto the couch, curling into a sideways ball, staring at the screen Julian is watching. After a moment, Julian comes to my couch. I move my feet so he has a place to sit. We stare at the screen in silence. After a few more moments, he speaks.

"You love him? That boy on the screen?"

"Yes," I whisper.

"Good looking kid, I'll give you that."

I smile, despite myself.

"I like the beard. Maybe I should try growing a beard. Whatdaya think?"

I shrug, and he gives me a small, pained smile. "All right, Veronica. What happened? If you don't mind me asking."

I shake my head no, happy to be talking about Phoenix. "We were in love," I whisper. "And then I did the unthinkable."

"Marrying ol' Malachi?"

"No. That was bad, but...I did it to save Phoenix and just about everyone else you saw on that screen tonight."

"Ah," Julian tosses his head back. "You tried to save him, and he feels it's his job to save you."

"Yes," I whisper. "I—I ruined everything."

Julian stares at me, and then he speaks. "Did you ever think if something is meant to be, it wouldn't be so hard?"

"Are you telling me Phoenix and I aren't meant to be?"

"I'm just sayin' you have a man up there," he points to the ceiling, "who is head over heels for you."

"Farnsworth?" I recoil at the thought.

"But I see the feeling's not mutual."

"How could it be? I mean, really. You understand. You were once where Phoenix is now."

"Yes, I was. And I was wrong."

I scan Julian's face, trying to read his eyes.

"Are you telling me we should just accept the injustices of the world, and all become pawns in Farnsworth's plot for domination?"

Julian smiles and shakes his head. "He's not plotting domination. He already has it. You could have yourself a nice life, Veronica, if you choose to overlook his indiscretions the way you are so willing to overlook Phoenix's."

"You can't compare them," I retort, sitting up straight, distancing myself on the couch.

"Really? Have you stopped to think what the New World might be like if Farnsworth didn't use blood as a commodity? It would mirror this place, Veronica. It would be just like HopeLess World."

"He kills children."

"So do I."

I move as far to the other side of the couch as I can.

"Now don't get dramatic. It's not on purpose. But my children are dying off out there same as his. At least his children have a chance at a good life while they're alive."

The image of the boy with the bird comes back to

me, and I shudder.

"You cold?"

I shrug. Julian gets up and produces a blanket out of a basket on the other side of the room. He tosses it to me, and then smooths it across my legs, exactly the way my mother used to do. I stare up at him with wonder.

"You're a smart girl, Veronica."

I scoff, but he goes on.

"Don't scoff at that. You are a very bright young woman. So listen to what I'm telling you. Principal Leader Farnsworth can offer you a good life—even with the uprising. It will be over soon. Trust me. And Farnsworth will win. He will protect you and provide for you. You will never be starving or destitute. All it takes is an adjustment on your part. You must decide to see the good, not the bad."

"He'll take my blood whenever he needs it."

"That's a small price to pay for what he's offering you."

"But you're a rebel," I protest. "How can you be telling me this?"

"Because I was wrong, Veronica. And I'm afraid that boy on the projection might be wrong, too."

I inhale sharply, and Julian pats my foot as he speaks.

"As awful as it sounds, maybe there isn't meant to be equality in life. Maybe some of us have, and some don't. And as long as you have, you'll have the luxury of helping others."

"But what about—"

"Love?" He smiles and runs his hands down his thighs. "Love is one of those things, Ronnie, if I may call you that."

I nod.

"You can pick whom you love by choosing to see whatever you want in that other person. There is no inherent good or evil. We are all a manifestation of our surroundings. That's all. Including that man upstairs. He didn't begin the Lettings or the Couplings. But he saw what his father did, worked. So he went with it. And love? Well, sometimes the feeling of being loved is more important than who you are in love with."

He stands and stretches, nearly touching the ceiling. "Coming up?" he asks. I turn to the projection, hoping to catch one more glimpse of Phoenix, but he is gone. "Ronnie? Are you with me?"

"Yes," I nod, standing. "I'm with you."

Chapter Thirteen

I walk the upstairs hallway silently. As I pass Farnsworth's room, I realize his door is cracked open an inch or two. Without knowing why, I peek inside and see him leaning against a windowsill, staring out. He is dressed in silk pajamas, and he leaves his shirt opened. He would look like he was posing for a portrait if it wasn't that he seems so deep in thought.

"Hello, Veronica." He speaks without moving.

I start at the sound of his voice. "I'm sorry, sir," I whisper. "I was just—"

"Don't be." He continues to face out the window. "Have you ever wondered how things can sometimes go so terribly wrong?"

My eyes grow wide, and I snicker. "Yes, sir. I wonder that all the time."

He turns to me, smiling. "Yes, I suppose you would."

We stand there for minutes, staring at one another. He appears pensive and concerned. The stillness of our surroundings and the softness of the bedroom light makes Farnsworth seem…almost human. For some reason, despite my anger, tonight I see him as a man, and not just a monster. He looks back out the window.

"Well, goodnight, Veronica." He surprises me with his abrupt ending to our conversation.

"Good night, sir." I turn away, flustered.

Down the hall, I see Julian smile at me before he retreats into his bedroom.

****

I wake the next morning with that old duplicitous feeling of hope. While I slept, hope seems to have come and settled in the small of my back, whirling itself like a tempest of energy. I can barely contain my excitement. Farnsworth has agreed to broadcast the good works we will be doing as a counter to Phoenix's broadcast of the war. More importantly, we are going to be able to offer some hope—no matter how small the kernel—to these people in HopeLess World. And maybe, in doing so, we can offer some hope to the people of the New World, as well. In a hurry to dress, I rummage through my bags and discover a pair of jeans, and a black tank top that is meant only to be layered under a jacket. It is as close to my regular uniform as I can find. I bound down the stairs to find Farnsworth and Julian already hunched over a dining room table, eating toast with something red smeared across it. I glance at the bread and narrow my eyes.

"It's jelly," Farnsworth tells me. "Would you like to try it?"

"No, thank you. I just really want to get to work."

"Work?" Julian questions, raising his eyebrows at me.

"Yes. Helping those people we came to help. Broadcasting our works to try to make peace with the rebels taking over the New World. Like we discussed last night…?"

"Of course," Farnsworth answers.

I take a deep breath, happy there's no argument from him.

"But you should eat, Veronica. You've eaten nothing for quite some time."

Again the image of the man with the blood smeared across his face comes to mind. "I—I can't," I murmur.

"You have to eat something," Farnsworth tells me. "You'll never have your strength otherwise."

"Fine." He is right. I lean over the table and grab two pieces of toast.

"Jelly?" Julian asks.

I shake my head furiously, the jelly looking too much like blood. I stuff the dry bread into my mouth and dust off my hands. "Ready?" I ask, my mouth full.

Farnsworth chuckles. "I suppose so," he acquiesces, pushing himself back from the table. I head toward the door, but he stops next to me and stares at my clothing.

"What?" I ask, checking myself up and down.

"It's really not appropriate for my wife to be wearing…"

I brace myself against the word, wife, and then I speak. "We are heading into the hot sun to help feed poor people living in squalor. I promise they don't want to see me dressed in one of those white suits Grace packed for me."

"Maybe not, Veronica, but still…" His words trail off. "This is important work we are doing, and I am the Principal Leader. You really should consider—"

"Fine," I agree, just to get us out of Julian's house faster. "But I'm not wearing something ridiculous."

"I would never expect you to," he tells me, smiling.

Within four minutes, I have myself up the stairs and changed into tan dress pants and a white button down shirt. I hate the idea of wearing white, but there's little option in my wardrobe. Grace tries to get me to wear white beads around my neck, but I have a limit. My wedding ring is quite enough jewelry for me.

"Don't say anything about the white shirt…" I mumble as I reenter the dining room.

"I wouldn't dream of it, except to say you look very beautiful."

"We're going to feed starving people." I stare him straight in the eye. "I don't need to look beautiful."

"Very well, Veronica, very well."

"You should change too," I tell him.

"I should?" He is startled.

"Into something you can work in. Lose the jacket. Wear your running suit or something."

Within minutes, Farnsworth has changed into a light blue dress shirt and some tan colored pants. Other than our trip to the waterfront, this is the closest to casual I've ever seen him. I cringe when I realize we are dressed similarly, but I refuse to waste one second more on costume choices. I wait in the hallway, and Jerold comes forward with my vest.

"Is this really necessary?" I ask.

"Completely, ma'am."

We suit up and gather as a group.

"Where is the food?" I ask Farnsworth.

"They're preparing it now."

"But we're taking the food from this house? That's counterproductive. Where's the food from the New World?"

"That's coming, my dear," Farnsworth answers, smiling.

I roll my shoulders, trying to shake off the

endearment.

"It's a long trip."

"Why didn't we bring it on the airplane with us?" I ask.

"It just doesn't work that way." With that he ends the conversation, and finally, we enter the vehicle.

"Where do we go first?" I ask. "Are we heading to that same neighborhood you showed me yesterday?"

Grace and Patty glimpse at one another, panicked.

"Maybe someplace a bit tamer to start," Farnsworth suggests.

"But those people really need food," I protest.

Farnsworth pats my hand, and I pull it back, quickly. While we sit, they load a second vehicle with the prepped sandwiches, and something Julian calls a "projection camera," to film our good works. We head out.

****

Unfortunately, it is not long until we find people begging at the side of the car. We roll to a stop. I try my door, but I am unable to get out.

"I'm sorry, Mrs. Farnsworth, ma'am, I need to exit the car first." Jerold hops out of our vehicle and surveys the area.

Finally, keeping the people back a safe distance, he lets me exit our vehicle. Farnsworth stands at the side of the car as I march up to our food truck and open the back. I'm happy to see the stacks of premade sandwiches, although I worry there won't be nearly enough. My gut aches, but I smile as starving person after starving person takes sandwich after sandwich. Julian follows me with the camera. A woman with four young girls thanks me. I ruffle one girl's hair, and the other three hug me, tightly. I wipe a tear, thinking of my four girls immersed in a fight, thousands of miles away.

Hour after hour passes. The mass of people who need food seems endless. Farnsworth is with me, his sleeves rolled up, handing out drinks and the wrapped sandwiches. We sweat uncontrollably, but Jerold refuses to let us remove the vests. I smile at person after person, the happiest I've been in—I don't know how long. I move quickly, probably too quickly, and as I go to get another sandwich from the food truck, I turn, smack into Farnsworth. We bump into each other, and I lose my grip on the sandwich. I juggle it back and forth, unable to get a hold of it, until Farnsworth grabs it, just before it hits the ground. A nearby crowd applauds as Farnsworth takes a goofy bow, and we laugh together for the first time ever.

Our ample food supply dwindles, but we haven't even begun to serve the communities who need it most. "We need to reload," I tell Farnsworth.

"We've done enough for today," he assures me, squeezing my hand.

"No, we haven't." I snap my hand away and raise my voice more than I intend. I take a step back from him. I collect myself and try to remain calm. "We've barely scratched the surface, sir. We need more food. Why else would we have come here?"

"You're right, of course," Farnsworth allows.

"Can we get the food, now?"

"Already been radioed in," Julian informs us as he walks up to us. He does not step out from behind the camera. Hopefully, we will have some good footage to project into the rebel camps in the New World. "Thanks to him." He points at Farnsworth.

"I knew you would never quit," Farnsworth tells me, wiping the sweat from his forehead. "No matter what I say."

"Well…uh…thank you." I nod at Farnsworth, and without meaning to, I break into a real, genuine smile.

He smiles too, and then walks back to the vehicle to rest. I watch him go and turn to Julian, who has finally set the projection camera down. He rubs his arm, sore from balancing the camera.

"Just don't broadcast me smiling at Principal Leader Farnsworth, please."

"You should have told me that one before," Julian responds, rolling his neck in circles.

"What?"

"Ronnie." He stops stretching and turns his full attention to me. "It's too late. This is live."

"Live? What do you mean, live?"

"I'm afraid that smile was just circulated throughout every rebel camp in the New World."

"And the laughing before?" I whisper, horrified. "When Farnsworth caught my sandwich?"

"Yes." Julian nods, solemnly.

I can only imagine how this will look to Phoenix.

"Damn it," I curse, my breath rushing in and out of my body. I scowl at Farnsworth, and then fix my eyes on the ground. "This is a disaster."

"Is it?" Julian asks.

My eyes dart up to him.

"Ronnie, I don't know if you saw what I saw last night on the projection…but I saw a beautiful woman snuggled up tightly against the boy you claim to love. Seems to me you may be chasing someone who's already gone."

I swallow my tears as the relief vehicle pulls up, carrying more food.

Julian pulls a rag from his pocket and wipes his sweat as he speaks. "What's important is they all see you are trying your best out here."

I nod.

\*\*\*\*

After an exhausting day of feeding as many starving people as we could find, we huddle into our vehicle, glad to be sitting down. The vehicle rolls forward as I stretch my long legs, careful not to kick Grace or Patty. My knees make a popping sound. I know we've put in a long day, but thinking about it, I realize we haven't even made a dent. I turn to Farnsworth. "What about the boy I saw?"

"What boy?" Farnsworth asks.

"Yesterday. On the way here. The boy who was…eating…a…" I am unable to say the words.

"What did you see, Veronica?" Julian asks.

"A boy eating a raw bird. And a man stole it from him." Retelling the story makes me sick all over again.

Grace clears her throat, and Patty fidgets in her seat. I turn to face out the window.

"I'm sure we can get to him tomorrow," Farnsworth assures me. He pats my knee and puts his head back against his seat.

"Tomorrow?" I ask, pushing his hand away.

Everyone in the car sees me reject Farnsworth. They all have the decency to look elsewhere.

"Yes." He opens his eyes. He doesn't appear overly happy with me. "Tomorrow we'll be sure to bring him a sandwich."

"Stop the car," I demand.

Everyone looks at me, wondering what I am doing. "STOP THE CAR, I SAID!"

Jerold raps on the glass partition, and the driver slams on his brakes. I struggle against my door.

"Sir?" Jerold asks.

"Let her out."

Mercifully, my door unlocks, and I fall out of the vehicle and onto a street somewhere in HopeLess World. I stumble forward, gasping for air as I hear Patty assuring everyone I have left the vehicle only to vomit. Jerold stands near me as Farnsworth walks over to me.

"What is going on, Veronica?"

I turn to him, livid, my eyes blurry with tears, my hands shaking. "Tomorrow?" I whisper. "Tomorrow?" I shake my head and storm off.

He catches up to me. "Veronica, I'm afraid I don't understand. I thought you would be pleased we will be back tomorrow for more charitable works."

"Well of course we'll be back tomorrow," I snap. "That's the reason we're here, isn't it?"

"Then what, Veronica? What is going on?"

I can tell Farnsworth is confused. It is so unlike him to have a confrontation—especially on a street, and especially with me. I begin pacing.

"I guess I can't blame you," I mumble. "Because you've never been hungry." I stop pacing and confront him, staring him square in the eyes. "But do you have any idea what it's like to wait another twenty-four hours when you're starving? Do you?"

"No, Veronica, I don't." Farnsworth speaks quietly.

"Of course you don't." I walk away from him,

mumbling.

"Then tell me," he calls after me.

I turn back to him, and he takes a step toward me.

"Don't discount me, Veronica. Tell me. Explain it to me so I can understand what it's like. So I can understand what you've been through. Please, Veronica."

They are the most honest, heartfelt words I have ever heard from Farnsworth. I walk back to him, slowly.

"I can't explain it. And thankfully for you, you'll never experience it. But we need to bring that boy food. Now." I head back to the car.

Farnsworth follows me and sits quietly next to me.

"Sir?" Jerold asks.

"Back to City Center." Farnsworth speaks softly, gazing out the window.

Grace and Patty look up at him, their faces etched with worry.

Jerold leans forward, adjusting his suit jacket. "But it's almost dark, sir."

"I know."

Chapter Fourteen

We roll into City Center to an ominous glow illuminating old rusty barrels. "They need to stay warm at night," Jerold explains.

Julian rests his head in his hand as we pass by the broken sidewalks, littered with filth and filled with lost souls. Our vehicle rolls over broken glass and abandoned tattered rags, as the previously deserted street fills with angry young men.

"You need to tell them." I speak to Jerold. "You need to explain we are here with food."

Within moments, the vehicle is pelted with stones.

"It's too dangerous. Sir?"

"Wait, please," I beg. "Let's just find that boy…"

Rock after rock pelts us, and someone overturns a barrel in front of our vehicle.

"Sir," Jerold warns. "Sir, I'm going to have to call this…"

"Crack!" A gunshot hits hard against my window. I duck, as Grace and Patty cower.

"I'm calling it," Jerold announces, and he raps on the partition. "You're okay ma'am." Jerold uses a quiet, soothing tone when he speaks to me.

I nod, terrified, fighting hard to calm my breathing.

Our vehicle speeds away, faster and faster, until we are far from City Center and the one boy I desperately wanted to have helped.

\*\*\*\*

We walk into the house in silence. I rub my shoulders, stiff from the heavy vest, and silently climb the stairs to my room. I clamber into a bath that Grace has already prepared, curling up my legs to squeeze all of me in. Lying there, I know there is no easy answer. No matter how much food we supply this world with, they will never sustain it when we are gone. But…will we ever be gone?

Naturally, my uneasy thoughts turn to Phoenix. I wonder what he saw today and what he thinks of it. Of me. My mind wanders to my hidden book. Could this be one of the books Phoenix once told me about? My thoughts linger on Phoenix, and I wonder if what Julian said to me is right. Has Phoenix moved on? Have he and Brooke become a couple once again? Couple…just the word makes me think of my unfulfilled duty. When will Farnsworth call on me to Couple? Despite the warm water, my body breaks out into tiny bumps all over.

I pull myself from the bath and dress in clean clothes. There is no sense in trying to sleep. Farnsworth and Julian know I am awake, and they're expecting me to come watch the projection, I'm sure. I comb through my wet hair and take a deep breath. I walk down the stairs and into our meeting room to find both men, riveted, staring at the screen.

"It's positive," Julian assures Farnsworth.

Farnsworth just grunts his response. I walk in and the men part. There, staring at me from the projection is Phoenix. The projection cuts away from him and cuts immediately to me, smiling and laughing with Farnsworth as we hand out sandwiches.

"Ugh," I moan. "I seem so ridiculous and vapid." I turn to both men. "Why? Why would they only show the parts that make me look silly?"

"They're trying to make you the enemy," Julian answers.

"Yeah, well, we're helping them with this," I nod to the camera lying on a table. "What a stupid idea that was…" I plop down onto the couch as Brooke steps up to speak.

"We weren't sure," she adjusts her green military jacket, "about Veronica Billings, but this video is all the proof we need. While we are fighting a war, she is off smiling and flirting with her new husband."

People scream angry words. She puts up her hand to silence them.

"So we are no longer giving her the benefit of the doubt. She is once again the enemy we always knew she was."

She holds up her gun and Phoenix stands perfectly still, biting the inside of his cheek.

"The people have chosen," she continues. "And you have chosen right."

More supportive hollering is heard, and again, she quiets them.

"In the meantime, while our rebel forces are securing the New World, you will continue to follow Phoenix and I as we serve as your leaders." She turns to Phoenix, and he offers a small, pained smile. Then she says something to him I cannot hear, and he smiles at her. It is an honest and real smile. The kind usually reserved for me.

Brooke reaches down and takes Phoenix's hand, and she lifts it high into the air, intertwined with hers.

She whispers to him, and he smiles once more. Then she leans over to kiss him on the cheek. He turns just in time to catch her kiss on his lips. They pull apart, and she looks as surprised as I do. The crowd hollers appreciatively as Phoenix wraps one arm around Brooke's waist, and with the other, raises his gun high into the air. Brooke appears absolutely giddy as the feed is cut, and once again he is gone.

Neither man speaks; they simply turn slowly toward me.

"Well," I whisper. "I guess I'll be going to bed. There is a lot of work to do tomorrow." I glance at each of them briefly before I walk out of the room, and slowly, climb the stairs.

****

When I reach the top of the staircase, I cannot will myself to go to the solitude of my bedroom. I cannot face this alone. Instead, I walk into Farnsworth's room and curl up on the windowsill.

After a while, he gently pushes open the door to his room.

"I see why you like looking out this window," I offer. "Even in the darkness, you can still see…" I don't even bother to finish my thought.

"Yes. A lovely view, considering everything." After a pause, he continues. "Are you okay?" He asks in such a way it sounds as if he really cares.

I shake my head. Through broken words, I try to speak. "I just didn't want to be alone. Do you mind?"

"Mind? Veronica, I have always wanted you to come to me. Always. I'm just sorry you have to be hurting this badly to do it."

I nod, fighting hard to keep the tears back. "I'm an

119

idiot," I whisper.

"No, you're not." He steps into the room.

"Can you close the door?" I ask, gazing over his shoulder.

He obliges without comment. "You are not an idiot, Veronica. Even the smartest of people get hurt sometimes."

"Julian tells me we can choose whom we love just by adjusting our attitudes toward them. Do you believe that?" I raise my eyes to him, aching and vulnerable.

"I wish I could say yes. But only you can decide that." He hovers near the door.

"Do you think he loves her?" I ask, as if I'm talking to an old friend.

"I don't know." He steps closer to me but hesitates.

"You can come in," I whisper. "It's your room."

Farnsworth walks in and sits on the edge of his bed, facing me.

I stare at him, completely overtaken with emotion and grief. "I just—" I try to make words, but instead, tears fall in their place.

Farnsworth stands and crosses to me. He wraps his arms around me, and I try to push him off, but he resists against my struggle. Harder he holds me still, until I let myself fall against his chest, weeping. I don't know how long he stands there, holding me as I cry against him, but I am thankful for it.

I feel light-headed and weak on my feet as he eases us both to his bed. We sit on the edge of the bed, his arms still wrapped around me. He does nothing for himself; he doesn't bury his nose in my hair, or try to lay me back next to him. He simply holds me. After my tears have run dry, I pull back from him. He smiles at me and reaches across to get a tissue from the table by the bed. He hands it to me. I look up at him and for the first time ever, I realize how handsome he is.

"How did any of this happen?" I whisper, but he puts his finger to my lips. I nod, my eyes resting on his once again.

Then he leans forward, and his lips find mine.

Chapter Fifteen

I pull back from him, surprised. He waits patiently, judging my reaction. I'm certain he is waiting to be slapped or spit at. But frankly, I don't have the energy for either. Instead, I just sit there, stunned.

This time he reaches for me. He leans forward, as if he plans to kiss me once again. I stare at him, unable to move…unable to speak. His hands find my hands, and he holds them. I shiver at his touch—his hands are nearly as cold as my soul. Our wedding bands clang together, awkwardly. I am distanced enough to methodically process our actions. His kiss is so very different from Phoenix's. It's cold and troublesome. Farnsworth's kiss stirs nothing inside me, there is no desire for anything more…but there is obligation. I know that.

Farnsworth lifts his hands to my shoulders, and I shudder, as if a piece of ice just slid inside my shirt. He is stronger than I expect, but I feel no connection to him. It is as if I am watching myself experience this. I have turned off from my emotions, and I could walk away unfazed, at any time.

He pulls back for a moment. "What are we doing?"

"Sir?"

"I think we can abandon that title here, don't you think, Veronica?" He smiles a confused smile.

"Yes. Of course. What are you asking me,

Malachi?"

He turns my hands over and runs his thumb across my palm. I close my eyes and try to remain calm.

"I guess I'm asking if that kiss was about me, or about him?"

I nod, looking away. Memories of Phoenix flash before me. I imagine swimming side by side in our lake. I remember the oppressive summer night, and the feel of our first kiss in the back of the army truck. I can practically touch the granules of sand as I think about the beach and his hands on my hips as he pulls me tight up against him. I shudder, knowing the exhilaration of our bodies touching. I close my eyes and breathe him in. I wrap my arms around myself, pretending they are his strong arms, offering me refuge and promising me he will be there, always. Promising me nothing will break us up, ever. But something did—him. I open my eyes and feel them glaze over, knowing I have to do something to forget Phoenix and make the hurting stop.

"It was about you," I whisper.

"I wish it were." He lifts his hand and strokes my cheek, gently.

I freeze, but force myself to try to nuzzle against it, desperately wanting to believe it belongs to someone else.

"I wish, more than anything right now, it was only the two of us here."

"It can be." I close my eyes again, but he pulls his hand away. I take it back from him and lead it toward the strap of my tank top. My hands tremble uncontrollably, and I have an aching feeling in my gut. My breath is running up and down inside my body, screaming to be let go, but I keep it locked up tightly and contained completely. I stare at Farnsworth, and I'm beginning to perspire as I wait for him to slide the strap off my shoulder.

"Are you…?"

"You have slated me to Couple with you…I thought you wanted to." My voice is low, and my words are choppy. I can barely look at him.

"I do want to, Veronica. More than anything. But are you sure?"

I still can't face him.

"Veronica?"

I finally meet his gaze, and the look in my eyes must answer his question.

"That's what I thought." He drops his hand.

"I will try. If we have to do this—"

"Have to, Veronica?"

The memory of Phoenix's arms wrapped around me overtakes my body. I place my shaking hands on top of Farnsworth's. My hands are now as cold as his.

His eyes fall to my hands. "Are you nervous?" he asks.

"Yes." There is no sense in lying now.

"I'm not going to push you, Veronica."

"I know that."

"Then why are you so terrified?"

I shrug slightly and bite my bottom lip. I see the glimmer of understanding in his eyes.

"This is not just about me or him, is it?" He searches my eyes. "Veronica, are you…?" He stands and moves away from the bed. He turns back. "You mean you've never…?"

I shake my head. "No, never. I've only ever kissed someone. Just one someone. Only a few times."

"You mean you and Phoenix…never?"

"Never." I sigh at the mention of his name.

"All that time he was with you? In his cabin?"

I just shake my head.

Farnsworth resumes his spot on the bed right next to me, and leans forward, resting his forearms on his thighs. "I had no idea, Veronica. Truly. I just assumed…"

I feel my face flush, and I begin to squirm, uncomfortably. "Well, what about you? Does your condition…affect you?"

"Affect me? Yes. But not in that way."

"So then, have you?" I ask, boldly.

He smiles a large, generous smile at me. "Yes, I have. Of course. Many times."

"Oh," I eke out. My eyes drop to the floor in front of me. I find it hard to take a breath. I could not feel any more stupid than I do right now.

Farnsworth reaches out and takes my hand. "It's not like that. But I'm twenty-four years old, and I'm the Principal Leader. I have had girlfriends before."

I whip my head away.

"I guess having a girlfriend or boyfriend is not a luxury you—or any of your friends—has ever known."

I turn back to him, my jaw set tight. "No sir, it's not."

He looks at me, raising his eyebrows.

"I mean, no, Malachi. It's not."

"Let me ask you a question, Veronica." I can see by the way he smooths the creases in his pants, it is his turn to be vulnerable. He clears his throat. "What if, way back when, you had fallen in love with me and not Phoenix?"

I raise my eyes to him.

"Would you have seen the good in me? Would you have known he's not perfect, either?"

"I don't know," I whisper. "Honestly, despite what Julian said, I don't know if I could ever have fallen in love with anyone but Phoenix."

Farnsworth gives me a tiny smile. He reaches up and smooths my hair with his hand. I can tell he's made a decision. "I think we've had a long enough day. What do you think?" He nudges his shoulder against mine, like he did that day at the waterfront.

"You mean, you don't want to?"

"Of course I want to, Veronica. But now is not the time."

I nod, feeling myself blush again. "I should go," I whisper, feeling mortified and abandoned. In just one night, I have been rejected by the man I love, and the man I loathe.

"No." Farnsworth speaks softly. "Stay with me. Here, tonight. Just lie with me."

"But we—"

"Veronica. Sometimes we can stop being who we are. Just for an hour or two. It's okay to need someone. And it's okay that someone is me."

I nod and lie back on his bed. He lies next to me, his eyes staring at the ceiling. I turn away from him and curl into a ball, my arm tucked underneath a pillow. He does not touch me.

"Thank you," I whisper. I am asleep before I ever hear his reply.

Chapter Sixteen

The next morning, I wake with a start to find Julian hovering over me, projection camera in hand.

"What are you doing?" I yell, sitting up, trying to get my bearings.

A still asleep Farnsworth wakes beside me.

"That should be a nice little good morning for the New World, don't you think?" Julian smiles a wide smile. I see something caught between his teeth.

"What are you doing?" I repeat, jumping out of bed and rushing for the camera.

"Not so fast, Veronica." He pulls the camera away and clicks it off. "I'm through shooting for the moment. And besides, it's already been broadcast. Your boyfriend has seen you fast asleep, curled up next to your husband. The man he's been plotting to kill."

"What's going on?" I ask. I turn to Farnsworth. "Malachi?"

"Oh you guys must have had some night for her to be calling you that without any prompting." Julian slaps his hand against his leg.

"Shut up," Farnsworth growls.

Julian becomes stoic.

"Malachi?" I press him for an answer. "What's happening? What does he mean?"

"Shall I tell her?" Julian smiles at Farnsworth. "Or would you like the honors, sir."

"Tell me what?" I glance at Farnsworth who is sitting on the edge of the bed.

He turns away.

"Well, I guess I've got to be the one then."

"Speak carefully, Julian," Farnsworth warns, staring dead ahead.

"What are you talking about?" I demand.

"What your husband didn't tell you was the truth."

I scowl at Farnsworth. He gets up and walks to the window, looking out.

"What truth?" I look at Julian.

"Any of it. For one thing, he didn't tell you the real reason he's here. You think it's to help some decaying civilization? Smarten up, Veronica. He's here for his own personal gain. Like always."

I turn to Farnsworth. "Malachi? What is he talking about?"

Farnsworth remains silent.

"I'm talking about your trip out here. You're here to trade blood for food."

"What?"

"All those people you saw walking around out there. There's a bunch of men who'll fight off any rebel threat just for the promise of a sandwich. And once that's done, there are plenty of girls who haven't blossomed yet. Girls you get to lead to the next Lettings."

"What are you saying?"

"And in return, Farnsworth will send me supplies to help me save my dying country."

"You're insane," I snap.

"Maybe."

"But what about your promise for a better world?"

"Does this look like a better world to you?"

"But you tried. You wanted to break free from Farnsworth and protect your people." I lean against the edge of the bed, clutching the blanket in both of my fists.

"You believed that? Oh Veronica, the only reason I left was to try to match Farnsworth's success in a world of my own. It was 'HopefuL World,' because I was hopeful. I never had noble aspirations."

"Are you even my father?" I ask. My eyes flood with tears.

"Yes." He nods. "Yes. That I am."

"Did you love my mother?" Tears choke my words. "Did you?"

"I had a fondness for her. Really. But she was always so idealistic. Like you. She couldn't support me in my endeavors."

"To become a tyrant." I stand, staring straight at him.

"Yes."

"Why did you film us? This morning."

"My end of the bargain. I have to say, you suggesting the projection feed was a gift from God."

"God wouldn't waste his gifts on you."

Julian glances around. "I guess you're right about that."

"And you," I growl, turning to Farnsworth. "I—I trusted you. I told you things I've never told anyone else. Ever."

"I know that," Farnsworth states, flatly. "I'm sorry."

I motion to the bed. "Was this part of your plan? Huh? Was it?" I face both men.

"Farnsworth knew he'd need a nudge to get you to agree. So I nudged a bit. It wasn't nearly as hard as I'd imagined. You're pretty fickle, Veronica."

"Fickle?" I scream. "I love that boy on the projection. And he broke my heart. And he breaks it again every time I see him. I—I just needed a friend. And Principal Leader Farnsworth pretended to be one."

"I didn't pretend, Veronica. I wanted to be there for you."

I whip around to him. "You're not my friend, and you don't love me," I hiss. "You don't even know what that word means. Neither of you do." I stare at both men for a moment and then storm to the bedroom door.

"Where are you heading, Veronica?" I hear concern in Farnsworth's voice.

"Anywhere I damned well please. And as far away from you two as I can get."

Farnsworth steps forward. "I would remind you, you are still my wife. As long as that ring is on your finger…"

I yank the ring off my finger and hurl it at Farnsworth. It bounces off his shoulder, but he doesn't flinch.

"With or without that ring, we are bound by law—"

"Whose law? Yours?" I toss my head back, laughing.

"Yes, mine," Farnsworth snaps. "And it's the only law that matters. As I think we've proven by this cesspit Julian created." He raises his shoulders and breathes deeply. He exhales, audibly. "As I was saying, ring or no ring, we are bound by law"—he speaks loudly over my guttural protests— "and you still have a duty to me—"

"Oh, stick it, Farnsworth."

He recoils from my words, and his face reddens. Julian snickers.

"You too, *Dad*," I mock. I turn back to Farnsworth. "You. I owe you nothing. I am here because of manipulation, no other reason."

"And to keep those little girls alive."

I step forward, closer to Farnsworth. I soften my voice when I speak to him. "I don't believe that anymore. I saw something in you last night, something I never knew was there. I saw goodness. I saw that you could care for someone else."

"It was part of his plan, Veronica." Julian's voice is stern.

I turn to him. "Yes, it was. But he could have pushed me. I—I don't know. I might have said yes. Then he would have gotten what he wanted, and succeeded in his plan. But he protected me for some reason. And for that, and only that, I am grateful." I turn to Farnsworth and look him straight in the eyes. "So I know if you kept us from that last night, just to protect me, then you won't kill the girls I love. I'm certain of it."

"Don't be so certain about Phoenix, however," Farnsworth states.

"I'm not. I don't trust you a bit when it comes to him. But I'm still grateful. And for that reason, I will give you a pint of my blood so you can stop tapping poor Grace."

Farnsworth takes a step back. "How did you know?"

"I figured out she was an 'O'. She has been looking

pale and even weaker than usual, but you have been looking better and stronger, so it wasn't hard to put together. Even for me."

"Veronica," Farnsworth whispers.

I put up my hand. "Please. No phony pep talk. I know I'm not smart. I know who I am, and I'm okay with it."

"But you're wrong," he protests. "You are actually too smart for your own good."

I give him a small, calculated smile. "No, sir, I'm too smart for your own good."

Farnsworth nods at me.

My eyes level on his. "I'll give you my blood this morning, before I leave."

"Leave?" Farnsworth steps closer to me. "But where are you going?"

"Back to the New World, of course."

## Chapter Seventeen

"The New World?" Farnsworth asks. "But how will you get there?"

"I'll walk."

"You can't do that, Veronica," Julian chimes in. "It's impossible."

"Watch me." I begin to leave.

"You're running away like a child, Veronica." Farnsworth smirks at me, pleased with himself.

"No, sir. I did run away like a child. And now I'm going back to try to fix it."

"It's a two month walk," Farnsworth warns. "Two months. You'll never be able to carry enough food and water. You'll die a couple of weeks in."

"I'll have to take my chances." I clench my fists and remain strong.

"You don't know what you'll run into out there," Julian advises. "The horrors, the dangers that will surround you at every step."

"They can't be any worse than the ones surrounding me here." My words are soft, and I feel sadness shaping into a fog around me. I glance back at Farnsworth one last time, before I slip out his bedroom door.

\*\*\*\*

"Veronica," Grace wipes a tear. "I don't want to see you do this to yourself."

We are in my bedroom in Julian's house. Patty has just left with a pint of my blood for Farnsworth, and I am busy wrapping gauze around my left arm to protect the new puncture.

"I have no choice." I hop off the bed, unfazed by Grace's words. There is a quiet but strong knock on my door. Grace bows out as Farnsworth walks in.

"If you came to see if I've changed my mind, the answer is no."

"I didn't think you would." He sits on my bed, watching me lace my boots.

"Grace brought them for me. Maybe she's not all bad," I mumble.

"Very few of us are," Farnsworth muses.

I turn to him.

"I wish I could fly you back, Veronica. I really do." I nod.

"But you know with the rebel takeover, it would be impossible. We got out just in time."

"I know that," I whisper.

"Veronica, before, you told me I don't know what love is. Do you?"

I turn away and busy myself with my backpack. I have buried the book deep inside.

"Do you, Veronica?"

I stop. "I don't know. But I think it's this feeling inside that drives me to wherever he is."

"That's not love, Veronica. That's just desire. Love is something else entirely. Love is the end of loneliness."

"It has to be more than that," I whisper.

"No, not really." He smiles at me, sadly, and then walks back to the door. "I wish you would reconsider staying." And he is gone.

I finish packing my backpack as best I can and make my way downstairs. Jerold, Lester, and Patty all nod goodbyes to me. Patty crams some medical supplies into my overstuffed backpack, and I thank her. They leave the room when Julian enters.

"I know you probably don't care what I have to say—"

"You got that right," I retort.

"I deserve that. And anything else you've got to say. But I want to tell you something."

"Why should I listen to you?"

"Because I'm your father."

I can't hold back a peal of laughter. "Really?" I ask. "Really? Now you're going to get parental on me?"

"No, I'm not. I'm not even going to try. Seems to me your mom did a pretty fine job of raising you all on her own."

"My mother has only ever been wrong about one thing—telling me I'm the spitting image of you."

"Are you sure about that?" He lifts his eyebrows, and it sends a chill down my spine.

"Yes. Yes, I am certain." I shake my head, pushing past him.

"I guess you're right. Ronnie, wait."

I stop.

"I just want to tell you one thing. Something I've learned in all the years of living I've done."

I raise my eyes to him.

"Ronnie, listen. It's going to get tough out there. You don't know what you'll face on your journey and, worse yet, you don't know what will be waiting for you when you make it to the other side. Frankly, I don't even know if you'll make it. But I do know if I were a betting man, my money would be on you."

I shift my weight from foot to foot.

"I want you to know something, Ron. The greatest foe we face is not uncertainty, but uncaring. In the grand scheme of things, the universe doesn't care what we do—we're inconsequential. So we have to fight against it—and for something—with everything we've got. But I guess you know that already."

He walks out of the room and comes back carting a rifle with a strap. "It's all I have, but it's yours."

I take it from him.

"I have only two extra rounds of ammunition, so shoot wisely."

I nod, slinging the gun across my back. I raise my eyes to his. And then, I am gone.

****

Three days have passed.

I am so painfully and oppressively lonely, I wonder if I should go on. I got out of HopeLess World unscathed, thanks to Jerold explaining the safest escape route for me. I follow my compass, and head due east. The only thing that keeps me going is hope. I have never needed that old friend more than I do right now. Thanks to hope, I know, eventually, months from now, I may make it back to my girls…and Phoenix. Whether or not they'll want me, is something else entirely.

I stumble forward, rationing my protein bars and drinking fresh water any time I encounter it. I have yet to touch the canteens in my backpack, which make my backpack incredibly heavy, but it's probably good, because the area I am stumbling into seems parched and hot. Thankfully, I picked up a stick some way back, and

I use it to help me walk. As far as I can see, there is only flat terrain, covered in reddish sand, and it does not look welcoming. I glance north then south, hoping for a reprieve, but there is none. I can't waste time heading in the wrong direction, I have to conserve as much as I can.

Using the stick to help support my weight, I venture out over the hot, red sand. It is difficult walking, and I realize the challenge to stay upright on the uneven terrain will slow me down even more. I curse under my breath and push forward, trying to remember to breathe. The sun beats down on me mercilessly, and I chuckle to think I ever considered the sun at camp to be hot. I pull a sweater out of my backpack and drape it across my head to offer some relief and protection. I can feel my skin burning, and stop only to pull on long pants and a long sleeved shirt, anything to protect me from the scorching rays. Not even an hour in, I have nearly polished off one canteen of water. I begin to wonder if Farnsworth was right. Maybe I won't survive.

Pushing that horrific thought out of my brain, I walk on. Eventually, I see the sun setting behind me, and I know I have survived another day. The sun sets quickly, and a cold front washes over me. My teeth begin to chatter uncontrollably, both from hunger, and cold. I devour a protein bar as I push forward. Eventually, I spy a rock up ahead, and I force myself to it with all my might. I fall next to the rock, heavy and exhausted. I close my eyes and slow my breathing. When I open them, I think of Phoenix—this spot I've chosen next to the rock reminds me of the lean-to we shared during that thunderstorm. The thought of

Phoenix warms me and makes me feel protected, but the memory of the thunderstorm makes me panic. I couldn't imagine being out here, alone, in a thunderstorm. My hands grab at the sand, and the parched earth surrounding me tells me I have nothing to fear. I relax a tiny bit.

Shivering, I fall asleep to thoughts of Phoenix, and I wake to the blazing sun, burning my face. "Day five," I mumble. I pull myself up, devour another bar, and push on.

By nightfall, I seriously consider I may die out here. This time I have no rock to rest near, so I pick a random spot and fall against my backpack. Sleep comes quickly, and again, I wake to the burning sun on my face. But this time, I am not alone.

"Hissssss..." It is a snake about a yard long. He slithers back and forth, wrapping himself around my backpack, his tail vibrating in a tell-tale rattle.

I desperately want to run, but I am afraid to make a move. Carefully, I grab my gun as the snake slithers nearer to my boot. My hands shaking, I lift the gun. Even though I'm a pretty good shot, the tremor in my hands makes me terrified I will miss, even at this close range. The snake inches closer. I fear he will coil around my leg, and I will miss my chance, or worse, I will shoot myself and bleed to death out here. All of my precious O, seeping into this unforgiving ground.

In no time, the snake is on my boot. Holding my leg as still as possible, I suck in my breath, and in one swift movement, I kick my boot with the snake, and shoot. By some miracle, I hit him square in the side of the head while he is in midair. The dead snake falls to the sand with a thud. I let the gun collapse, and I burst into tears, allowing myself to sob. After a couple of minutes I'm better, but I still can't shake the feeling of snakes crawling on me, so I jump up, running my hands up and down my body, checking myself. I use the stick to prod the backpack. Thankfully, I am alone, but I doubt I will ever get to sleep tonight.

On and on I walk, down one hill and up another, my feet stumbling forward. I know I will be dehydrated soon, so I force myself to drink, even though I see no way to replenish my water supply. The sun begins to set, but this time it is no longer a marker of how far I've come, but rather, a harbinger of what may be. And this scares me more than anything. I collapse on the ground, and again my thoughts turn to Phoenix. I wonder how he is and what he is doing. I pray he's okay, because even if he truly doesn't love me anymore...that won't stop me from loving him. I know this, because I tried. I tried with Farnsworth. I really, really tried to forget Phoenix. Or, at least I tried to cover my aching sorrow with the attention of someone else. But it didn't work. Not for me. I don't know how Phoenix moved on so quickly. I don't know how he could love Brooke the way he loved me...unless, of course...he never really loved me at all. Pictures don't lie, I saw how close he is to Brooke. They are cut from the same cloth, made for each other. The tears slide out easily, and thankfully, sleep comes quickly.

This time I sleep for only minutes before I hear a noise. I sit up, startled, and cradle my gun. I strain to hear what sounds like two or three motorbike engines. In the distance, I see a vehicle moving quickly across the sand, heading straight for me. I raise my gun to fire.

## Chapter Eighteen

I stand to get a better shot. I point my gun at the oncoming vehicle that appears to be two motorbikes, held together by a seat. It comes at me faster and faster, bouncing across the sand. I debate the clearest shot, and decide to aim for the driver's head. Someone in the vehicle stands and waves his arms.

"No," he yells. "No!" He waves his arms furiously.

I keep my gun pointed at him, trying to size up the situation.

The vehicle stops a few yards from me, and the man in the passenger's seat jumps out. He walks over with his hands in the air. "Away, away?" he asks.

I don't answer.

"HopeLess?" His words are broken. "Away, away?" He points over his shoulder in the direction of HopeLess World. "You? Away, away?" He makes a motion of two fingers walking against his palm.

I finally understand. "Yes." I nod. He smiles at me, and I lower my gun.

"Come." He waves me on, smiling. "Come. To food. You—" He points at me and makes a cutting motion against his throat. I point my gun at him again, but he is unfazed. "Yes, yes. You die. Alone."

He gives me a big smile. I debate my next move, but he is right about that. I will die out here alone, but with them, at least I have a chance. If that was, in fact, what he was saying to me. I throw my backpack over my shoulder and follow the man to the vehicle.

"Sit," he offers, pointing to the seat. He climbs in back. The driver is another man, but he doesn't smile or say a word.

"No way," I say. "I sit in back. The gun stays pointed at you. Try anything and you're both dead."

"Yes, yes," the man agrees.

I climb in, and we are off. We drive for hours, and I continually check my compass to be sure we are heading in the right direction. We are. Sleep wants to find me, but I fight against it, afraid to let go of the gun. Eventually, I begin to see trees.

"We left the sand?" I ask.

"No sand. Desert—no." He seems very pleased.

"Desert," I mumble to myself. I am thrilled to be away from the desert. Out here, at least I have a chance to find food and water. I am certain I nod off, but no harm comes of it. The men stay in front, driving. Eventually, after a few more hours of sleeping on and off, we turn and change our direction. "North," I mumble. "We're going north." I shout to be heard over the engine.

"Yes, yes." The man turns in his seat and smiles.

"But I can't go north. I need to head east."

"North—village."

"Village?"

"Village. Food."

"How far?"

"No more than less than one hour."

I smile at him. "Where are you from?" I ask.

"Yes, yes. Village."

I sit back and let them drive me off course for no

more than less than one hour.

\*\*\*\*

Sure enough, forty-five minutes due north, we pull up to the perimeter of what looks like a small, quiet camp—not so different from my camp. There is no movement around the small cabins, and I wonder if this has all been a trap. The man and the driver jump out before me, and I raise my gun, trying to ward off any unwelcome advances.

"Yes, yes. Village. Food, yes?"

"Food, yes," I answer, pointing my gun upwards and following them to a small building that resembles a mess hall. I glance at the quiet man, wondering why he does not speak. He avoids eye contact, but leads the way into the mess hall. As we enter the building, a bell chimes on the door. There is a long counter on the opposite side of the room with stools stacked next to it, and a few small tables and chairs scattered about. An older man and woman exit from the back room, rubbing sleep from their eyes.

"Can I help you?" the older man asks, studying me.

The man from the vehicle steps forward. "Food, yes?"

"She needs to eat?" the older man asks, still eyeing me.

I wonder at the phrase "needs to eat."

"Yes, please," I offer, carefully tossing my gun to my back. "I have been traveling…from HopeLess World. Do you have anything I can eat? I can give you this." I pull out an empty canteen. "In exchange."

The older man and woman glance at one another.

"For the food, I mean."

They all remain quiet.

"Um, it's really all I have…"

The woman steps up and takes pity on me. "We don't want your canteen, dear," she takes me by the shoulders. "And you are welcome to eat. Sit, please."

She turns me around, and I sit at a small wooden table with two chairs. There is complete silence while she brings me a plate filled high with potatoes and vegetables, covered in a red tomato sauce. My driver and his talkative companion step outside as she drops the food in front of me and strolls off, her flowing skirt swaying as she walks. Her long grayish-gold hair lies in spindly spirals down her back, and she adjusts the shawl she has draped across her shoulders as she sits, opposite me.

"This is delicious." I tell her in between mouthfuls.

The woman reaches out and squeezes my hand.

"But where did you get this?"

"We made it."

"But all the vegetables…"

"We grew them."

"Really?" I turn my eyes up to her. "I tried growing food once for my—" I stop myself. "Anyway, it didn't work."

After I inhale everything on my plate, I sit back. "Thank you. Really. I haven't felt this full in…" My mind jumps to one of my last real meals—my pre-Letting breakfast that Willy had prepared for me. My mood darkens, thinking of him. "But um, I wish there was something I could offer you in return."

"We don't take from each other here," the older man states, breaking his recent silence. He pulls something hard and pointy from the bib pocket of his overalls, and my body stiffens. I stand, preparing myself to fight back. He tilts his head quizzically, as he pops the pointy end into his mouth. I now see the opposite end has a tiny bucket attached. He strikes a match and holds it to the small bucket. He puffs out a cloud of smoke.

"You know how I feel about that pipe," the woman reprimands in a warm and fuzzy tone.

"Ah-yup," he answers, puffing away. She gives him a light, girlish giggle, and he smiles before turning his attention back to me.

"We give others what they need, and take only what we need."

"Really?" I raise my eyebrows in disbelief. "How…how do you make that work? And how did you come to live out here?"

The man gets up slowly, still puffing his pipe, and walks into the back room. I'm afraid I've asked too much. The woman comes around to my side of the table and sits next to me.

"I'm Darla." She pats my hand that's resting on the table. "That there was Leroy." She points in the direction of the back room. "I'll answer your questions, honey. But first—"

We are interrupted by the sound of the door opening. A youngish woman, with long, curly black hair, and giant brown eyes slips inside. She moves as if she is unwelcome here. She stands in the shadow and nods to me.

"Who's this?" the girl asks.

"A new friend." Darla answers without turning in the direction of the door.

"I don't much like new friends."

"It's none of your concern."

The young woman sneers at me and then backs out. I squint at Darla, and she closes her eyes for a moment.

"Well," she sighs. "I guess first I'm going to have to answer that one question you're probably wondering about. Her name is Constance. She lives with us. But unlike me and Leroy and the others, Constance ain't so happy here. That's all there is to say about that." Darla adjusts herself by rocking back and forth in the chair. "Now, I would like for you to answer my question." She drapes the shawl dramatically over her shoulder and leans back in her chair. "So, tell me, how does the Principal Leader's wife become stranded in a desert so far away from the New World?"

I hear my hurried breath and avert my eyes, trying to control the panic settling on me. I think of making a run for the door, but imagine Constance, perched outside, ready to attack me. I feel my gun resting at my feet, wondering if I should grab it.

"There's no need to do anything rash," Darla offers, as if she's reading my mind. Her fingers are busy playing with the fringe ends of her shawl.

I stare at her, surprised.

"Come now." She smiles a soft, lovely smile that makes her nose crinkle. "How did you end up here, Veronica?"

I take a deep breath. "After my forced wedding, we abandoned the New World because of the rebel attacks and flew thousands of miles to HopeLess World."

She nods, understanding.

"There, I confirmed I was once again a pawn in Principal Leader Farnsworth's game. So I left. After I had walked for days, I found myself in a desert," I remember the word, "and then those two men brought me here."

She nods along.

"And you?" I ask. She sits forward, resting her elbows on the table, something that would have made my mother crazy. "How did you end up here?"

"Love," she tells me.

"Love?" I question, wondering if this delightful woman is just a bit unstable.

"Yes, love. The same thing that's driving you back to the New World."

"How did you know?" My heart is pounding so fast, I'm certain she can hear it.

"Oh, Veronica…" She leans across and pats my hand. "It's written all over you. Like a map. You are trying to make your way back to that rebel boy. The handsome one."

I smile generously without even meaning to.

"Yes, that one." She sits back, her shawl falling to her elbows, exposing a soft white blouse embroidered with yellow flowers. Flowers I know well.

"Are those…dandelions?" I ask, timidly.

Darla only smiles her response. She gets up and takes something from the back of the long counter. She sets it on top of the counter and within a minute, a projection of Brooke appears before me.

Brooke looks beautiful as always, but she is uneasy today. Maybe it's because she stands alone. He is nowhere to be seen.

Darla lowers the volume on the projection and pushes a few knobs and buttons. I sit still, unsure of what to do next. It is only a moment until Brooke steps down, and Phoenix takes the stage.

"Oh, he is a looker, isn't he?" Darla smiles at me.

I can't answer her. My eyes are flooded with tears as I listen to Phoenix ramble on about their near victory. A large, heavy tear spills down my cheek.

"Oh, Veronica." Darla clicks off the projection. "Love can make us do the darndest things. All of us. Including that boy."

My chest heaves as I imagine his rediscovered love for Brooke.

"Look at you. Love is making you walk thousands of miles to get to the person you just can't live without."

I fight to regain some composure. "I just…just want to bring him a book. To—to help him."

She smiles a knowing smile at me.

"You love Leroy?" I ask, turning toward the door from which he had exited.

"With every ounce of my being."

"And he loves you?" I lift my eyes to hers.

"Yes."

"You're lucky," I eke out, my throat tight.

"So are you."

"I had love, but I lost it. I was…I was so stupid."

"Veronica," she leans forward, pushing my empty plate aside. She takes both of my hands in hers. "You are so young." She sighs. "Veronica, don't you understand? Your heart beats from conception, but it is merely a reflex. Your heart isn't complete…isn't…full until you have found romantic love. Didn't you ever notice how full and…" she searches for the word, "okay you feel when he's near?"

I nod, agreeing.

"That's love filling your heart." She reaches out and gently strokes my hair. "It's not as easy to lose love as you think. Once love has found you—real love—it can never unfind you. No matter what you do. It would be like your very essence abandoning you. It can't happen. Love…love is the soul of your heart."

## Chapter Nineteen

I close my eyes, and the image of him is so vivid, I cannot sit still a moment longer. I stand up quickly and grab my backpack.

"I suppose it's pointless to ask you to stay and get some rest."

"Yes."

"Would you like a ride as far as we can take you?"

"Yes, please."

"Before you go…" Darla disappears into the backroom for a moment. She comes back out carrying two small, rectangular envelopes. Each has a different word written on it. One says "carrot," and one, "tomato." "Take these." She tucks them into my hand.

"Thank you, Darla. But I already told you, I have no ability to grow a garden."

She shakes her head, smiling. "Oh Veronica, you don't make a garden grow. Love does."

My gaze drops to the seeds in my hand. "Like I said, I have no ability to make a garden grow." My eyes fill with tears.

"Oh, pshaw." Darla waves off my last statement with the flick of her wrist. "When the time is right to plant, you'll know. Until then…keep them with you."

"Thank you." Still clutching my seeds, I throw my arms around her and embrace her. She hugs me back, warmly.

"Now let's get you going." She adjusts my sweater, and then leaves with my old canteen. She comes back with the canteen filled with fresh water. "We should stop at the bathing spot first. Getting clean will make the journey more bearable."

I nod, agreeing.

"Come on." She holds her hand out for me to follow. "The sooner we get you ready, the sooner you return to the New World."

****

With my hair dripping wet yet still wearing my filthy clothes, Darla sees me into that same small vehicle she tells me is called a "buggy." Leroy packs us with another few containers of fuel, and then speaks.

"I've told them to drive you east, until they run out of fuel. They are to refill twice. Then, I'm afraid, you'll have to take it from there. They will conserve the other containers for their trip back. If you're lucky, you'll hit water before they have to return. They are going to switch off driving, so you won't need to stop much."

My stomach clenches. I knew they weren't driving me all the way to the New World, but I am terrified about being on my own again. Darla must sense it.

"Veronica." She steps forward as Leroy steps back. She takes both of my hands and looks up into my eyes. Her eyes twinkle like a young girl's. "You will be okay."

I nod, unconvinced.

"Yes it will take conviction and fortitude, but both of those you have. In spades."

I smile, unsure of the expression, but it seems like the proper moment to smile. Out of the corner of my eye I see Constance. She hovers in the distance. "Is she coming with me?"

Darla drops my hands and turns over her shoulder in Constance's direction, and then back to me.

"No." Darla seems bothered by Constance's presence, but she gives me her full attention. "As I was saying, it will take conviction and fortitude. And it will also take a bit of magic. But you have that, too."

"Magic?" I question.

"Of course." She takes my hands again and squeezes them. "Forgive my constant espousing for love, but Veronica, someone has to teach you—the only real magic in life is love."

She kisses my hand, and I climb up into the back seat of the buggy. Leroy raps on the seat, and we pull forward with a start. I gaze back over my shoulder at Darla and Leroy, wondering if everything I just experienced was a dream.

****

After one day's drive, I see storm clouds ahead. We are in an open-top vehicle, making us certain victims of the weather.

"Rain, rain," the man who speaks says in a sing-song voice.

"Yes, rain, rain…" I mutter grouchily, suddenly terrified. I know we're driving right into the storm, and to be in an open-top buggy means we will be drenched. What's more, I see a lightning strike, directly up ahead. "Damn." I mutter my thoughts to myself, not wanting to appear weak to the two men who are driving me. You never know when one or both may decide to turn on me, and I'll have to prove my strength.

The vehicle slows down. "Why are we slowing?" I ask loudly to be heard over the still running engine and the rumble in the distance.

"Rain, rain," the man repeats.

I steel myself against my fear. I need to get to Phoenix, and that is more important than any irrational fear. I close my eyes and breathe deeply. It's only rain, I tell myself. What's the worst that could happen? A lightning strike, my brain answers back. I breathe deeper. Yes, but if I was meant to be dead, I would be dead by now. Of that, I am sure. How strange, the thoughts that comfort me now. I open my eyes. "We'll lose too much time if we stop," I tell the men.

The driver examines me in the rearview mirror and raises his eyebrows. He seems surprised.

"We need to keep going. Please."

"Rain, rain, wet, wet."

"I understand…but…there's something much more important out there. Past the storm. Please. Please keep driving."

They pull our vehicle over, and I slump down in my seat, defeated. The two men jump out of the buggy and grab a large plastic sheet from the storage area in the back of the vehicle. They each grab half and pull it up and over the top of the buggy. It falls lightly on the rollover bars, and grazes my head a bit. It hits the driver's head as well, and he reaches up to push it away.

"Rain, rain," the man answers.

The driver leans forward, gripping the steering wheel tightly, and we roll forward.

Excitement and nervousness tingle in tiny droplets throughout my body, mimicking the rain tapping lightly on our plastic cover. "Thank you," I tell them.

The driver just glances at me in the mirror, and we

are off.

**\*\*\*\***

Soon, we are caught in the rainstorm. Huge droplets of rain attack the feeble windshield and flimsy cover, like maggots burrowing into a dead carcass. The wind howls fiercely, and it's become my job to hold onto the plastic cover as best I can. I tuck it into any nook or crevice I can find, and hold on tightly. The man who speaks holds an edge too, but he doesn't seem bothered by the rain. Suddenly, BOOM! A huge crack of thunder claps over our heads. I jump, but try to remain calm. I catch the driver glaring at me in the mirror. I close my eyes and breathe deeply, thinking of Phoenix.

Another boom of thunder claps and then another. We can barely see because of the sheets of rain pummeling the windshield. The driver leans forward, straining to see where we are going. I silently pray we do not go off course, or worse. Lightning cracks dangerously close, one hitting a tree stump only about a quarter of a mile away. The temperature has dropped low, and I huddle into myself, trying to stay warm. We hit ruts in the roads, and water splashes up at me.

"Ugh," I exclaim, surprised. The rain pummels us, unceasingly. It's begun to sound like gunshots ricocheting off the car. "Hail," I yell, though I'm not sure why. I am frozen, my teeth are chattering, and my hands are turning white from the cold and the tight grasp I have on the plastic. I pull the plastic down further, for more protection, and the hail pelts us through our thin cover, leaving tiny little red welts behind. The sky is dark gray, and I feel like I'm trapped in my lake—unable to know up from down. If it weren't for the possibility of finding Phoenix sooner, I would be seriously rethinking my decision.

Suddenly, we hit the biggest rut of all, and we all fly up out of our seats. Luckily, the vehicle keeps moving, but I'm achy and sore and terrified. I close my eyes and think, This must be what it is like when God has forsaken you. No sooner do I think the thought, I regret it. I know how much worse it could be.

Mercifully, we make it through. Up ahead, I see the last glimmers of the sun, tired from an exhausting day battling rain clouds. I know exactly how it feels.

**\*\*\*\***

We drive another three and a half days, stopping only for necessary breaks. We are lucky with finding old roads and cleared passages, so we maintain a good speed. Then we are surrounded by the mile-high trees of the east. The men pull the buggy over.

"What's going on?" I ask.

"We're out of fuel." It's the driver who has never before spoken to me.

"You can speak?" I turn to him, surprised.

"Yes, I can speak." He furrows his forehead answering my question. "But I only speak when I feel like it. Unlike my friend here." He points at his driving companion. "He'll speak to anyone about anything."

"Yes, yes."

I smile at my two travel companions. We all hop out of the buggy, and the men begin busying themselves with refilling the fuel for the buggy. I wait for them to finish.

"Thank you," I tell them. "Thank you for finding me in the desert and for bringing me to your camp." I shake hands with the chatty man first.

"Bye, bye," he tells me.

"Bye, bye" I answer, smiling. I turn to the other man. "Thank you."

He looks off as he shakes my hand, and then he turns back.

"Veronica," he lets go, and stuffs his hands into his pockets. "You know how some days you wake up to a gorgeous pink sky but you know…you know the uh, the rain is close behind?"

I shudder in response.

"Yeah," he mumbles, trying to laugh it all off as he shuffles back to the buggy. He speaks to me as he climbs into the driver's seat. "Well, uh, good luck making your way to the New World."

"Thank you." I stare at the man, utterly confused. I shake my head as he starts the engine. "Wait," I yell after him. "What does that mean?"

"Don't forget about us," he adds. He points off in the direction of the east. "I can see water." Then he starts the buggy and drives away, leaving me to wonder why strangers always speak to me in such cryptic ways.

****

With the man's words still fresh in my brain, I begin to walk. What did that mean? What does any of it mean? Why am I always solving puzzles? First it was my mother with her secrets, then Grace with her obscure statements, and then Darla, and now this guy…? Why can't anyone speak to me like I'm a normal human being? Sure, I've led more girls to the Lettings than anyone else in the history of our world, and yes, I fell in love with the rebel leader and then married the Principal Leader, but does any of that have to make me so…different? Such a freak? I stop short, answering my own question. They speak to me cryptically, because they don't know how else to speak to me—I'm an enigma, and with the exception of my mother, no one is sure if I can be trusted. Trust. I shudder at the word, unable to comprehend how Phoenix can't understand I trust him above all others. The thought of him propels me forward, and I begin to move again. Knowing the water of the east is close, I decide to head north. I don't know how long it will take me, but my journey of over two months has already been condensed to just one week.

Within a few miles, I find the remains of what must have been a multi-lane road, like the one that leads from camp into the New World. This road is broken and filled with large gaps in what is left of the blacktop, but at least it serves as a guide to where I am heading. I walk, unfazed, glad to be out of the buggy and moving my legs, which have grown very stiff from all the sitting and bouncing. As I walk, I imagine scenarios. I envision stumbling into Phoenix on my path, what would I do? What could I say? I wonder about Lilly, Violet, and Raven too. Is it possible they have also turned on me completely? It couldn't be. I remind myself they are only children, and they don't know any better. Then I think of Lulu, and a chill sets over me. I begin to panic only when the road has ended, and night begins to fall. I have conserved my flashlight as much as possible, but something about being this near to the New World makes me long for the welcoming guidance of that tiny beam of light. Of course, as soon as I switch it on, I realize my flashlight also makes me an easy target for anyone who may be passing by. But who else would be here, in this place where, despite the ground beneath my feet, the world seems to have ended?

I stumble against a broken piece of blacktop and switch my light back on, quickly. I cannot afford to fall and break a bone. Not now. Not when I'm this close. Braving the light, I push onward, exhaling when I feel the road under me once more. Bracing myself, and using all my will to fight these irrational fears swirling in my brain, I press on. Since I sat for so long, I know I'll be able to walk a good part of the night.

On and on I push, feeling the first slickness of autumn leaves under my feet. Autumn leaves are beautiful, but they're also an omen of the bone-chilling cold that is to come. I steel myself against this fear as well—only this fear is neither irrational nor unfounded—winters can be deathly cold. I shiver as an evening breeze washes over me.

Hours later, I fall, exhausted.

I wake, alone but okay. My backpack is still on my back, I must have passed out from exhaustion. As the sun rises, I see by following the road, I have climbed a good part of a small mountain. It is a steep mountain, and the path I am keeping to is not very wide. Although I have no fear of heights, I hug the inside edge of the path, because I do most certainly have a fear of plunging to my death. I walk a bit farther and feel the sun warming my face. Although I have glued my eyes to the broken road before me, I allow myself just one peek in the direction of the sun.

Then I see it. A sight so beautiful, I hear myself gasp. It is nothing short of awe-inspiring. Tears make a surprise appearance in my eyes as I experience a longing for Phoenix so intense, I have to squat down to steady myself. Gazing out at my view, I wish, beyond anything, he were here to see it with me. There, laid out before me, is the widest valley I have ever seen. For miles and miles the valley stretches out before me; wild with trees, and yet tamed by huge fields of grass. Its beauty overwhelms me, as does its vastness, and I wonder, who do I think I am? What makes me think I can survive this journey? I'm just a girl—a not very smart, completely gullible girl—who fought for the wrong cause and then fell in love with her enemy. The feeling of defeat that overtakes me makes me sink to my knees, as I wonder why I should even bother to go on.

The nearest field is entirely visible, and I stand to get a better view. Just as I do, I spot a fawn, completely unsure of her legs, trying to take what must be her first steps. I shake my head, laughing out loud with joy. My emotions are so raw, I climb from depression to exuberance in the matter of a breath. I clamp my hand over my mouth, knowing something this wonderful has to prove there is still goodness in the world. Tears roll down my cheeks as I watch the fawn stumble across a field to join another, larger deer.

"Her mother," I whisper, transfixed.

Even from this distance, I can see both deer turn to me at once. It is as if they can hear me. "Hey," I murmur, putting my hand up to them. The mother deer nuzzles the fawn and then gives a gentle nudge, pushing the fawn forward, closer to me. The fawn moves with greater and greater agility, and suddenly, they both stop, staring straight at me. They bend down and begin to graze on something yellow.

"Huh," I gasp, placing my hand on my racing heart. "Dandelions." I only whisper the words, but I know she will hear it. "Hello, Mom." My words are made choppy by my flowing tears. Somehow, in the middle of nowhere, she has found me. And in finding me, she has saved me once again.

Chapter Twenty

The next seven days are a test of my mind, body, and conviction. But finally, when I am certain I cannot take even one step more, there, in front of me, is the city of my youth—fortuitous timing. I finished the last of my protein bars yesterday, and I have only a tiny bit of water left. My backpack has become frighteningly easy to carry. I need food, water, and rest…immediately.

I gaze up at the skyline of my city. In stature and girth it still resembles the city I once knew, but I can tell its soul is really only a memory of what it once was. It no longer has an underlying pulse, that frantic feel of life—no matter how miserable it may have been. Long gone are the working smokestacks that spewed endless black coal into the gray sky; no more are the streets filled with young men scurrying to and from their shifts at the factories, too tired to raise their eyes from the pavement. Now, there is emptiness.

What I see now scares me more than the thriving city ever did—I see a desperation growing that will soon, if not stopped, tirelessly and relentlessly expand, until this city, my city, morphs into HopeLess World. I close my eyes and shake my head to destroy the thought that Farnsworth may have been a decent Principal Leader, considering everything. After all, I have the singularly unique perspective of having seen both sides of our world...literally. I force my eyes open, suddenly frozen, realizing I may be the only living soul who knows this, and therefore, by the process of elimination, I am thereby appointed the one person who must do something about it.

Oh, crap.

What's more, as I carefully approach the city that holds every memory of my childhood, I am more and more certain there is a force bigger than me, and even bigger than Phoenix, that has brought me here. I walk on, the gun held tightly in my grasp, my hands growing sweaty from fear and concentration. I don't know what's in here, this city. Is there anyone left? Have all the inhabitants gone to fight with Gunnar? If anyone is left, will they shoot me on sight? Or worse? Will they take me to Gunnar—considering here, my blood is still worth something?

There is no part of me that wants to enter the city, but I see no way around it. There is water on all sides of the city; and crossing through the city is the shortest route into the New World. The small bridge I have to cross to enter the bottommost part of the city is only a mile or so ahead. After all of this, here I am. There is nothing to protect me now. There are no tall trees in which to hide. There is only me, and broken pieces of pavement. Some of the pavement is so damaged by the sun, it looks as if it has deep grooves shaped into a pattern of stripes—like the stripes that flank both sides of my hips—those stripes that joined my body as a permanent decoration around the age of ten.

"What are those things?" Gretchen asked me one day while we were wading into the lake.

"What things?"

"Those stripes on your hips?"

I checked to see what she was talking about. Sure enough, peeking out from my swimsuit, on both sides of my hips, were the tiniest white stripes that appeared almost iridescent against my tanned skin.

"I've no idea," I answered her, wondering deep inside if these stripes had something to do with the fact I had blossomed a week before but never told her. Were they markings of the secrets I kept? I opened my mouth to tell Gretchen the truth. It wasn't that I wanted to keep this secret from her; it's just that I was afraid if I told someone...anyone...then everything would somehow change. I knew it was too soon for me to be sent to the New World, so I couldn't imagine what else they would have in mind for me. But whatever it was, I knew I didn't want any part of it.

"Well, I like them," Gretchen said, falling back into the lake and then popping her head up. The water matted her feathery eyelashes in a way that made them resemble two Woolly Bear caterpillars. "They look like racing stripes."

"Racing stripes. I like that." I smiled at her, and she took my hand. Together we flopped back into our lake, letting the warm summer sun wash over us, obliviously happy—neither of us having any idea what the blueprint of our lives had in store for us.

****

As I walk closer to the city, I reach up to wipe away a lone tear. Sure I'm mad at her, and yes, much of this is her fault...but I sure do miss her. Missing Gretchen exacerbates my loneliness, and walking toward the shell of the city I remember from my childhood only intensifies the feeling. Once I had my mother. And then Gretchen. And then, Phoenix. But now I have no one. No one but me. I have morphed into this…being…a being who is neither male nor female, but simultaneously, both. I am all I have now, so I'd better start liking me.

The closer I step to the small bridge, the angrier I become. I was wrong. I can't exist as a being, and I'm not okay. Frankly, I am angry. Very, very angry. Phoenix walked away from me without a fight, and then he had the audacity to blame me. He claimed I went with Farnsworth willingly. Well, at least I had a reason: to protect my girls…and him. What was his reason for leaving me without a fight?

I ready my gun without meaning to. I hold it higher, sweat pouring off my body. I have to control myself to keep from running forward, searching for Phoenix and my girls. A moving target is a more noticeable one—but it's also harder to hit. I reach up to wipe the sweat that's itching my forehead and get immediate relief. I wish I could appease all of my angst like that—just scratch it away—because right now this impulse to get to them somehow, for some reason, angers me. Just for a moment, I would love to forget my girls and even, Phoenix. I would love to act irresponsibly. I could never have stayed with Farnsworth and indulged in the excesses that go along with being Mrs. Farnsworth—all of those things he kept pushing on me—I never wanted the riches or the niceties that are fading fast thanks to the rebel movement. All I wanted, all I want is peace. Peace for our world, peace of mind, and peace within my life. I want the dirt and reality and honesty. And for some reason, I understand I will never, ever, feel this covetable peace until this damned book I have carried all of these thousands of miles, is tucked safely in Phoenix's grasp. And then, after I hand him the book and look him in the eye once more, we can part.

I slip on a leaf but steady myself before I fall. A few trees have miraculously survived, even this close to the city. They are spindly, but here. Just like me. I glance up to see the leaves are a deep red—the color of blood. Summer is over. The seasons changed, and so did I.

****

I slip through the unmanned guard gates at the bottom of the city without incident. There is no one left to care about the inhabitants of the city. Not that anyone ever did. But once, Farnsworth had stations set up to keep the inhabitants of the city in—to make sure our precious blood was contained.

Thump, thump, thump. I walk over the bridge and into the heart of downtown. Thump, thump, thump, the pain in my head echoes my footsteps. My mouth begins to prickle from dehydration. There are still skyscrapers all around, but the once constant whirl of the factories has been replaced by an eerie quiet that can only be described as an oppressive hollowness—a hollowness that makes me feel as if I am walking in a cemetery, amidst freshly fallen, broken bones. I shudder with the soft breeze that passes by. I turn my face upward, seeing the view of my youth, a graying sky peeking around the tips of tall buildings.

"Hey, Mom," I whisper. "I made it…now what?"

I snicker to myself when I realize I really have no idea what to do next. More accurately, I know what to do, but I have no idea how to do it, and even more frighteningly, I have no idea what will happen next. One thing I do know, twilight is approaching, and the city is not the place to be alone after dark. I consult my compass and turn east. Although I know the city well enough to travel without assistance, I'm not taking any chances. I'd hate to have come this far to get lost now.

As I walk farther uptown and toward the east side, I begin to see signs of life. In one building, a woman hangs a bed sheet out a low window.

"Hey," I call to her, hoping she will have pity on me and offer me some water. Instead, she ducks inside, never to be seen again.

A few more people gather on a street corner, huddled around a glowing barrel. It sickens me when I realize how much this resembles HopeLess World. Exhausted, I trudge on, and either no one notices me, or they don't care. Unfortunately, the sight of a person walking with a rifle in her hands must not be surprising. I press on and pass an old bar that appears deserted. A stool props the door open slightly, and I peek inside to see overturned stools. When I was young, I saw men in here, drinking something yellow, but the men are long gone. My breath hitches for a moment when I remember the men would gather here to listen to Farnsworth's Message to the People. I wonder if they may still have a projection screen, and if, by any chance, it will broadcast Phoenix.

Hunger, fatigue, anger, and desire are driving me to make rash decisions. Having no idea what's waiting inside, I push open the door, desperately needing food and water, and more than anything, wanting to find that projection screen. I stomp across the room and make my way to an oversized bar. I rummage around behind it, dodging a skinny rat, and stepping through months-old garbage. There is no food or water to be seen, but finally, I find a small black square that could be a projection box. I drop it onto the counter.

"Come on," I whisper, pressing knobs and buttons over and over in random order, trying to find the magical sequence that will allow me to see Phoenix. I bang on the box and lift it into the air to inspect underneath. Nothing. I am loud and vulnerable here, and I'm making idiotic decisions. It's clear my brain has let starvation take control. Frustrated, I try banging the box against the counter a few times.

"That's not going to work."

I snap my head up to see a man standing there, facing me. He is tall and thin, with gray hair, and intense brown eyes. I raise my gun.

"I am Veronica Billings." My breathing is loud and hurried. "I need water."

He nods and throws me a canteen he has stashed in his back pocket. Without taking my eyes off him, I manage to unscrew the cap with one hand while I hold the gun with the other. I sniff the contents and then drink so quickly, I nearly drown myself.

"Thank you," I whisper, gasping. "I am making my way back to the New World to fight with Phoenix Day and his revolutionaries. If you don't do as I ask, or try to stop me in anyway, I will kill you if I have to. Don't make me have to."

"Got it," the man tells me, raising his hands in the air. "Listen, I'm Gary. You may not remember me, but I knew your mother—"

I cock the gun.

"No! No!" He waves his hands, pleadingly. "No,

please. Not in the Coupling way. I used to sell her your protein bars. That's all." The expression on Gary's face changes, and his eyes drop down to his feet. He shuffles a few inches to the left, stepping out of a tiny puddle.

"Did you just—?" I point to the floor with my gun and then aim it back at him.

"I'm not very good with confrontation," he explains.

I shake my head, trying to regroup. "Um, what's her name?" I ask, staring down the barrel of the gun at him. It's still difficult for me to talk, but I force the words. My hands are trembling, and I fight hard to control them. "My mother. Her name."

He lets his hands fall timidly, but I can tell he is sure of his answer. "Morgan. Her name was Morgan."

I lower my gun and swallow hard. My throat tightens thanks to his word, "was." I nod. "Yes," I eke out.

"I didn't know her well," Gary continues. "But I remember she was always happy and optimistic. Even in the worst of times."

I give him a faint smile. That sounds like Mom.

"Why are you here?" I ask, facing the gun away from him. "Why aren't you fighting?"

"Well," he chuckles to himself. "No offence, but it's kind of hard to know who the good guys are these days. I wouldn't know whose cause to fight for."

I nod at him, understanding. "Have you been following the war? Can you tell me anything?"

"I've been doing my best to stay uninvolved. In case you didn't notice, I really don't like confrontation." Gary shoves his hands into his pants, clearly embarrassed. He pulls them out almost as quickly. He wipes the side of his hand against a dry area of his jeans.

"Where is your food stash?"

"Don't have one." He avoids eye contact.

I stand up straight and tighten my grasp on my gun.

He lifts his hand. "Okay. I have a canned food stash in back."

I feel the gnawing emptiness in my stomach and look over my shoulder. I nod toward the back room. "I need something to get me through. Please. Anything." I hear my desperate tone and realize hunger and exhaustion are beginning to win over logic. I cannot afford to appear weak.

Gary hesitates. Of course he doesn't want to give up his supplies. I lift my gun, although I am terrified by what other bodily excrements he may expel.

I speak hurriedly. "I'm heading to the New World to rejoin the fight I was abruptly taken from. I need to help Phoenix Day and save three…maybe four girls." I swallow hard, praying Lulu is still there for me to protect. "I need food and a place to sleep for just an hour or two."

The man hangs his head for a moment and then faces me. "Wait here." He lifts his hand as if this will somehow, magically, make me stay still. It's clear he doesn't want me to see how much food he has hidden.

"Go ahead," I point toward the backroom with my gun. I don't care how much food he has, I just need some of it.

He steps around his pee puddle and disappears. Seconds later he reappears with a can of corn and an opener. "It's not much, but…" he shrugs, opening the can and handing it to me.

"Thanks." I grab it with one hand and tilt the can back, devouring the corn.

"Um, as far as a place to rest, I'm sorry, but I told you I was a coward." He smiles nervously, his lips quivering. "I—I really don't think you're going to shoot me, and I don't want to invite trouble in here. Just standing here talking to you is making me extremely uncomfortable." He reaches up and scratches at the side of his head furiously, as if he has a terrible lice infestation.

I nod along, grossed out, knowing I would never lay my head on anything around here anyway. I take a step backward.

He smile-laughs at me. "Us cowards, we always fear the worst and prepare for it, so we're not real good at sharing. But having a coward for a friend can be a good thing."

"Why is that?" I shift my tired body from one foot to the other. "I'm too exhausted to play games." I reach around and rub my sore shoulder. "Do you have a point?"

"I have some free advice."

"To hide out like you?"

"No." He laughs as if I've said something extremely witty. "I'm…well, I'm afraid I'm a coward, but you, Veronica, you're a warrior. Or at least that's what I've heard." He places a foot on an overturned stool, seemingly suddenly possessive of his bar. As if he imagines I'm going to claim the months-old garbage and scrawny rat as my own.

"The advice?" I straighten myself, standing an inch or two taller.

"As I was saying, cowards may not have your

Cathrine Goldstein

bravery, but we do have an uncanny ability to stay alive and avoid danger." His face glows like he is proud of his achievement.

Staring at him, the image of the rat pops into my head. There is some resemblance between the two of them.

He continues. "In addition to being hoarders, we're hiders. From everyone and everything. So even though I don't follow the war, I make sure I know where the fighting is at all times."

"Where is it?" My voice is low and guttural. I hear the demand in my tone. He steps backward as I step forward.

He speaks quickly. "The battle is spilling out of the New World. It will be here soon. Some rebels have already set up camp in the city."

"Has—"

"I don't know. But since they are leading the revolution, I would imagine they would still be in the New World, where the greatest numbers of people have gathered."

I nod. "It's like the end of our civilization all over again."

"Yes." His chin is down, but he raises his eyes to me as if he's letting me in on a secret. "You may not have to go searching for the fight. The fight may find you. You can set up camp and wait it out. They'll be coming." He scratches the side of his head. "There will soon be total anarchy on the streets. Only this time there may not be any Givers to save us. That is, unless you decide to save us all, Veronica Billings."

I start at his words. He must be joking.

"For right now, find a safe house. We all do. A

place you can raid for food and then rest for a couple of hours. There are still untapped safe houses all over the city. Then you'll be better prepared to fight." He looks away and then directly at me. "Choose correctly, Veronica. Because I would imagine if you don't..."

His words simply trail off and his eyes drop back down. He is right. If he chooses the wrong house to hide out, the most he'll risk is a beating. But if I choose the wrong house...

His words interrupt my thoughts. "Hopefully, you'll choose correctly."

My brain comes alive with synapses so loud, they sound like thunder inside my head. Is there any way I could ever choose correctly? Is there anyone whose instinct would be to keep me alive? But if I push on into the New World, I will surely collapse before I find the fighting. I sincerely wonder if I may die right here and now. No. I refuse to die. What a waste of all my effort.

"Thank you," I mumble.

"It's the least I can do." He releases a small scoff, knowing what he said was the truth—what he did for me was the very least he could do. He raises his head. "Good luck."

I turn to go.

"Veronica?"

"Yes?"

"You are the spitting image of her."

I breathe in sharply, my eyes aching. I think of Julian. "I wish that were true."

The coward smiles at me. "It is. It has to be. I...I think you're the one."

His gaze is fixed on me, and I chew my bottom lip, trying to remain stoic. I breathe in deeply, longing for my mother, longing for Phoenix, desperate for guidance.

"Veronica, I think you're the one who will find a way to save us all."

My eyes grow wide at his declaration. I take a deep breath and sigh. "I wish that were true…too."

Chapter Twenty-One

I rush from the bar still ravenous, but even more determined. There's no way I'm going to sit still and wait it out like the coward suggested, but I will find a safe house to scour for food and water…and then, I can search for Phoenix.

My feet pound hard against the concrete, moving faster and faster north. I know there is only one house that could ever represent a "safe" house to me. Sure it's juvenile and even pathetic, but I have to take a chance somewhere, and for me, that somewhere is the place I lived with my mother all those years ago.

I pass many semi-empty buildings and know any one of them could be a safe house, but now I have this unexplainable need to get to my old home. Yes it's irrational and childish, but I cannot will myself to stop anywhere but there. Time and again my mother has come through for me; of course the only place in this city I would trust would be the home she made for us.

As I walk, I chase away troublesome thoughts. What if I never find the frontline? Or worse, what if I find Gunnar first? Or what if I find Phoenix, and he won't even talk to me…? I truly do not know which I am honestly fighting for: our country or our love. Does it matter? But it does matter, because there is no love left. He made that very clear. I glance around my old city, slowing—come to think of it, there's not much city left either…so, what am I fighting for?

I begin to stumble down the street. Now is not the time to doubt myself or give in to bodily weakness. "No," I hiss through clenched teeth. "You will not lose your nerve. Not after nearly three thousand miles." I close my eyes and breathe deeply. I open them and move in double-time. I will get this book to Phoenix if it's the last thing I do. Even if we can't save us, I pray to God we can save him. I point my chin down, steeling myself against my thoughts and the chilly night. I lace my fingers through the straps of my backpack, letting the gun rest gently along my side. I move as quickly and stealthily as possible.

Block after block, I walk, passing building after building. My stomach continually tries to pull me toward any abandoned building, but my heart refuses to stop anywhere but home. I see only a few people here and there, stragglers out searching for food. No one bothers with me. Soon, the already familiar streets begin to look like home. Flanking the river is the huge, oblong building guarded by the many broken flagpoles—a chemical factory that spews its discharge straight into the water. A few more miles will bring an entrance to a bridge leading to the New World. This entrance used to be so heavily guarded, we pedestrians and general city inhabitants were told never to walk here. We were made to walk a few blocks farther in. I heed that advice today, in the hopes of staying hidden. Quietly, I duck down a street and then turn north. Faster and faster my body moves, trying to outrun my brain, which keeps reminding me this will probably all be for naught.

Before I can decide against it, I break out into a

shadowy sprint, finding refuge in basement stairs and dark, deserted alleys. Before I can decide not to, I turn down my street. There it is, hidden in shadow, the place I spent ten years of my life—where no less than seven families inhabited the brown colored building where my mother and I survived in the basement apartment.

The same crumbling steps lead to the same front door, a door we never used. Although we lived in the bowels of the building, I always thought we were special, because we had our very own entryway that led right into our tiny living space. The same door that made me feel special, also worried my mother. She would triple check the bolts on that door every night. I would watch her from my tiny cot pushed up against one wall of our room, wondering if there would ever be more than this for us. She would always turn to me and smile. "Goodnight my angel," she whispered every night for ten years.

Without meaning to, my brain draws a comparison between our tiny home and the room I inhabited in Farnsworth's mansion. What would my mother think if she ever saw that room? Did she ever imagine one person could have so much, and could she have fathomed those excesses would be offered to me?

I stop short, unable to move, thinking of the very last time I walked this street, when the Harvester came to take me away. I shudder intensely under the dim streetlight, and wonder how many girls Phoenix had taken from their mothers during that brief time he was a Harvester. I walk slowly, knowing I probably shouldn't even try that small apartment door, wondering if I'll be lucky enough to be able to push in the window—the one below ground level, the one that terrified my mother, but to me, signified freedom. My breath is labored as I step slowly toward our house. I wonder who lives here now, or who did before the revolution seemed to have uprooted everyone. Where are all the people? I wonder as I close in on the house. Certainly some are here. I see movement upstairs, but where are all the others?

Staying low and in shadow, I make my way to the far side of the apartment. I squat down by the filthy opaque window but can see nothing. I pull my sleeve over my palm, and taking a deep breath, I wipe away at years of grime. It takes two or three passes, but I can finally see well enough to make out a few unmoving shapes inside—one of them being my childhood cot.

Staring at that cot, memories flood over me. I can see my mother standing next to our small electric kettle, boiling water to keep us warm, rubbing her hands vigorously over the steam and warming a small plastic bottle meant for me to slide into my cot to help keep me toasty through the night. I gaze to the right and see the same small round table where she would fix me oatmeal for breakfast. I see a piece of clothesline draped from one side of the room to the other—probably the exact same clothesline my mother used, to hang our newly scoured clothing. The thought of her this close nearly suffocates me, and I push the side of my hand into my mouth to silence my sobs.

After I calm myself, I get back to the business of seeing who, if anyone, is inside. Best I can tell, the apartment is empty. Using all of my strength, I am able to wiggle the window free. I turn back over my shoulder to check no one is following me, and certain I'm alone, I try to crawl in through the tiny window. Of course my gun and my backpack trap me on the outside world, so reluctantly, I ease both off. I toss the backpack into the room first, then I throw my legs in and slide down inside, carrying the gun. I know I have just taken the biggest gamble ever, because if anyone were to walk through that door, I would be trapped with no means of escape. Which means, I would be dead.

"It's okay," I assure myself in this foreign, quiet, breathy voice. "It's okay."

I make my way around the apartment as if I've never left. I immediately head to the kitchen sink and turn the faucet. A small trickle of brownish water falls, and I stick my head into the sink and lap at the water. As soon as I'm done, I fill my empty canteens and then turn to the cabinets, scouring empty shelf after empty shelf, hoping for a can of anything. Finally, tucked far in the back, I find the smallest can of corn—identical to the one the coward had shared.

"Really?" I mutter, but I'm too famished to care. I reach for the drawer where my mother kept the can opener and voila! It is there. I race to open the can with shaking hands, each turn of the can prolonging my agonizingly ravenous stomach. Finally, the can opens, and I lift the corn to my mouth and shovel it in. I manage to devour the can without stopping to chew. Once again, the corn only fuels my hunger, and I seriously contemplate heading back downtown to the bar of the Peeing Coward, to pilfer some of his goods. Instead, I find a container of oatmeal so old it may have been left by my mother. I have an odd connection to the container and hold it for a moment, thinking more about her than my hunger. Finally, I pull off the cover and begin to shovel bits of dry oatmeal into my mouth. I move too quickly and very nearly choke on the powder the oatmeal has made in my mouth. I search for something, anything, to wash it down. I turn on the faucet, cup the brownish water into my hand, and slug it back as quickly as possible. It is there, bent over the kitchen sink, that I hear the door handle jiggle.

I freeze. I will my breathing to quiet until it veritably stops. For a moment, only a flash of time really, I allow myself to fantasize it is Phoenix who is going to walk through that door. And without asking, he'll walk to me, lift me into the air, and carry me to my old cot.

I shake my head. No, that would be too convenient for us. If...when...I find Phoenix, it will be in the midst of complete turmoil. It has to be. There will be no easy answer for us.

I snap to and rush to get my gun. I crouch low in the far corner, aiming my gun at the door. I don't want to shoot anyone, and I gaze at my backpack, feeling the eyes of Gandhi jump off the book and through the green canvas, directly into my soul. I shake my head. Sweat drops into my eyes, stinging and blurring my vision. My legs fight me, not wanting to hold this position after having walked a million miles. Nonetheless, I force them to stay still. I hold my racing breath as the handle turns. Someone forces the lock, and then click! Whoever is there is about to make his or her way inside.

I hold as still as possible, but it is impossible to stay hidden. I curse under my breath, sure I am an idiot for choosing this house. Thinking about it, when was this house ever a safe house? It was the place my mother and I nearly starved. It was the place where she was called to Couple. It was the place the Harvester found me. This isn't home. This is the crux of some of my worst nightmares.

I stand slowly, aiming my gun at the door, praying I don't have to shoot, and I won't be shot. I contemplate charging past the intruder, I have the element of surprise on my side. Finally, as if taking one's time pulling off a plastic bandage, the door jiggles again. Whoever it is outside is having an extremely difficult time entering. So this is my chance. The enemy at the door has stalled so I can get away. I'm certain of it. Faster than I ever thought possible, I push the small table under the window and climb up. Why my brain thinks the thoughts it does…I focus on how my mother would disapprove of me stepping on the place we once ate.

I throw my gun and backpack through the window and out onto the street. I hoist myself up, my body fatigued, my arms rebelling—not wanting to support my weight to drag me through the window. I kick to fight my way up and…Clamp! Someone grabs my foot.

"Huh," I gasp, refusing to look back. I kick furiously, but slip back down toward the table. The person yanks harder on my foot.

"Hey," the person growls. "What are you doing here—?" It's a man's voice. "Where are you going in such a rush…?"

He pulls harder still, and I thrash about, kicking fiercely, but still he doesn't let go. My arms ache and sweat pools on my body. My arms want to give out, and I feel my body and spirit falling. Finally, I slip down another bit and feel his grip lessen slightly—he must think he's won—and crack! I kick backwards with all my might.

"Ow…Damn it."

The pressure is off my leg. I must have kicked him right in the nose. With one final desperate burst of energy, I hoist myself up and climb through, scratching my arm on the window casing as I go. I grab my gun, throw my backpack over my shoulder, and run as fast as I can, escaping before I am found. I knew that window meant freedom.

I run for blocks until finally, sure there is no one behind me, I stop and throw myself against the nearest wall, desperately trying to catch my breath. I hinge forward at my waist, trying to suck in enough air and ease my head up to peer out into the blackest of nights. My thoughts even blacker, I wonder what I'm going to do next.

\*\*\*\*

High on adrenaline and fueled with a tiny bit of nourishment, I decide to make my way to the front line. It is a short walk to the bridge, comparatively. Over and over my mind wants to stop me. It reminds me how very…improbable all of this is. The chances of finding Phoenix and being able to hand him a book—which could very well mean nothing—well, all of it sounds ludicrous. Still I walk on, nearing the bridge. I begin to cross over without incident. Every now and then, I have to pull at the waistband of my pants, trying to keep them from sliding uncomfortably low on my hips. There is no doubt the endless walking, and the lack of food, is wrecking havoc on my already thin body. The only thing about me that has grown stronger is my heart—kept alive by thoughts of Phoenix.

I near the summit of the bridge when I wonder if he thinks of me nearly as often as I think of him, and if he would, in fact, take anything I am offering. Can I help him become the man he once was? What I want, more than anything, is the chance to be together again. But even more important than that, is to let him find himself, again. I know he no longer wants to be with me. But maybe, maybe there is the tiniest part of him that can forgive me and love me once more. It's a long shot sure, but the distance representing this probability cannot be as far as the distance I traveled to find him. Since meeting Phoenix, I've understood love is a worthy opponent of reason, but now I realize it's even more. Love is reason's greatest foe. With that thought in mind, I cross the bridge and enter into the New World.

****

I head north, and it is not long until I encounter fighting. I grip my gun tightly and walk through small pockets of men engaged in hand-to-hand combat. Consistently, I see the men of the New World outmatched by Gunnar's rebels. It will be an easy victory for Gunnar. Frankly, I'm surprised it's not over yet.

As I walk on, the air thickens with the feeling of danger. Darkness shrouds me and my infamy some, but I am certain I am an easy target. Fear comes to rest on my shoulders, and I move faster, unable to outrun this terrifying feeling. My senses heighten, forcing me to analyze everything more than I should, my breathing rapid. The small pockets of combat grow into larger groups, and inevitably, at every turn, someone is taking a beating. A man dressed in a vest and dress pants vomits blood as he takes a punch to the gut. I want to run to him and help, but I know I'll be no match for the three men holding him. Instead, I force my eyes down and keep them glued to the street. The scene around me is violent and sickening. I want to stop and help every person I encounter, but I know there is only one way I can help. There is only one way for my help to be a feasible option—and that is to be rid of Gunnar. And to be rid of Gunnar, I need help. I need Phoenix.

I head to the area of the broadcast, hoping...praying...he will be there. Soon enough, off in the distance, I see the lights that hang above the stage where I had stood, side by side with Raven and Phoenix, not even a month earlier. How different it seems now. As I approach, I realize they are in the midst of a broadcast. My heart quickens in time with my feet. Soon, I break out into a full-fledged run. A crowd of angry, surly, dirty, abused men, women, and children surround the stage. I push through them, continually unaware of what my next step will be.

Then I see them—the unlikely comrades, together on the stage. Gunnar is approaching the microphone, with Brooke close at his side. Lulu stands next to Gunnar, and there, hovering at the side of the stage, are Raven and...Phoenix.

"PHOENIX!" I scream, risking my life as I rush toward him.

"RONNIE?" Phoenix jumps off the stage and pushes his way through the crowd.

Before I even realize what is happening, Phoenix lifts me in the air, holding me in his tight embrace.

## Chapter Twenty-Two

"Run," Phoenix implores as he sets me down on the ground.

"Raven?" I ask him as we push our way out of the crowd.

"She's with Brooke, she'll be okay."

The crowd surveys us curiously, unaware of what to do. A few men rock on their heels, ready to attack. Another small group points at us, and suddenly, the sound of the crowd yelling increases to such a decibel, it rushes at us like we are caught in the most treacherous of rivers, about to pass over a dangerous waterfall.

Phoenix grips my hand tightly as the surrounding crowd closes in on us. My backpack slips from my shoulders and falls to the ground. I pull back from Phoenix, and he turns to me.

"My backpack…"

"Leave it."

I shake my head and break his grasp. I try to fight my way back the two or three steps to grab the pack, but a large man blocks my way. I look up at the man's face and he smiles, a space showing where his two front teeth should be. He reaches toward me with short, grubby arms. I recoil, and suddenly Phoenix pulls me back, lunges around the man, and grabs my backpack. He slings it onto his shoulder like it weighs nothing, and somehow, he finds my hand again. I catch a glimpse of the stage and see Gunnar is glaring at us, probably desperately trying to understand what is transpiring.

"Stop them," Gunnar commands, sounding surprised his followers didn't think to stop us themselves.

We are away from the large man, and we pass through the group, dodging and slipping like fish in a river. We are nearly free when…CRACK!

Startled, I turn to see where the gunshot came from. There is Gunnar on stage, holding a gun. He points it into the air. He is alone with Lulu now. In the chaos, Brooke must have taken Raven and run.

"Raven's safe." I exhale, and Phoenix nods. We are all still, staring at the stage.

"That is your leader," Gunnar announces, pointing at Phoenix, "and he is consorting with the enemy."

Phoenix tightens his grasp on my hand. "Even so, Gunnar," Phoenix answers him. "She doesn't deserve to die."

"No?"

I can tell Gunnar is enjoying toying with Phoenix over the possibility of my death. Even if Phoenix feels nothing for me anymore, he wouldn't want me dead. That, I'm sure of. He's never wanted anyone dead. I steal a glance at him out of the corner of my eye. Well, at least that was true of the old Phoenix, anyway.

"Who does deserve to die then?" Gunnar opens his question to the crowd.

"No one," I chime in.

"Oh really, Mrs. Farnsworth?" The condescending tone Gunnar uses proves he enjoys calling me this.

The crowd murmurs and shoves in response. I am pushed closer to Phoenix.

"Gunnar," Phoenix speaks sternly. He steps forward to address Gunnar directly. "We are at a crossroads. I won't let you kill her."

"I'm well aware of that."

"But for the first time ever, I don't know what the next step is."

I turn to Phoenix, amazed he can express exactly what I am feeling.

"Well let me enlighten you then." Gunnar walks across the stage and grabs Lulu by the hand.

His abrupt action startles her, and I flinch with her reaction. I pull away from Phoenix and try to move to Lulu, but Phoenix grabs me and holds me still.

Gunnar walks downstage with Lulu in tow. He steps to the microphone and clears his throat. "This fight has gone on much too long."

This is the first time I can ever remember agreeing with Gunnar.

"And one of the reasons for that," he continues, "is because of your leader—Phoenix Day."

Mumbling ensues. I turn to Phoenix and squeeze his hand. He squeezes back but remains stoic, staring straight at Gunnar.

"His…indecision…and continual obsession with Veronica Billings—also known as Mrs. Farnsworth, our enemy—has put our entire operation in jeopardy. Time and again. Therefore, there may be nothing left to do but declare them both our enemies." He claps his hands, and the audience tentatively applauds along with him.

My breathing has become audible, but Phoenix remains calm, still staring straight ahead at Gunnar. I can't let him go through this for me. He has come so far, I can't ruin this for him.

"Phoenix," I murmur, barely audible.

He shakes his head, still focused on Gunnar. "Fine," Phoenix answers through his teeth. "Topple Farnsworth alone, and you'll have what you've always wanted, your time to be Principal Leader. Isn't that what you want? To be Farnsworth? Stop the hypocrisy, Gunnar. Tell the people the truth. Tell them you plan to move into Farnsworth's mansion and do exactly what Farnsworth has done all of these years."

"And what about you, Phoenix? What do you plan to do?"

The crowd is silent. Waiting for his reaction.

"I—I don't know." Phoenix drops his head, finally breaking his focus on Gunnar.

"You heard him people," Gunnar smiles a wide, victorious grin. He looks down at Lulu and she stares up at him, smiling back. Gunnar faces the crowd and nods toward Phoenix. "He doesn't know what he'll do. He doesn't know what to do." Gunnar sneers and points at Phoenix directly. The hungry, desperate crowd mumbles uneasily. "Luckily for us, I know exactly what to do."

I stare at Phoenix, waiting for his retort. Instead, he keeps his eyes focused on the ground before him. Something needs to happen.

"Oh, really?" I shout, challenging Gunnar.

Gunnar glares at me with such contempt I take a step backward. Lulu is scowling at me as well. Her beautiful blue eyes narrow and her cheeks puff up with what can only read as indignation. Phoenix's eyes dart up at me.

Despite the hostility I feel from the crowd, I press on. "You know exactly what to do. Then why not tell us."

Gunnar does not answer, but I see his chest rush up and down, anger seething out of him.

"Come on, Gunnar." I push, aware this may end very badly.

"I don't owe you an explanation." Gunnar hisses.

"No, you don't," I concede. "But you do owe all of these people—all of your loyal followers—an explanation. Maybe you'll oust Farnsworth. Then what? What is your plan, Gunnar?"

Mumbles are heard from the crowd.

"I don't answer to traitors."

"Then answer to your followers," Phoenix adds.

I exhale, seeing a glimpse of the real Phoenix shining through.

"You've got a plan, right Gunnar?" he asks. "Tell them. Share your plan with them. After all, it is contingent on them, isn't it?"

"I don't know what you're talking about." Gunnar's voice is low and measured, but it booms through the microphone.

"No?" Phoenix steps forward, closer to the stage. "Why don't you tell these good people how you plan to restore order through threats, and use these unknowing people to reestablish blood as your primary commodity, Gunnar?"

Gunnar is staring hard at Phoenix, his hands clenched into fists.

"Tell them. Explain how you will pick and choose. Tell the people." Phoenix stands tall and shouts at Gunnar. "You'll pick those who are able to live in the

New World with you. The rest will serve you just as they had served Farnsworth before you."

I flinch, thinking of HopeLess World, and what could potentially happen here. Even unshakable Lulu studies Gunnar, uneasily.

"Of course not," Gunnar answers through clenched teeth, trying desperately to wear a smile. He has none of the decorum or smoothness of Farnsworth. I can see the shiftiness in Gunnar's eyes, even from here. Gunnar sways back and forth, seeming unnerved. Something Phoenix has said affected him more than he's letting on.

"Then what are you going to do, Gunnar? You have a plan. Enlighten us." Phoenix will not back down.

Despite my delight that Phoenix seems like the person he once was, I have that gnawing feeling inside that tells me we are heading into dangerous territory— and directly into an on-coming, unstoppable storm, fueled by anger and embarrassment.

"Phoenix," I whisper. "He's crazy. Let's not push—"

"I am going to rule equally."

"Nice answer, but how?" Phoenix presses.

"Yes, how?" someone in the crowd asks.

Gunnar whips his heads back and forth, seeming unsure. "I will come up with the answer."

"Not good enough," Phoenix demands. "How are you going to keep us going? How will you restore commerce without blood? Who will you trade with? Where will the money come from?"

Looking at Gunnar, I can tell these are questions he is unprepared to answer.

"I—I," he stutters.

"You don't know," Phoenix reprimands. "You

have no plan and you never have." Phoenix turns to the crowd. "He will reestablish the Lettings just as soon as he's in power. And to keep the Lettings running successfully, he'll have to reestablish the Couplings too."

The crowd mumbles.

Phoenix continues, "Some of you will escape, but others won't be so lucky. There aren't any girls left to serve you. Now you will be serving each other."

The crowd turns to one another and suddenly breaks off into tiny family units. Whatever unification had been achieved, has now been eradicated.

"Shut up," Gunnar shouts at Phoenix, but the crowd has already turned on Gunnar.

"No more Couplings," one of the women screams.

"You said no more Lettings," someone else counters. The crowd grows angrier and moves toward the stage.

"Trust me," Gunnar begs, separating himself from the mob. "I have a plan. I just can't share it yet."

The crowd boos and hisses. Phoenix and I move in the opposite direction of the stage.

"Lulu," I whisper to Phoenix, and he nods.

Phoenix pulls me with him as he walks us to the side of the stage. We make our way through the loud, angry mob and stand nearly parallel with Lulu.

"Lulu," I whisper to her. She doesn't hear. "Lulu," I repeat louder.

She turns my way but narrows her eyes at me.

"Come with us, Lulu. Please. You can't trust him." I am leaning on the stage, reaching my hands out to her.

She shakes her head. "You're one to talk about trust," she hisses at me.

"Lulu, please." I am begging her. I search for any sign of Brooke, hoping she can talk some sense into Lulu, but she is nowhere to be seen. Despite my need for help, I am thankful she is not here and has taken Raven to a safe place. "I saw the way you looked at him. You're beginning to doubt him. You know it. Lulu, please—" I implore, reaching out for her.

Some of the crowd has made its way onto the stage, cornering Gunnar.

"I will not reestablish the Lettings," he pleads, trying desperately to mask his terror with charm.

It doesn't work. Instead, he sounds pathetic. The crowd moves closer to him. Finally, they are within touching distance, and someone pushes Gunnar's shoulder. I see the fury in his eyes, and I have that really bad feeling in the pit of my stomach.

"Lulu," I plead. "Please, please come with us. You can't trust him. Be mad at me, but come with us, please."

She shakes her head and stands her ground.

"Lulu—"

"—I will not be Farnsworth," Gunnar is yelling. "I will not reinstate the Lettings—"

The crowd is shouting over each other.

"You can't trust him."

"Stop him!"

"No more blood."

"How will we eat?"

"What will we do?"

"How will we survive?"

"Oh God, oh God…" A woman falls, weeping.

"People, please, stop." Gunnar sounds desperate, and his words accomplish nothing.

The people shout and push and cry. I try to climb onto the stage to get Lulu, but there is such chaos, someone unknowingly stomps on my hand as I climb up.

"Ow…" I pull my hand back, shaking it.

"You okay?" Phoenix asks.

I nod, my hand throbbing. "Lulu," I cry.

Phoenix jumps up onto the stage, pushing his way through to get to Lulu. She is caught up in the crowd and so much smaller than the others, I'm afraid she will suffocate for sure.

"Lulu," Phoenix yells, reaching toward her, but she continually backs away, her tiny body and her giant loyalty stuck with Gunnar.

"Lulu," I beg. "Please."

The din grows to a roar as people shout, scream, and cry.

"It's all over," a woman wails.

"No, no, no—" someone else cries.

"This can't be."

"People," Gunnar tries to regain control. "People, you need to trust me—" He is cornered, pushed to the back edge of the stage.

"We're not going to trust you."

"You lied to us."

"What now?"

"You promised no more Lettings—"

"Or Couplings—"

"And there won't be. You need to let me explain—" His voice is a low growl. I know this isn't good. You can't corner a lunatic like Gunnar.

"Liar…"

"Traitor…"

"We trusted you."

"Kill Gunnar!"

"ENOUGH!" Gunnar screams, stepping forward.

Phoenix has reached Lulu, but she purposely moves out of arms' reach.

"You want to know what will happen? I'll show you." With that he grabs Lulu, and the two of them break off from the crowd.

My stomach aches, filled with a horrible feeling. He is just too untrustworthy.

"This little girl," Gunnar raises Lulu's arm into the air as he speaks, "is one of a few last remaining O's. Would I do this if I was planning on more Lettings and Couplings?"

"No, no, no—" I murmur, climbing onto the stage and running toward them. I feel like I'm fighting my way through rushing water as I watch Gunnar raise his gun and point it at a very confused Lulu.

"Gunnar, no," Phoenix yells. "You've made your point."

"I don't think I have."

"Ronnie?" Lulu is terrified.

"I'm here, Lulu," I yell, fighting through the thickening crowd. "I'm here."

"Ronnie?"

"Right here," I push my way past as Gunnar smiles, and I hear a resounding BAM!

Gunnar shoots Lulu point blank in the chest.

\*\*\*\*

"Nooo!" I scream, falling forward. "Nooooo…" I throw myself onto Lulu, wailing.

Phoenix is next to me, feeling for Lulu's pulse.

"Lulu, Lulu, stay with me—" I cry, pressing my

hand tightly to Lulu's wound. Her blood is gushing through my fingers. She is losing blood faster than I can contain it. "No," I sob, holding Lulu in my arms.

Phoenix applies pressure to her wound. He looks at me, and I can see it in his eyes.

"No," I sob, rocking Lulu like the child she is.

Phoenix tries in vain to resuscitate Lulu. Over and over he places his mouth on hers, pumping at her heart. It is useless. She is gone.

"Phoenix, no…." I cry, falling against him as I hold Lulu.

"That's O," someone announces, and suddenly, we are surrounded by a pack of hungry animals. "Gunnar told us she was an O."

"We need that O…"

"What if he reinstates the Lettings?"

"What if he doesn't? We need that blood."

"I need O. Let me at it."

The growing mob closes in on us, snatching at Lulu—seeing her death as their gain. People topple over us as they push their way closer. Someone pulls a knife and tries to cut Lulu, obviously wanting more of her blood. It is such a frenzy, no one even considers how to contain the blood if they were to get it. The knife wielder dives forward. I turn my shoulder to block his way and protect Lulu, and he stabs me on the shoulder.

"Ugh," I wince through the pain. "Phoenix," I cry, and he pulls Lulu from me, carrying her like a babe in his arms.

"Stay with me," he tells me through clenched teeth.

I nod and hold Lulu's hand as we push through the crowd. My shoulder throbs almost as deliberately as my heart. We are stopped by a band of people who won't let us pass. With every step we take forward, they try to push us back. Phoenix's hands are occupied with carrying Lulu.

"Just give us the girl before we lose all the blood," one of the men tells us.

"Hand her over," demands another.

Phoenix tries to dart past them, but they continually move to block his way. "Ron?"

"I'm here," I tell him, raising my gun. My shoulder aches as I aim at the people blocking our way. "Move," I yell, fighting them back with the rifle. "Move!" I poke someone in the abdomen and nearly cry out from the pain in my shoulder. I am certain the blow from my gun hurts me more than it hurts him.

We push our way through the mob, and make our way down the steps of the riser.

"This way," Phoenix tosses his head over his shoulder as we run.

I follow him to a small green truck with a covered back. I jerk open the door, cringing from pain, and he places Lulu inside the tiny backseat, carefully but quickly, then tosses my backpack on the floor. Before I can think, Phoenix climbs into the driver's seat, and I climb in next to him. Immediately, he pulls off his jacket. He uses his teeth to tear the bottom seam, then rips off a piece of material. He pushes it against my shoulder and takes the rest of his jacket and ties it around me to hold pressure on my wound. Then he slams his hand against the dashboard and fiddles with some wires under the steering wheel. I face out the window as the mob begins closing in on us. Instinctually, I climb into the back and hold myself over

Lulu to protect her.

"Uh," I exclaim when someone slams their hand against our window.

They start pushing against the truck, rocking it back and forth, like they are trying to roll it.

"Phoenix…" I whisper, breathlessly.

"I've—got it."

The truck turns over, and we both exhale. We move forward slowly, the truck parting the crowd. Finally, we are free of the mob, and I climb forward into the passenger's seat. I turn to Phoenix, and he turns to me. Neither of us smiles. He focuses on the road, and together, we once again race off into the unknown.

Chapter Twenty-Three

Pushing the truck as fast as it can go, we drive for an hour without speaking. The ride is rough and bumpy, but we are making good time. Phoenix checks the rearview often, but thankfully, no one is following us. I continually look over my shoulder, praying for a sign of life from Lulu, but there is none. I reach back and place my hand on hers. I pull away when all I feel is ice-cold death.

"Ron…" He speaks without taking his eyes off the road.

"She was only a child. A baby, Phoenix."

"I know."

"She should be playing dolls, and swimming, and running around in a field of dandelions." I turn to Phoenix. "Why is there so much death where there should be life?"

Despite the fear and pressure we are feeling, he reaches out and takes my hand in his. He feels so warm and comforting tears spring into my eyes.

"You don't have to…" My voice is only a whisper. "I—I know you don't feel that way about me anymore. You don't have to try to make me feel better."

Phoenix yanks at the steering wheel, and we come to a rough, jarring stop. I jolt forward in my seat, but Phoenix throws his arm across me, blocking me before I hit the dash. I stare at him with disbelief as he turns to me, letting his arm drop.

"Phoenix, we can't stop…we don't know who's following— "

"Is that what you think? That I don't love you anymore?"

My eyes flood with tears, and I look down at the seat between us. Those few inches of cracked leather feel like an impassable gully. All I can do is shrug in response. He shakes his head and pulls the truck back onto the road and up to speed. We drive the rest of the way in silence.

****

We speed past woods I think I recognize. "Phoenix?"

He jumps at my voice, both of us accustomed to the quiet and the racing sound of the engine.

"That's the way to camp." I point out the window.

"We can't go to camp now."

"But Raven and Brooke—"

"They'll be okay."

"No," I turn to face him. "No, Phoenix, they won't. If Gunnar heads that way, who knows what he'll do." I hear the anguish in my voice.

"He won't."

"But—"

"I said he won't." Phoenix grips the steering wheel and clenches his jaw.

"Fine," I mumble, my throat tight as I choke back tears.

Phoenix shifts in his seat. "Look," his voice is softer as he explains. "Gunnar is too much of a coward to act on his own. He needs followers to act, and right now he has none. Those people back there are so confused—consider what they just tried to do to…"

"I know…" I squeeze my eyes shut, attempting to forget the horror we just encountered.

"My best guess is he's heading to Farnsworth's mansion. It's what he's always wanted anyway—to live there." His words are tinged with disappointment. He focuses hard on the road and continues.

"But Phoenix—"

"The people turned on him when he…before, with…Lulu…" Phoenix's voice trails off, and I hear the pain in his words. He clears his throat. "It wouldn't be smart for him to do anything to the other girls. There's no point. It will alienate what's left of his followers. The girls are safest with Gretchen and Margaret, at camp."

"But Lilly and Violet, they're at the mansion. Farnsworth has had them all this time—"

"Is that what he told you?"

I nod.

"No wonder…" Phoenix turns to me. "Lilly and Violet are at camp. They have been for a while. They're safe there."

"He lied again." I shake my head, completely relieved and yet hardly able to comprehend the idea the girls are safest with Margaret and Gretchen—the former head of my camp, and my ex-best friend—two women who abhor me.

Phoenix tightens his grip on the wheel and looks away. I can tell this is the end of this conversation.

"Okay." I stare out the opposite window.

"Really?" He turns to me, and I face him.

"If you think they're safe, then okay."

"Thank you." A long pause fills the truck cab.

"Besides, we can't exactly go into camp with…" He glances over his shoulder and turns back, his face painted in sadness.

"I know."

He offers me a small, sad nod.

We are quiet again.

\*\*\*\*

We drive for another hour, and finally, we pull up to a tiny cabin, hidden deep in the forest.

"Your cabin," I whisper.

"As far as I know, no one has discovered this yet."

We jump out of the truck. I am so stiff from sitting, I try to stretch my arms, but the pain in my shoulder stops me. "Ugh," I cry, grabbing my shoulder.

Phoenix walks up behind me to examine the cut on my shoulder. "It's worse than I thought. The pressure helped contain the bleeding some, but you may need stitches."

"It'll be fine. I'm used to bleeding," I joke.

He smiles a small smile. "We need to clean it up."

"Her first—please."

He only nods. Phoenix takes a deep breath and quietly opens the back door of the truck. Lulu is lying there perfectly still, her skin even whiter than usual.

I gasp, putting my hands to my face. Aside from Buzzcut, and the two boys Brooke shot in the woods that day, I have never before been so near death. I keep waiting to see signs of life in her. I look for a gentle movement in her chest, a flickering of her eyelids…but there is none. I search for anything normal amidst this, the greatest of abnormality. Without a word, Phoenix disappears to the side of his cabin and comes back carrying a shovel.

"Isn't it too soon for that?" I ask, my eyes wide.

Phoenix says nothing, but walks to me and gently places his hand on my cheek. He strokes my cheek softly, and I close my eyes for a moment. Then he steps away and walks quite a distance from the cabin. I find him behind an old maple tree, digging.

"The ground is soft here," he tells me. Sweat pours off his forehead and stains his T-shirt. "And there's nice shade from the tree, but I'm far enough not to hit roots." He stops, leaning against his shovel. "And, come here for a sec."

I walk over to Phoenix and stand next to him. I inhale deeply and smell…him.

"Look." He points over my shoulder.

I turn, and behind me, through the thick trees, I see a beautiful break in the woods, creating an unused path. The path is lit up by tiny droplets of moonlight that fall through the trees, making it seem as if the path is twinkling.

"It's perfect," I whisper, still facing away from him. I turn back. "Thank you."

He nods again and resumes digging, wiping the sweat off his forehead with the back of his forearm. I leave to check Lulu and fetch Phoenix some water from my backpack.

I return with a canteen, and he takes it from me. He untwists the cover and finishes the water off. He hands it back to me and smiles a small thank you smile. I nod in response. He works another hour or so, and all too soon, he is through. He tosses the shovel onto the ground far from the hole he's dug.

He walks to me and reaches out to take my hand. "It's time." His words are gentle but horrible, all at the same time.

"No," I murmur. I put my free hand against my stomach. "Shouldn't we just give her a little time? Just in case—"

"There is no more time, Ron. It's over."

I nod, biting my lip, trying desperately to be strong.

He squeezes my hand as he speaks. "We need to let her rest. It's the best thing we can do for her, now."

I steel myself against my sorrow, and together, Phoenix and I walk to the truck. Lulu is so peaceful, looking like she did when she would float on her back in our lake on a hot summer day. For a moment, I can almost believe—then I see her eyes. Her eyes tell the truth. Her soft, blue eyes are fixated on nothing but stare straight ahead. They are frozen with the expression of surprise over Gunnar's actions. As if she will never forget. Seeing death is bad enough, but knowing the fear of death will be forever in her eyes— that's simply too much.

I let a small moan sneak out of my chest, and Phoenix hurries to close her lids. But he's too late. That vision of Lulu will be forever with me. Gently, he lifts her from the truck and once again carries her like a babe in his arms. Her lifeless arm falls away from him, and her pale face rolls out toward me. I force myself to swallow my sobs.

Phoenix stops and waits as I tuck Lulu's arm back up on top of her, then he carries her to her grave. He squats down next to the hole he's dug, and places her into the grave, carefully. Watching her be placed in the earth is so final; I can no longer contain my sobs.

"Oh God," I whisper, falling down onto the ground next to the hole.

Phoenix walks to me and lifts me up. He pulls me to him, and I bury my face in his chest. This time, I give myself over completely, not like when Farnsworth tried to comfort me.

I sob against Phoenix. "It's not fair," I mumble into his chest.

"I know," he whispers, stroking my hair.

"She was a child. And that…that lunatic just…" I can't finish my words. I am so angry I ball my hands into fists. "Ugh," I yell, as I beat my fists against Phoenix's chest. He barely flinches. The pain in my shoulder is excruciating, but the pain in my heart is so much worse. He lets me stay here, flailing against him, until the anger is out. My arms drop from exhaustion, and I press harder against him as I cry even more. He holds me without saying a word. Finally, my tears slow, and I pull back from him. "Sorry," I mumble.

"Shh," is all he says. Sure I am stable, he crosses back to Lulu. He tucks her hands up nicely on top of her chest and smooths her hair away from her face. He disappears into his cabin and comes back with a blanket. He wraps it around her, covering the blood soaked clothing. "Do you want something to place with her?"

"Yes." I glance around but see nothing. Finally, I settle on a spray from a pine tree with a few pinecones still attached.

"That's beautiful." He is squatting next to me.

I lean over Lulu and wipe the blood from her face. I lay the garland on top of her, then I stand, and Phoenix stands with me.

"You want to say something?" he asks.

"I don't know what to say…"

"Sometimes words really do fail us, don't they?"

I stare at him.

"There are only a few, real words in life, Ron. Words you can always trust."

I nod, understanding. "Goodbye Lulu." I squat down next to her. "I love you, and always will."

We stand in silence for a few moments. Finally, he turns to me.

"You must be starving."

I shake my head.

"Well, I am. There is food in the cabin. Would you mind going in and preparing something?"

I narrow my eyes and wonder if he's lost his mind—how could he think of food at a time like this? And then suddenly, I realize. He is trying to spare me from watching Lulu being covered in dirt.

"Okay," I eke out. I turn to the cabin and then back to him. "Thank you."

"You're welcome."

I begin to walk away.

"Ron?"

I stop, and face him. "Yes?"

"After this," he bows his head toward Lulu, "we uh—we need to talk."

"Yes."

He lifts his shovel, and I walk away.

## Chapter Twenty-Four

Within a half an hour, Phoenix joins me in his cabin.

"I…all I found was this." I hold out two cans of pasta in sauce. "I couldn't open them. Sorry."

Phoenix takes the cans from me and cracks each open with his pocket knife. He sticks a fork in each, and a small smile turns up the corners of his mouth, just for a second—like he remembers the first time he fed me in this cabin—when I had dug into the food, forgetting a fork. Phoenix plops down on the lone chair opposite the bed, and leans forward against his legs, cramming food into his mouth absentmindedly. I sit on the edge of his bed and peer into my can. My stomach flips. I'm ravenous, but the color of the sauce makes me think of blood.

"I'm sorry," I mumble, putting the can down. "I—I can't eat this."

"Why not?" Phoenix puts his food down and comes over to look into mine. He realizes what I see. "I'm sorry, Ron. Here." In a flash he is up and back, holding a box of crackers. "These might be better."

I take a tiny bite of the cracker, but I can't eat. He's watching me, and I can tell he understands.

He glances at his own clothes. "What do you say we get cleaned up first?"

"Okay." My voice is weak and distant.

"Okay." He stands and produces two thin towels that look more like small bed sheets.

I sit, running my hand across Phoenix's bed, feeling the rough texture of the brown blanket of the Harvesters. "This is the same blanket that was here last time—"

"Yes." He stands still, clutching the towels, waiting for me to move.

"It's probably been here as long as you have."

"Yes." He stares at me, trying to understand. He reaches up and scratches his beard.

I glance up at him. "Why do things get to outlast people?"

"Oh, Ron." He walks to me and sits next to me. Our legs touch, but he pulls his away abruptly— probably feeling the invisible yet painful barrier Farnsworth has built between us. Phoenix speaks. "Things can't outlast people…"

"Of course they can. Look at this blanket. It'll still be here, lying on this bed, probably long after we're gone."

"That's uplifting," he teases.

I stare at him blankly, and he nudges my uninjured shoulder.

"Hey. Ron. What I mean is, a thing can be forgotten—or replaced—tomorrow, but a person will live on inside us forever."

I nod, grateful for his words.

"And I bet you outlive this blanket. What do you say? It'll be moth eaten and frayed down to a mere nub long before you leave this earth." He places his hands on his knees and turns away for a moment. "And you leaving this earth is a thought I don't want to have."

My eyes dart up to his. "Really?"

He smiles slightly, and tiny crinkles form around his eyes. "Come on." He pats my knee, rather brotherly. Well, what I imagine a brother would pat my knee like, anyway. "Let's get you cleaned up. Do you have anything to change into?"

I shake my head and then rethink my answer. "Um, a couple of things," thinking of my last clean pair of underwear. "But no pants or shirt."

He crosses to a pile of clothes on the floor and grabs a white and green plaid shirt. "Come on."

I follow him out the door.

****

We are standing outside of his cabin, but inside a tall wooden box with no top. "This is a makeshift shower," he explains. "It's a little chilly out, but it's the best I've got."

"It's great." I didn't see the shower on my last visit. To keep warm, I hold the towel to me, tightly.

Phoenix pumps water from the ground, and it flows up and out a tap on the wall. "I can build up enough pressure so you can get a quick shower. Best to just turn off the spigot unless you're rinsing off." He barely looks at me while he speaks.

"Um, okay," I mumble.

"If you remember, there's a sort of latrine over there." He points in the opposite direction of the shower and cabin. "When you're done with your shower, we can wash your clothes and let them dry overnight."

My eyes dart up to him on the word "overnight." So he's expecting me to stay not just through the day, but the night also. He fidgets with the shower, and I can tell this whole conversation is difficult for him as well.

"Okay," I very nearly groan. It takes all of my energy just to stand here. I lean against the shower wall.

"Well, I, uh…" He walks to me and unties the bandage he had supplied for me. My shoulder aches as the pressure is released.

"Ugh," I wince.

"You okay?"

I nod through a grimace.

"We'll get that taken care of. But right now, I'll uh…I'll leave you alone. I'll be right in the cabin if you…need anything." He turns abruptly and shoves his hands into his pockets. He drops his head and walks off into his cabin.

I strip out of my clothes, desperately wanting to be clean, but at the same time, the feeling of washing her blood from me is like losing Lulu all over again. It's another connection gone. But I have to get clean. And I have to address my injury. I don't need an infection right now.

I turn the water on as he showed me, and feel the glorious, albeit chilly, water run down over me. I wince when the water hits my shoulder, but seeing Lulu's blood run down my body and into the earth below makes me nearly numb. Quickly, I turn off the water and grab the soap Phoenix has supplied for me. I lather my hair in the soap and wash my entire body clean— wishing I could wash away the memories of my day. I turn the water back on and step under its spray, closing my eyes and shivering. The water hurts my injured shoulder, but cleanliness wins out over pain. I am ever so grateful I had packed a few sparse toiletries in my backpack, and I can at least begin to make myself feel female again. Suddenly, in the midst of preening, I can feel something, or someone, and I jerk my head over my shoulder to peek in the window of his cabin. He is there but turns away, aware I caught him staring at me. I'm not the slightest bit embarrassed, because the shower walls cover everything but my head. But I do wonder why he was watching me…

I finish my shower, towel off, and grab my dirty clothes. I do my best to scrub them in the water. As I wring out the clothes, I am astounded by the amount of blood Lulu must have lost. Once my clothes are fairly clean, I lay them over the sides of the shower to dry. I slip into my clean underwear and his shirt. Although I am tall, his shirt hangs mid-thigh. I collect my backpack and head into the cabin.

"Oh." Phoenix appears startled to see me.

"Sorry, did I surprise you?"

"Uh, no. No." He shakes his head and looks off. "I'm going to shower too. Will you wait here?"

I can't imagine where else I would go, but he sounds sincere so I answer him with a nod.

"Good." He grabs a towel and clean clothes and heads out to the shower.

I peruse his tiny cabin, thinking of the last time I was here and how things have changed. For one thing, the pictures of me are down. Realizing this is like a blow to the gut. It's obvious he doesn't love me anymore. I sit on the bed waiting, but the memories of his kiss flood over me, and I have to get up. I pace back and forth, across the cabin floor—to the chair and back to the bed, over and over—wondering if my seashell is hidden somewhere here; willing myself not to peek out the window at him. After three passes, I can't help myself. From across the room I peer out the window, but I can barely see the shower stall. I creep closer to the window, trying to maintain my distance. My heart is racing, and my palms break out into a warm sweat. My shoulder throbs, but I ignore it as I inch even closer. Finally, I am at the window, and I stare out, boldly. I know I won't see any of him, I'm not trying to…it just makes me feel better to know he's near. I look at the shower wall, waiting to see his head pop up, but I see nothing—

"Bam!"

I jump startled.

"Sorry," Phoenix tells me. "The door slams. I should have been more careful."

I stand with my hand on my heart, trying to calm myself. "Uh-huh." I fight to calm my breathing, but I'm still lucid enough to notice he's wearing an olive green t-shirt and jeans. He looks like—my salvation.

"See anything interesting?"

"Un-uh." I shake my head.

"Too bad. I did." He smiles the first real smile I've seen from him since I've been back.

I smile back, blushing.

"Let's take a look at that shoulder, okay?"

"Yeah."

He stands there staring at me, and I realize my shirt is covering me completely.

"Oh…" I unbutton my top two buttons and slide my shoulder out of the shirt. I'm certain I hear his breath catch.

"We uh, we need to clean this up."

Okay, so the reaction was because my wound is disgusting, not because I slid my shirt down a few inches. I have to get a grip. He produces a bottle of some kind of liquid and a rag.

"Luckily, the bleeding stopped. But that means you'll have to miss out on the pleasure of me gluing you shut again."

"Hm," I grunt. The glue episode makes me think of Brooke, and I wonder if she lives here too.

"I'm going to put this on, it will burn. Probably a lot."

"That's okay, and I'm sorry to bother you with this. I just can't reach—"

"You never bother me, Ron. I want to take care of you." He speaks these words so softly, I'm not even sure I hear them.

I freeze, not daring to breathe.

"Ready?"

I inhale sharply. "Okay."

He places the soaked rag to my shoulder, and my skin screams in protest.

"Ugh." I grit my teeth.

"It'll pass." He blows on it. "It hurts like hell for a few minutes, but it will fight that infection."

I nod, waiting for the pain to pass. The burning subsides.

"You've got a pretty good gash. Thankfully, it's not deep, so it won't interfere with your arm's range of motion."

"Okay."

"Now I'm going to put some medicine on it and bandage you up."

His proximity is making me lightheaded, so I don't speak. I feel a slick cream being spread across my cut, and then pressure as he bandages the wound.

"All done." He tosses the extra supplies on the tiny

table by the chair.

I turn around to face him.

"Come." He reaches out and takes my hand, which suddenly feels like it's filled with dancing bubbles. "We need to talk."

\*\*\*\*

We sit on the bed, next to each other, but not touching. We are both quiet for whole minutes. Finally, he stands and walks away. He turns back. "Before anything else, just tell me one thing. Did he hurt you?"

"What?"

"Farnsworth. Did he hurt you? I don't care about what transpired, as long as you're okay. So tell me. Honestly. Did he hurt you when you two—"

"No. No, Phoenix." I stand and walk to him. "We never…I never Coupled with him."

"What?" His eyes are fixed on mine. I can see a spark of hope behind the permanent worry that is etched in them.

"Sit. Please." I take his hand and gently lead him back to the bed.

"I wouldn't blame you, Ron. I—I was such an idiot—"

"Phoenix. Listen. The night I saw you kiss Brooke—"

"Ronnie, I'm sorry. I was—"

I put my hand on his hand. He looks down at my touch and stops speaking.

"Please," I tell him. "Let me finish." I take my hand away, knowing I can't afford a single distraction if I'm going to get through this. "The night I saw you kiss Brooke was one of the worst nights of my life. Not just because of that, but also because of some things I saw on my trip. And, because I found out I am cut from evil cloth..." My eyes drop down to the bed between us.

"What are you talking about?"

"It seems evil is in my blood."

"I don't understand—"

"I'll explain it all. I promise. Just let me tell you this first..."

He sits up straight and takes a deep breath.

"I had been watching you before that night, and you seemed to have disappeared. The Phoenix I knew was replaced by a man talking about victory and killing. I felt like you were...dead."

His head hangs between his shoulders, and he stares at the ground and nods.

"So that night, the night you kissed Brooke on the projection, I thought my world had ended. I thought the Phoenix I knew was gone, and I assumed this new you and Brooke were a couple again." I toss my hands in exasperation. "I would have done...anything...to make the pain go away. So I made my way to Farnsworth's room."

Phoenix takes another deep breath, and his body stiffens.

"And I sat on his windowsill, waiting. When he joined me, I fell apart. I had just met my father—my real father, Phoenix—"

"What?"

"Yes, and he told me you had moved on."

"But how?"

"I'll explain that later, too. So I just lost it. I can't remember ever being that upset in my life. Including today. So Farnsworth tried to comfort me. He held me, and I cried into his shoulder. He sat me down on his bed—"

Phoenix stands and paces, running his hand through his hair. "What did he do?"

"He…he let me finish crying, and then he kissed me. And I kissed him back." I sit, unable to move, balling the brown blanket in my fists. "Just because I wanted to get even with you, or forget you, or I don't know what."

Phoenix stares at me.

"But it was awful—plastic, and cold, and unfeeling. No matter how hard I squeezed my eyes shut, I couldn't change him to you. So I figured I deserved the horrible kiss and whatever may go along with it, because I married him…"

Phoenix glances down at the ground.

"So I put his hand on my shoulder. I knew I was slated to Couple with him. It was inevitable. And I knew my mother had survived the Coupling houses, so I could survive this too."

"And—?" Phoenix speaks through a clenched jaw.

"And he told me he knew this was all about you, Phoenix." I stare straight into Phoenix's eyes as I speak. "I was shaking, and he asked why I was so nervous. When he guessed I had never Coupled before, he was shocked, to say the least. But he stopped. He didn't push me. And I was eternally grateful, because honestly…I don't know what I would have done. He asked me to stay with him, and I did. We were both fully dressed, and I slept with my back to him. It felt good not to be alone. I'm sorry."

Phoenix studies me, his eyes intense and determined.

I stumble over my words. "I…I know it's over

between us, and I know you don't love me anymore, but the whole time I was in Farnsworth's room…" I let my words and my head drop. I speak into the floor. "I just kept trying to imagine you were there with me. That Farnsworth wasn't there. That it was you, Phoenix."

"Me…?"

My voice is low and breathy. My eyes make their way to his. "That it was you I was going to…" My eyes search his, pleading.

"What?" His word is like a gentle caress. "Tell me."

"…Couple with."

He takes a sharp breath, his eyes locked on mine. He walks to me and places his hand under my chin. Gently, he guides my chin upward and lifts me to my feet.

"The stupidest thing I've ever done in my life, Veronica Billings, was to let you go."

I gasp, and my knees suddenly feel weak. I am caught in the intensity of his eyes, like an animal caught in a trap.

He wraps his arm around me, steadying me. "I would do anything, anything if I could keep you locked up here, safe and happy—out of harm's way—"

The only reaction I can muster is a nod.

"But I can't. We're both people who have a journey we need to honor."

"Yes," I whisper.

"I can't excuse my actions, but I will tell you this. I was overcome with jealousy. I didn't want you marrying him. I don't want you married to him. If you are married to anyone, I want it to be—"

I stare at him, my eyes wide.

"Sorry." He breaks his hold on me and steps back.

I wobble, but find my balance.

He drags his hand across his chin and turns to me. "The only thing that matters to me is you. And the idea of you with someone else…even if it's to save me— maybe especially if it's to save me…" he shakes his head. "I can take any pain, any torture, as long as I know you are with me."

"I am."

He nods and an uncomfortable thought comes to mind.

"Are we…going to break Brooke's heart again? Did you tell her you loved her?"

"No."

It's awkward, but I have to know. I rock on my heels, feeling like a child engulfed by his oversized shirt. I pull the sleeves down over my hands. "Then…why the kiss?"

"I had just seen the projection of you laughing with Farnsworth. It hurt."

I nod, understanding all too well. "Farnsworth and I were in an awful place. He did something goofy. I'm sorry."

"Ron, I would so much rather see you laughing than crying, even if it's with someone else." We smile at each other, and his stern expression softens a bit. "Brooke slapped me across the face as soon as they turned off the projection."

"Oh good." I chuckle. "You deserved it."

He laughs softly, and the corner of his mouth turns up into a sideways grin. Then he locks his eyes on mine and crosses to me. Trapped by the intensity of his stare,

I feel myself flush. He takes my hand and leads me to the bed. I stand in front of him as he sits, holding me gently by my wrists which are engulfed by the oversized cuffs. He reaches up and tosses my still damp hair behind me. "How's your shoulder?"

"F—fine," I stutter, not feeling any pain at this moment.

He reaches around the baggy shirt and lets his hands clasp about my waist. Material gathers in his grasp. "I lost myself when I lost you. But just seeing you here—feeling you…" he squeezes my waist.

"I was worried about who you'd become, with all the talk of victory and killing. It's not you, Phoenix."

"No," he bows his head. "It's not." He lets his head fall forward against my stomach.

I run my fingers through his hair, gently. Even through the shirt, his beard tickles my stomach.

"I sided with Gunnar, because I thought it was the only way. I've always hated his methods, but he was gaining power quickly, and I thought it would be better to be with him than against him. What an idiot…" His head rocks back and forth, gently. "It's all such a mess…I don't know if I can ever find me again." He looks up at me. "But I do know having you with me is the only chance I have."

"We can find you again."

"It's not too late?"

"It better not be. I just traveled three-thousand miles—mostly on foot—to find you. I went through a thunderstorm."

He smiles at me, his eyes bright. "Yeah?" He traces his finger down the side of my cheek, my eyes closing, my body aching for his touch.

"You're what got me through. Again." My voice is barely audible as he lets his fingers linger on my chin. "I'm not giving up on you. You're still in there, Phoenix."

His thumb slides upward and brushes my lips. I want to tell him I know he's still there because I see it in the way he took care of Lulu, and in the way he takes care of me, but I am suddenly unable to form words.

He stands now, our bodies close, his fingers caressing my lips. His hand comes to rest on my cheek as he leans down to whisper into my ear. "I promise you, Veronica Billings, if you're willing to give me another chance, I promise we will find us again, too."

I raise my eyes to him, relishing the feeling of our intimacy. I close my eyes and breathe deeply. "I think we already have."

Cathrine Goldstein

## Chapter Twenty-Five

He wraps my cloth-covered hands with his. My breathing is rapid as he lets go of one hand and tosses the rest of my hair so it hangs down my back.

"I know you're still married to him—"

"I threw my ring at him and stormed off."

"Bastard. He should have risked his life to follow you and make sure you were safe."

I smile as Phoenix reaches out, smoothing my hair. I close my eyes, lost in the moment.

"But you are still bound by law. His law. And no one can free you except him."

I nod, solemnly. "And you are still connected to Gunnar." The words send a shiver down my spine.

He drops his head and then resumes stroking my hair. "I know. So it sounds like we have a lot to talk about. A lot to work through."

I nod, enjoying the feel of his strong hand stroking my hair. "But I don't know if I'll be very good company right now. Lulu just...my heart aches."

"I know. So let it ache here, with me." He places a finger under my chin and gently lifts my eyes to meet his. He speaks softly. "My mother once told me in the light after the darkness of tragedy, you will find perspective. The sun will rise tomorrow morning. Let's not let Lulu die in vain, Ron. Let her death serve to help us find our perspective and our way back to each other."

"Is that being selfish?" My heart aches from pain and throbs from possibility.

"No. She's gone, and there's nothing we can do about it. But together, we can right us." He smiles, and the crinkles form around his eyes.

It's all…too…my eyes flood with tears, and I turn away.

"Hey?" He strokes my hair even more gently, trying to see into my eyes. "Ron? What is it?"

I can't bring myself to make eye contact. "You know that moment when you get hurt—injured, I mean—and you think 'that hurts' but you know the real pain is still to come…?"

"Yes."

"I'm afraid we're in that moment."

He says nothing, but brushes my hair back from my face softly, and lifts my chin. "Maybe. So let me be with you when that moment hits."

I nod and manage a small smile. But then the tears come again, violent like the waves I've seen at Farnsworth's ocean.

"I'm sorry…" I whisper through my sobs. I fall against him, my body convulsing from the horror I feel. He holds me for an endless amount of time, until finally, I take a deep breath, sure there are no tears left. I gaze up at him, trying to see through blurry, puffy eyes.

"Shh." He holds me tightly. "You're grieving, Ron."

"I just can't stop thinking about her last moments. How horrible they were."

He nods.

"And even more, her last days…or weeks. What it was like for her to be with that lunatic. Did she eat? Was she cared for at all…?" I shake my head, unable to think about it.

"I understand. I feel incredibly guilty for ever bringing Lulu near that maniac…"

"You were protecting her—it was the only option you had…" I grow dizzy, and my legs give out beneath me.

Phoenix grabs me with his arm around my waist and steadies me. "Hey," he whispers. "Listen to me."

I look away, staring off.

He shakes me gently to get my attention. "Ron, listen. What matters is that you never gave up on her. And you loved her through it all. And most importantly, you were there for her, at the end. She didn't die alone in some horrible place. You were right there, with her, letting her know she was not alone."

My eyes dart up to him, grateful. "Thank you," I whisper. "I think that would be the worst. To think she died alone."

"Yes."

"And…" My words trail off, and I sigh.

"What?"

"Is it bad that I don't want to be alone right now? That I want to be here with you?"

He doesn't answer. Instead, he reaches up and pulls his shirt over his head. My eyes fall across his bare chest that is so toned and muscular, I gasp. I stare at him, completely unsure of what we're about to do.

"Phoenix?"

"Trust me, Ron."

I nod, my hands suddenly shaking. He takes them

into his hand and lifts them to his mouth. He kisses my fingers softly.

"You're grieving right now—I would never take advantage of you. But…"

I take a deep breath.

He lets go of my hands and reaches out toward the still unbuttoned top two buttons of my shirt. The collar lays open, and his fingers trace the hollow of my throat. "You look gorgeous in my shirt."

His eyes are locked on me, and I feel overpowered but safe all at once. There's a strange ache in my body, answering to the hunger in his eyes.

"It is by far the most beautiful you have ever looked."

My eyes dart up as he reaches out to touch the next button. He studies me as he slowly begins to unbutton. My entire body warms, and I bite down hard on my bottom lip. He abandons my button to run his fingers across my lips once more. I try to remember to breathe. As he reaches down for the next button, my breathing becomes shallow and rapid. His eyes are locked on mine as he works my shirt. His hands are level with my breasts, and he moves his head to the side, questioning me with his glance, as if he's waiting for me to stop him. I don't.

He moves to the next button, and I close my eyes. I feel dizzy and unsteady on my feet—but in a whole different way than before. He has me unbuttoned almost to my bellybutton, although I'm still covered. Still staring into my eyes, he finishes unbuttoning my shirt. He begins to open it slowly.

"Phoenix…" I reach out and grab his hands, instinctually.

He stops. I am both terrified and enthralled.

He raises his eyebrows. "No?"

I don't answer. The heartbeat pulsing in my head drowns out my thoughts.

"Ron?"

I let his hands go and breathe deeply. I close my eyes for a moment and then open them. I smile nervously, biting the inside of my cheek. I take another breath and manage to nod slightly. He smiles at me and reaches out for my shirt again. He opens it gently.

"Phoenix…" I am sweating and my breathing is shallow, as my body waits for his touch.

His eyes dart down from my eyes to my opened shirt. "You are so incredibly beautiful—"

I squirm slightly. "I'm sure Brooke is so much more—"

"Shh." He closes his eyes and shakes his head.

He reaches inside my shirt and wraps his arms around my waist. He pulls me to him, and we stand, chest to chest. I am so overcome, I feel faint.

Tears come into my eyes once more, but this time they are not only tears of sorrow, they are also tears of joy and tears of relief. He pulls me closer and holds me tighter. I cry into his chest, my tears expressing things my words cannot.

With hardly any effort, he lifts me up in his embrace, and I wrap my legs around his waist. Gracefully, he carries me to his bed.

Careful of my shoulder, he guides me down onto the bed. He stands over me, smiling, and then he slides in next to me. He is up on his elbow, by my side, but still perched above me. He wraps his free hand around my waist. He moves me so I feel his bare chest against mine. Then he reaches up and strokes my cheek with his hand.

"Are you okay?"

I can't speak. I only mumble some affirmative response and nod. He smiles. I can feel his arm muscles taught, holding him next to me. The smile leaves his face.

"What?" I murmur.

He stops and takes a sharp breath. "I meant what I said. I wouldn't care if you had…Coupled with him…but, Veronica, we need to free you from him, because from tonight on, this," he strokes my cheek again, "I want this to be only for us."

My breathing is so rapid I feel as if I might pass out. I nod. He places his hand on my bare belly.

"This," he whispers, pressing against my abdomen softly, "I need this to be only for me."

I draw in a breath sharply, his words making me dizzy. "Yes," I manage to eke out.

He smiles a strong, sexy, overprotective smile. "It's incredibly possessive of me, but I don't want anyone else to ever be this close to you."

I nod, my eyelids only half-opened.

"Not physically and not mentally. Okay?"

"Yes…" I close my eyes, lost in the intensity of the moment.

He slides his hand around my waist, pulling me to him, holding me tighter. I feel his muscles straining. Something…needs…to happen.

"I want to be the one you come to, Ron. For all of it. I would rather die than ever feel what I felt before—when you were with Farnsworth. Nothing could be worse than feeling like you left me. And even worse, knowing I was the one that drove you to do it. I would welcome any physical pain not to feel that mental…anguish again."

"I'm sorry," I whisper, a tear leaking out of the corner of my eye.

"Hey. Hey…" He wipes my tear. "It's not your fault. It's mine. But I'm going to make it right if you let me."

"You already have."

He strokes my cheek once more and then slowly, finally, he leans down and kisses me.

His kiss is soft, and I can tell he means only to kiss me the one time—but I wrap my arms around his shoulders. I feel him begin to back away, but I hold him fast, pulling him closer. I ignore the screaming pain radiating out from my shoulder.

"Ron…"

He looks so serious I can tell he's fighting his every impulse. I don't let go. Instead, I try to pull him on top of me.

"Ron…" He warns me with his voice.

"I—I just want you to kiss me again."

He smiles, and complies. This time he nudges my nose with his before kissing me on my forehead, my eyelids, my cheeks, until he makes his way to my lips, where he kisses me ever so softly, over and over. Despite my efforts to roll him on top of me, he keeps his body wedged next to mine. He pulls back.

"Again," I whisper breathlessly, and he smirks.

This time he lands his kiss directly on my mouth. Finally, he gives over to me…his mouth opening mine as he kisses me forcefully, his short beard scraping against my face. I dig my fingernails into his back, my body arching off the bed. I lean upward to match his intensity, and we are locked together, my arms wrapped around his back, his hands pressing into the mattress on either side of my face.

Still kissing me, he sits up and pulls me up with him. He is on his knees, his hands cradling my face, my hands resting on his chest. I move my hands down, tracing the swell of his arm muscles, and he drops his hands to hold me around my waist, pulling me closer. My shirt slips off one shoulder, and I try to wiggle out of it, but he grabs it fast and pulls it up onto my body. He breaks our kiss and leans back, resting on his heels.

"I, uh…" He jumps off the bed that squeaks when he moves, never meant to support two people or any sort of activity.

I am still on my knees, watching him. He paces around the room. I plop down and sit cross-legged. My shirt is still opened, but I am covered. He paces for whole minutes without speaking.

Finally, I have to ask. "Did I do something wrong?"

"What?" He turns to me. "Seriously?"

I shrug in response.

"Of course not, Ron. Of course not." He walks back to the bed and sits next to me. He yanks on the knees of his pants when he sits, and I can tell he's uncomfortable.

I snicker slightly.

"Think it's funny, huh?"

"No." I shake my head, but a grin spreads across my face even though I am dealing with my own pleasurable level of discomfort.

He drags his hands across his face. "The thing is,

Ron, I don't know how much longer I can stay in control. And when we kiss like that...I uh...I really have to fight..."

"Do you think there'll ever be a day when we won't have to stop...?" The words slip out, and I clamp my hand to my mouth.

His eyes level on me. "God, I hope so." He leans over and gently pulls my hand from my mouth. He strokes my hair, and we both smile small smiles. Then his eyes narrow as he examines me.

"What is it?"

He is focused on my face, and I put my hand up to my mouth again, trying to figure out what he sees.

"Your mouth, cheeks—they're all red and chafed from my beard. I'm sorry. I'll shave it off for good."

"No," I answer much too quickly, putting my hand on his arm. "No. Please. I—I really like it."

"Really?" He reaches up and runs his hand across his beard.

"Yes. It's so...I don't know." I breathe deeply. "It's uh, incredibly masculine. It makes me..." I shrug, and bite the corner of my lip, hoping he understands the rest.

"The beard stays then." He slaps his knee. His voice is definitive.

"Good," I giggle.

"Good." Those beautiful crinkles form around his eyes when he smiles. "All right," he asks. "Should we try this again?"

I nod, enthusiastically.

He laughs. "I meant the talking part."

"Oh. Uh, sure. But the kissing's a lot more fun."

"Yes it is." Still keeping his distance, he uses his

body to maneuver me, and together we slide back down on the bed. "Your shoulder okay?"

I nod and lie there, gazing up at him. "This doesn't feel much like talking to me."

"No?"

"Nope."

We both smile.

"There's a lot to talk about. I think I need one more kiss to sustain me." He strokes my cheek with the back of his hand—his hand is rough, but his touch is so incredibly gentle.

"I have stories that'll probably go on for most of the day and night," I whisper, turning my face so I can kiss his fingers.

He sighs a definitive sigh. "Well, in that case…"

He leans down over me, still careful to keep his distance, and gently guides my mouth toward his. He lowers his mouth to mine and kisses me completely…then he pulls back and looks me deep in the eyes, nodding…and with that one look, I know Phoenix is the only man who will ever be allowed to kiss me again.

Chapter Twenty-Six

Just when I think I may very well combust, he flips onto his back and lies there, staring at the ceiling. He reaches up and runs his hands through his hair. Boldly, I let my hand find its way to him, and my fingers trace the ridges of his abdomen. He lets a sigh escape from his mouth, but he doesn't stop me.

"That uh, feels…good," he mumbles.

"Um-hm." I am lost in his scent and the feel of his incredibly strong body.

"Uh, really good." He rolls onto his side and reaches around outside my shirt to rub my back.

"Mmm," I murmur. I tip my chin up, and he kisses me again.

"That sound you make…it drives me a little crazy."

"Mmm…"

"All right." He sits up quickly. "I—I…let's get something to eat. I just felt your ribs through my shirt."

I roll onto my belly, knocked over by his sudden movement.

"That's what you were thinking about?" I am leaning on his makeshift pillow, watching him. I bend my legs at the knees, my feet swaying back and forth in the air. "While you were kissing me?"

"No. Of course that's not what I was thinking about while I was kissing you. But I can't be thinking about what I was thinking about. Okay?"

"Yup." I giggle slightly.

He laughs and shakes his head at me. "You're a bad kid."

I flinch when I hear these words. Although he meant them playfully, deep inside I'm afraid they're true. He doesn't notice the concern and remorse rising within me. Instead, he is beaming.

"Here." He props up his pillow. "Hop up."

I sit up against the pillow. He grabs the box of crackers and some water, and washes the red sauce off the ravioli.

"I really think you should eat." He sits next to me, holding the box and the can of slimy, washed ravioli out for me.

My shirt is still unbuttoned, but I'm not at all exposed. As exciting as it is to be in Phoenix's bed, wearing his opened shirt, it's also incredibly comfortable. I take the can of ravioli, allowing myself to forget everything except this moment.

"Thanks." I take a few crackers in my free hand, and we both eat. As soon as I shove a cracker into my mouth, I realize how ravenous I am.

"So, spill it." He speaks between bites. "How did you find your father?"

"I'm warning you, this conversation will make us lose our appetites." I wipe the cracker crumbs from my hand and twirl a ravioli in the can.

"I'm not scared."

"No, I'm sure you're not." I let my eyes fall across his incredibly strong chest, and then I clear my throat and collect my thoughts. "Well, Farnsworth took me to meet him. Apparently my father, Julian is his name, broke away from Farnsworth and Farnsworth Sr. years ago. He tried to set up his own world—in a place so far from here supposedly you can only get there by airplane."

Phoenix nods.

"You know what an airplane is?"

"Sure."

"How come everyone knows everything except me?" I mumble, frustrated.

"Give yourself a chance, Ron. Farnsworth doesn't exactly give girls an education."

"How I wish that would change." I gaze off. "Along with just about everything else in our world."

"Yes." Phoenix holds my hand for a moment and then we resume eating. "So he is a rebel, then? Julian?"

"Yes. But for all the wrong reasons. Kind of like Gunnar, I guess. He wanted to have everything Farnsworth had. But he failed, miserably. His land was supposed to be HopefuL World—but instead, they call it HopeLess World."

"I know HopeLess World."

"You do? I never even knew anything existed past the New World." I am exasperated.

"That was the plan. You weren't supposed to. No one was supposed to. That's how they kept us all in check."

"His world is a mess—his people are homeless and walk the streets aimlessly. I saw..." My words fall away, and my stomach twists into knots. I put my ravioli down.

"What?"

I just shake my head.

"Ron? Tell me, please." My words come quietly. "I saw a young boy, no older than my girls...he was on the street. He was…he was eating a raw bird, Phoenix."

"Jesus."

"Yes. And what's worse is a grown man came and snatched it from him. I tried to go back to find the boy and give him something—just a sandwich, but it never happened. And I know feeding him one time won't make a difference, but I had to try…"

Phoenix nods, understanding.

"It was maybe the worst thing I have ever seen."

He strokes my arm.

"And…" I approach this timidly.

"What?"

"Well, the things Julian told me, they were mostly all lies, of course. He tried to turn me against you so I would side with Farnsworth. It seems they had a deal. If Julian pushed me to Farnsworth, and got me to…" I drop my eyes to the bed but I go on, "Couple with him willingly…then Farnsworth would reward Julian with reinstating trade with the New World, which, ultimately, would benefit both parties."

"That makes perfect sense."

I'm feeling braver now. "So Farnsworth's proclamation of love…it was just to set me up. I was useful because of my father."

"He told you he loved you?"

"Yes."

Phoenix stands and pretends I need water. "And, um, what did you say?" He's not looking at me.

"Nothing. I ran away."

Phoenix turns to me and snickers. He hands me water I don't need, but I take it and thank him with a smile. He sits with me again.

"But here's the most unsettling thing, Phoenix.

What if Farnsworth isn't as bad as we think?"

"What?" He turns to me, his eyes narrowing.

"Just hear me out. It was something Julian said. I told Julian that Farnsworth kills children, and he said, 'So do I.' Then he elaborated, explaining his kids are on the street, dying from starvation and dehydration. Farnsworth's kids have food and a fairly decent life—"

"Until they're killed." His voice is forceful. "Until they're killed, Ron."

"Yes. But is it possible that like me, Farnsworth isn't fully aware of the ramifications of his actions?"

"Are you kidding?" Phoenix's voice is loud, and he jumps to his feet. "I don't know what load of crap he fed you, Ron. But that man kills young girls when he's done draining them for their blood."

"Yes. You're right." I feel my cheeks grow hot, but I know there's something to this. I push on. "But Phoenix, Farnsworth didn't start the Lettings, or the Couplings. And maybe he knew what was happening in HopeLess World, and saw what happened to a civilization that had no commodity."

"I can't believe you are saying this." Phoenix crosses his arms in front of him and shakes his head.

"I know. And I understand if you're appalled by me and what I'm saying. All I'm telling you is what I saw."

"You suddenly believe Farnsworth's a good guy?"

"No." I walk to Phoenix, taking his hand, and he drops his aggressive stance. "No, Phoenix. The way Farnsworth considered those girls to be disposable is unforgivable. All I'm saying is maybe he's not as bad as some."

Phoenix stares at me blankly, reluctant to agree.

I release his hand and sit back down on the bed. "I know what death means." My eyes flood with tears, and I pick at the worn blanket on the bed, pulling at the tiny pills.

"Yes?"

"It's the end of hope."

"Ron?"

"Maybe that boy I saw, Phoenix—maybe he was already dead. Maybe he died a horrible, disgusting death, years ago. It's just his heart forgot to stop beating. Maybe he would have given anything to be in my camp, eating three meals—no matter how meager— swimming in a lake, and catching crickets and fireflies. Even if it did mean certain death at such a young age. Because that boy, no matter what anyone tells me, that boy was already dead. And if Hell exists, Phoenix, he was living in it."

Phoenix bites the inside of his cheek, and his nostrils flare as he takes a deep breath. "What gave you this new…perspective?"

"See what I saw. You have to see it, Phoenix. We have to do something about it."

"I'm afraid I'm not in much of a position to save anyone right now."

I stare at him, my eyes glazing over.

"Wait a sec—" I hop out of bed and grab my backpack. "I've been carrying this my entire trip. I took it out of Julian's house. Here—" I pull out the book, and a bag of seeds drops onto my toe and nicks it. I rub my foot.

"Seeds?"

"No." I speak as I pick up the packet of seeds and cram it into my backpack. "Those were given to me by a woman I encountered in my travels. They have a world they started too, Phoenix, a small community, a place where they all live, helping each other."

"There are more?" He raises his eyebrows, questioning. "Really? They help each other? Sounds idyllic."

"Yes." I nod, enthusiastically. "But there was a girl there who wasn't happy. They all seemed to ignore her, but I think there was more there than they admitted. The lead woman, Darla, gave me the seeds. She told me I'd know when and where to plant. Until then…" I hand Phoenix the book.

"What is this?" He turns it over in his hand, sitting up in bed.

"Once you told me you had read some books by the ancients, and they made sense to you. And you modeled your Peaceful Revolution on the writings of some of those ancients. So I thought this might…help you find your way back."

"I don't know if I can, Ron." His words are quiet, but he flips the book open. It opens to a page I had bookmarked. He reads, his eyes devouring the page, and then shuts the book. "It's Gandhi." He turns to me, his eyes grateful and filled with excitement. "He says exactly what I've been feeling—he would lay down his life for what he believed in, but there's no reason to justify taking another man's life."

"I just saw it and read that and thought of—" Before I can even finish my sentence he's scooped me in an embrace.

"Thank you." He pulls back for a moment, his eyes running up and down me. "Thank you, Ronnie."

"You're welcome." I smile at him, but the feeling

in the pit of my stomach tells me I need to say more. "And there is something else. I am afraid to even tell you this, but—"

"Afraid?" He reaches out and holds me by the shoulders, fast. He turns me to face him. "Ron," his tone is much gentler. "I never, ever want you to be afraid of me."

I smile at him, understanding.

"So what is it?" He loosens his grip on my arms.

"Well, I kind of glazed over it before, but…when I was at my lowest point—he—Farnsworth—he could have pushed me to Couple."

Phoenix closes his eyes and inhales deeply.

"But he didn't. I thought that showed some decency in him. And when I was leaving, I called his bluff. I realized he was never going to harm Raven, Violet, and Lilly. And he acquiesced."

"And you didn't know they were with me."

"No."

"You didn't know I would free them…" He looks away.

"It wasn't about that—" I speak quickly. "Look, I had to depower Farnsworth somehow. I realized as long as I'm not begging him to keep the people I care about alive, he has no power." I grab Phoenix's hand. "But Phoenix, that doesn't include you. He wants you dead."

"Who doesn't?" He scoffs, and I tilt my head, frowning.

"That's not funny," I whisper.

"Hey." Phoenix takes me by the hand and pulls me to him. "Are we caught up?"

"I think so." I yawn, my adrenaline finally starting to drop off.

"Tired?"

I nod. A chill washes over me, and I shiver.

"Cold?"

"A little."

Phoenix walks me back to the bed and wraps his blanket around me. "Come here."

He opens his arms, and I snuggle against him, careful of my sore shoulder. He holds me for a long time, neither of us saying a word, neither of us needing to. The feel of his strong body around me lulls me into a safe, peaceful place.

"Think you can sleep?"

"Mmm." I nod, my eyelids heavy.

"Good. You must be exhausted. Good night, Ronnie."

"Night..." I am just about to nod off when a thought hits me. "We can't leave that boy, you know. The one in HopeLess World..."

The warmth of his body and the sound of his heartbeat overtake me. Just as I am about to drift off, I hear him whisper those three little words I so desperately need to hear.

"Yes, I know."

And I am gone.

## Chapter Twenty-Seven

"Ronnie?"

"Mmm." I turn over and wince when I roll onto my injured shoulder. "It can't be time—"

"Ronnie, wake up. Get dressed." Phoenix tosses my still damp clothes at me.

"What time is it?"

"Four a.m."

"Have you been up?"

He nods. "For awhile, reading the book you gave me. And watching you…sleep."

I smile. "Well, you can watch some more." I yawn and stretch my arms. "Ow." I grip my shoulder with my good hand and rub. "I need more sleep…" I squeeze my eyes shut.

"Ronnie, we're not alone. We have company."

I sit up, fast. "Who is it?" My heart races so quickly it wakes me up instantly. "Phoenix?"

"I'm not sure." He's clutching his gun, facing out the window of his cabin. "No one knows about this place. I'm certain of it. You're the only person who's ever been here."

"I am?"

"Yes. Are you dressed?" He turns to me, but I'm still in his bed, huddled back against the pillow.

"I don't want to move…" Somewhere my brain thinks if I don't react, it won't happen. "I just want to stay here. Hidden."

"Me too, Ron. But please. You need to get dressed."

I can see the concern in Phoenix's actions. He paces from one window to the other, trying to decipher our situation. I dress quickly, reluctant to abandon his plaid shirt, but I tear myself out of it and toss it on the bed. I shiver in my tank top and thin shirt.

"Keep it," he whispers, smiling. "It looks incredible on you." Although he is trying to be carefree, I hear the concern in his voice. He turns back out the window.

I slide on his shirt and wrap my arms around myself, terrified. "Phoenix?"

He puts up his hand to quiet me. He crouches low next to the window and reaches over to grab my gun. "Here." He tosses me my rifle.

I grasp it tightly.

"Come here." He motions for me to squat down behind him, and I do. We are so close I can smell him—the combination of sweat and soap that permeates his clothing. Despite the danger we are potentially facing, his scent calms me. I breathe him in deeply, and he reaches around and squeezes my hand. "Scared?"

"No," I lie.

He squeezes my hand again and then grasps his rifle once more. "It'll be okay," he whispers.

And somehow, despite everything, I believe him. I still believe him when I hear the voices, approaching the cabin quickly.

"If I can get you free, you follow the path next to where we buried Lulu. It will take you to the water. Walk east toward the New World. Find Brooke." He pauses and strains to see out the window. "There's a chance she could be in the city. The fighting is moving that way."

I nod, remembering what the Peeing Coward had told me.

"I wish—I wish I knew definitively. If you find her, and she's too close to Gunnar, find Bryce."

"The one who tried to kidnap me? From the attack at camp?"

"Yes. I don't have time to explain." Sweat beads on the back of Phoenix's neck. "You can trust him."

There are a million things I want to ask and say. I want to protest and insist I stay with him. Instead, I nod feebly. "Okay," I whisper.

"Thank you," he whispers back.

The outside voices are growing closer and closer. They are the voices of men—two men speaking to each other. I brace myself for a showdown with Gunnar. But as the men keep speaking, I recognize the voices.

"It's Farnsworth and Julian," I whisper to Phoenix. "What?"

"I'm certain of it. It's them. Somehow they came back East and found us." Panic begins to overtake me. I remember something. "That night, Phoenix…when I was in Farnsworth's room…"

"Yes?" Phoenix is speaking through clenched teeth.

"He was surprised we hadn't Coupled because of all the time we spent alone in your cabin. They know about it, Phoenix. At least Farnsworth does. I'm sorry. I should have told you sooner."

"It doesn't matter." Phoenix's cheeks puff in and out as he breathes.

"Phoenix?"

He doesn't respond.

"Phoenix?" I hear the demand in my voice. "He wants to kill you, Phoenix. They both do. You have to run. They won't kill me. I'm too…linked to them."

"I'm not running, Ron." Phoenix's voice is low and definitive.

"I know." I am devastated.

"I am staying here. I want you to—"

Our words are interrupted by the outside voices.

"Phoenix?" It's Julian.

I can't imagine what he wants with Phoenix, though.

"Phoenix?" he repeats.

Why would they think he was here? And how did they find him?

"We know you're here. Didn't think you were this much of a coward."

I see the muscles in Phoenix's neck tense. He grips his rifle tighter.

"Come on out, son. My name's Julian Billings. Might recognize my last name. I'm afraid I've come with some bad news. We need to talk."

Phoenix turns to the side, poised to strike. I see his profile.

"They're baiting you," I warn.

Phoenix takes a deep breath and nods.

"He's intimating I'm dead."

I can see Phoenix processing this information, deciding what to do next. The voice grows closer.

"Come on, Phoenix. Let's talk. Man to man."

I am itching to confront Julian and Farnsworth, but I owe it to Phoenix to stay put and follow his plan.

They are at the cabin door now. "Phoenix? C'mon, son. You asleep?" Julian rattles on the cabin door.

I shut my eyes tightly, knowing it will only be a few seconds until they find us.

Phoenix must know, too. He stands tall and points the gun at the door. He motions for me to stand near him, but behind the door. I move to where he asks and wait, my breath rushing in and out, surrounding me with a chilly blast. I am preoccupied, momentarily, by the coldness of my breath—shouldn't my breath be warm against the chilly night? Then I remember I am Julian's child, and I have to wonder if my very soul is made of ice. Phoenix inhales deeply and places his hand on the door. He holds his rifle in one hand, and in one fluid movement, he yanks the door open and aims the gun at the two men waiting outside.

"Well hold it now, son."

I peek through the crack in the door and see Julian with his hands up, but no Farnsworth. This is not good. They were traveling together. I am sure of it. This must mean they brought reinforcements who are waiting to ambush Phoenix.

Phoenix steps forward, pushing Julian backward.

"You don't want to kill me, son."

"Why's that?"

"Because I've got some sad news you need to hear."

"I'm listening."

"You know my daughter, Veronica."

I see the muscles in Phoenix's body tighten. He raises his gun higher.

"And I can see by your reaction you love her, very much."

I bite the inside of my cheek, wishing—praying that is still true.

"Well, I'm sorry to have to tell you this, but Veronica is lost. Somewhere out there." Julian uses his hand to motion to the vast, dark emptiness.

I shudder in response, aware of how true that could be.

"Why are you telling me this?" Phoenix asks, unmoving.

"Because we need you, son. We need you to help us stop Gunnar and secure Farnsworth as the true and only Principal Leader."

"Why would I do that? I spent a lifetime trying to stop Farnsworth."

"But at what cost?" Julian counters. "The end of civilization—once again? Do you, Phoenix Day, really want to be the one responsible for the second annihilation of our species?"

"We weren't annihilated."

"Maybe not entirely, but close."

"What do you want?"

"Help."

"I'm in no position to help anyone. So why don't you just go on your way and leave me alone to grieve."

"Nice touch, Phoenix. But I don't believe it." Farnsworth steps out of a shadow.

I was right, Farnsworth was hiding, and he is traveling with two bodyguards. I have to squint to see, but I am certain neither guard is Jerold or Lester.

"Farnsworth." Phoenix acknowledges him. "I don't know what you're talking about."

"Well, why don't you start by dropping the gun?"

"Not gonna happen."

Farnsworth's bodyguards raise their rifles in response, and Phoenix points his gun back and forth, between them.

"I'll tell you what's not *gonna* happen, Phoenix. You're not *gonna* win." Farnsworth is his usual cocky self. "I know Veronica is in there." Farnsworth stares past Phoenix and toward the cabin.

I flatten myself against the wall behind the door.

"I know, because if you truly thought Veronica was missing, you would have dropped everything to find her. But your instincts made you stay put. You're protecting her, as usual." There's a note of disdain in Farnsworth's voice. "And that means she's right inside."

"You're just not as smart as you think, Farnsworth." Phoenix's voice is calm. "She married you. Not me. So shouldn't you be off looking for her? Why'd she run from you? And why'd you come to me? What do you need me for? Reinforcement? Aren't you man enough to take care of your wife yourself, Farnsworth?" Phoenix replants his weight from one foot to the other, his voice snide.

I peek through the crack in the door, and even from here, I can see Farnsworth glare at Phoenix.

Julian howls a laugh, slapping his knee. "He's got you there, Malachi."

Phoenix holds his gun steady. "So what is it you want from me? To find your wife and return her to you? Are you insane?"

Farnsworth says nothing. He just points to the cabin. "She's in there. I know it." Farnsworth turns to his guards. "Get her."

Farnsworth glares at Phoenix, his face cold. How

could I have defended this monster, only hours before?

As the guards push past Phoenix I glance around for anywhere to hide, but there's nowhere. I stay planted behind the door, knowing it's as close to a hiding spot as I will find. Phoenix enters, right on the guards' heels. I no longer have a clear view of the action, I can only see out the open side, where the door is kept away from the wall because of my body. I see intermittent moments, when someone walks into my line of vision. I hold my breath and wait.

"She's not here. I already told you." Phoenix keeps his voice calm and measured.

I hear the two guards overturn Phoenix's cot and topple his books.

Farnsworth speaks. "Of course she is, Phoenix. You two are like magnets—drawn together. But just wait until I turn her around. Magnets can also repel each other you know."

"The only thing repelling Veronica is you."

The guards have the cabin ransacked in a matter of a minute or two.

"Is that so?" Calmly, Farnsworth steps into my line of vision and nods to the door where I'm standing. Farnsworth doesn't look my way, he just stands, stoically staring dead ahead.

Silently I count: one, two, three, four, and yank! A guard pulls the door away from me.

"Huh," I fall forward, tripping over the guard. Phoenix catches me and pushes me behind him.

Farnsworth steps forward. "Mrs. Veronica Farnsworth. I have been worried sick about you."

Phoenix pushes me farther behind his back. He holds the rifle steadily with just one hand. I stay quiet.

"Don't you have anything to say for yourself?"

I raise my chin, trying to appear defiant, while fear squeezes my heart so intensely, I am afraid it will forget to beat.

"Veronica?"

"She has nothing to say to you."

"Is that true, Veronica?"

I nod my head in a calculated move, trying to conceal my terror. I'm not scared for me. I'm scared for him. Suddenly, Farnsworth notices my shirt and glowers at us. Trying to be subtle, I shrink back into the protective space Phoenix has made me between his back and his arm.

"So, I see we may be too late. Seems Mrs. Farnsworth did find the strength to Couple. It just wasn't with me."

"Nothing happened, Farnsworth." Phoenix keeps his composure. "I'm capable of controlling myself." The muscles in Phoenix's arms strain as he holds the rifle with one hand, and me behind him.

"Really?"

"Yes." Phoenix takes a deep breath.

"Well then, it seems you and I can have another go at it, what do you say Veronica?"

Before I can speak, Phoenix drops his stance and steps forward. "Make no mistake, Farnsworth…" Phoenix raises his arm and cups his hand toward Farnsworth's throat like he might strangle him.

The guards move closer to Phoenix, but Farnsworth puts up his hand to stop them. "You were saying?"

"Make no mistake, Farnsworth," Phoenix speaks through his teeth. "Veronica and I may not have

Coupled…but I promise you, when she decides the time is right, it will be with me."

"Huh," my breath catches in my throat.

Phoenix drops his hand from its threatening position and steps back to me. Despite everything, his words create a strange sensation that courses through my body, ending in flushed cheeks and a completely inappropriate smile. I stare at my feet and shuffle them, back and forth, trying to calm myself, trying to keep myself from kissing Phoenix.

"She's still married to me," Farnsworth grunts, observing my reaction through narrowed eyes.

"So let me go." I compose myself and step out from behind Phoenix.

Phoenix grabs at me to pull me back behind him, but I break free and walk toward Farnsworth. Farnsworth's eyes soften at the sight of me.

"Let me go, Farnsworth. You have what you want. You have Julian and trade with his world. With Julian's help and us, you can topple Gunnar. Topple Gunnar and…sadly…you'll have things back exactly as they used to be."

"That's what I'm afraid of."

"What?" I shake my head, confused.

"That everything will be exactly as it was. And that means it will be without you."

I whip around to face Phoenix to see if he can make sense of this madness, and he nods slightly, as if he understands Farnsworth perfectly. Confused, I turn back to Farnsworth.

"But I don't love you. I—I love him." I know it's gutsy to throw that out there, but it needs to be said. I walk to Phoenix, and he wraps his arm around me, protectively.

Farnsworth glares at us. "I can make you stop."

"You married me and took me to the other side of our world. I walked back to find him. Do you really think there is anything you can do to stop me from loving him?"

"He can kill Phoenix," Julian chimes in.

I narrow my eyes at him. He is made of pure evil. But now is not the time to deal with him.

Farnsworth puts up his hand. "This, Julian, is the reason your world failed before it ever started. You're just not smart enough."

Julian's cheeks turn a flaming red. Although I hate to admit it, there is something I get from my father—I understand the feeling of not being smart enough.

"We won't kill Phoenix." Farnsworth looks back and forth from me to Phoenix. "Killing him would make him a martyr. And she will love him all the more."

I inhale deeply, grateful Phoenix's life will be spared, but also terrified over whatever is about to come.

"But hurting him…well, Veronica can never stand to see the people she loves get hurt."

"You left my girls alone—"

"Yes. But I promised you I would never leave him alone. I will risk your misery if it means you come back to me. So…"

Farnsworth snaps his fingers. One guard steps forward and grabs Phoenix by the arms. Phoenix doesn't fight. The next guard walks up to Phoenix and bam! Punches him hard, in the gut. Phoenix crumples forward, the wind knocked out of him.

"Phoenix," I moan, helping him up.

"It's okay, Ron. This is it. He's testing us now."

I confront Farnsworth, staring straight into his eyes. "Farnsworth…" I warn him with my voice.

"What? What are you going to do, my lovely Veronica?"

"Nothing." I clench my teeth and stand firm.

"Again." Farnsworth tips his hand forward like he is about to bow, and the guard punches Phoenix again.

"Ugh," Phoenix exhales through clenched teeth.

I rush to him. "Phoenix?" I rub his back. "Phoenix, it has to stop…"

"It's okay, Ron." Phoenix straightens himself up and speaks through a tightened jaw. His cheeks puff in and out, and his face is red. He looks directly at me. "Listen to me. It doesn't matter what happens here. What happens to me—"

"Phoenix, you could die here. Because of me." The agony I feel is reflected in my voice. I reach out and touch his cheek.

"Shh, Ron. Please." He smiles a faint smile, and I can tell he's struggling to breathe. I owe it to him to shut up and listen. He continues. "It doesn't matter. And I will no longer fight back, not like this, anyway. It's Ahimsa. And someday you'll understand. But right now I am telling you, I would die for you, Ron."

I move forward in protest, but Phoenix shakes his head. "I would die for you. But it is not your job to die for me. Not physically or mentally. Do you understand?"

"If you die, I would already be dead."

"No. You have a journey. So much bigger than you can possibly imagine." He smiles sweetly. "I've always known it. And I think now, so do you."

I nod at him feebly, feeling somehow peaceful. I turn to Farnsworth. "It's enough. You've made your point. Please."

"Really?" Farnsworth raises his eyebrows, questioning me. "Are you going to deny him? Are you going to tell me you don't love him?" He snaps his fingers, and the guard punches Phoenix once more. This time they let him drop to the floor.

"Phoenix." I fall onto the ground next to him, trying to help him up. We are a mess of arms and sweat and agony.

"It's okay, Ron." Phoenix is strong, but I can see the pain in his face.

"We can't do this." I plead with Phoenix. "I can't do this."

Phoenix reaches out and strokes my hair. "Yes, you can. You are the strongest person I have ever known."

"Again," Farnsworth commands.

One guard drags Phoenix to his feet while the other strikes him. This time, after the punch, the guard pulls his hand back and rubs his knuckles. I glare at him with disdain.

"Ready to give up, Veronica?" Farnsworth resembles a hungry, wild dog, salivating.

I cringe when I look at him and turn to Phoenix. "Phoenix?" I implore.

Phoenix shakes his head.

"No," I snarl through clenched teeth, turning to Farnsworth. "I'm not ready to give up. I don't love you."

"Very well." Farnsworth nods, and the guard strikes Phoenix across the jaw. There is blood dribbling from Phoenix's lip.

"Stop it," I demand.

"You can stop it at any time, my dear."

I turn to Phoenix. His lip is cracked open, and his cheek is swollen.

He shakes his head. "No, Ron…"

I know denying Phoenix, even as a complete fabrication, will devastate him. I also know to deny my love now will give Farnsworth all the power. Forever after he will understand beating Phoenix will make me conform. I smile at Phoenix.

Farnsworth stares at us like we've lost our minds. "Again," he commands.

This time the guard punches Phoenix across the opposite cheek, and Phoenix's head drops forward.

I run to Phoenix and lift his head, stroking his cheek, gently. "I'm sorry," I whisper. Then I release his head carefully and walk to Farnsworth.

Farnsworth's eyes light up as I approach. He surely thinks he is victorious.

I speak slowly and carefully. "I love him. And I loathe you. But I also pity you, because all you can do to him is to inflict physical pain. And that won't stop him." I turn back and smile at Phoenix.

Phoenix's eyes are lifted, and he meets my gaze. He lifts his head a bit to smile back.

I turn to Farnsworth. "So beat the crap out of him. Just remember, when payback comes…and it will…you'll never be able to survive what Phoenix can. One little cut, Farnsworth…"

I raise my eyebrows and pretend to grab a knife that isn't in my pocket. Farnsworth flinches. I smirk at him.

"So one point goes to you, Mrs. Farnsworth." Farnsworth smiles in a way that unnerves me. "Too bad I can move in for the checkmate at any time."

"And what's that?" I stand up straight, trying to remain strong.

"The girls."

"They're at camp now. They're safe."

"Are they?"

"You promised—" I step in closer.

"Yes, I did. And I could offer all sorts of clever retorts, like 'so did you'."

"I only promised to be your wife to keep them alive," I mutter. I glance over at Phoenix. "All of them."

"Yes. Well, I've kept up my end of the bargain, despite your…indiscretions. But I can't control madmen."

"What?" I have that horrific feeling in my gut, and I grab at my waist. My eyes dart over to Phoenix and back to Farnsworth. "What?"

"Oh, haven't you heard? Gunnar is on his way to camp to retrieve your girls. Left around midnight. Seems he heard I was here and amassed yet another loyal group of followers." Farnsworth rolls his eyes. "It's getting rather…trying…all of it."

"No," I gasp, moving farther from Farnsworth.

"I'm afraid so."

"Why didn't you tell me sooner?" I demand, stepping closer to Farnsworth.

This time he doesn't flinch. Instead, he reaches out to stroke my hair. I reach up and slap his hand away, but he is faster than me, and grabs my raised wrist with his opposite hand. He holds my wrist tightly, and we stand, staring at one another, my cold breath racing in and out of my empty soul. That's it.

"Let. Me. Go." I speak quietly and under my breath.

After another moment, Farnsworth releases my arm, and I step back, my eyes fixed on him, fury growing inside me.

"You can't face him alone, Ron. You need backup." Phoenix can tell I have been called to action. His words are remarkably clear considering the beating he is enduring.

"There's no time," I mumble, as I grab my backpack. My shoulder aches and my wrist burns, but I refuse to rub it. I will not give Farnsworth the satisfaction.

"Make time," Phoenix instructs. "Gunnar will see you and shoot the girls just to make you suffer. Then he'll shoot you."

I recoil, horrified, knowing Phoenix is right.

"Find Brooke. Go together. Move fast, Ron. I will get to you as soon as I can."

I nod, knowing there's not a second to waste. I hurry around Farnsworth and retrieve a nearly full canteen. I stop and face Phoenix. He smiles at me and nods. Then I run out the door before anyone can catch me.

## Chapter Twenty-Eight

I keep running, straight through the path by Lulu's grave and come upon the lake, just as Phoenix promised. I hear footsteps behind me, but they are not gaining on me. Rather, with every step I take, the footsteps seem to diminish. I believe whoever is chasing me has become tangled in the overgrowth. Still, I don't want to take any chances, so I refuse to slow down. Soon, I am certain I have outrun my tail, and I'm distanced enough from the cabin that I no longer hear the punches. All I can do is pray they've stopped, because I've left. Unable to keep the quick pace, I slow down but keep moving east, as Phoenix instructed, completely unsure of what will happen next. I know I will make my way to the New World, but how will I find Brooke...or Bryce? And how will they react when they see me?

After a journey that feels short in comparison to my last trek, I know I have a choice to make—forge ahead toward the New World, spending endless hours more to finally stumble into the war-torn edges of their once-thriving society—or turn and head to the much-closer city. I can't even consider that camp is the closest of all. Phoenix warned me not to go alone, and he is right.

I freeze, experiencing déjà vu. I have done this before. I know what waits in the New World—

Gunnar's rebels, a score that needs to be settled, and people who need a leader. But not right now. Something in me turns my feet in the opposite direction, and Phoenix's book jumps to mind, telling me I cannot force or control results, I can only work toward my goal. Maybe I will be able to help the people of our country, but it won't happen until I've taken my journey and fulfilled my destiny. I'm not meant to go to the New World now. I'm sure of that. Instead, something insanely intense is pulling me back to the city. My city. Maybe she's there. Phoenix said it could be an option.

Pound, pound, pound—I run forward. This would be a really bad time to be wrong. I take a deep breath and follow my instincts. Certainly time is against me, but desperation is my enemy.

Faster and faster I jog, until I come to a bridge connecting the city with the edges of the woods. I swallow hard when I realize this is probably the path I followed when the Harvesters took me from my home and brought me to camp. I shake my head and press on, amazed there is no one confronting me. Nonetheless, I decide to stay in shadow as best I can. I move swiftly, my backpack and rifle jostling as I go. I follow a highway I remember, my immediate plan only as far-reaching as my next step.

I duck under a barbed wire fence and make my way onto the flat, two-lane bridge. I look up to find empty watchtowers, where guards were once posted twenty-four hours a day. A chill washes over me, and I tighten Phoenix's shirt around me. Then, up ahead, maybe two or three blocks from me, I see a small pocket of fighting, but nothing too intense. It seems nearly everyone has lost his or her passion. I'm not sure they even remember what or whom they are fighting for.

I pass them without trouble, and see a larger group of people, all varying sizes, huddled together, swaying. I walk toward the group, staying as low and unnoticeable as possible. A ruckus is unfolding on the street corner, but best I can tell, the angry people are confronting each other with words, not guns. I have to take my chances with them—maybe, just maybe, they will know Brooke and where she is. Their voices grow louder.

"I told you—"

"What do we do now? Where do we go?"

"Veronica Billings would know what to do."

I flinch when I hear my name. How do they know me? I suddenly remember I am married to the Principal Leader. I shake my head, trying to rid myself of that thought.

Then the strangest thing happens as if it was all orchestrated. One of them spots me. "There she is!"

"Our prayers are answered." A woman falls to her knees, her hands clasped, as she sways forward and backward.

"Veronica," another yells, and this small group crowds around me.

I am taller than everyone, and looking down at them, I realize they are all women. Some have wide scarves wrapped around their heads; others are barefoot and ragged. They push me forward, in very deliberate movements. They have a plan. They keep repeating words like, "finally," and phrases like, "thank goodness." I wonder over and over what they are saying and why. I try to move away from them, but they keep me corralled.

"I need to go," I explain. "Do any of you know Brooke—the rebel leader?" No one answers. "I am needed somewhere. I have little girls who are relying on me—"

They pay no attention to my words, but rather, one smiles and grabs my hand. She pulls me forward as if she's been expecting me. Swiftly, the group moves me to a tall, thin apartment building with a façade once made of beautiful stonework.

"In there," one woman prods. She nods in the direction of the house.

"I—I can't," I stutter. "I need to find Brooke..." but my words are lost. They keep motioning toward the house. I glance at the house and then back over my shoulder at them. The women have formed a semi-circle around me, and I realize a few are carrying rifles. I have no choice.

"Keep going," that same woman urges.

Deciding there is no other option, I turn briskly and jog up the steps that lead to the house. I reach for the door, my pulse pounding in my ears, drowning out all sounds behind me.

The word: "Ambush...Ambush..." reverberates through my ears, replacing the relentless beating of my quickened pulse. I shake my head. No one knew I was coming. There couldn't be an ambush. It makes no sense. It's not logical. But neither was my decision to come to the city, nor their reaction toward me. But still, an ambush would be farfetched. Even for my life. Grasping on to this tiny bit of logic in my otherwise illogical life, I push open the door.

"Ronnie!" Raven rushes into my arms.

"Raven?" I hold her close, and tears stream down my face.

The door slams behind me as Brooke jogs toward me. "Is he with you?"

"No." I shake my head, still holding Raven. I stroke her hair. "Farnsworth has him. Where are Violet and Lilly?" I squint to see in the semi-darkness.

"At camp, with Gretchen."

My moment of fleeting optimism dissipates. "They're not safe there," I exclaim, holding Raven at arm's length. "Not now."

"It's the only place we could put—"

"Gunnar is on the run. Farnsworth just told me Gunnar is headed there."

"What? Farnsworth told you? And we believe him?"

"There's no time to explain. Phoenix agreed with Farnsworth. We have to get to camp to stop Gunnar. Even someone as competent as Margaret—"

"Who?"

"The woman who runs the camp. She can only do so much. What can anyone do against a homicidal maniac?" I gaze down at Raven and pull her to me again, holding her tightly. "Brooke, if he gets to those girls first…" my words trail off, and I squeeze my eyes shut, trying to block out the horrible images in my brain. When I open them, I see Brooke staring at me, her gorgeous cow eyes softening. I feel mine harden as I let Raven go. I grab my rifle and pull it into my two hands. "You named me an enemy of the people."

Raven steps to my side, right up against me. It's clear where she's putting her allegiance. I slip my arm around her. Brooke's eyes widen, and she shakes her head.

"Well you do get right to it, don't you?"

I remain stoic. My jaw set tight.

"Don't tell me you took that personally?"

I stare at her blankly. Raven looks up at me, but I continue to glare at Brooke.

"Jeez, Louise. We were siding with Gunnar, V. You really have to learn how to be more manipulative."

"Thanks, I'll leave that to you."

Brooke shakes her head again and exhales audibly, but I am undaunted.

"I could have been killed…a million times over." I tighten my grasp on the rifle, but she just smiles at me.

"Yeah? And which one of us is exempt from that?" Brooke tilts her head and scrunches up her face. "What was I supposed to do, V? You married Farnsworth." She holds out her hands in complete disbelief. "And what that did to Phoenix…" she shakes her head. "He is a shell of the man he used to be," she mumbles, quietly.

"No, he's not." I bite my bottom lip and feel my chest heave up and down. "He is the same man he always was. He's just…lost."

Brooke and I exchange a look, and reflected in her eyes I see the pain I am feeling. What I don't know is if the loss she feels is because of her love for him as a leader, or her love for him as a man.

"You think he can be the leader he once was?" Her voice is shaky when she asks this. Vulnerability is not Brooke's strong suit.

I glance at my watch and see the seconds flying by. We have no time for this conversation, but I owe her this much.

"No doubt." I am unwavering in my answer.

Brooke nods and focuses on the ground. She kicks at the tattered rug with her toe. A small cloud of dust wafts up around her army boot. "I guess now that you're back, it all makes sense." She smiles to hide the hurt in her eyes.

I offer a small smile and breathe deeply. I can feel her pain.

She squares her shoulders, keeping her emotions in check. "Now if we're through catching up, let's go stop this damned thing once and for all."

"Yes," I agree.

She turns on her heels and disappears into another room of the house. Raven and I follow close behind.

****

Brooke leads us into a sizable kitchen. Raven grabs some protein bars from a stash on the counter, and flops onto the black and white tile floor to eat.

Brooke turns to me. "Gunnar disappeared immediately after that debacle with Lulu?"

I can tell, like me, she is trying to estimate how far he has traveled. "Midnight."

We are all exhausted and pressed for time, but we look at each other for a moment, neither of us saying anything. She breaks the solemn mood by stretching up on her tippy-toes to retrieve a map from a high shelf.

While she fights to unroll the map and contain it on a round kitchen table, I quickly scan my surroundings. My guess is this was once a very plush three-story house—but through the years, family after family inhabited the place, abusing the cabinets and wearing down the rugs to the nubs. A peek into another room to see the remains of a blood red velvet couch and stained, torn, drooping window curtains, proves this to me. My eyes come to rest on a large oak desk in the front room. I notice the sides of the desk. "Bullet holes," I mumble. My eyes fly up to see the walls are also riddled with bullet holes. I give my attention back to Brooke in the kitchen, and her eyes level on me. Then I realize. "This…this was a Coupling house."

Brooke shifts her weight from foot to foot and focuses hard on the map before her. I grab one side of the map to hold it open for her.

"About time," she mumbles, running her finger across a block by block detailed image of the city.

"Did shooting the desk help?"

"It didn't hurt," she answers, never diverting her eyes from her paperwork.

"We're here." Brooke speaks definitively, and I can tell our conversation is over.

While she processes the map, I can't help but conjure horrific images of my mother in just such a house, who knows how many times, doing God knows what, with whom. I shudder, knowing I am the result of that effort, and I make a silent pledge, here and now, that I will not let her suffering be in vain. I am the product of a Coupling, and I will see to it there was a reason for my birth. A reason my mother was locked in a tiny room with Julian. The thought sickens me, and I force my mind to something else…anything else.

Brooke taps her finger against the map. "Would anyone like to get to work?"

Raven joins us and we follow along with Brooke's assessment.

"If he's on foot, Gunnar could probably get to the camp within sixteen or so hours. He doesn't know the woods like me. When I led us, we did the trip in a lot less time."

She raises her eyebrows, baiting me, and I give a strained smile, biting my tongue.

"Adding the walk from my camp to yours…" She traces the path with her finger. "I think we've got about eight hours. Conservatively."

"Eight hours?" Raven asks, fully grasping the intensity of the situation.

"Yup."

"Eight hours to save Lilly and Violet and find Phoenix," I add.

"Is that enough time?" Raven asks, her gorgeous blue eyes fixed on me.

I look deeply into her eyes and see him. "It has to be," I answer. I glance at Brooke. "It has to be."

Brooke nods back. "So stop wasting so much time with the dramatic responses, and let's get moving." Brooke grabs the map and lets it roll onto itself. She immediately goes to work, loading two backpacks with protein bars and waters. She holds out her hand for my backpack and stuffs mine with the same. She shoves the map into her backpack. While she works, she exhales, audibly. When the packs are crammed to the brim, she slides hers on, then hands one to Raven, and mine to me.

"Let's go," she snaps, her head swiveling back and forth from Raven to me. "I'll get the troop. We have help." She seems like she's about to say something else, but then she stops. "Time, Raven?"

Raven checks her watch. "Seven hours, fifty-five minutes."

"Damn," Brooke mumbles. "Too slow." She slips

her hands through the straps of her pack and raises an eyebrow at me. "Ready?"

I nod, knowing neither of us could possibly be ready for what we are about to embark on. She leads the way to the front room. Raven and I follow close behind.

"This is our meeting area," Brooke tells me.

Three women stare at me.

"Is this the troop?" I shift my weight from foot to foot, uneasily.

"I have reinforcements," Brooke answers, rolling her eyes. She unhooks a walkie from her belt and shouts orders. Immediately, a few more women burst through the door toward us, most carrying guns—then another few, and another. As they come at me with guns drawn, I force myself to stay still, remembering this group is on our side. Raven sticks by me as Brooke's troop gathers 'round us. I tower over all of them. That's when I stare at their faces and realize...

"They are *all* women," I exclaim.

Brooke turns to me and frowns.

"Brooke? You have women working with you."

She shrugs and smiles, despite herself. "The men who've been ruling our world and trying to change our world...trying to overtake our world...have made such a mess of it. I thought, what the hell, we can't make it any worse."

I turn to Raven in disbelief. She just smiles.

Brooke reaches up and tucks a lone piece of wavy hair back behind her ear. She arches her back. She looks gorgeous, but weary. She catches me staring at her. "Are we going to get going, or are you going to stare at me all day? If I wanted people staring at me, I could have men working for me. They're stronger and—"

I shoot her an exasperated grimace, and she turns to her troop.

"For those of you who don't know her, this is Veronica Billings."

Many of the women glance at each other. Murmuring ensues.

"Yes, she is married to Principal Leader Farnsworth—"

Someone pulls a gun on me. I raise my hands reflexively, but Brooke raises her gun in response. She turns to me, and her jaw drops open. She blinks slowly and purposely. It's obvious she's stunned my reaction was flight instead of fight.

"But as you can see, you don't need to fear her." Brooke rolls her eyes at me.

"Brooke…" I raise my eyebrows in an effort to make her hurry.

"As your leader, I am telling you, you must listen to her. She is on our side. Together, we have a plan to rescue two little girls before Gunnar can capture them."

The women raise their guns in a collaborative gesture.

Brooke turns to me. "Veronica?"

The group tightens in closer to us, waiting for their orders. So it's my turn.

I look from Brooke to Raven, and then my gaze falls on the faces of every woman in the group. Every one of them waiting for the answer. Every one of them has lost someone dear to her—every one of them has a husband, or a brother, or a sister, or a child, who needs her. Although my allegiance with the head of the Peaceful Revolution and marriage to his enemy, our

Principal Leader, makes me more high-profile than these women, it strikes me we are all the same. They love their men like I love Phoenix, they love their families like I loved my mother, and they would die for their children just as I would lay down my life for Raven, Lilly, or Violet. Every one of these women is the savior of someone else. And this group of saviors is looking at me to lead them—to share my plan. If only I had one.

Chapter Twenty-Nine

I swallow hard. "My best guess is now that Farnsworth and Julian have Phoenix, they'll head toward the New World. It's the only place they know and it just makes—"

"Who's Julian?" Brooke interrupts.

"He's...uh...my father." I stare at my feet while I speak.

"Your father?" Her eyes widen with disbelief.

"You know your father?" Raven rocks up onto her toes and bounces in anticipation, excited by the prospect of someone knowing her father.

"Yes. I don't have time to explain everything now, so you'll have to trust me. Do you have transportation?" I turn to Brooke when I ask this.

"Of course."

"Then we have no choice but to head directly for camp. We have to hope we arrive prior to Gunnar. Then we can take Lilly and Violet and go. Any other girls, too."

"He won't harm the others."

"He's not being rational," I warn.

Brooke tilts her head in concession. "Fine."

"Then, once we have the girls, we get them to a safe place and figure out how to rescue Phoenix."

"Oh, great," Brooke snaps. "His favorite thing."

"Do you have another option?"

"Yes. Leave him alone, and let him be the man he is meant to be." She turns to her troop. "Load," Brooke commands, and within a minute or two, the all-female troop has pulled the trucks around front and loaded them. We move swiftly down the front steps and pile our packs and guns into the trucks.

"That man…" I warn Brooke, "the man Phoenix is right now, is a man who is being tortured and will probably be left for dead."

Brooke shrugs.

"A shrug? Really?" I try to make my way to the driver's seat, but Brooke pushes me out of the way.

"My truck, I drive."

"You learned how to drive a truck, huh?"

She narrows her eyes at me as we climb into the cab. We settle as she starts the ignition. I sit next to her, fuming, obsessively rapping my fingers against the door handle. Raven sits behind us. We pull out with three trucks following close behind. I start gnawing at my fingernails.

"Okay, that's just disgusting. Quit it." Brooke looks from left to right as she crosses an intersection. The streets are still deserted.

"So sorry to bother you," I hiss.

"All right, V. Enough. You know why you're so angry with me?" Our truck races forward as we speak.

"Because you think you know everything and won't mind your own business?"

"No. Because I'm right. And you know it. But you don't want me to be right. You want me to agree with you and say, 'Yes, let's go rescue Phoenix'." She glances at me quickly and then forces her gaze back on the road. We pick up speed. "And the thing you're most angry about is that I understand him better than you do."

I slouch in my seat, breathing heavily, suppressing a scream.

"I mean…" She shakes her head. "How can two people who claim to love each other know so little about one another?"

I lean my head back and stare out the window, my eyes suddenly filling with tears. She's right.

Minutes go by. "Look. I get it." Brooke's voice is softer now, almost friendly. "You love him, so you want him. And you think that should be enough. Believe me, you're preaching to the choir on that one. But the truth is, no matter how much I understand that boy—he doesn't love me. He loves you. And you love him. And with that, I would think, comes the responsibility of learning who he is." Brooke slows the truck as we creep through an eerily quiet part of the city. "We can't take any chances here."

I nod, aware there are probably factions of rebels hiding in the shadows, and a speeding truck will draw unnecessary attention. The glow of the early morning sun reminds me of HopeLess World, and serves as a harbinger of what could be.

I think about Phoenix's remark about me having a journey. I think of his. I squint at Brooke.

"You know," she speaks louder as the truck gains momentum, and we near the western edge of the city. "I am the last person to believe in cute little sayings or that crappy, schmaltzy love stuff…"

I face Brooke, wondering what else she could possibly add.

"But my mother once told me something that stuck

with me all these years." She looks out her side window and then dead ahead. "She told me in the word 'heart,' is the word, 'hear'." Brooke shrugs. "It's ridiculous and dopey, but that may be why it is so perfectly fitting for you."

I tilt my head at her.

"If you love him V, you need to hear what he is saying to you."

****

Brooke's words resonate through my brain as we pull out of the city and across the highways leading from the New World.

"What happens if he gets there first?" Both Brooke and I jump slightly at the sound of Raven's voice.

I had very nearly forgotten she was here, huddled in the back seat. I shoot a sideways glance at Brooke.

"Ronnie? What happens if Gunnar gets there first? Please. Tell me."

I just can't answer her. Instead I shake my head, trying to plaster a false smile on my face.

"He won't." Brooke looks at Raven in the rearview.

"Thank you," I whisper to Brooke.

Brooke focuses back on the road. "So stop asking such stupid questions, okay?"

I stare at Brooke and drop my shoulders in disbelief.

"'K." Raven shrugs, seemingly unaffected by Brooke's candor. "Ronnie?"

I turn in my seat so I can face Raven.

"You promised to tell us about your father."

I know I hadn't promised, exactly, but it would probably do us all good to get our minds off of the girls at camp. And besides, Brooke and Raven should know who we're dealing with.

"Um," my eyes drop down to the seat, and then I raise them to face Raven. I take a deep breath. I have nothing to be embarrassed about. He is the one who made the evil choices, not me. I am merely his offspring. "He—my father, Julian—he was sort of Farnsworth Senior's Gunnar. But he got farther than Gunnar will. Julian started another world on the other side of our land. A place none of us knew existed. At least I didn't. You?" I turn to Brooke.

"Un-uh." Her eyes grow wide. "Really? I never knew of anything except the city and the New World."

I bite the inside of my lip and nod, feeling a bond with Brooke. I am relieved to know I am not the only one who was ignorant to all this. But I am surprised Phoenix didn't share his knowledge with Brooke.

"V?" Brooke raises her eyebrows at me. Obviously, she wants to know more.

"Anyway, this other world, it's a horrible place, filled with starvation and misery. But he, Julian, is a tyrant, and that is the world he created."

"No way?" Raven is completely invested.

"And you're sure he's your father?" Brooke has her doubts over just about everything.

"Unfortunately, yes. He claims to be. And he looks just like me. So…seems you were right about me all along."

"How's that?" Brooke furrows her brow.

"Seems I really am made of pure evil."

Brooke doesn't respond, but focuses on the road ahead. I begin to see trees whizzing by. We must be leaving the immediate area of the New World. I shift in my seat, our truck racing toward camp, a place that should feel like home, but instead, offers me only the feeling of complete and utter dread.

After what feels like forever, Brooke glances at me. "He loves you, V. You. Phoenix Day could never love a girl made of pure evil."

We exchange small, pensive smiles.

The truck races on.

Chapter Thirty

As we near camp, I feel exactly as I did when I fled the New World by helicopter, and again when I visited HopeLess World—fearful, incapable, powerless, and hopelessly unequipped for the task that has been thrust upon me. So I'd better figure out something quickly.

"How does Gunnar feel about you at the moment?"

Brooke jumps slightly. She has been concentrating on making our way through the woods, and my voice must have startled her.

"Last I knew he thought we—Phoenix and I—were with him." She clears her raspy throat and slugs at some water.

"He believed you?"

"As long as Phoenix was away from the influence of—" She stops short.

"Me…" I eke out.

"Yeah. He thought Phoenix had come back to his senses. And truthfully, Gunnar's at a loss by himself. He needs to be ruled. All he's doing is rushing aimlessly forward and—"

Brooke focuses on her driving, and I steal a glimpse at Raven who is quietly staring out her window. I can't imagine how this must feel for her—to lose a friend and then witness that friend die—all the while knowing thanks to her blood type, she is the next likely target. I'd love to tell her otherwise, but she's too smart to fool.

"What about Phoenix's Peaceful Revolution?" I ask. "Gunnar didn't seem to buy into that."

"He didn't. He reminded Phoenix it was a disaster before, and frankly, once Phoenix thought he'd lost you—"

"He lost himself," I add, sadly. My eyes fill with tears, and I sigh.

"Yes." Brooke smiles at me almost as a friend would. "Look, V. It's not like we're working with a script here. We're all doing whatever it takes to stay alive and hopefully regain control of the country."

"You have no idea how out of control our country is—"

Brooke raises an eyebrow, inquisitively. "Maybe not. But what I do know is if Gunnar sees us together, any groundwork we made controlling him is over. If we get there too late—you have to stay back, and let me try to handle him. He trusts me as much as Gunnar can trust anyone. He conceded to let me be a leader—and frankly, he hates you. With a passion I have never seen in anyone, ever before." She stops and looks away, then she turns to me, and something flashes in her eyes. She tosses her head elegantly and forces her eyes back on the road. "Let me rephrase. He hates you more than I have ever seen anyone hate. But Phoenix loves you with even more passion than Gunnar hates." She grips the steering wheel. "Why is that, V? Why do you bring out all this…passion in these men?"

"I don't know," I whisper.

She examines me for a moment. "No, I don't suppose you do."

"We're close," I murmur, spotting familiar

landscape. My concern for Phoenix and the girls is making me fidget.

"Yes," she agrees hurriedly, twirling a rogue piece of hair absentmindedly and then gripping the steering wheel once again. "Now what the hell are we going to do?"

\*\*\*\*

I look around, collecting my thoughts. "If Gunnar is here, we may not know it. He could be hiding out somewhere, waiting for his chance. Phoenix pointed out Gunnar probably wouldn't do anything to the girls unless he was benefitting in some way. And to benefit, he has to be broadcast so people can see him. Keep the projection away, and we'll keep Gunnar under control."

"Don't pull right into camp," I continue, staring out the window. "Park here." I point to an area about a half mile from the dirt road entrance. Brooke pulls over, and the other trucks follow. I jump out and grab my gun. Raven follows me. I squat down to talk to her. "You can't come with me."

"I don't want to leave—" She pouts like the eight year old she is.

"I don't want you to either. But if Gunnar sees me, he will make rash decisions. Please."

She nods.

"Once I find the others I'll figure out where to hide you."

Raven sighs heavily. "What a waste of my talents," she mumbles.

I rush Raven into the third truck and inform the women in that truck to stay put, with the engine idling. Best case scenario, we get the girls and get away ASAP. Worse case…no, I'm not thinking of that. I arm the women in the second truck and tell them to follow me. I set them up in a perimeter around the camp entrance. There is only one way in and out by vehicle.

"Shoot if you see Gunnar," I instruct them.

Brooke raises her eyebrows at me as we walk toward the camp.

**** 

The camp is quiet. Too quiet for afternoon. "Something's wrong," I announce in a hushed voice, holding up my hand to slow everyone.

"Maybe Margaret changed the schedule—"

"Impossible. Margaret would never change a schedule. She lives for schedules. She would fight to keep things as normal for the girls as possible. There's someone here."

We split up and begin to ease toward the cabins. Two or three women hang behind us, wielding rifles. I motion for Brooke to meet me beside the cabin I had reserved for Farnsworth in what feels like a lifetime ago.

"It may be Farnsworth and Julian," I tell her. "They were the closest to camp. They found us at Phoenix's cabin."

"You were in Phoenix's cabin?" Brooke asks, turning to me. Her face has fallen, and for the first time ever, I see defeat in her eyes.

"Brooke, this is not the time—"

She nods and blinks back tears.

"We need to focus here. Farnsworth and Julian were the closest, but I think Farnsworth would be heading to the Letting facility, because he would be in desperate need of a transfusion by now."

"Okay."

"That leaves Gunnar. My every instinct is telling me Gunnar moved faster than we thought, and he is in there. Waiting. Waiting for me."

I stand and pull my gun around to the front of me.

"What are you doing?" Brooke whispers loudly. "Are you insane?"

"He wants me. He's always wanted me. He may be content to play a game of cat and mouse for a while—and that would give you the chance to get the girls and get away."

"And you?"

"I'll figure something out."

"Well, you'd better."

"Why, Brooke…are you worried about me?"

"Of course not. I'm worried you'll do something dumb and get us all killed, or worse yet, you'll get killed, and I'll be left to pick up the pieces. Again."

A searing pain radiates across my stomach. I hate that I had left Phoenix in pieces. "Got it."

"Where do you think Gunnar will be?"

"The mess hall."

"You sound pretty sure of yourself."

I shake my head, thinking how I'm not sure of anything right now. "My cabin is too personal. He dislikes me too much to be near my things. Plus, it's small. And the Infirmary is too small as well. If I'm right, he'll want to make a grand statement, and he'll need space to pull that off. Cover me."

I begin to move forward, and Brooke reaches out to place her hand on my arm. I look down at it and then up at her.

"You've got one shot. Be right, V."

I nod and dash off.

****

I hurry to the mess hall purposely, my gun drawn in front of me. I pass cabin O and my mind is flooded with memories. Immediately, I think of Lulu, and my heart aches. I think of Raven waiting in the truck—and all I want is to send Raven away—someplace safe, so she can grow up healthy and happy. But first, we need to make her a world where she can do that. I steel my nerves.

"Gunnar?" I call, nearing the mess hall. "Gunnar? I know you're in there." I wait outside the mess hall, afraid if I was to go in, I may very well walk into a trap. I try to peer through a window, hoping to find Gunnar alone, the girls stowed somewhere safely. I see nothing. I hear nothing. I wait for whole minutes, never taking my eyes off the mess hall door. I sense Brooke coming closer, but I'm careful not to let my attention be swayed. Despite the chill, perspiration forms on the back of my neck and drips down into the small of my back. It tickles me, but I don't dare move to relieve myself.

"Gunnar," I repeat. "I know you're in there. Come on out and face me." Still nothing. For a fleeting moment, I begin to doubt myself. Could I be wrong? Has Gunnar already taken the girls? Is the eerie quiet and sense of dread I am experiencing because…because Gunnar has already been through here leaving a trail of carnage in his wake? I shake my head. No, that can't be it. He's in there. He's just too much of a coward to face me. Or else…or else he is preparing…something. I swallow hard and move forward one more step.

I put my head down and breathe deeply. I am nearly at the steps of the mess hall—and simultaneously, I pray I will, and will not, find Gunnar inside. If he is there, waiting, I am banking on the idea he will want me to suffer. This will buy me some time, anyway, and during that time Brooke can rescue the girls. My footsteps are quiet, but my heartbeat is deafening. Before I can think twice, I jog up the stairs and reach out—but just as I begin to yank open the door to the mess hall, I'm interrupted by the sound of a truck moving my way—quickly. I whip around to see two trucks speeding toward me.

I turn back to the door and then to the trucks, wondering if this is the ambush I was both fearing and dreading. I squint to see into the trucks, wondering if Gunnar is inside. I do not know which way to turn, not knowing which side—the mess hall or the trucks— could possibly be safe. I draw my gun and point it at the trucks, and behind me, I hear laughing. The laughing grows louder and louder, and I know that sadistic laugh could only belong to one person. Still facing the trucks, I back myself toward the door. My hand reaches out behind me and grabs the handle to the mess hall—I hear the click of the door and take a deep breath. The trucks are before me now…I am about to make my move into the mess hall, when suddenly, chaos ensues.

"Veronica." It's Julian, jumping from one of the trucks. He moves slowly, considering the situation, and I wonder if he is not as young as I had first imagined. Farnsworth is behind him. The other truck belongs to some of Brooke's female army who followed Farnsworth and Julian in. I search frantically for Phoenix, but my heart falls when I don't see him.

"Where is he?" I hold my ground, but my words demand an answer from Farnsworth. I hear the

277

desperation in my voice and take a breath, trying to smother it. They walk toward me, but remain on the path.

"I'm certain I don't know of whom you are speaking." Farnsworth answers me in his most reassuring voice.

"You do know you…you…bastard."

Farnsworth wheels around to face me. He steps closer, grinding his teeth. He is still a few feet from me, but he leans in, as if the words he speaks are meant for my ears only.

"Veronica, you are still my wife, and as I explained to you before, I will not be spoken to in that way."

"Then tell me what you did with him."

"Ah, you must mean Phoenix, the former leader of the Peaceful Revolution."

My eyes find Farnsworth's. I can barely say the words. "What do you mean f-former?"

"I only mean the Peaceful Revolution fell apart, didn't it."

I exhale, wanting to defend Phoenix, but I'm too relieved to speak. I shake my head, focusing on what's here, before me. I know in my gut Lilly and Violet are inside the mess hall with Gunnar. Then I realize Julian is carrying something—the projection.

"No," I yell to Julian. "No projection. It's what he wants."

Julian smiles.

"Julian," I repeat. "The projection, Gunnar wants that. It's his way of showing everyone he means business. The girls will be killed if he knows the whole county is watching him. He can prove he'll end the Lettings if he kills the last O's."

Julian raises the camera to aim it at me. "Don't you think I know that?" He laughs as he speaks.

I feel my face flush and anger boil inside me. "You want to kill them?" I screech.

"I don't care what happens to them." Julian is careful not to run the projection while he says this. "But it's pretty clear to me Gunnar will be the victor here, and I'm in no position to side with the losers. But…I've also got a deal with Farnsworth, just in case. All those poor, lost, useless souls just ambling about HopeLess World—that boy you worry so much about—they'll all be useful now…for the Lettings and the Couplings."

"You rat," I spit. "Go to hell."

"I will do just that," Julian gives me a cocky smile and raises the projection camera again. "Just as soon as I return home."

"Where is Phoenix?" I demand, turning to Farnsworth. Farnsworth shrugs, and I raise my gun. "Farnsworth? Where is Phoenix?"

"He ran the first chance he got." Farnsworth crosses his arms, and he seems pleased that Phoenix is nowhere to be found.

"More like limped off…" Julian adds with a chuckle.

I can't help myself, I leave my position and walk down the steps of the mess hall and over to Julian. Without thinking, I take the barrel of my gun and prod Julian in the abdomen. Hard.

"Argh," Julian grunts as he falls forward, catching himself.

"Turn off the damned projection," I demand.

Julian stands upright, fury dancing in his eyes. He drops the camera to his side, then reaches out, and before I know what he's doing—bam! he slaps me across the face—hard. I step back, dazed, clutching my cheek.

"Julian," I hear Farnsworth chide. Farnsworth moves nearer to me in a protective move.

"You listen to me, little girl." Julian is up close to me.

I feel his hot breath on my face, but I refuse to step back.

"And you are a girl. Understand me? Just a…a girl. And this is a man's world, and a man's fight. You've overstepped your boundaries one too many times. Just like your mother with her free thoughts and opinions. Why the hell do you think we won't give you an education? Huh?"

Through his pockmarked face I see his dark skin turning crimson.

He continues. "I'll tell you why. You were made for two things only. To give blood when we need it, and to Couple whenever we want it. And it's your job to Couple with whomever you are told to Couple with. I am sick of playing these games. I've had it with you."

He lurches forward to grab my gun, but I step aside and he tumbles forward. Through this exchange, Brooke, and the women of her army, have begun to circle us. The remaining trucks pull up, and voices grow louder as angry women begin to run around. As Julian steadies himself, I lunge forward and manage to knock the projection camera out of his hands. Before I know what has happened, Raven reaches down and grabs the camera.

"No," I shriek. "Raven, you need to go. You can't be here."

But through the noise and unrest, Raven can barely hear me. The camera records my every move.

"Can't you do something?" I ask Farnsworth, my voice demanding.

"What can I do?" Farnsworth lifts his hands in quiet despair. "I have no one here to help me."

"Where are your bodyguards?"

Farnsworth points to Julian who is hovering back, away from this exchange. "He's all I have now."

"You're still Principal Leader," Brooke barks. "Act like one."

I know the camera is rolling, and this is not setting the right tone. I have to interject. "Look, I don't want to fight with you but—"

"Fight?" Farnsworth smiles at me, a charming, but overly white-toothed smile. He knows he is on show. "Why would we fight, my love?"

"Love?" I cringe at his words. My body aches from trying to remain calm—my soul wants to annihilate Farnsworth, but I fight to remain in control. "I am not your love." My words are soft but filled with contempt. I scowl at him.

"Oh," Farnsworth smiles an even more patronizing smile and walks closer to me. He stands in front of me, and we stare, eye to eye. "Still angry with me?" he asks, turning to face the camera as he speaks.

"For torturing the man I love?"

Farnsworth whips back around to face me. He motions for Raven to follow him with the projection; she does so, seeming confused and scared. Farnsworth narrows his eyes, and his lip turns up into a snarl, meant only for, and seen only by, me.

"A lover's spat," Farnsworth turns back to the

camera, assuring his viewing audience in his smoothest voice. He raises his hand and runs a finger across his scalp as he turns back to me.

I face him, feeling the look of contempt freeze on my face. Then he shifts toward me, and in a completely shocking move, Farnsworth wraps his arm around me. I try to wriggle free, but he is stronger than me, and he holds me tightly. I stare at him, my jaw slack.

Farnsworth must read the surprise on my face, because he leans in, closer. He nudges against me and acute pain radiates from my injured shoulder, nearly matching the hatred I feel toward him.

"You're not the only one who's full of surprises," he whispers, seeming very sure of himself.

Utterly confused, I try to separate from him, but Farnsworth smiles and waves at the camera. He squeezes my arm, angling for a response from me, but I remain stoic. He leans over and whispers into my ear.

"Don't be an idiot, Veronica." His breath is cold against my neck. "Think. Think about what is going to happen here. You are still my wife."

I turn to him, my face inches from his. "I left you—"

"You little fool," he smiles as he speaks. His words are quiet, but his demeanor is grandiose. "You didn't leave me. No one has ever left me. You are bound to me unless I free you. You'll have nothing with him. Ever. Because no matter what time you may steal to be together, I will always be there—as your husband—blocking your intimacy—if not literally, at least, figuratively. You know you will never be free of me, Veronica." He reaches out with his hand and smooths my hair.

I cringe but try hard not to recoil.

"And you know you will never feel free to be with him while you carry your obligation to me. And what about him? You think the great Phoenix Day really has that much self-control?" Farnsworth slides his hand down and grabs the lapel of my shirt. He snickers. "He didn't touch you because deep down, in his most unenlightened places, he is repulsed by you. Because every time he looks at you, he sees me."

I gasp, finally breaking free from him.

Farnsworth motions for Raven to move away. Once she does, he shakes his head, smiling. "Poor Veronica. Once you were wanted so…" he takes his time with his words. "So…badly…by two men, and now…well now, you repulse us both."

Then through the turmoil, I hear my name, whispered in a sing-song. "Veronica? Oh, Veronica. *Killings*?"

I turn, to see Gunnar standing in the door of the mess hall. Violet and Lilly are huddled together on one side of him. I squint to see he has a handgun, wedged into the side of Violet. Lilly stands next to Violet, clinging to her sister. They are both too terrified to cry.

"Silence," I demand, holding my hands up, trying to quiet everyone. I have one job only. And that job is to get those girls out alive.

Quietly, Margaret and Gretchen also walk out of the mess hall and stand on the opposite side, far from Gunnar. Gunnar holds out his free arm to Gretchen, and she walks to him. He folds his arm around her, and she closes her eyes. When she opens them, she meets my gaze.

"I'm sorry," Gretchen whispers to me, and Gunnar

pulls her to him, shaking her as he does.

The two of them stare at me, but I can tell they are not truly together. Raven keeps the projection running.

"Veronica Killings," Gunnar hums. "How nice of you to join us. And how convenient for me."

I am stunned by the blanket of silence that has fallen, covering the chaos of only moments before.

"What do you want, Gunnar?" I tighten the grasp on my rifle, and as the anger and fear course through me, my cheek stings. That's okay…I'll deal with Julian later.

"I think you know."

"Enlighten me."

Brooke stands near me, her gun drawn on Julian. Raven holds the projection and records every moment of this for the country to see.

"I want you dead, Veronica."

Although I knew this was the answer, I start when I hear these words. Some mumbling begins but ends as soon as Gunnar holds up his hand. I swallow hard and take a deep breath.

"I know, Gunnar. But why?" I shift my weight from foot to foot, trying to remain strong.

"Because someone has to pay for what has happened. Someone has to take the blame for all the killings."

He faces the camera as he speaks, and I wish I could tell Raven to turn it off.

"By more killings?" I counter. The longer we stand here, the more time I have to formulate a plan. A cold breeze washes over me, and I let it cool my cheek. I inhale.

"By killing the right people."

"You killed a child." I wish I could pull my gun on him, but it would be a disaster. I see the amusement in his eyes, the happiness on his face. I was right…he does enjoy this.

"That was a terrible, unfortunate incident." Gunnar is speaking to the camera, blatantly lying.

"You're a liar," I hiss. "You've got your gun pulled on a child right now."

"Only to make my point. And to see how far the great Veronica Killings will go to protect these girls."

"You killed Lulu, a child, to prove you will end the Lettings. And even that isn't true, is it?"

"Of course it is."

"No." I nod to Brooke, and she pushes Julian over toward Gunnar until the two are standing side by side. "You were going to use the people of his world," I nod, this time to Julian, "and you were going to reinstate our world as it was with Couplings and Lettings. Only this time, you would live in Farnsworth's mansion, and he"—I point to Julian— "would get to make HopeLess World, hopeful again."

The two men stare at me, grinning, but I refuse to lose my confidence. "The only problem is we're here to stop you."

"And who would that be?" Gunnar asks. He hands another gun to Julian who wedges it into Lilly's side.

I grimace as she gasps.

Gunnar drops his gun from Violet and walks toward Brooke. "You and this beauty over here?" He places his hand on Brooke's hair. She tries to break free, but he grabs her and holds her still.

"Gunnar," Brooke speaks in a low, threatening voice. "Don't be a fool. We've been on the same team."

"Oh bull!" Gunnar lifts his hand that's holding the gun, and strokes her cheek with it. She cringes with his touch. "You know, the only reason I let you think I was buying your act—that you and Phoenix were with me—was to be near you."

Brooke narrows her gorgeous eyes and pulls back. She smacks his hand away.

"Oh, you can step back now..." Gunnar smirks at her, and I know the worst is yet to come. "But one of my first acts as Principal Leader will be to sentence you to a Coupling. With me."

"Huh?" Brooke takes an audible gulp of air and steps away from a laughing Gunnar. She takes her gun off Julian and points it at Gunnar.

"Brooke, no..." I warn. We're losing focus. "This is what he wants..."

"Well this...and so much more..."

Gunnar steps closer to Brooke, and she raises her gun. He puts his hands up, laughing. "Kill me, and he kills them," he counters, pointing to Julian.

Brooke turns to me, confused and terrified.

"Don't do it Brooke..." I watch as she fights to breathe.

She lifts a shoulder to wipe a drop of perspiration on her neck.

"Brooke—"

Before I can say another word, a new truck comes barreling into our circle. Before the truck even comes to a complete stop, Phoenix jumps out.

## Chapter Thirty-One

"Well if it isn't Phoenix rising from the ashes," Julian muses.

"Stop." Phoenix speaks forcefully and definitively, walking toward our circle. "Stop all of this."

I am so relieved Phoenix is alive and here, but my heart aches when I see his bruised face. Raven turns the projection camera to face Phoenix. Farnsworth stands by, idly, watching his future unfold around him. Phoenix has his rifle slung across his back. He walks into the center of our group, calmly. He raises his hands and turns in a circle, commanding attention.

"What do you want?" Gunnar asks, abandoning Brooke.

She exhales.

"As if I didn't know." Gunnar stares at me as he says this.

"I want you to go away. Farnsworth is Principal Leader, not you." Phoenix turns to Farnsworth.

"Wait," I step forward. "I was wrong to believe there is any good in Farnsworth, Phoenix."

"His actions were cowardly, yes but—"

"Not just that. He made an alliance with Julian— using the poor people and children of HopeLess World. They were planning to use all of those starving people to fight the war in the New World, and then continue on with life as it always was. Julian can't be trusted. And

287

therefore, neither can Farnsworth."

Farnsworth raises his eyes to me, and I meet his gaze, sadly.

"Is this true, Farnsworth?" Phoenix speaks directly to Farnsworth. "You made an alliance with Julian?"

"What I did or did not do is none of your concern. I am still Principal Leader, and as such, I have a responsibility to my people." Farnsworth turns to Phoenix and speaks plainly. "I have to keep them alive, Phoenix."

"But not by selling them out."

Farnsworth nods slightly. "I admire your passion," Farnsworth is calm as ever as he speaks. "But you have a much greater nemesis than I." He nods toward Gunnar and Julian.

"Put the gun down," Phoenix tells Julian.

Gunnar laughs.

"You don't want to kill children, Gunnar. That's how all of this started, remember?" Phoenix speaks in a relaxed, brotherly way.

"There's no turning back now," Gunnar answers. "I said I would become Principal Leader, and when I did, I would abolish the Lettings and the Couplings. And I got dragged into a dark place today…" Gunnar speaks slowly, acutely aware the camera is on him, "…where I threatened to force someone to Couple."

Phoenix glances at Brooke, sure it is her. She looks off.

"And the only way—the only way—to prove I will put an end to the Lettings, is to do away with those last O's." Gunnar speaks calmly, like he was asking Phoenix about the weather.

Phoenix leaves the circle hurriedly, and jogs back

to his truck with all eyes and a camera, fixed on him. He opens the back door of the truck and another little girl jumps out. This one is maybe only six years old. She takes his hand, her eyes wide as the fullest moon. Together, they walk back to the circle. They stop in front of Gunnar.

"This is Clara," Phoenix tells Gunnar.

My mind is racing as I try to imagine what is happening. "Clara, Clara, Clara…." It pops into my brain. "Lulu's sister," I blurt.

"Yes." Phoenix turns to me and back to Gunnar. "Gunnar…" Phoenix warns. "Clara is also an O."

"Impossible," Gunnar snipes.

"No. Not impossible. She is Lulu's little sister. No one knows about her, because she fell through the cracks when this second revolution started. Imagine how many more girls there are?"

Gunnar scratches his head. "They are all documented. By blood type."

"The ones the government knew about, yes. But there are secret offspring of unarranged Couplings. And there will always be more. No good can come of this, Gunnar."

Phoenix smiles at Clara and gives his attention back to Gunnar. "These are children, Gunnar. Children. The very people you claimed you wanted to save. And now look at you."

Gunnar's face turns red, and he stares at his shoe.

"The country will turn on you, Gunnar," I add these words carefully.

Slowly, the women of Brooke's entourage start to hiss and boo Gunnar.

"We all hate you."

"There's no hope for you."

"You're nothing but a coward."

I try to quiet the women—sure this will fuel Gunnar's fire.

"Killing children is not the way…" Phoenix warns, gently pushing Clara over to the group of women who surround her protectively.

"This is all rubbish." Farnsworth steps forward. "I am Principal Leader, not Gunnar and not Phoenix. Me. And I will decide what will happen from this moment on."

His calmness under pressure reminds me of Margaret. I glance over to find Margaret still holding her post next to Lilly and Violet. She has not moved an inch from them—not even when the guns were pulled.

"They are right, Gunnar—everyone will despise you." Farnsworth continues in a more relaxed tone. "You don't want to kill children. Believe me, I know." His words fall on deaf ears, as Gunnar begins to pace. "You have never known the meaning of a sleepless night until you are responsible for taking the life of a child."

Phoenix and I exchange a look before turning back to Farnsworth, stunned by his honesty.

"Mine is an elite club, Gunnar. One I never wanted to join, but once I did, I learned there is no quitting. And for this club, Gunnar, the dues are so high, it costs…well, it costs you your soul."

I blink back tears, understanding completely. He can see it. Farnsworth comes to stand by me, and everyone is momentarily silent.

"I'm sorry." Farnsworth's words are merely a whisper, and this time he is not conscious of the camera. This time his words are meant only for me.

"Let the girls go, Gunnar," I plead. "You don't want them. You never have."

"You're right." Gunnar speaks in such a calm way it stuns us all.

I see Phoenix ready himself, ready for the trick Gunnar is about to play.

"You're all right, actually. I did what I did back there...but I don't want to kill children." Gunnar motions for Julian to lower his gun, and once he does, Lilly and Violet sprint to Gretchen, hiding behind her.

I exhale, but that feeling in the pit of my stomach suddenly feels like a punch to the gut.

"What I want to do is kill Veronica."

With that, he pulls his gun and fires.

****

All I feel is the cold, hard earth beneath me, and the wind knocked out of my chest. I hear nothing for whole minutes, although I am aware Phoenix is above me, talking to me. I examine my left arm, and see blood flowing freely from bicep to fingertip. I wait for the pain, that excruciating pain that is overdue, but it does not come.

Damn is all I can think. That means the worst is still to come.

I begin to hear snippets of sounds: Phoenix asking me if I'm okay; the women screaming; Raven with her projection camera rolling. I focus on Phoenix, asking me over and over where I am hit. I look at him like he's crazy. Can't he see the blood on my arm? I lift my left arm with no effort. No pain. Something is not right. I wonder, for a moment, if I'm dead and experiencing my last sensations. I smile at Phoenix, glad they are with him.

I shake my head and start to awaken from my daze. I realize only seconds have gone by, not minutes, as I had thought. I check over my body, suddenly understanding I am not hit. That means the blood is not mine. But whose? I move around frantically and begin to push people aside. I fight my way to my hands and knees and see Farnsworth there, about six feet away, propped against a large stone. The blood is his. I crawl to him. His breathing is labored, but he smiles when he sees me. Within a moment, Phoenix is next to me. I stand and pull Phoenix's plaid shirt from my body, and Phoenix grabs it, tearing at it, making a tourniquet to try to stop the bleeding. Surprisingly, Gretchen makes her way to us quickly. She does not speak, but dives in, helping Phoenix. She is steady and competent. I always knew Gretchen would make an excellent Caregiver.

"Oh, I appreciate it," Farnsworth whispers. "But we all know that's not going to do one damned bit of good."

"We don't know..." Phoenix interjects, ignoring Farnsworth and beginning to tie up Farnsworth's shoulder.

Farnsworth winces from the pain, and Gretchen dabs at his forehead with her sleeve.

"Thank you, Phoenix." Farnsworth places his hand on Phoenix's while Phoenix works. "But we do know."

"It's a small wound," Phoenix tries to dismiss Farnsworth.

"I'm a hemophiliac." Farnsworth smiles. "You know that, Phoenix. The best we can do is sit here and let me bleed to death."

"No," I protest.

"Ah, my lovely Veronica." Farnsworth dismisses Gretchen with a wave of his hand.

Gretchen retreats, and finds her way back to Margaret. Farnsworth reaches up and touches my face with a bloody hand. I don't pull away. My eyes find their way to Phoenix and he sighs, sitting back on his heels, relinquishing.

"Would you, would you two stay?" Farnsworth asks, laughing to himself. "I know we haven't exactly been friends, but you two are all I have."

"Of course we will." Phoenix sits down next to Farnsworth in a gesture of peace.

"Oh, my dear Veronica. Whatever will happen now?"

"I don't know," I whisper, trying to conjure up images of heaven similar to those I used to say existed in the New World. I can't do it—right now candy growing on trees seems about as realistic as the possibility of Farnsworth getting into heaven.

"I mean, with our country?"

"Your country, sir, and I don't know."

"Veronica, please. Please. Not now. No more, 'sir', please. And it's your country too. Could you..." he takes a labored breath. "Could you please call me by my God-given name?"

"Okay, Malachi," I whisper, unable to imagine the country is what he wants to speak about while on his deathbed.

"Veronica, you'd better know—or figure it out soon. You will be in charge now." It is growing increasingly difficult for Farnsworth to speak.

Phoenix's eyes dart up to me.

"No," I shake my head vehemently. "No."

"Of course you are, dear. You're my wife."

I cringe at these words, suddenly realizing my future with Phoenix will end here and now. As long as Farnsworth refuses to release me, I will be bound to him forever. That is the law of the New World exactly as he had written it; exactly as Farnsworth foretold. My last chance to be with Phoenix is dying away before my eyes. How ironic. The man we wanted dead—the man whose death would ensure our freedom, now assures my confinement.

I stare at Phoenix, tears in my eyes. Phoenix only smiles a small smile.

"Get Raven," Farnsworth instructs Phoenix, as he fights for air. I wonder how much longer he has. While Phoenix is gone, Farnsworth speaks to me. "Come closer," he whispers.

I lean down over him, my hand resting on his bleeding shoulder. He smiles at me.

"I release you, Veronica, from your duties as my wife."

"Huh," I sit up, and he grabs my hand tightly.

"But be smart, my dear. Don't tell anyone but him. No one. If you do, you will no longer be Principal Leader. And this world needs you. Gunnar will self-destruct. But stop Julian. He is your greatest enemy right now. But to do that, you must distance yourself from the rebels."

I begin to speak.

"All of the rebels, my dear. All of them. Especially him."

"Especially me what?" Phoenix is here with Raven, but the projection camera is off.

"I have freed her, Phoenix."

"What?" Phoenix's expression changes to one of euphoria. "We need to have you say that on cam—"

Farnsworth holds up his hand to quiet Phoenix. "Wait." He struggles for a breath. "If she is still married to me at the time of my…demise…my death will make her Principal Leader. But no one who fought with me will trust her if she sides with you."

"So even in death you separate us?" Phoenix snaps.

I narrow my eyes at him.

"The choice is hers," Farnsworth coughs. "Be with you and there will be nothing but chaos. Step up as Principal Leader, a real Principal Leader, not that sham you tried to pull off before, and find a way to make peace. Find a way to stop Julian and open trade—find a form of commerce other than blood." Farnsworth struggles to sit up, and Phoenix helps him. Farnsworth adjusts his bloody jacket and winces. His eyes fall on me. "I've always wondered who would come to my funeral. Have you ever wondered that?"

"No." I shake my head, fighting a chill.

"I've always hoped I would be pleasantly surprised." He motions for Raven to turn on the camera. She does, and Farnsworth looks into it.

"This is Principal Leader Farnsworth the Third." His voice is shaky but calm. "I am coming to you with my last broadcast as Principal Leader." He chokes up for a moment, but manages to smile his trademark white-toothed smile and continues to speak. "With me, in my last moments of life, is my beautiful wife, Mrs. Veronica Farnsworth."

Raven turns the camera to me, and I stare into it. Farnsworth reaches up and takes my hand. I don't move. The camera focuses on him.

"I am hereby announcing from this moment on, Veronica—as long as she remains Veronica Farnsworth—will be the new Principal Leader, to be contested by none." His eyes make their way to mine. "Do you have anything to add, Veronica?"

I look at Phoenix desperately, his eyes blazing with anger and fear. How can I make a decision like this? If I deny my position and admit I am free from Farnsworth, I am handing these people over to Gunnar and Julian, and leading them to certain death. But if I accept my title as Principal Leader…I may never be with Phoenix again. How do I choose? I close my eyes and the image of Darla pops before me. I need to believe in the magic of love, and pray it will bring a miracle.

"Veronica?" Farnsworth is deathly pale.

"No," I whisper. "I have nothing to add." My eyes fall to the ground before me, and I am unable to lift them to Phoenix.

"Very well." Farnsworth smiles at me, clutching my hand. "Follow her, my people. She stands for all that is right and will fight against those injustices that, although I didn't begin, I have upheld."

He nods, and Raven clicks the camera off. Phoenix squats down by us once more. Tears flow freely down my face. I reach up and wipe them with the back of my hand, smearing tears and blood everywhere. Despite everything, I have to know.

"Why did you take the bullet for me? I could have survived it."

"But what if you hadn't?"

"Then, so what? So you would have gone on as Principal Leader, Phoenix would have helped you against Gunnar and Julian—" I stop short, flummoxed by Farnsworth's smile.

"I do think you will be an excellent Principal Leader, Veronica."

"But that's not the reason he took the bullet for you." Phoenix speaks quietly, looking directly at me.

"It's not?"

"No," Farnsworth smiles at me as he strokes my hand.

"No." Phoenix repeats. "He did it, because he loves you."

Farnsworth nods slightly, gives my hand one last squeeze, and then he is gone.

Chapter Thirty-Two

In the distance I hear one lone gunshot, but I am too numb to wonder about it. I decide a single shot is the proper send-off for our neither fully good, nor fully bad, leader.

"Malachi?" I ask, shaking him slightly. "Malachi?"

"He's gone, Ron."

I glance up at Phoenix, suddenly frozen. I am terrified by all of the death that surrounds us. "How, how can there come a day when there are suddenly no more tomorrows?"

"I don't know…" His voice is soft, but he is unable to look at me.

It is too much, and I am done. "This is wrong," I mutter. "He was wrong. We were wrong." I stare at Phoenix. "Our whole world is wrong."

"Yes." He agrees with me, but I see the pain clouding his beautiful blue eyes.

A few of the women from Brooke's troop pull up to us in a truck. Quietly, Phoenix helps lift Farnsworth into the back of the truck and gets the body settled. Phoenix slaps his hand against the back of the truck when Farnsworth's body is loaded, and the truck rolls forward. I stand abruptly, nearly losing my balance. Phoenix stares as the truck drives off. Neither of us moves for minutes.

Finally, my eyes scout the area that was my home

for so many years. I know the location is the same, but I recognize nothing. I see terrified girls hovering about. I see women who are floundering, their families lost. I examine the rock I stand near and see blood, and death, and carnage. Desperately, I look around for Brooke— but she is nowhere to be found. In my heart I know the gunshot had something to do with her, I just don't know if she was on the giving or receiving end. All around me is a broken world, and I need to fix it. Thank God Lilly and Violet are free, but there are still so many seemingly insurmountable obstacles. My eyes come to rest on Julian, who has slunk to the background through all of this chaos. I will start there.

Just as I begin to walk forward, Phoenix reaches out and grabs me by the arm. He turns me to face him. "This was our chance, Ron. Why?" His blue eyes are fierce and intense.

I feel them burrow into me, and I can barely breathe, let alone talk. "Y—you said yourself, we each have a journey—"

"Yes. And it's high time we planned that journey together. I am sick to death of this, Ronnie. I nearly lost you countless times…and just when we have the opportunity to be…us, you are compelled to throw it all away."

"I'm not throwing it all away." I speak louder than I mean to. "I'm lost, Phoenix. Lost." My voice grows soft as the tears roll down my cheeks. "But I have a job to do. And maybe thousands of people are relying on me to do that job well. And to do it, I have to heed Farnsworth's warning. Can't you understand that?"

"Oh, I understand." He nods and checks his anger, but he speaks through a clenched jaw. "I can't believe—cannot believe, that after all of this"—he gestures with his hands, making a giant circle— "after everything…after that night in my cabin that—this…this is where we are again."

"Phoenix."

"No. No." He raises his hand to stop me from speaking.

"But—"

"No, Ron. No. I'm sorry, but I am just not sure I can stand by, again, waiting, as you single-handedly save the world, again."

"Phoenix? What are you saying to me?" I grab his hand, lost in his eyes.

"When, Ron?"

"When, what? When will my duty be over? My journey?"

"No. That I get. I understand who you are. You saved those girls, and I…" He reaches up and drags his hand across his beard, his eyes twinkling; he smiles as he fights back tears. "I admire the hell out of you for it."

"We saved them together."

"But you had the…fortitude to make it happen."

"Then, what? Please, Phoenix. Please help me understand."

"When, Ron, when do we get to stop being led around by Farnsworth? He's dead, and still you'll believe whatever he tells you." He laughs, in spite of himself. "But why not, right? You've always believed him, ever since you were a little girl. You followed him blindly. And even before he knew about me, he warned you about rebels. He was the sophisticated Principal Leader who rewarded your every move with accolades until you were old enough to be rewarded with his name. And I was just the rebel he warned you about. And soon, he didn't even have to warn you about me—I failed all on my own. No wonder you think his way is the only way."

"That's not fair—" I choke back tears.

"No?" Phoenix reaches out and caresses my cheek with his thumb. I close my eyes and open them when Phoenix continues speaking. "I'll tell you what isn't fair: us, or our lack of us. You married him when you said you loved me. And now you're throwing us away again, because that's what he told you to do."

I shake my head violently, terrified by what Phoenix says to me, and even more terrified that I understand his point perfectly.

Phoenix drops his hand from my cheek. "What I want to know is, when will you ever stop trusting him over me?"

I stare at Phoenix, fighting the tears aching in my eyes.

"Ron?" I turn to see Raven standing there, the camera pointing at me. "You need to say something. We'll lose our audience if you don't speak soon."

I nod, taking a deep breath. I raise my chin. Here it is, decision time. I can either save my life with this one person, or save countless lives by letting him go.

"I have to do this," I whisper to Phoenix. "Will you wait for me? Please?"

Phoenix just smiles a smile that doesn't answer my question. But I know the truth, he has been waiting for me all his life, and at some point, he'll be done waiting.

Raven clicks on the camera and points it at me. I glance at Phoenix who stands there, clutching his gun, staring at me. I look directly into the screen.

"Ladies—uh," I clear my throat. It feels swollen and achy. I take a deep breath and try once more. "Ladies and Gentlemen of the New World, the city, and beyond, I am here to tell you that tonight, my…my husband, Principal Leader Malachi Verrell Farnsworth the Third, has passed away." I catch a glimpse of Phoenix who remains stoic. I take another deep breath and compose myself. "Therefore, I will step up and assume the position that has been thrust upon me. And in doing so, you will now refer to me as, Madame Principal Leader Farnsworth."

Out of the corner of my eye, I see him. Phoenix turns his back to me, and begins to wander away.

\*\*\*\*

The women of Brooke's troop move forward and form an impenetrable boundary around me. Phoenix couldn't reach me now if he wanted to, but sadly, I know he doesn't want to. I stare out at the field Phoenix has crossed, as his silhouette disappears into the afternoon sun. Once more he has left me to my duty— my duty to Farnsworth. But no matter how I dissect it, he has still left me…again. After he promised he never would.

Every ounce of my being wants to run after him— but I'm not sure if it's to scream at him, or jump into his arms. One thing is certain, to him, I have just recommitted myself to Farnsworth—the one thing we both thought could never, and would never, happen again. I stare out at faces wearing expressions of confusion, shock, or admiration. I look back at Phoenix, moving farther from me with each step he takes. My breathing grows shallow, and anger begins to churn in my belly. I feel its warmth radiate out, down my hands that ball into fists. All I want to do is to scream and cry and...fight.

Suddenly, I understand.

I pull my gaze from Phoenix and face the camera again, but this time, I don't say a word.

Quietly, I take the gun from around my shoulder and place it on the ground next to me. Then I climb up on top of the rock that became Farnsworth's final resting spot. The women stare at me, some sway back and forth on their heels, others mumble. The girls stare as well. Even Margaret, who refuses to abandon her position on the steps leading to the mess hall, has inched closer to see what I am doing. I drop down to a seated position and cross my legs under me. I breathe deeply and close my eyes, letting my hands come to rest on my knees. I'm not sure I am doing this correctly, but I remember this action, or inaction, from the book I gave to Phoenix. I open my eyes and continue to sit for whole minutes, breathing in and out, mentally calming myself. I sit and wait. For what, I am not sure.

Then, something beautiful happens. Each one of the girls, Lilly first, then Violet and Clara, make their way through my protective entourage and sit down on the blood-soaked grass before me. Raven follows us with the camera. The older women still themselves and quiet their questions, looking at one another. Then one woman repeats my action, she takes her gun from around her neck, and lays it carefully next to mine. She sits cross-legged, next to Clara. Two more women join her. A third takes off her gun, places it on the ground, and spits on it. She kicks dirt onto the gun, mumbling something about her hatred for war.

Once they settle, the moment is so peaceful, an onlooker would never guess what had transpired here, only minutes before. If only I could find that serenity in my heart, but I know peace will elude me personally as long as there is tension with Phoenix. Tension—oh there's more than tension with Phoenix. I am angry. I grit my teeth, momentarily pushing aside my feelings for him to concentrate on what I am trying to accomplish here. And then, maybe, maybe he will understand it is all the same.

The silence that falls over us represents nothing less than hope. Our moment of solidarity is magic, like those first days of spring, when the sun graces us with favorable temperatures, and the grass begins to push its way through the ice and snow. I feel like that blade of grass, reaching up to the warmth of the sunlight, knowing full well my roots are still encumbered by a cold, all-encompassing enemy. But at least there is a promise of a better tomorrow—and that, that possibility, is called hope.

We sit for minutes more, the cool autumn breeze giving way to a sharper, winter wind. I fold into myself, wishing I was still wrapped in Phoenix's plaid shirt, even if all it could offer would be a false sense of security. I'd take that right now. I remember the feel of the shirt, and how every time it brushed against my skin I imagined his touch. What I would give to have Phoenix here with me, his arm wrapped protectively around me. It would give me the perfect opportunity to punch him in the gut.

"No," I whisper to myself. "No anger." I try to quiet my mind, but it races with questions—how could he not understand? How could he abandon me again?

How? After what he said…? I shake my head, unable to fathom how I am once again here; unable to comprehend how Farnsworth can control me posthumously.

Little by little Brooke's entire troop has joined our passive resistance. A good-sized stockpile of weapons has grown, and is wedged against the rock. Woman after woman has tossed her weapon onto the pile, some delaying, but all ultimately joining us in our peaceful protest.

Although I am miserable over my latest fight with Phoenix, the camaraderie I feel with my fellow citizens has lulled me into a false and irrational sense of peace. My eye catches Margaret and Gretchen, still standing on the front steps of the mess hall. I wonder if they will ever join me. I scan the campground, and when I am certain we are ready, I stand, feeling terror and anticipation replace my very blood. I try to calm my raging heart. It is time. I nod to Raven, and she turns the camera to focus in on me.

"Citizens of the New World and beyond, as your Principal Leader, I am here to tell you the fighting is over." I hear my words, and I feel as if I'm standing above myself, staring down at me. "Yes. You heard me. The fight in the New World must end. Former Principal Leader Farnsworth is deceased, and the rebel whom we have all feared, Gunnar," I punctuate his name, "has run like the coward he truly is." I take a deep breath and let it out, slowly. "He must be stopped, but in a nonviolent way. We will deal with him when needed." My words flow naturally now. "However, I am sorry to say we face an even greater foe—a man, who, regrettably, shares my bloodline. But violence is not the answer there, either."

"Actually," I jump down from the rock and walk forward, toward the camera. "Violence has never accomplished anything." Out of the corner of my eye I see them, Brooke and Phoenix, walking toward me. I feel a prickly warmth, like a heat rash, beginning in my gut and traveling up my torso. The feeling travels quickly, like sharp, yet warm water being splashed against me. I feel simultaneous anger and relief at the sight of them. What could their return possibly mean? I narrow my eyes at Phoenix. If I ever get a moment alone with him… No. Deep breaths. That's all I can do right now. I take one more breath and focus on my job at hand. "Therefore, change will happen—but we will learn from our ancestors, and from the Peaceful Revolution led by Phoenix Day." I speak this last part through clenched teeth.

Phoenix walks closer to me, and his mere presence makes me heady. I close my eyes and try to regain my composure. I steal a glance at him and wonder if we can ever lay down the weapons between us and start anew.

"And now is the time for us to make peace and rebuild. Like our ancestors before us. Lay down your weapons. Stand with me for peace and freedom. Our old way of life"—I shake my head for emphasis— "it is gone. The killing must stop. Here…today."

The women clap in agreement.

"There will be no more killing children for their blood." I smile at Raven. "And there will be no more killing, period. That is why we implore every man, woman, and child who has sided with Former Principal Leader Farnsworth or the rebel group, to lay down his or her weapon." I am taking a huge gamble here, but I know it is right.

Phoenix is suddenly there. He lays his gun down on top of the pile and stands next to me. I exhale, tears springing into my eyes, and at the same time, I fight the impulse to push him away—forcefully. He knows what I'm doing. That's why he's here. It is his time to win. We stand side by side, the ultimate authority and the greatest of rebels, praying others will follow suit.

"This is Phoenix Day," I smile at the camera and then turn to Phoenix to glare at him.

He nods at me, a smile plastered on his face, studying me with his eyes, but I can tell he is not the slightest bit surprised by my reaction.

"The leader of the Peaceful Revolution. He has joined me in this quest for solidarity and peace." I spit these words at him, their meanings heavy between us.

He raises an eyebrow, daring me. So he's in the fight. And what a fight it will be. Looking at him, my shoulders drop slightly, and I feel myself soften. It is not the time for personal issues. Now, as I tried to tell him before, is the time for something much bigger than the sum of the two of us. I offer him the chance to speak.

"Phoenix?"

He nods, knowing despite our—or my—pettiness, his time has come. He is closer to me now, and my body grows weak from his proximity, but I bite the inside of my cheek, trying to remain strong. Not now. This is not the time to give in to desire or fear. This is not the time to crumple into a mess of tears or relief. This is the time to be strong. When it comes to our relationship, if you can call it that, we've got a greater task ahead of us than merely finding civil accord.

Saving our world in a peaceful, nonviolent way will be easy compared to working out all the kinks between us. I know he knows it too.

Phoenix speaks directly into the camera. "Fighting does nothing but destroy. The killing stops now. We need an answer, and the answer is peace."

A lone person claps in the distance. Slowly, that person is joined by another, and yet another. People hug, and a silence sweeps over our small crowd in a show of unity.

"It is Ahimsa," Phoenix announces, and then he reaches down and grabs my hand, raising it, to show our solidarity.

I want to rip my hand from his grasp, but I decide that would not be a very peaceful course of action, and we need to set an example here. Despite my anger, my palm grows warm and sweaty, and my body aches for his touch. Then I think of the projection I saw not so long ago, and I remind myself this is the same move he made with Brooke to prove their togetherness. It is a business decision, nothing more. I squeeze his hand so hard he snaps around and glowers at me. I grin slightly.

Despite our personal unrest, I am awash in the feeling of success. However, I know our moment is only veiled in peace—real peace cannot exist with Gunnar and Julian on the run. I search for Julian, and my heart drops when I realize he is gone. My best guess is that he will head for the airplane and back to HopeLess World. I just have to be fast enough to stop him.

I turn back to the camera. "At this time, I have no choice but to attempt to right our world. To do this, I will try to carry on my late...husband's...legacy," I mumble the word 'husband,' but still I catch Phoenix frowning at me, "and venture to a place far beyond our comprehension—to a land on the other side of our country. A place most of us never knew existed. I will not travel alone…" My eyes make their way to the ground and then up to him, tentatively. I clear my throat and focus. "But while I am gone you will be in survival mode, fixing your houses, picking up the pieces of your broken lives. Food will be rationed to avoid looting and pillaging." I stop short, noticing my little girls, and then my eyes find their way to Phoenix once again. Standing here next to me, he feels like a tall, strong, force surrounding me. I look back into the camera. "Listen." I speak to the camera as if it were a friend. "I'm not made to be Principal Leader. Not really."

A collective gasp is heard.

"Ron?" Phoenix whispers into my ear. "Ron, don't be rash…not because of me."

I turn to him, certain only he can hear. "Shouldn't everything I do be because of you?" I feel my eyes rim with tears. "That is, if this was really real, and not just some warm blip on the radar of the life of the great Phoenix Day."

"A warm blip?"

Then I say the thing I never should. The one thing I can never take back. "He died for me, Phoenix. Died… for…me. And you couldn't give me the decency to try to figure it all out before you went running off in your trademark hotheaded huff."

"What?" Phoenix speaks much too loudly. He stares at me, and the look in his eyes is one I have never seen before. It's a mixture of hurt, guilt, anger, and sorrow. It's a look I don't like in the least. A dull ache throbs in my throat, and I am aware all eyes are on us. I turn back to the camera and try to pick up my conversational tone, although it's not easy.

"I am a rebel," I announce to the sound of more gasps. "Through and through. And as such, I am not meant to be Principal Leader. But there is someone here, someone who can lead you with calm and diligence. Someone, who in the worst of times will be level-headed, someone who will not be swayed by personal feelings," my eyes dart up to Phoenix, "nor politics. Someone who will only have your best interest at heart…Someone…" I say this slowly and calmly.

Brooke and Phoenix stare at me, probably unable to imagine what I am doing. From behind the camera, I see Raven's knowing smile plastered on her face.

"Someone, who can do what I cannot—and that someone will watch over the day to day operations. Therefore, I have an announcement to make. As of this moment, I am relinquishing myself as Principal Leader."

"Ronnie?"

I glimpse at Phoenix, knowing his concern for me is genuine. I turn to the mess hall and back to the camera. "As of this moment I am no longer your Principal Leader, and I announce my successor to be Margaret, the Head Leader of this camp. Margaret?" I hold out my hand to her.

A stunned Margaret glares at me, probably certain this is some demented joke.

"Are you sure?" Phoenix whispers.

"Yes." I breathe deeply. Pretty darned near close to sure, anyway.

Margaret gasps, while Gretchen stares at her and

smiles.

"Go," Gretchen prods.

Margaret steps forward, uncertain of what I have said.

"Margaret?"

She walks up beside me.

I turn back to the camera. "I have never seen a leader so cool under pressure and so capable," I explain. "Margaret has been a solid worker for the government for many years, never overstepping, and always reliable. Margaret also does not care for me all that much, so I am certain she will keep me honest—reporting to me on what is and is not working." I turn to Margaret, but she stares dead ahead, focused on the people before her. "Before I will pass the reins of power, the only requirements I have are that Margaret rules with a peaceful mind, and not a mindset of war, and she institutes the abolishment of the Lettings and the Couplings. Will you do that, Margaret?"

She regards me coolly out of the corner of her eye, and nods in response.

"Excellent." I smile at her, and the girls squeal in delight, hugging one another. I fight back a sob of happiness trying to burst from my chest.

The members of the camp break into spontaneous applause, Brooke being the last to join. She chews the inside of her lip and puffs out her chest. I may have to do some serious damage control there. Margaret finally turns to me, and I extend my hand. She takes it.

"Why?" she asks, as we shake.

"Because it's right. And…because you're right. You will be an excellent Principal Leader, Margaret." I lean in and whisper so only she can hear. "Don't let me down, Margaret."

She looks down at the ground for a moment and then leans back toward me. She meets me eye to eye. "No, Veronica…I won't let them down."

I nod and smile. "I knew I was right," I answer her, my relief manifesting into a grin.

Finally, she cracks a small, but very serious, smile.

Chapter Thirty-Three

Phoenix has not moved from his spot right next to me, so Gretchen steps around him to walk over to me. "You sure you want a Principal Leader who hates you?" She smiles.

"It wouldn't be the first time," I answer, offering her a small smile back. Honestly, there is too much swimming in my head right now to try to figure out my relationship with Gretchen—if there is a relationship with Gretchen. Despite it all, I can't help but feel a little bit sorry for her. I know what it's like to bet everything on love, just to have it all fall apart.

Brooke saunters up waving her walkie in her hand, and Gretchen steps back, hovering at the edge of our small group.

"I'll be damned." Brooke slaps Phoenix on the shoulder so hard, his chest jolts forward slightly. "I was just on the walkie, and the reports from my camp say the rebels in the New World are joining the Peaceful Protest. People are refusing to fight, and without a central figure to fight against...I'll be damned—everyone is simply laying down his or her weapon and trying to start anew. We're on our way to fixing this place once and for all." She scans Phoenix's eyes for a reaction, but I can tell she sees none. "It works, Phoenix. Your Peaceful Revolution...it works. I had my doubts but..."

Phoenix rubs his shoulder and considers what she is saying, as if he's realizing this for the first time.

"I suppose it does, doesn't it…?" He stares off into the distance. He stands up straight, taking a deep breath. He looks proud, and he should. He also looks incredibly strong, and lean, and masculine. And that darned scruff on his chin, not quite a beard, but not clean-shaven, is making my anger dissipate almost as quickly as my focus.

"Margaret, huh?" Brooke eyes me coolly.

Behind her, I spot Margaret already at work, giving orders. I focus on Brooke. "Brooke, you couldn't really expect me to name you Principal Leader?"

Phoenix is watching us, his eyes fixed on me. His gaze makes me squirm.

"Why the hell not? If you were just gonna throw away all…that…power. Geez, V." Brooke shakes her head, scrutinizing Margaret, then turns to me. "I'd sure look a lot better in Farnsworth's mansion than any of you would."

"Yes, I'm sure you would." Despite the frustration and grouchiness growing in me, I smile at Brooke's pouting. "But I need your help, as usual. We still have Gunnar to tackle."

"Gunnar's gone." Brooke's eyes grow cold when she speaks.

"What? Gone? As in, ran away?" My heart is pounding.

"Ran away," she scoffs. "I'm too good a shot for that. Too bad for him. He should have known."

Brooke stiffens, trying to appear cold and unfeeling, but I know better. The terror she felt over Gunnar's threats drove her to action.

"H-he's dead too?" The gravity of the situation makes me ask the obvious.

"Yes, V, he's dead." She speaks slowly, exaggerating each word, just to be sure I feel stupid and understand, all at the same time. She rolls her eyes. "This one, Phoenix? Really?"

I glance at Phoenix who does not react. She notices.

"Ohhh," she nods and smiles. "Revolution getting the best of you two, huh?"

I ignore her question. "Are you okay?" I ask her.

"Of course I'm okay, why wouldn't I be? I'm not the one who got shot." She tilts her head when she speaks.

"It's just, you killed someone and—"

Brooke's eyes narrow, and she drops her carefree demeanor. "Not someone. Gunnar. And he deserved to die. And you, of all people, know this."

I just nod in response.

Margaret walks over and interrupts. "I need a full briefing on the size and state of the country."

"Uh—okay. Now?" My eyes survey our worn and beaten camp. I shift my weight from side to side.

"Tonight." Margaret smooths her jacket sleeves as she speaks.

"But we need to move faster than that. We have to go forward," I explain. "Julian has probably absconded with the airplane by now—"

"So why don't you get a running start?" Phoenix blurts. He turns to me, his eyes blazing. "I'm sure the great Veronica Billings, or whatever your name is at the moment, can outrun a mere airplane."

"Huh!" I gasp at him in complete shock, my jaw

open.

"Whoa," Brooke mumbles, stepping back.

I narrow my eyes at Phoenix. "Why don't you drop this façade and just admit you hate me." My breathing is fast and hard, through my clenched teeth.

"Ron I—"

"I see," Margaret interrupts, her eyes passing from Phoenix to me and back.

Phoenix stares at the ground.

"Despite whatever 'this' is, our focus now is only on our country."

"When isn't it?" Brooke asks, rolling her eyes.

Margaret takes a step toward Brooke. "If you choose to work with us," Margaret eyes Brooke calmly as she speaks. "Then I would appreciate a bit more team spirit. Or you can feel free to keep your comments to yourself." Margaret straightens her jacket.

"Is she serious?" Brooke asks, but Margaret ignores her and focuses on me.

"As for your concern about the airplane," she pronounces the word carefully, "Julian has done no such thing. The moment you named me Principal Leader, I got on the walkie to hunt down some connections. I grounded the airplane, so there's no way he will have access."

"You've done that already?" I look at her, my eyes wide with admiration.

"Of course. Among other things. Seems I have an ace in the hole."

I turn to see Raven standing there, smiling.

"I uh…" Raven kicks the ground with her foot. It's obvious whatever she is about to say is hard for her. "I think I have a job here." She glances up at me. "That is, if it's okay by you. Because if you need me—"

"A job? With Margaret?" I turn to Margaret.

"She's a whiz at this old-fashioned technology," Margaret explains. "And since your only goal in life is to keep these girls safe, I thought you would be happy if they stayed with Gretchen and me here," she scans the camp, "or in the New World, until such time as you complete your...quest."

Gretchen smiles at me.

"Uh—yes," I choke out, my eyes growing blurry with tears.

Margaret sees me and nods. "Then it's settled. Tonight you come to brief me, and I will set you up for your travels." She lifts her hand and motions vastly unsure of where it is we need to go.

"West," I interject.

"Fine. West. You will leave for the West tomorrow. With your team."

My team?

"Until then, there will be a public funeral for former Principal Leader Farnsworth the Third. Do you wish to speak? As his widow?"

"Uh—no." I glance at Phoenix.

"Very well then. I have the funeral planned for this evening. After that, we will head to my quarters, wherever they may be," she mumbles. She surveys the area again—and I can tell she sees what I see— devastation. "On second thought, we'll head to the mess hall, to eat and discuss the next plan." Margaret is so used to giving orders, she turns before we can comment. She turns back. "And then, I highly suggest you two talk this out," she waggles her finger back and forth between Phoenix and I, "before you board the airplane together tomorrow."

"Oh, we will," Phoenix assures Margaret, his chest heaving with angry breaths, his eyes locking on mine.

Despite my anger, I feel a pull toward him, one that threatens to paralyze me. The feeling starts in my knees and radiates upward, deadening my arms, and leaving me gulping for small, rapid gasps of air. The pain in my injured shoulder subsides as I close my eyes and will myself to stay strong. I am not going to cave or apologize.

"Good." Margaret wheels around and is off.

"And that's that," Brooke mumbles, snapping my focus back.

"Veronica?" It is Margaret calling. Her voice carries the same irritating shrillness it always did.

I hunch my shoulders up to my ears. "What did I do?" I mumble, feeling frustration in every part of my body.

"The right thing," Gretchen assures me.

I feel Phoenix's eyes on me as I leave them and go to find Margaret.

****

Farnsworth's funeral is spectacular. It's been thrown together quickly, but it really doesn't appear that way. We were each assigned a job we needed to complete before the funeral, and everyone rose to the occasion. As I assisted Margaret with the layout and flow of the funeral, Phoenix built Farnsworth a beautifully crafted casket. Phoenix was shown to some wood we were storing in an old cabin, and within a matter of two hours, he had built an extremely presentable casket. How I wish we could have done the same for Lulu. Margaret has chosen the nicest of places for the funeral, atop the highest hill in the camp. Gretchen and I always hated climbing that hill to do bed checks, but now, looking out, I see how picturesque it is.

The evening is chilly—we used to call these nights the threatening nights—although it was not yet terrible, we knew the weather would soon become our greatest enemy…or so we thought. I stare at a shivering Gretchen, who is fighting to keep her ponytail behind her shoulder, as she sets up chairs for the audience. She looks so small and weak, my mind jumps to the past, to other nights in autumn just like this—to all those endless evenings we spent huddled in blankets, crowded around space heaters, trying to keep each other warm. I smile, remembering the stories and the gossip we shared, late into the night. I remember complaining about what a pain Margaret was, and I remember Gretchen's tales of freedom and what it really meant. The reminiscence should make me warm and happy, but instead, it adds to this unshakable longing I'm feeling. I try to clear my head, but I shudder at the memory.

Just then, Phoenix, who is single-handedly carrying the casket, passes me. He's in that same t-shirt and jeans, and I can't help but notice his straining muscles as he balances the empty casket on his shoulder. His eyes follow me as he passes, and I shudder for an entirely different reason. I'm sure he notices. He leaves without a word, tending to Farnsworth.

It's time. Still in desperate need of a bath and a change of clothes, we are ushered to sit down. I am sent to one side of the hill, closest to the mess hall, and Phoenix sits mirroring me, but on the opposite side, closest to the waterfront. When this projection airs, it will send a clear statement that Phoenix and I are on a unified team, but we are not together. I glance at my blood stained, filthy clothing. Margaret had ordered me to change, but I fought her hard on this point.

"Let them see it," I implored. "Nothing will change if they forget. They are a nation of babies—remind them, Margaret. Remind them of the horror."

She nodded, conceding.

I glance over at Phoenix who is also in his filthy clothing. Since he no longer carries his gun, he seems unable to know what to do with his hands. He finally decides to lean forward on his thighs and clasp his hands together. He reaches up for a moment and drags a hand across his scruff. My breath catches, and I sigh it out. His eyes dart over to me, and I turn away quickly, hopefully before he notices the blush threatening to overtake my cheeks, neck, and chest. I shiver, suddenly overwhelmed with the memory of being in Phoenix's cabin. I steal a peek out of the corner of my eye, as he sits up, looking incredibly uncomfortable.

Lilly, Violet, Clara, and Gretchen file in next to me. I search for Raven, but I cannot find her. At first I panic, and then I remember Margaret has her working, and she is most certainly running the projection. I sit back and try to relax as Brooke, and a few women of her troop, sit next to Phoenix. I scan our tiny audience and find the first few rows of seats are occupied by Brooke's original, all-male army. As they heard of the success of the Peaceful Revolution, they swooped in to camp, ready to follow any command Brooke gave them. At the end seat sits Lucus, Brooke's greatest fan and ally. He has his arms folded across his chest, staring at

Brooke. He is clearly the leader of her troop when she is otherwise occupied. He watches her every move, but she doesn't even seem to notice him.

Between us stands a podium that was taken from a corner of the mess hall, and in front of that, placed on the hill, is the closed casket, holding Farnsworth's body. I tremble when I look at it, and Violet reaches over to squeeze my hand. I wish this would just be over. Then, as if someone is granting my request, the rest of our tiny crowd takes their seats and we begin. I glance around, knowing everyone is sitting here either out of curiosity, respect, or obligation. I have a small twinge in my heart that hopes it is not the former or the latter. A few people look as if they have come from the New World, though I'm not certain. It was once so much easier to tell people of the New World from those of us from the city or camp. But it's not that way anymore. Now, people seem equally devastated.

Margaret stomps up the hill. She is a bit winded, so she takes her time walking to the podium, catching her breath. She is certainly more presentable than the rest of us—well, all of us except Brooke, who is flawless in every situation. Margaret is clean, but still wears her army green uniform. I notice it does not fit her as tightly as it once did. She arrives at the microphone, and Raven begins the projection.

"Ladies and Gentlemen…" Margaret omits the description of where people are from, her goal being to unify us, not separate us further. "Tonight we come to you…"

As Margaret's words drone on, I find myself gazing at Phoenix. I pay no attention to Margaret, but rather, all of my attention is focused on this boy—this man really—whom I so desperately want to be with, but who makes me so…angry at the same time. Can't he understand me? And why can't I understand him? Why?

My eyes fall on the casket. Between us lies a body that has inhibited our progress, time and again. But Farnsworth is gone now and no longer able to force a physical wedge between us. But…but what happens when two people who have bonded over a mutual hatred of a great foe, lose that foe? Have Phoenix and I lost our common cause? Will we still be "us" without Farnsworth? Was our fight against Farnsworth the reason we were together…and, now that Farnsworth is gone, what does that mean for us?

"Veronica?" I snap to and see Margaret is addressing me. "Would you like to place the flower?"

The flower. Right. Damn. I had forgotten she was expecting me to place a flower on Farnsworth's casket. I was supposed to hunt down a connection that could take one from Farnsworth's garden and bring it to us. My eyes drop down to my empty hands, unsure of what to do. Part of me wants to cry on his casket, the other part, to spit. Phoenix eyes me curiously, but there's no part of me that thinks he wants me to fail. But I will fail without a flower, and I certainly cannot pull a flower from thin air. In an instant, Lilly, Violet, and Clara jump up and run off, holding hands. Raven follows them with the projection.

"Girls?" I call after them.

Margaret regards me coolly, and I simply shrug. Surprises are not Margaret's thing. A few minutes later, the three girls stand before me, pink cheeked and smiling. Violet's breathing is fast, I can tell they must have run a good distance in no time at all.

"Here." Violet holds out her hand.

I can't pull a flower out of thin air, but it seems my girls can.

"Violet?" I look down and see she is squeezing a flower tightly in her grasp. My eyes widen as I stare at what she has.

Her tiny fingers fold around not just any flower, but a dandelion.

I squat down before her, tears flooding my eyes. "Violet? Do you, do you know what this is?"

The other two girls circle around me, and Raven closes in tightly with the projection.

"Un-uh." Violet shakes her head. "Is it okay I picked it? We just wanted to help. And—"

I see the two other little faces, staring at me, smiling.

Before Violet can finish speaking, I pull her to me, careful not to crush the dandelion. "You picked it?" I ask.

"Yeah. Just back…behind the cabins." Her words are muffled, as I hold her close. She points over her shoulder and giggles.

I laugh along with her, pulling all the girls to me, including Raven, who tries to balance the projection camera as I hug her. I catch a glimpse of Phoenix, smiling.

"Ron, the projection," Raven protests, pulling back.

"Sorry, but it's a *dandelion*!" I exclaim, my eyes filling with tears. I turn to see Phoenix and a few others on their feet. They understand the meaning of a dandelion. I wipe away a tear.

"Ron?" Raven is confused.

I look over to see Margaret, staring, her eyes wide. She clearly wants me to get on with this. I stand and wipe the back of my hands across my cheeks. I walk over to Margaret.

"Can I? Can I say something after all?"

She nods and steps back. The girls sit back down, and I step up to the podium, still clutching the flower.

"Ladies and gentlemen," I begin. A giddy feeling climbs up my shoulders, battling my anger and sadness. My words want to come out in short, forceful blurts. My exuberance very nearly keeps me from speaking, but I try to contain myself. I take a breath and continue. "Most of you know who I am, in one capacity or another. But what most of you don't know is that today, I hold in my hand, the greatest symbol of hope many of us have ever seen."

I hold up the dandelion, which is beginning to wilt in my grasp. Rumbling is heard throughout the audience.

"What I show you is a dandelion. A flower we thought became extinct with the ancients."

More grumbling.

"In fact, there were once so many dandelions, the ancients considered them nothing more than weeds—and they purposely chopped them up and poisoned them."

"No," someone calls out, and I nod in agreement.

"I know. It is hard to imagine this perfect little burst of sunlight—like holding the actual sun in your hand—could ever be considered a pestilence. But it was." I shake my head. "What it represents today…" I choke up for a moment and push on. "What it represents today is hope for a brighter tomorrow. Ladies and gentlemen, this flower was just picked here—at this camp—the very camp that once served only to house young girls waiting for the Lettings. Well today, we said no more, and good-bye to the Lettings. And this…" I hold up the dandelion, "this is our reward. I have seen other dandelions in my travels, but never have I seen one so close to home." My eyes dart to Phoenix. "And this one dandelion means there is a chance more will come. Which, my friends, means," I clutch the podium with two hands, "we once again have hope—not singularly, but as a nation. And that will make us undefeatable. So through your time of rebuilding, through this very, very confusing time, remember this flower, and remember the hope it offers us."

I leave the podium and place the dandelion on Farnsworth's casket. From his death stems our hope, at least for us as a nation—I look up at Phoenix—even if not for us personally.

Chapter Thirty-Four

It did not take long to brief Margaret, so I decide to grab a shower, eternally grateful to be free of Farnsworth and his blood once and for all. I throw myself into the weak stream of water, and a strange thought hits me as the watery blood runs down my arm—how much of this blood had once been mine? I shudder, remembering the Lettings and my obligation to Farnsworth. As the blood makes its way down the drain, I can't help but think of Lulu. The tears come freely, chasing the drops of blood into the swirling water. I take a few extra moments to let myself cry, and when I'm done, I feel…worse. There is so much that has gone wrong, not the least of which is my relationship with Phoenix.

Once I'm clean and dressed in an army green jacket, fatigues, and a black tank top, I head directly for dinner. I take a deep breath as I pull open the door to the mess hall and walk in to all eyes on me—including his. Gretchen smiles sweetly, and Brooke shakes her head at me. I hurry past everyone and slink to the counter to grab a plate of food, then make my way back to the girls' table.

There isn't a lot of food left in the camp stockpile—mostly powered milk and a few cans of different types of pastas, but I think we are all grateful to sit quietly and eat. Phoenix sits on the opposite side of the mess hall, hunched over his food, inhaling his dinner. I watch him as subtly as I can, my heartstrings tugging a bit when I realize how hungry he is. I understand his hunger. He's worked nonstop all day, and if he feels like me, there's this emptiness, this void inside, that can't be sated. I steal another glance at Phoenix then stare at my plate, pushing the pasta rings back and forth with my fork. I've been working all day too, but I'm not the slightest bit hungry. Something about blood and death really kills my appetite.

Sitting here picking at my food, my thoughts drift to Willy. I keep expecting to look into the kitchen and see his smiling face. I stare into my glass of powdered milk and think about the many times Willy had added an extra scoop of milk for me, insisting I needed to eat more, because I was so much taller than the rest of the girls. I smile at the memory of him, half-expecting to hear his humming all the way out here, at the tables…the humming that had so often soothed me as a kid. I stare at my plate and feel Phoenix's eyes on me. I look up just as he looks away.

Soon everyone has finished eating, and I feel Phoenix's unrelenting gaze on me. Now the game is ending, and there's no denying he's ready to make his final move. I sit here, my breath hurried, my body glued to my seat. Phoenix stands, but I am unable to do the same—my body suddenly weighing thousands of pounds. Within a few seconds, Phoenix is before me, and I consciously have to remind myself to breathe. It takes all my will not to let my eyes travel up his clean t-shirt, across the scruff on his chin, to dive into the warm, peaceful serenity of his incredibly blue eyes.

He stares straight at me. "We need to talk."

I stare back at him and raise my eyebrows in a dare. "So talk."

Phoenix scans the mess hall. Brooke, Gretchen, the girls, and a few other people are milling about.

"Not here."

"Where?" I refuse to budge.

"I have an idea. Come." He stands to the side, waiting for me to follow him.

"Come?" I force my eyes open, wide. "Seriously?"

He squares his shoulders, facing me once again. "Seriously."

There is no humor in his expression. He lifts his hand as if waiting for me to stand and follow him out. I feel the anger growing inside me, and I fidget in my seat.

"Uh, Phoenix, I don't know what you think you're doing, but you can't just boss me around—"

"I most certainly can."

"What?" I stand up, and we are almost eye to eye, although there is a table between us.

"Oh good. You're up."

His eyes flicker, and I plop back down into my seat, crossing my arms in front of me. He's enjoying this, and there is no way in hell I am going to let him win. I stare up at him, and he narrows his eyes at me.

"Veronica, let's go."

I set my jaw and take a deep breath. I speak through clenched teeth. "Like I already said, you can't boss me around—"

"Oh, I most certainly can boss you around."

"Have you lost your mind?" Despite the chilly temperature, I feel a droplet of sweat make its way down the back of my neck.

"No, I've gained a ranking. I'm your superior now, and as such, you listen to my ord—"

"My what?" I stand again, my voice louder than I mean it to be. A hush falls on the mess hall, and I feel all eyes on me. My cheeks heat with anger and embarrassment. I walk around the table and stand as close to him as I dare. "My superior? A superior what? You have got to be kidding me." I laugh at the absurdity.

Phoenix remains stoic.

"This has gone from ridiculous to ludicrous." I shake my head and move, trying to distance myself.

Phoenix grabs me by the hand, and I whip around to face him.

"I am your superior, because Margaret put me in charge of our reconnaissance mission…"

I glare at Margaret and try to pull away, but he holds me, fast.

He raises his voice slightly to still me. "And as such, you do as I ask."

"If you think, for one minute…" I step in closer, my chest heaving with my breath.

"I don't have to think about this, Veronica. I know."

I stare at him, my eyes wide, my jaw slack. "You know what?"

"I know what you need. Now come." Phoenix holds up his hand for me to follow him out.

****

I am sitting next to Phoenix in a small cart Margaret uses to get around camp quickly. He drives us hurriedly across the grounds, and I sit perfectly still, my arms crossed in front of me. I am bounced around,

329

nearly flying out of my seat, and I am certain he purposely tries to hit every rut in the dirt path.

"Ugh," I whine, my arms wanting to flail out to the sides to keep my balance, but I refuse to let go. I refuse to uncross my arms or to let him think he's won in any way. I will sit here, petulant and stubborn, and I will not give in. I am cramped next to him in the little cart, so I hug the side as much as possible. Every time we hit a rut or bump, I'm jostled in my seat, which causes me to slide closer to him.

Phoenix glares at me out of the corner of his eye, and I scowl back.

It's dark now, and it's eerie traveling through the woods with only the cart's low beam headlights to mark our way. I don't care. I sit obstinately, unmoving. In the distance, I hear an owl hoot and a rustling of dried leaves. A chill washes over me, so I close my eyes to let it pass. Despite the cart, the trek to the waterfront has never felt longer. Finally, we arrive, and I sit still while Phoenix pulls a blanket from the back of the cart. I raise my eyebrows and scoff.

"I hope you're not planning a romantic evening." I nod toward the blanket.

He tilts his head at me. "What I'm planning is to talk this through. But if you want to stand, or get sand all over your butt, that's your choice."

"Fine. Take the damned blanket."

"Oh, I was going to."

He stares as I glare at him.

"Come," he tells me.

I don't move.

"Veronica. We can do this the easy way or the hard way."

"Are you threatening me?"

"I'm warning you."

"And what would the hard way be?"

He turns out to the lake and then back to me. "Are you coming?"

"You didn't answer my question. What would the 'hard way' be?"

"Oh something like this—" With that he throws the blanket over one shoulder and walks to me. Without a word, he swoops down and lifts me.

"Quit it!" I fight against him, but he holds me fast. "Phoenix, quit it."

He hoists me up over his shoulder and walks me to the beach. My head is dangling down his back, and I pound against him, my hands balled into fists. When we're a few feet from the water, he drops me down hard and glares at me. I stumble, but gain my balance, smiling victoriously when I don't fall. I brush myself off and face him. He rubs the spot on his back I was just beating against, his breathing, labored.

Although I'm angry, I'm in awe of his sheer strength. "Damn, you're strong."

"Yes."

I rub my sore ribs. "You shouldn't have done that."

"I would have stopped if you said to stop."

"I said, 'Quit it'."

"Not the same thing." He turns away and then back. "I'll always stop if you say stop. I hope you know that."

"I do." I look down at the beach beneath my feet and desperately want to feel the sand slide between my toes. I cross my arms again.

"Could you please stop that…?"

Cathrine Goldstein

"What?"

"That, crossing your arms." He mimics me.

"Oh, it bothers you? Sorry." I purposely cross them tighter and stare at him.

"Let me put this another way. Veronica, please uncross your arms before I tie them behind your back."

"You wouldn't...."

"Wouldn't be the first time, would it?"

I drop my arms to my sides.

"Thank you." He spreads the blanket out on the beach and sits. He bends one knee up and drapes his arm across it. He stares out at the water. "It's so beautiful here."

I keep my distance but mutter a, "Yes."

"I think this may be my favorite place on earth."

"Really? But we always fight here."

"Not always." He turns to me and smiles a small, but genuine, smile. "Come sit with me, Veronica. We need to talk."

He holds his hand out and looks at me in a way that makes my stomach ache. I've never seen this look from Phoenix before, and I'm afraid I know what it means. My breathing comes faster, and I realize, no matter how mad I am, if he is telling me we're over, I'm not ready. I walk closer and sit.

"Thank you."

I nod. "Why...why are you calling me that?"

"What?" He tilts his head, confused.

"Veronica."

He laughs and picks up a stone on the beach. He throws it out into the lake, and it lands with a plunk. "Because it's your name."

"I mean, as opposed to Ron, or Ronnie, like you

332

always do."

He stares at me and sighs. "Veronica seemed like the best option. If you only knew the names I've wanted to call you—"

He catches me off guard, and I laugh, covering my mouth with my hand.

He joins me. "It's good to hear you laugh."

"You too." I shrug. "So why, 'Veronica'?"

He turns away. "Honestly, I don't know…" He shakes his head and runs his hand across his chin.

I inhale sharply.

He turns to me. "Actually, I do know. I've been calling you Veronica to distance myself a bit."

My breath catches in my throat, and I feel the tears welling. "That's what I thought."

He gazes at me with those incredibly smart, vibrant eyes, and every ill feeling I've had dissipates. Suddenly, all I want is to make this work. That's all I've ever wanted.

"What do we do now?" I ask the question while I'm staring at the blanket between us, unable to look him in the eyes.

He leans over and places his finger under my chin. He tilts my chin upward until we are looking eye to eye. Once again, I pray he will produce my seashell, but he doesn't.

Instead, he speaks softly. "I don't know." He reaches up and strokes my hair.

"Is it…are we…fixable?" My tears spill forth, and I'm unable to stop them.

He doesn't answer. He drops his hand, and stands. He walks down to the waterfront. I follow after him.

"Phoenix?"

He turns to me slowly.

"Do you want to fix us?"

It feels like forever before he speaks. "I don't know."

Phoenix looks back out over the lake, and I turn and run.

## Chapter Thirty-Five

"Veronica? Veronica, wait." Phoenix is on my heels, he is faster than me, and I know I'll never outrun him. Defeated, I stop. He grabs my arm and spins me back toward him.

"What, Phoenix? What?" I am exhausted, and my words come softly and slowly. "If you feel bad about hurting me, just think of it as payback for all the times I've hurt you."

"I don't want payback, and I don't want to hurt you." Phoenix grabs me by both arms and stares into my eyes as he speaks. I feel weak and defeated, but his touch gives me an electrical charge that keeps me going.

"Then let me go," I plead. "I—I don't know how much more I can take."

"I'm not letting you go, because I need to explain. What I said before…Ron…"

My tears flow faster with his mention of my nickname, and he reaches up and brushes one away. He smiles.

"What I said before was true." He holds me tightly as I try to break free of his grasp. "I don't know if I want to fix us."

"Phoenix," I feel weak, my knees suddenly unable to support me.

"Ron, wait. I don't know if I want to fix us as is.

Not as Phoenix the leader of the Peaceful Revolution, and Veronica Farnsworth. I think it's time we say good-bye to those two people and start over, not as something else entirely, but as the people we really are."

"Together?"

He drops his eye contact and breaks his grasp on my arms. It seems to take forever for his hand to find its way to mine. He leads me to the blanket, and I follow, willingly. We sit side by side.

"How did you feel growing up with a last name?" His question catches me off guard.

"I don't know, I never thought about it."

"You never thought about it, because you had one."

I turn toward him. "Phoenix, what does any of this mean?"

"Veronica, we're on the cusp of something great here. Our world has the potential to become what it once was, and maybe better." I see the sparkle in his eyes while he speaks. "If Margaret does her job correctly, which I think she will, it'll be a brave new world for all of us."

I nod. "Yes, and?"

"And we will have opportunities—you'll have a chance to do things your mother only dreamt of. People—all people—will have the chance to be in love, and marry, and have children, not based on blood type, but based on love."

I stare at him, my eyes wide.

"And when the next generation talks about Coupling, they won't mean a required action that occurs in a Coupling house, they'll mean two people who decide to be a couple. Like...boyfriend and girlfriend, or husband and wife."

"Yes," I whisper, caught up in the dream.

Phoenix turns away.

"But, Phoenix, what does any of this mean?"

"It means, I want you to have the opportunity for all of it."

I nod, swallowing hard. "But you don't want to be the person I do it with." I stare out at the water.

"It's not that, Ron." He puts his hand under my chin, and guides me back to face him. "Not that at all. But I have nothing to give you, and as Farnsworth's widow, you have the opportunity to be cared for the rest of your life—"

"How did this conversation go from love to money?"

"Because when our world changes, which it will, it will also mean a sort of class system will go into effect. People will have the freedom to love whomever they want, but with that freedom, comes responsibility. People will now be responsible for their own welfare. Our government will not be overseeing or supplying our needed goods. We will have to work to make money, and that money will be what supports our families. And Ron—I'm…I'm a rebel. People may not remember my Peaceful Revolution brought them their peace, but at those hard times when they're longing for the good ol' days, they will remember I was the troublemaker who started it all."

"Do you seriously think I care about material goods?" I am so hurt I recoil from him.

"No but—"

"There's no 'but' here, Phoenix. You either think of me like that or not."

"It's not that easy—I want you to have—"

"What? Things?" I stand, anger clouding my judgment. "The gowns Farnsworth forced me into? The overly manicured flower gardens he maintained?"

"No," Phoenix snaps, standing. "I want you to have a name. Okay?" He paces away from me.

"I do have a name," I insist.

He crosses back to me, anger blazing in his eyes. "Oh, you have too many names," he barks. "That's not the problem."

I stand up tall and square my shoulders. "I have one." I watch Phoenix pace beside the blanket. "You know he released me, Phoenix."

"Yes, but no one else does. So we would live in…" his words trail off.

"Well maybe if you hadn't run off, again, we could have—"

"I didn't run off." He runs a hand across his hair.

"What would you call it?"

"Gaining perspective…and following that gunshot. You had everything else under control. You didn't need me to stand there and listen to you talk as…Mrs. Farnsworth."

I can tell this is incredibly difficult for him. "I have only one name, Phoenix, it's Veronica Billings."

"But what if I want you to have another?"

"What?"

"Don't you see? These children were—the children of the Couplings—you're the exception, Ron. The rest of us don't know our fathers, and we have no names."

"I wish I didn't know my father." I stare at him, trying to read what's in his mind—trying to see my future. "And Phoenix, I gave you a name."

"But it should have been me who gave you a name." He steps back, shaking his head. "Veronica, the name you devised, it was touching and…beautiful, but it's not real. And if we were to have gone on…"

My body trembles in response to his use of the past tense. I try to move, but he grabs my hand and holds me.

"If we were to have become…more…I would have had nothing to give you. Not like Farnsworth did. I have no home, no money, and if we were ever to…hell, I'd have no name to give our children."

I gasp, backing away, flushed. I stand for full moments, staring at him. "But Phoenix, I don't need those things. And the name, it doesn't matter. There will be generations of people with no family name."

"Yes. And that will be the dividing line. That will keep us on the outside, always."

"Then maybe that's where we belong."

"Not we, Veronica. You have a name. I don't want to ruin it for you."

"But Phoenix, all I want—all I have ever wanted, was a chance for an education—and you."

"It's so easy to say that now—when you've never known anything else…"

"I've seen plenty of how the wealthy people of the New World lived. And I've seen how the devastated people of HopeLess World live. So don't tell me I don't know." I step closer to him, seething. "I do know, Phoenix Day. A hell of a lot more than you'll give me credit for."

"I give you all the credit in the world. But Veronica, it's not enough—"

"Yes, it is enough. But I don't think it's enough for you."

"What does that mean?"

"This little act you're giving me—it's just that. An act. I think what's really going on here is you're not angry with me, you're angry with Farnsworth—"

"He should never have forced you to marry—"

"Not about that. You're mad at him for dying."

"What?"

"Oh face it, Phoenix. Your entire personage is built on destroying Farnsworth. And he's dead, so now there's nothing for you to rebel against."

"That's not true." He is facing me, his jaw muscles clenched.

"You are the leader of the Peaceful Revolution and it worked—but now you're terrified, because you have no idea who you are now there is nothing left to fight for."

"You are so far off base—" He begins pacing.

"Am I? Really, Phoenix? Tell me. Tell me there wasn't some tiny part of you that tried to keep Farnsworth alive so you could maintain your purpose."

"How dare you."

"Tell me. Tell me I'm wrong."

"I'm not buying into this—"

"I don't believe for a second any of this is about giving me a name—who cares? I think it's all a convenient way to back out of the commitment you made to me. So let me make it easy for you, if you want out just say it."

He remains quiet, his shoulders rising up and down in time with his hurried breath.

"Phoenix. Do you want out?"

His nostrils flare as he breathes.

"Just say it." I shake my head. "I never, never thought I would ever say this, but Julian was right…you are a coward."

Phoenix crosses to me and grabs both of my upper arms. He holds me tightly, without hurting me. I stare into his eyes and see the anger and resentment, but I never, not for a moment, feel unsafe.

"If you need to find your purpose," I whisper, "go. Don't make me the reason you are not fulfilled or free to live your life. You'll resent me so much, we'll forget everything we once had."

He nods at me and drops my arms. He steps back from me and turns toward the foot path.

He stalls for a moment. "For the record, Veronica, it's not about me, it's about you."

"What is?"

"The reason we can't be together. Tomorrow we leave on a mission to bring hope to HopeLess World and to bring down your father, and I can't trust you will act without feeling."

"Will you?"

"I'm leading an army, Veronica. And I need them to trust me, and respect me, and do as I command. And you know better than any of us that we're entering enemy territory. I need to be on top of my game. And to have you there—not just as Veronica Billings, daughter of Julian Billings and widow of Principal Leader Farnsworth—but to have you there as my…my…"

"Your what?"

"It doesn't matter, because it can't happen. I need to have a clear head, and not have my judgment obscured. You need to mean the same as everyone else out there does—the same as Brooke, or Lucus, or anyone. I can't favor you, or I may very well risk everyone else to keep you safe. Can you understand that?"

I don't answer him.

"Okay. So the best I can do is to pretend I have no feelings for you, and pray that eventually, they go away."

I nod, my throat tight, my eyes aching.

He turns back toward the path. "We have to leave in a few hours. You...uh, you take the cart." He hesitates. "Be careful down here please."

I nod and look out over the water.

Chapter Thirty-Six

The sound of my sobs are drowned out by a voice behind me.

"Oh, the hell with this."

I turn just in time to have Phoenix swallow me up in his arms. He holds me, suspended in the air, and I wrap my legs around his waist. He kisses me, and I let my hands fall through his hair. Effortlessly, he carries me to the blanket and somehow manages to set us both down without breaking the kiss.

When he finally pulls back, he holds me at arms' length, staring at me, wild and hungry. "You are my drug, Veronica Billings. I am better because of you, and I am worse because of you—but I am alive because of you. But the only way this will work is if you respect my authority tomorrow and all the days following. Do you understand?"

"I don't get a say?"

"No."

I feel my eyes widen as he turns away and then back.

He speaks calmly, but forcefully. "What I mean is, of course you do when I ask for it. But we will be an army, not a team. All of us. And as such, my word will be law. Do I make myself clear?"

Something in the way he says this causes an unexpected reaction in me. I shift myself around and bite my bottom lip. "Yes." My breathing is coming faster and shallower. The tension between us is so thick it covers us like a dense fog.

"It comes down to trust. Even when you think you're the only one who has the answer—you have to trust I may have one too. Can you do that?"

I nod.

"Veronica?"

"I can try."

"You have to do better than try. For this to work, all of it, you have to trust me in every way—"

"I do, Phoenix." I place my hand on his arm.

He looks down at it and then up at me. His eyes have darkened.

"What do you want?" I whisper, my body warming.

"Give up the control, Ron. Start tonight. Give it to me. Let me know you trust me, unconditionally."

"I do—"

He puts his finger to my lips. "No. I don't want to hear it. I want to know it."

"How?" My heart is beating so fast my breath is coming in short little gulps. There is one way I can prove my trust...

"Phoenix?"

"Shh." He leans forward, and his lips brush against mine, gently. He pulls back, his eyes focusing on me, feverishly.

Within a breath, Phoenix reaches over and cradles my face in his hands. He pulls me to him and kisses me softly, over and over again. I feel the sob build in my throat as I move closer to him. I reach out and grab his biceps; his muscles tighten as he holds me. Gently, he pulls me even closer to him, his lips locked on mine, and he eases me back onto the blanket. His mouth opens mine, and he hovers above me, kissing me like I feed his very soul.

He takes my two wrists in his one hand and plants them over my head, stroking my face with his free hand. My body is on fire as he reaches up and separates my hands, pinning each over my head, holding me against the blanket. I can feel his strength—I can tell he is careful not to hurt me or my still-injured shoulder, but I am certain I cannot break free. He leans down, and I kiss him harder, a moan escaping into his mouth, knowing I trust him implicitly. Wherever Phoenix leads me tonight, I will follow…willingly.

Again he puts my two wrists into his one hand, freeing his other hand. While he kisses me, he lets the fingers of his free hand trace my jaw, and travel down my neck, drawing small patterns on my collarbone. He leans onto the side of me, letting his fingers trace a line down the center of my torso, before landing on my bellybutton. He flattens his hand against my concave tummy and kisses me harder. I squirm beneath his kiss, fighting to get my hands free, wanting desperately to pull him closer to me.

"Huh," my eyes fly open as he breaks our kiss and gathers the material of my tank top in his hand. He tugs my tank top free of my fatigues. Again he flattens his hand against me, but this time it's against my bare belly. I squirm, sliding lower on the blanket, trying to force his hand higher. He stops and smiles at me, and I am lost in the intensity of his eyes. He lets my hands go. I pull them down, rubbing my wrists.

"Why? Why are we stopping?"

Cathrine Goldstein

He leans back but stares at me. "That's what you thought? I was going to force you to Couple to prove your loyalty and trust?"

"Not force. It would not have been forcing."

He smiles. "I've already broken every rule I made for myself." He shakes his head. "My feelings for you are bad enough, but Ron, if we were to…I could never leave you to fend for yourself. My every instinct would be to protect you and you alone."

"Oh." I sit up and turn away, suddenly uncomfortable.

"What is it?"

I shrug.

"Veronica?" His voice is warm but determined.

"It's…it's just something Farnsworth said. He said the reason we don't Couple is because I repulse you…because every time you look at me, you see him."

"He said that?"

"Yes."

"Bastard." Anger flashes through Phoenix's eyes. "Honestly, I never knew he was that cruel to you. If I had—"

"It was only at the end."

"But still, it doesn't make it right."

"Do I repulse you? Is that why we aren't—"

"I want to be with you more than you could possibly imagine." He strokes my cheek, gently. "But I also want to give you a life, a life for the two of us, together."

"You want that?"

"Selfishly, more than anything."

I smile at him. "Me too."

"So let's go conquer this last part of our journey,

and then, then we can focus on us."

"But…"

"What?"

"This last part of the journey, it's really about you, isn't it?"

"What?"

"You want me to be some passive, little soldier who doesn't think or—"

"No. I want you. But I want you safe." He leans forward and strokes my hair, gently.

My insides warm, and I nuzzle against his hand.

"Ron, haven't you ever noticed the butterfly? It's not nearly as beautiful at rest as it is in flight. You are that butterfly, and I would never pin you. But I will do whatever I have to, to protect you, always."

I break out into a smile.

"What?"

"You uh, you did kind of pin me." My cheeks burn, and I can't force my eyes off the blanket.

"Not in the metaphorical way. And Ron," he lifts my chin so I look into his eyes, "best I could tell, you liked it."

A shiver overtakes me, the cool fall air settling on us.

"Are you cold?"

"Just a little." I answer him with my eyes half opened, reliving the bliss of the moment before.

He wastes no time. Within a second, he pulls me to him and wraps the blanket around us. It is incredibly secretive and exciting. His arms hold me tightly.

"So maybe we haven't Coupled, but we are a couple. Here, tonight. And maybe that's even better."

"Maybe." I tease. "But I don't think so…" My

words are soft, and I feel his arms tense as I speak. The warmth of the blanket together with his embrace is making me heady. "You and I, Phoenix…we're always better together than we are apart. Always."

"Yes."

"So I think if we've learned anything, it is…the only danger we face is in being apart, not together."

"I want to take care of you."

"I know that. But taking care of me doesn't mean keeping me from life. It means being there for me. It means being with me…"

His eyes widen, and I can see the glimmer of shock, hope, and understanding.

We sit like this for minutes more, protected by the magic of a harvest moon. I think of his hands holding mine, pinned above my head, and my body aches. I want more. I turn my chin up to him, and he leans down to whisper into my ear.

"If we go down this path, Ron, I…uh, I'm not sure I can—"

"Then don't."

In a flash he finds his way back to my belly. My breath catches as he places his burning hand against my skin. Then, shrouded by the safety of the blanket and the night, he slides me down onto my back.

"Phoenix," I whisper, raising my mouth to meet his.

He holds himself inches above me. "I know." He lowers himself on top of me, and I feel the weight of him press against me.

My body shudders.

"Are you nervous?" he asks, stroking my cheek.

"No."

He gives me a sideways glance.

"A little," I admit.

"I would never hurt you…"

"I know."

"Trust me," he whispers into my ear.

His words make me ache for his touch. I barely remember to breathe.

"I love you, Ron."

"I love you, too."

The rest of the night is ours alone.

****

The sun begins to break over the lake, and Phoenix stands, facing the water. Careful to wrap me in the blanket, he leaves and walks purposefully toward the lake. He begins to wade and then dives in, his arms above his head. He pops up for air, moments later, and I bask in the silhouette of Phoenix Day, illuminated by the glittering rays of the rising sun. My eyes never leave him as he dives in, again and again, fighting his way through the cold water.

I sit, unmoving, experiencing a feeling of peace I have never before encountered. I pull my eyes off Phoenix to look at my hands, but I barely recognize them. No longer are they the hands of a lost, reactive little girl, now, they are the steady, sure hands of a young woman—a young woman who, despite the unknown obstacles that lie ahead, knows she is loved and safe.

I feel grounded but elated. Giving myself to Phoenix, and knowing how protective he is of me, doesn't make me weak…rather, it makes me feel stronger and more capable. I stare at him thinking how odd yet wonderful it is to be free to choose the one person who will be by my side—always. I know I have chosen well.

I remember once accepting that a moment of happiness may have to be enough to sate us for our lifetimes, but now, now that I know this feeling—I am certain one moment will not do. I will search for this feeling over and over.

I want a lifetime of happiness with Phoenix, and I know we can have it as long as we are together.

I trust that.

Trust.

Such a strange little word really, and yet, it seems, without it, nations can fall and couples can divide. I look out at Phoenix, and he holds up his hand to me. More than anyone, I know the overwhelming odds we will be up against in just a matter of hours. I know the evilness we must battle.

I close my eyes and take a long, deep breath of the cool, foreboding air. Yes, the odds are seemingly insurmountable, but we have triumphed over impossible odds before—including in our relationship. And now, more than ever, we are equipped to face what comes our way—because we do it as a couple.

He walks back in from the water and over to me. I open the blanket, and he slides in next to me. The feel of the cold water makes me shiver, and he wraps his arms around me, protectively. He turns my back to him, and I let my head fall onto his shoulder. He leans down and kisses me on my forehead, cheek, and slowly, he makes his way toward my lips.

****

So maybe I can't believe we can right all wrongs, or even that our world will get better…but I trust

Phoenix, and I know we can trust each other. And that, at least, is a beautiful beginning.

## A word from the author...

A dark, gritty, New York City girl at heart, I stretch my comfort zone every summer and head to camp in the deep woods to work on The Letting series. I find it is worth every non-air-conditioned, bug-bitten moment, because I have fallen in love with Phoenix and Ronnie, and I hope you will too...

I am the author of *The Letting*, Book 1 in The Letting series, and I also write romance and steamy women's fiction novels. I began my career as an award-winning playwright, and I am a proud member of RWA, PAN.

I am addicted to Luna bars, decaf coffee, yoga (yoga clothes), and I find my best writing ideas come from sweat sessions on my treadmill. I love the works of many authors, and these days I read a lot of Shel Silverstein and Mo Willems—which brings me to my reason for reading these modern masters, the absolute loves of my life: my two young girls, and my husband (who reads grown-up books too.)

To find out more about Phoenix, Ronnie, and me, and for updates on The Letting series and more, please visit: www.CathrineGoldstein.com